DEADWORLD

DEADWORLD

J. N. Duncan

KENSINGTON PUBLISHING CORP.

http://www.kensingtonbooks.com

KENSINGTON BOOKS are published by

Kensington Publishing Corp.
119 West 40th Street
New York, NY 10018

All Kensington Titles, Imprints, and Distributed Lines are available at special quantity discounts for bulk purchases for sales promotions, premiums, fund-raising, and educational or institutional use.

Special book excerpts or customized printings can also be created to fit specific needs. For details, write or phone the office of the Kensington special sales manager: Kensington Publishing Corp., 119 West 40th Street, New York, NY 10018, attn: Special Sales Department, Phone: 1-800-221-2647.

Kensington and the K logo Reg. U.S. Pat. & TM Off.

ISBN-13: 978-0-7582-5566-2
ISBN-10: 0-7582-5566-7

First Mass Market Printing: April 2011

10 9 8 7 6 5 4 3 2 1

Printed in the United States of America

This book is dedicated in loving memory of my grandmother, Olive T. Jackson, an author herself, whose inspiration got me started on this long road to publication at the ripe old age of fourteen.

Acknowledgments

I would like to thank my wonderful agent, Nathan Bransford, the editor team of Audrey LaFehr and Martin Biro at Kensington for making my story so much stronger than its original form. A special thank you to all of the lovely women in the Maumee chapter of RWA for providing inspiration and support, and a special nod to Kat, who had a dream that she bought my book in a bookstore long before it ever sold. And last but certainly not least, to my family and specifically my wife, romance author Tracy Madison, for putting up with all of the vagaries of a two-person author household. Without you all, this book would not be the book that it is today.

Prologue

A misty rain swirled down into the darkness between the two brick buildings. Flattened against one cold wall, Archie Lane huddled next to a stack of sagging cardboard boxes, peering out of the narrow alley at the sliver of sidewalk illuminated by a nearby streetlight. This was not how he had envisioned running away. There had been no envisioning to speak of, really. All he had wanted was to escape the smack down going on in his parents' living room, where Dad had the leg up on the cursing scorecard and Mom was on pace to set a new "thrown objects" record. Now the midnight sounds of Chicago's suburbs were frightening him even more.

They were not strange sounds. Archie recognized most of them, from the sounds of tires on wet pavement to the screeching yowls of two cats duking it out, but in darkness, all things magnified in the wrong direction. Every shadow contained lurking doom. Body parts lay rotting in every container. Every passing car was his dad hunting for him. Surely, he was destined for the belt with this one. That threat had been very explicit after the last time.

The problem was where to go? Every friend he knew would have parents who would turn him over and make a phone call. His grandpa would let him stay, if only he could remember how to get there. He was also a thirty-minute ride by car. On foot that might take all night, if he even knew what direction to go in.

Archie's concerns had turned more immediate as the rain began to fall. It was getting cold. His long-sleeved shirt offered piss-poor protection, and, worse, he was starving. Where did street kids go when they were hungry and wet?

Archie hadn't the slightest clue. He did not know a single street kid. If he could find one, maybe they could tell him. At worst, maybe he could find a store to hang out in for a while, maybe steal a candy bar or something to fill his rumbling stomach. There was a Kroger not far from his house, but the darkness had confused his sense of direction. It was not on the old downtown strip where he found himself now. It was . . . somewhere else.

Archie thrust his hands deeper into his jeans and ventured forth. He would just have to ask someone. It couldn't be far, and it was open twenty-four hours. He could wander around until the sun came up and maybe, if he was really lucky, sneak back into his room without anyone being the wiser. Mom and Dad would be passed out by sunrise. As long as Dad didn't come in to kick at the foot of his bed to see if he was sleeping, all would be good.

At the alley's opening, Archie stood at the corner and poked his head out. There were only a few cars parked on the street. Further up at the corner, a couple walked quickly down the opposite sidewalk, huddled under an umbrella. Boy! They were in a real hurry, looking back at something, but Archie could not tell what. The intersection ahead appeared empty. Not fifty feet down the sidewalk, a car door opened, and a man stepped out. Nice car. Nice suit. He popped open an umbrella and looked up in Archie's direction, eyes hidden behind dark, round glasses.

Archie ducked back into the darkness and watched as

the man began to walk toward him. He hardly looked dangerous, but what Archie found disquieting, what spawned a gnawing worm in his gut, was that the slick-looking car eased along the edge of the street, matching him step for step. Archie took another step back into the darkness, just in case.

The man hummed a tune, some old-fashioned-sounding thing Archie didn't recognize. His footsteps were silent upon the wet cement. When he got close, Archie held his breath, freezing every muscle of his body, willing it not to begin shivering. There was no way the guy could see him there, melded flat to the brick wall, right? He continued to walk, stepping across the alley's opening, one step, two, but at the edge he stopped.

Archie's heart leaped in his chest. The man, not ten feet away, paused and then turned, the umbrella resting lightly against his shoulder. He looked directly at Archie.

"I dare say, young man. Whatever are you doing out on a night like this and dressed like that?" His voice was old, reminding Archie of his grandpa, but it had a smoothness to it that belied the man's age. "And huddled in that rotting, forsaken alley. Surely you must be cold?"

Stranger at night on a nearly empty street. Archie knew better. These weren't the sorts of people you talked to when alone. "Pervs will snatch you right off your own street!" his mother had been fond of telling him.

"Just, um, hangin' out," Archie said. "I was on my way home actually . . . from a friend's house."

A corner of the man's mouth curled up beneath the shadows of the umbrella. "I see. No ride home from your mum or dad? It's awfully late. Bad sort of folk out and about this time of night, Mr. Lane." The blue car came to a stop behind the man, its windows cloaked in glossy, rain-splattered darkness.

"It's okay," Archie said, the worm in his gut now

chomping gleefully at his insides. "I'm good. I don't have far to go." If he was quick enough, he might be able to bolt past the old guy. If not, one of those gloved hands could easily get a handful of shirt. The man's words suddenly sunk in. "Hey. How'd you know my name?"

"I know your mother, Archibold," he said, the other corner of his mouth twitching up to reveal a ghostly smile. "We met at the mall just the other day. I believe you were at the candy machines getting yourself a treat."

Archie nodded. "Oh. Yeah." His stomach rumbled at the thought of the handful of gummy worms he had gotten last weekend.

"Would you care for a ride home, Archibold?" When Archie remained silent, the man knelt down. "You ever ridden in a Rolls-Royce before?"

Archie shook his head. "Nope. It's Archie, by the way. I hate Archibold."

A deep chuckle rumbled out of the man's throat. "Archie it is. I've got soda inside, and I believe there might be something you could eat."

A ride in that car would be cool, no doubt. Free food and drink would be good, too. The worm paused in its hungry gnawing to shake its wary head. Don't ride with strangers. You just never knew, did you?

"I don't know. Actually, I think I'm good. My house isn't far at all."

He stood back up, looking down the street from where he'd come. "Almost two miles, Archie. That's a bit of a walk on tired feet."

"You know where I live, too?" Archie pulled his hands from his pockets. The worm was telling him to run, and the idea was making more sense by the second.

"Of course I do," he said, kneeling back down. A gloved hand reached up to pull the glasses down the bridge of his nose. "I could not have followed you here if I did not, now, could I?"

Archie froze, his body and mind coming to an ice-encased standstill. "Whoa, dude. Your eyes are glowing."

"They are." A black gloved hand reached out toward him. "It's a special trick. Can you see anything in them? If you look hard enough, you will see something very special indeed."

One step, followed by another. Archie felt his hand reach out to take the strange man's hand. There actually was something in the glowing, irisless eyes. Shadows, gray and swirling like fog, danced around inside them. Archie began to shiver.

"They look like ghosts," he whispered.

The man stood up, his hand clasped tightly around Archie's. "Very good, Archibold. You can see the other side. Would you like to go?"

The door latch clicked open, and Archie stepped toward the car. "Are they all dead over there?"

"Every last one, my young man," he said and pulled open the door. "You see, they are my ghosts, but to join them, you must be one as well."

"Oh." The comforting warmth of the inside of the car beckoned. It felt so good against his wet, shivering skin. "Don't you have to be dead to be a ghost?"

The gloved hand gently pushed Archie in the back, easing him into the black cave of the car. "But worry not, Mr. Lane. I shall take care of that."

The door slammed shut, and a moment later the Rolls eased back into the street.

Chapter 1

Beneath the serene, protective canopy of maple leaves, a boy reclined against the trunk, withered and bloodless, his skin two sizes too big for his depleted body. It was death in all the wrong ways.

Jackie Rutledge squinted at the chaos from the parking lot, frowning at the milling gawkers. A gaggle of reporters and cameramen huddled around their cluster of vans waiting to pounce on the nearest unwary law-enforcement officer. She absently rubbed at her throbbing temple. There should have been laws against committing crimes on Mondays.

The drifting scatter of clouds taunted her by blocking the late September sun only to laugh at her seconds later. Her sunglasses provided little relief from the pain induced from last night's bottle of tequila, and Jackie hoped that luck would bring a thunderstorm and send the crowd running. There was no luck to be found in this park however. Death had sucked it all away.

The enormous maple, its branches drooping nearly to the ground, was completely encircled with crime-scene tape. Some of the crew were walking around, combing through the grass. The local police looked to have been put in charge of crowd control.

Jackie walked over to her partner, Laurel's, car and accepted the triple-shot latte and four Tylenol. "Thanks for the wake-up. Why can't killers keep better hours?"

"Off shifts pay better," Laurel said and reached up to brush off some lingering sand from the dangling ruffle of auburn hair on Jackie's forehead. "How was the lifeguard?"

"My thighs still hurt, so I'm guessing it was good." Tequila shots blurred out everything beyond last night's walk on the lake. The guy was long gone when Laurel had pierced Jackie's skull with the seven AM wake-up. Plopping the pills into her mouth, Jackie swallowed them with the lukewarm coffee.

She took the FBI jacket offered by Laurel, who was now scanning the crowd past the pair of television vans parked at the curb of the parking lot, her blue eyes narrowed in concentration. Her voice was distant. "Wish my thighs hurt."

"So is this the same MO as the Wisconsin woman?"

Laurel did not answer. Her eyes were closed, and Jackie knew better than to keep talking. Laurel had her psychic radar on, checking for anything out of the ordinary. If this was related to the Wisconsin victim, odds were there would be something. Even with the length of time that she had been dead, there had been a "taint." For Jackie, some demented prick had drained the woman of her blood. Period.

She finished off the last of her latte and waited for Laurel. She was ready to get moving, more so to avoid the media that looked to be wandering in their direction.

"Something is off here," Laurel said, her voice barely a whisper.

Jackie cringed. Of course there was. "Not off in a 'spiked your morning coffee' sort of way, I hope?"

"There's some bourbon in the trunk." Laurel didn't smile

at the humor. She was too intent on something out in the crowd.

"Great. Off to a fabulous start already," Jackie said, but Laurel was shuffling across the grass to the other side of the parking lot where the crowd had gathered. Something had tweaked that little psychic nerve of hers, and Jackie knew when to leave well enough alone. She waved. "Go find your bogeyman, Laur." Turning around, she made her way toward the overhanging tree before any media might notice she was standing by herself.

The blanket of leaves and limbs pushed and swatted at Jackie until she found herself standing in near darkness, thin shafts of light shining down on a boy seated neatly against the trunk of the tree. A couple members of the crew were already milling around in the shadows.

"That you, Jack? Glad you could join us."

Jackie's mouth creased into a frown. Pernetti. He would be the one detailing the victim. As if her headache didn't already feel like someone cranking screws down into her skull. "Don't even start with me, Pernetti. I'm not in the mood."

"Boy, did you get laid or something? You're bright-eyed and bushy-tailed this morning."

For a moment, Jackie thought he might have actually noticed, but then common sense took over. Pernetti was not capable of noticing anything like that. "Kiss my ass. Just tell me what we've got here."

He knelt down next to the body. "Archibold Lane, age twelve. Some sicko sucked the boy dry. There's ligature marks on the wrists and ankles. Funky marks, though. It looks like zip ties. Other than the hole in the arm, there's nothing else visible on him. Scene so far is weirdly spotless."

Twelve. What was wrong with people? "Spotless? That's doubtful." These days, everyone left something to track. Unless of course you knew how to clean up after yourself, and knew how forensics worked, but even then, it was unlikely.

"Clean so far, Jack." He shrugged, pointing at marks on the boy's wrists. "Other than the marks and the hole, he's got a couple bumps and scrapes that anyone might get when they've been out and about for a couple days."

"Two? He hasn't been dead that long."

Pernetti stood back up, thrusting his hands into his pockets. "Runaway, according to the sheriff. Fled from Mom and Dad beating each other up and not seen until this morning."

She doubted very much that Mom was doing any beating up on Dad. It hit her then, a brief flash of a twelve-year-old running away from a "domestic dispute" nearly twenty years prior. Mommy certainly had not been doing any of the beating. Jackie took a deep breath. The smell of death was doing little to wash the residue of memory away. "Anything else?"

"Nope. Area still being gone over. Bowers and Prescott are out canvassing, but it's looking a lot like that Wisconsin woman we brought in a couple months back."

Jackie shrugged and pulled out a pair of latex gloves from her jacket pocket. "Maybe. Okay, move, Pernetti. I want a look." She didn't want one, really. There was almost nothing she would see here, she could tell already. The perp had been clean and careful. Even the ground around the body looked undisturbed. Still, she would end up lead on the case, and, if anything, she needed to verify Pernetti's own observations.

"Think we should track down those parents and see what they have to say. Let them know their son is dead because they can't bitch at each other like other civilized folks."

She did not bother glancing up at him. "Go away, Pernetti. You're distracting me."

Thankfully left in silence, Jackie gave Archie a quick look over and found nothing out of the ordinary. He seemed almost peaceful, if one could ignore that fact that he looked like a pasty, deflated version of his former self. The thought sent a shiver down Jackie's spine, and she decided she had seen enough for the moment. Putting her sunglasses back on, she stepped back out from under the tree to find Laurel seated on the hood of her car smoking a cigarette. That was the first sign of trouble right there. A healthy girl by nature, Jackie knew if you hit the stress button hard enough, Laurel would be reaching for that security blanket in the bottom of her purse.

Jackie knew any shot at the day getting better was vanishing with each puff of smoke.

Chapter 2

One hundred forty-four years was a long time to be a failure at something. Nick Anderson felt every last year of it as he looked over the heads of the crowd at the towering maple, wondering how long it had taken to find someone who looked like his son. The boy sitting under the tree was not an exact likeness, but the similarities were obvious. Cornelius was back, and this time Nick knew it was for keeps. The game was on for one final round, and if he didn't catch the bastard, Nick would be dead.

The circus atmosphere in the park did little to help. In the two hours since returning from his initial discovery to the park after finding the body, Nick had been talked to by every reporter and cop on the scene. There appeared to be little in the way of evidence, and Nick had not dared do anything to the body earlier. Evidence gathering these days was far too elaborate to miss his tampering with the body. The feds did not appear to have anything concrete going on. He had seen them in action enough to know, and he knew how Cornelius worked. There would be little for them to go on until things were explored a bit more. Immediate discovery was too boring for him.

A late-arriving fed caught his eye, a tough, slight-looking

woman in a black leather jacket, jeans, and hiking boots. He watched her pop some pills into her mouth and wash it down with coffee while they both looked out in his direction, scanning the crowd. There was an easy comfort to the way they interacted. Partners, Nick figured. The coffee drinker donned an FBI jacket and walked toward the tree, and Nick wondered if she might be the one in charge. Not a good sign. Female law enforcement were generally harder to handle. Their bullshit meters were far more finicky. He wondered how long it might be before he was having a conversation with her. A day? Two, perhaps?

The other one came toward the crowd, and if it was not for the FBI-emblazoned jacket, Nick would never have pegged her for law enforcement. She had none of the swagger or stern confidence most portrayed at a crime scene. She looked far too soft for that, far too kind around the eyes.

It was the eyes that grabbed Nick's attention though. She scanned the crowd, but her gaze was unfocused, miles away. He watched her, curious about what she could be looking for until she got within about ten feet of his spot. Those distant and vacant blue eyes came abruptly into sharp focus, and what little color she had slowly evaporated from her face. The cold, probing fingers of psychic energy pushed around him then, and Nick swallowed the bile that rose in his throat.

Christ! A medium.

He gave off a definite and profound sense of death, or so his assistant Cynthia claimed. She was a powerful medium in her own right and, after meeting fifteen years before, had told him he felt like a walking cemetery. Not the most endearing sentiment, but apparently true. Nick had hired her on the spot. She had taught him how to know when a psychic was looking around for the dead, opening themselves up to the spirit world. It was a very distinct feeling, and now here he was, face-to-face with one who worked for the FBI who was standing five feet away from him at a crime scene he would undoubtedly be tied to sooner, if not later.

She wobbled on her feet, pale as the death she must have been sensing. Nick could see she did not suspect him in the slightest, but she felt him, and it scared the shit out of her. It would have been a good time to casually shift off into the crowd.

"Miss? Are you okay? You look a bit pale." The gesture of goodwill was out of his mouth before he could stop it.

"No, no. I'm fine, thanks. Just lost in thought," she said, managing a friendly smile. "How are you?"

She had a sense of wholeness about her that Nick found striking. It had his mind conjuring up an image a century and a half old, sweet and bitter at the same time. His comforting smile faded. "Disappointed I have to see things like this. You sure you're all right? I thought you might pass out there for a second."

The scared look in her eyes began to dissipate, replaced with wariness. "Fine. Really. I imagine you've been asked, but have you seen anything unusual around here today?"

Nick caught the subtle inflection, but years of listening to such questions had honed his response down to nothing. "No, I haven't. I was just walking through the park and stopped to see what all the fuss was about, and I think I've seen enough. I'm not fond of the circus folks make of these things."

"No," she said. "Neither am I, but we'll catch him. Don't you worry."

Nick gave her a faint smile and nod before backing away and heading slowly out of the crowd. He waited until she continued her search in another direction. It was time to leave. A medium was going to be hard to deal with, and any snooping around would have to be very quiet. The time had come to inform everyone else. Shelby would be pissed he had failed to inform her earlier. Reggie would be eager for action, but then he was always ready. The dead were good that way. Poor Cynthia had not heard any of this story.

He picked up the pace once he reached the edge of the park, and Nick could feel the creeping pangs of hunger. It was time for some blood.

Chapter 3

Laurel did not look at Jackie when Jackie stopped a few feet in front of her. She sat on the hood of the car, feet on the bumper, her elbows propped on her knees. The cigarette between her fingers glowed for a brief moment in agitation before leaving her mouth.

Jackie sighed loudly and crossed her arms over her chest. "Okay, what gives?"

She finally flicked her gaze upward. "There's *something* here."

Jackie closed her eyes. Great. First a boy drained of blood and now something supernatural. She stepped up and sat down on the hood next to Laurel. "Give me one." She didn't really want a cigarette. Six months without and she had kicked the habit yet again, but it was one of those camaraderie things. "So what the hell is it?"

"Hush," Laurel said, putting a finger to her lips. "He's close and might hear you."

Whatever it was, it was dead. Being quiet didn't much matter for Jackie. Still, Laurel actually looked frightened, and that was enough to be worried about. The spooky stuff rarely did that, so when it did you paid attention. "Sorry. You want some pics of the area?" When she nodded, Jackie waved Denny King over and had him go run off a gigabyte's worth of photos in the direction Laurel had pointed. While he was doing that, Jackie grabbed her by the arm and pulled her off the car.

"Come on. Come get a look at our boy." It was best to get her mind off whatever it was that had scared her. It was not the first time supernatural shit had hit the fan, and much like the normal shit in life, Jackie knew you had to just wipe it off and keep walking. She prayed to herself that whatever was out there stayed away from the case.

Pernetti had thankfully vacated the scene when they stepped up to Archie. It was difficult to get the deflated-balloon image out of Jackie's head. Someone had just drained the life right out of him. What sort of person were they dealing with here? The familiar knot of self-righteous anger began to burn in her gut. This was a fucked-up guy they were after. The sort that needed a swift and permanent removal from this world.

"What an awful thing to do to someone, and a child at that," Laurel said, squatting down next to Jackie beside the body. "They finished with him?"

She nodded. "Yeah, think so. Go ahead."

Laurel reached out and laid her fingertips on the boy's hand. A moment later, she jerked back. "Shit. It's here, too."

"It?" Jackie stood, half expecting the boy to sit up from the tree. "What it?"

"The . . . spirit or whatever it was. Its residue is on the boy." She rocked for a moment on the balls of her feet and then tentatively touched Archie again, lingering longer this time. The firm set of her mouth turned into a frown.

Jackie stared down at her. "You want to tell me what's going on?" Laurel pulled back and gave her an "excuse me" look. "Sorry. I hate when your freaky ghost shit gets involved in a case. So are you saying the thing out there had something to do with Archie's death?"

She shook her head. "No, I don't think so. I don't even think it's the same spirit. This one is . . . bad news, Jackie. Really bad."

The knot in Jackie's stomach dissolved into something else. Trepidation. "And the one out there was nice in comparison to this?"

"Different." She got to her feet, leaning lightly against Jackie's arm. The effort had obviously drained her. "Whatever this is, it isn't here anymore. The thing out there . . ." Laurel dug her fingers into Jackie's arm for support and perhaps a little courage. "Goddess help me, Jackie. It was so strong. I felt like I'd opened a door to the other side."

"But you didn't see anything?"

"No. I barely kept from passing out. This sweetie of a guy noticed and snapped me out of it."

Jackie stepped back, staring at her partner. "Just happened to notice you were in some psychic trance communing with the dead?"

She gave Jackie a dirty look before glancing over her shoulder. Jackie turned and saw the local sheriff standing behind them.

"Agents," he said, nodding at them with a curious look. "Have you found anything useful?"

"No, nothing just yet," Jackie replied with a smile and stepped between him and Laurel. *Look at me, Sheriff, not the psychic.* "It's an incredibly clean scene."

He nodded. "Yeah, that's what it seems like to me. Like someone just dropped out of the sky and set the kid under the tree and then took off again. Nobody has seen anything that we can tell."

There was something all right, but ghosts were the last thing Jackie was about to mention. The blood-draining aspect to this case was enough to turn the media sharks into a frenzy. They didn't need any more help.

The sheriff excused himself, and the agents made their way out from under the tree. Laurel followed in a daze, glancing every few seconds toward the crowd. Jackie needed to take a few minutes to get updates from everyone and make sure the parents had been contacted. Someone was picking them up, and Jackie had a few choice words in mind for them. When Laurel absently bumped into her for the third time, Jackie turned on her.

"Is this as bad as you're making it look? Because you're starting to worry me here."

Laurel's mouth scrunched up. "Maybe? I don't know, Jackie. I've never felt anything like this before. It's like discovering an F6 tornado."

"A what?"

"Never mind. It's fascinating and terrifying at the same time. Okay?"

Jackie nodded. That made some sense but did not do much to ease the nervousness gnawing at her. Jackie didn't care for spiritual involvement in her cases. Spirits didn't follow the usual rules, and dealing with them generally fell outside typical crime-solving procedures. Worse, they were a foe you could not see or hear. Ghosts were annoying like that. "You want to go have another look around? I'm really not liking the fact nobody can tell how the boy was put there. We should check out those pics Denny took, too."

"Sure. Let's do that."

The crowd was nosy and morbid, and the continuing dance of clouds and sunlight was beginning to play hell with Jackie's head. She pointed a finger at the first reporter who caught sight of her. "Don't talk to me now. I'll make a statement when I'm done."

Laurel chuckled as the reporter stopped in his tracks and let them wander on. "I wish I could do that."

"Do what?"

"Pull up a look of murderous rage at will. It would be handy."

She shrugged and moved on, steering them around the back side of the crowded parking lot. Laurel knew as well as Jackie where she pulled that feeling from, and Laurel wisely said nothing further. They didn't speak at all while they made their way around the hundred or so loosely gathered people, casually scanning for anything out of the ordinary. Sometimes it was just a look someone would make, a momentary pause when they walked by or looked their way, and suspicion would be roused. But Jackie saw nothing.

Out of the corner of her eye, she kept watch on Laurel, looking for any signs of the weird "ghost trance" she would get into when she communicated with the dead. The maple stood in the center of the field like a green shroud of death. No way was someone going to be carrying a body under there without leaving any signs. A snapped twig, a footprint, there had to be something. Finally, they neared the loosely parked group of FBI vehicles. "Sense anything odd at all?"

"Nope. Sorry, it's gone now."

"What about your handy little helper? The cute guy."

"No. He's gone, but he wasn't a ghost, Jackie. He was as real as you and me."

"Probably. It's still suspiciously convenient," she said. "I'm also betting that a ghost didn't drain the blood out of that boy. Right?"

"They don't do that, but you're being paranoid."

Jackie smiled. "Yep. That's why I'm in charge. Now I'm going to go have a little chat with the oblivious fuckups known as Archie's parents and let them know—"

"Jackie," Laurel said, laying a hand on Jackie's arm. "Take the reporter. I'll talk with Archie's parents."

"You saying I don't know how to give them the once-over?"

Laurel gave her a little shove. "That's exactly the issue. Go beat up on the reporters. We both know problem parents are not your strong suit. We don't want to be in the papers for the wrong reason."

Jackie frowned but walked toward the TV reporters anyway. It paid to have a perceptive partner at times.

Chapter 4

Nick's hands slipped on the doorknob to the offices of Special Investigations, Inc., the rather bland name for his investigation agency. A second try brought a painful wince to his face, but the latch withdrew, and he stepped into the soft light of the front office and was immediately greeted by the familiar cool cylinder slapping into his palm. Blocking his way in was the crisply dressed Cynthia, far more imposing than her 5'5" frame would suggest.

"Damnit, Nick! You look like shit. I should smack you. You do realize it's, like, after noon? When did you last drink? Six, maybe seven this morning?"

She spit out the words too fast for him to reply. After a moment of numbed silence, Nick unscrewed the cap and took a long draught, puckering at the bitter taste. It made lemons taste like pure cane sugar. One of these days, the guys at the lab would figure out a way to sweeten the stuff. He shrugged. "Thank you, Cynthia. Always prepared."

She rolled her eyes and walked back to her desk, her soft, full mouth drawn into an angry, thin line. A colorful bouquet of flowers obscured half the work surface. "One of these days, I won't be here, Nick. What are you going to do then?"

"Die, I expect." He smiled halfheartedly at her, but at least it was truthful. Four hours without, and the doorway to the other side began to pull at you with an ever-increasing force until your soul was compelled to flee the world of the living. It was a constant and inviting temptation.

"So you're a comedian now, are you?"

"Nope. Just honest, and thanks for being there. Really."

The taught lines on her face faded, and the hint of a smile returned. "Always will be, whether you're an ass or not."

"I'm far too fortunate."

She laughed. "Yes, you are. So is this the big case you've been dancing around telling me about for the past few months?"

There was that hopeful look in her eye, full of curiosity and a vague sense of worry. Nick had refrained from mentioning the case, the one bit of history he had been too reluctant to reveal to Cynthia over the years. She knew him about as well as anyone could, but the truth would have scared her, and that was the last thing he wanted to do. The time for secrets ended now, and Nick's stomach tightened at the thought of sharing the news.

"Yeah, it is. A dead boy drained of blood was found in a park this morning."

"Shit," she said, eyes going wide. "Another vampire?"

He nodded. "Yeah. Did you get a hold of Shel and Reg?"

"Of course. She'll be here by three, and Reggie will come when you're ready."

"Good. Thank you." Nick walked by and gave her shoulder an affectionate squeeze. It was impossible to fathom what things would be like now without her around. "I'm going to kick back and relax for a few before Shelby gets here. It's been a rather long day already." Cynthia looked up at him with expectant eyes, but there was nothing to say, not yet.

"Okay. Here," she said, handing him a note from off the desk. "Richard from the lab called, and I expect some . . . answers."

He took the note and gave her a grim smile. "You'll get them soon enough. What's with the flowers?"

"Pretty, aren't they?" She leaned forward and smelled them, smiling. "That sweet Mrs. Renfro sent them over."

"Ah." Nick appreciated the easy ones. Reggie had talked to the dead Mr. Renfro himself, who was hanging around because he had died without telling his wife about the lockbox full of cash he had been hiding in the backyard for the past thirty-seven years. The money had been significant and had certainly eased the pains of retirement on Mrs. Renfro. He had not had the heart to charge her for a two-minute phone call.

Pulling a cold can of Guinness from the mini fridge in the hall, Nick closed the office door and kicked off his boots. He pushed the shades up onto his head and savored the near darkness of the room. The beer was half gone before he managed to sit down.

Trust.

There was little of it to go around anymore. After 180 years of life, the principle of diminishing returns had reached its limit. One covenant of trust had never been betrayed, however. Cornelius Drake had said he would come, five times over, for deaths Nick had incurred back on that fateful day in the pouring rain, and, true to his word, he was here again to finish his twisted game of revenge.

The fifth and final set had begun at last.

Nick downed the last of the beer and crumpled the can into a ball like tin foil. His shot at the wastebasket hit the rim and bounced out. Leaning back in his chair, he closed faintly glowing eyes and sighed. "Yeah, I've got game, all right."

Chapter 5

"Okay, so what do you figure?" Jackie said, polishing off her ziti and meatballs with famished zeal. Her body had settled enough by midday to realize it had puked out all its nourishment. Laurel, on the other hand, picked mindlessly at a Caesar salad, pushing the leaves of lettuce around and nibbling on a crouton. Her glass of sparkling water had barely been touched.

"About what?" The absent tone indicated how well Laurel was listening.

"The case, girl. The weird vibes, the bloodless boy, freaky fucking ghosts." She finally caught Laurel's gaze. "What do you think?"

She stared at Jackie, hard and quiet, until Jackie finally turned away. "Don't take this case, Jack."

Jack? Christ, it was serious. The last time Jackie had heard her abbreviated name from Laurel's lips was on a four AM ride home from a brawl outside a bar. It hadn't mattered that the asshole had it coming. "You serious? Since when?"

"Yes, since my bad-vibe radar pinged off the map into next week somewhere." She leaned forward over the table for emphasis. "This is bad news, Jackie. Let Pernetti handle it. He's been whining to get his hands on leading something big. This case is . . . It's all wrong."

Jackie spit the mouthful of wine back into her glass. "What the hell, Laur? They're all wrong. It's our job to make them right again."

"No," she said, stern and quiet. "Wrong as in someone is going to get hurt."

"Oh." Jackie rolled her eyes, though she could not exactly laugh that one off. The last time that feeling had happened, Jackie's ankle had been snapped in a high-speed chase gone bad. At least the crash had involved the bad guys, too. "Well, we didn't sign up for the safety aspect of this job, you know."

Laurel shook her head. "No. This is not in the same realm, Jackie. This is 'don't touch with a ten-foot pole' sort of bad. It has a big glowing skull and crossbones stamped all over it."

"Really?"

Laurel frowned at Jackie's sarcasm, but then, how could she not make light of such things? She wouldn't leave the case to someone like Pernetti and his super-sized, glow-in-the-dark forehead. Seriously, the man had to polish the damn thing.

"You realize that sort of feeling is exactly the reason not to give it over to some goon like Pernetti?"

"I don't care. I'd rather see Pernetti get wheeled into the morgue than you, and need I remind you you're a goon, too? Albeit a much prettier one."

Jackie studied Laurel's expression. One didn't joke about seeing another agent in the morgue. It was bad karma. She knew from the last time a ghost was involved that if the shit really hit the fan, Laurel might actually fight her to get off the case, and that was not a scenario Jackie could win. Fighting Laurel would be like taking a bulldozer to the foundation of her being. The consequences would be too dire.

Jackie grinned at Laurel. "That's why I always win."

"Uh-huh. Get over yourself, goon girl, and promise me you will be very careful with this one."

The cell phone buzzed in Jackie's pocket, and she pulled it out to see that Denny was calling. She hit the button. "What's up, Den?"

"Hey, Jack, thought I'd let you know we found an old coin beneath the boy."

"You mean like something a coin collector would have?"

"Yep, looks that way," he said. "It's sealed up in plastic, but it looks to be very old if it's real. It's going downtown with the little evidence we have for now."

"Give it to the geeks when you get there. We'll be in soon. I want to see those pics you took also."

"I e-mailed them to you a few minutes ago."

"Already? How?"

Denny laughed. "Technology, Jack. You know, the cool stuff without triggers attached to them."

"Ohhh, funny, man. It's a good thing I like you, otherwise I'd have to inflict some bodily harm."

"Promise?"

Jackie smiled, clicked off the phone, dipped the last of her bread into the sauce on the plate, and ate it with a wide-eyed smile. "They found an old coin under our boy. So, why don't we go back to the bureau and see if the geeks can find out anything regarding that penny."

"Promise me, Jackie. Be very careful with this one."

Jackie could feel the heat of the finger pointing at her chest. The seriousness of Laurel's voice tightened her stomach. "Okay," she said, laughing off the tense moment, but she knew better. Laurel was never wrong about these things. "I promise."

Chapter 6

Nick sat against his mahogany desk, thumbs hooked in the belt on either side of the buckle that looked like two crossed revolvers. As the stress mounted, old habits tended to kick in, and the cowboy posturing was one of the oldest.

"Drake is back," he said, glancing quickly at each of them.

Shelby sported cutoff denim shorts that revealed a good inch or two of ass, and a white tank top with no bra. Her nipples pushed up right into the fabric to say, "Hello, how do you do." It was an annoying habit of hers, purposefully putting herself on display in front of him. Her dark hair had been drawn back into a simple tail, showing off the smooth, sensuous lines of her face, looking unchanged from the day he had met her seventy-eight years ago.

Reggie's transparent form sat in the old leather wingback in the corner. He was dressed in the same old, faded overalls, T-shirt, and leather work boots he had died in, forever Nick's right-hand man.

Cynthia sat in the chair immediately in front of him, her legs demurely crossed, gaze curious and calm. Only the arms crossed over her chest gave any indication of her seriousness. Nick knew that irritation lay ready in waiting, crouched just beneath the surface.

Shelby's relaxed nonchalance evaporated. "How do you know?"

"Someone found a twelve-year-old boy, drained of blood, sitting up against a tree in Garibaldi Park this morning. I felt Drake on him. I sensed Drake . . . a couple days ago but had no luck tracking him down."

Reggie made a low whistling sound, and Shelby straightened up stiff as a lightning rod. "Two days? And you didn't tell me?" She pointed an accusatory finger at Nick. "You asshole! You promised you would tell me the minute he was back again."

"There've been whispers lately," Reggie said in agreement. "But these days, the restless folks whisper about a lot of things, and, honestly, I'd not been paying attention to them. I suppose I should've checked on things."

Nick shrugged at them. Knowing two days ago would have served no useful purpose other than putting them in harm's way even sooner. "It wasn't clear, and more than likely you would have just gotten yourself in trouble before we realized what he is up to this time. I figured it was better to risk just one of us until absolutely necessary."

"Ah." Shelby's voice teetered on the fine edge of fury. "And if you'd managed to get yourself killed before letting us know what the fuck was going—"

"Hey," Cynthia's calm and cool voice interceded. There was a hint of fear. This was beyond Shelby's usual acerbic attitude toward Nick. She never got downright pissed at him. "Aren't we a team here? I mean . . . what exactly is going on? I'm a little disappointed to be left out of the loop on this, Nick."

He folded his arms across his chest, a futile attempt to ward off the negative emotions tightening up every muscle in his gut. How many times had he considered asking Cynthia to find another job, trying to find a good way of letting her go, and then not being able to do it? It was difficult to let go of someone who knew about the dark parts of your heart and accepted them anyway. And then part of it was just plain, old-fashioned honesty. He did not have the wherewithal to lie to Cynthia.

"Cyn. This case is potentially very dangerous, and it's also very personal," he said, forcing himself to look down at those wide, accepting brown eyes. "After today, if you decide to pack up and leave, there'll be no hard feelings from any of us. Honestly, I'd feel better if you did."

She leaned back, eyes narrowing. "You're serious."

"I'm not going to ask you to stay."

Shelby laughed. "Oh, come on, Nick. Like Cyn would refuse you anything."

He shot her a hard glance, which was met with equal fire.

"Why don't you just tell me the whole story and let me decide for myself?" Cynthia said.

Nick shifted against the desk. Nothing like having the two people you cared about most in the world seriously annoyed with you at the same time. "You have to promise me, Cynthia. If you have any doubts, any reservations at all about this after today, you will—"

"Christ, Nick. Just tell her already, and make it the short version. The last time you sat down and told this sob story, it took five and a half hours."

Except I was lying down in your bed and figuring I was dead. Nick bit off the reply that burned on his tongue. "Fine. The short version. Stop and ask me a question about any of this. Shel and Reg know the story."

Cynthia smiled. "Talk away, hon. I'm all ears."

Shelby walked out of the office and returned a moment later with two more beers. In the meantime, Nick turned to Reggie. "Reg, when you decide to leave, I need you to go check out the FBI headquarters downtown. Typical snoop run. I want to know who is on the case, what they've got, etcetera. Be careful though. They have a medium working with them now, and she's pretty strong. Might give the locals on the scene a look, too, just in case."

His silvery head nodded. "I'm all over it, boss. Was just waiting for the go-ahead." He waved his fingers at Cynthia and Shelby. "Bye, girls. Enjoy story time with Uncle Nick." His body slowly sank through the chair and vanished.

With a fresh beer in his hand, Nick opted to stand behind his desk to allow for some pacing. Telling Cynthia this information was just too nerve-wracking to be parked in a chair. Shelby was the only other person he had ever told, and look what had happened. Sadly, it was too late to turn back the clock two days and fire Cynthia. Even then, it was possible she had already been marked. Cynthia sat on the edge of her chair now, hands folded neatly in her lap. She looked more curious than anxious, and Nick wished he could make her feel the opposite. She needed to be worried. She needed to know that leaving was the best option, and sooner rather than later.

Shelby sipped at her beer, standing with nonchalant grace in the corner. "Anytime, babe. Drake's probably already planning number two as we speak."

"Shelby," he said but realized then that arguing was pointless. She was just looking for an excuse to jump down his throat for breaking his promise to notify her. Nick heaved a sigh and shook his head. "Anyway. The short-and-sweet version." A long draught on the beer wetted his already dry throat. "Short, at least."

"Nick," Cynthia said, forever the voice of tranquillity. "Just tell me, please."

"Right. I know." He blew out his breath again. It should not have been this hard the second time around. "I was a sheriff in Wyoming back in 1862."

And so his story began.

Chapter 7

Jackie leaned over Denny's shoulder, one hand braced on the edge of his desk. He had the crime-scene photos uploaded onto his computer, a spread of thumbnail pictures across the twenty-four-inch screen. Laurel stood in the corner of his cubby peering from the other side.

When he scrolled to the next set, Laurel pointed. "Stop." She stepped forward for a closer look. "Tenth one and the next few. Those look like the right area."

The tenth photo was enlarged to fill the screen, and Jackie looked at the faces of the crowd. Hands in pockets, pairs and small groups chatted with one another. Nobody that she could see had any of the telltale signs that might implicate something more than casual interest.

Denny looked up at Laurel. "See anything?"

"No. Did you shoot video first? These pics might be too late."

"Too late for what?" he asked.

"Her knight in shining armor," Jackie said.

"Being polite doesn't make you chivalrous," she snapped back.

Denny snickered and clicked through to pull up the

playback screen. "Here's what I've got. I shot it before I began taking the pics."

It was from the vantage point of the park grass, somewhere between the big maple and the parking lot. It started near where they had parked and panned slowly across to the television crews, zooming in gradually to pick up clearer images of the crowd standing at the edge of the grass.

When the view panned all the way to the other side, Laurel pointed at the screen. "Stop there."

Denny paused the video. Jackie could tell immediately who she was likely referring to. A tall, broad-shouldered figure past the crowd, walking away from the scene. "The big guy there, jeans and sweatshirt."

"Yep, that's him."

"Okay," Denny said and zoomed in closer. He clicked the play button again, and they watched him continue walking away. A few seconds later he stopped and looked back.

"Look at where his gaze is," Jackie exclaimed. "He's not interested in the tree at all."

Laurel straightened, crossing her arms over her chest. "Hmmm, you're right. He's looking back at us."

The still frame zoomed in more, and the image blurred. Denny began to go to work. "I'll get this cleared up and enhanced. It should give us a pretty good shot of his face to work with if you want."

"Do it," Jackie said. "Run it if you get a good one, and see if anything pops up."

"Sure thing."

Laurel shrugged. "He's probably just wondering if I'm all right."

"Maybe," she agreed. "But he could be wondering a lot more than that, too."

"Paranoid."

"Innocent."

"Ha! My title is better."

Jackie clapped Denny on the shoulder. "Thanks, Den. Figure out who he is, and I'll buy you a shot."

"I'm there."

She stepped away from the desk. "I want to see about that penny they found. Maybe the geeks can tell us what it is."

After acquiring the penny, Jackie and Laurel went down to the basement and tracked down Mark Hauser, head of the Geekroom, where all things information were acquired and processed. Jackie never ceased to marvel at the kinds of things the FBI was capable of finding out. It was almost disturbing.

"Hey!" he exclaimed, spinning around in his chair when Jackie knocked on the open door to his office. "What brings the FBI's sexiest agents down into the depths?"

Jackie took in the sprawling desk with its three thirty-inch monitors and grimaced. "Seriously, Hauser? Can you ever greet us without mentioning looks?"

"Why? That would be boring." He gave her a smug grin. "Besides, who else around here can get away with it besides us harmless geeks?"

Laurel laughed. "He has a point. Hauser's about as harmless as they come."

He pointed at Laurel. "Exactly."

Jackie thrust the bag containing the coin at him. "You guys are also the sneakiest, most conspiratorial bastards in the agency. Everything has a plan."

He plucked the bag from her fingers. "It makes us more interesting. What have we got here?"

"It's a coin found under a dead boy this morning. Only real piece of evidence we found at the scene, so I'm hoping you might give us some info on it."

"Cool. Let's have a look." He grabbed a pair of tweezers from a drawer and withdrew the coin from the bag. After turning it over a couple times, he arched his brows. "It looks like an Indian Head Penny, 1862. Perfect condition, by the look of it."

"Worth much?"

"One sec, and I'll find out," he replied and spun back around to type on his computer. About thirty seconds later he tapped his screen. "If it's real and as pristine as it looks, it'll fetch about twenty-five K."

Laurel whistled softly. Jackie could hardly believe it. "For a damn penny? Wow."

"Coin collecting is serious business, Jack," he said. "And this was just found on the ground beneath a dead body?"

"Yep."

"Robbery gone bad?"

The image of loose, gray skin washed through Jackie's mind. "Don't think so. We think it was left on purpose."

"Really." He nodded and reexamined the coin. "Someone sending a message, perhaps?"

"What sort of message requires killing a twelve-year-old boy?"

He winced. "Ouch. That sucks. I'll look into this and see if I can find anything—coin collectors, auctions, that sort of stuff. Maybe something will pop."

"Thanks," Jackie replied. "Let me know the second you find something."

Back on their floor, Jackie sat down at her desk to the sound of Denny's voice coming from the other side of the cubicle's wall. "Check your e-mail, Jack. Got some interesting stuff on your guy."

"Already? Nice going, Den. Thanks."

"Anytime."

Jackie turned on her computer and accessed the e-mail, downloading a picture of what turned out to be a photo ID card. Laurel leaned over her shoulder, her head next to Jackie's.

"He's a PI?"

"So it would seem," she said.

"Man, would you look at those eyes. Those have to be colored contacts."

"Maybe. So why would PI Nick Anderson be interested in the body of a dead boy from the Chicago burbs?"

"Coincidence?"

Jackie shot her a skeptical glance.

"It's been known to happen, you know."

"Not in my lifetime." Jackie scrolled to the next page, where another picture greeted them.

"Whoa, he cleans up nice," Laurel said.

It was a newspaper clipping dated over a year earlier. Jackie scanned through the article. "Nicholas Rembrandt Anderson? What the hell. Hey, Denny!" she shouted. "Are these the same guy?"

"Yeah. Interesting guy. Wait till you see the next page."

"CEO of Bloodwork Industries," Laurel said. "Wonder what that is?"

"Curious, isn't it? I think we might want to have a little chat with Mr. Anderson."

"He donated two million dollars to the children's hospital."

"So he's a saint."

"Bet he likes tough FBI types."

Jackie smirked. "Rules you out then, doesn't it?"

"Screw you. I'm tough in the ways that matter."

"Like an Annabelle's cream puff."

"Oh, Annabelle's! We're stopping, right? Where's this Anderson guy located?"

"Um, I don't know where this address is," Jackie said, pointing at the screen.

"Just type it into Google maps."

"What?"

"Oh! Look at this." Laurel had scrolled to the next screen, which was another newspaper clipping. This one was dated April 1970.

Jackie stared at the picture. It was the spitting image of Nick Anderson. "Wait a sec, that can't be right. That the same guy?"

Denny's voice piped in again. "It's his dad, keep reading."

"Creepy," Laurel said. "Looks just like him."

"Acquitted of murder." Jackie tapped the screen. This was getting better by the word. "In the slayings of five people. . . ."

Laurel chimed in at the same time. ". . . who were drained of all their blood."

Jackie leaned back in her chair. "Holy shit. Coincidence, my ass. We really do need to go have a chat with this guy."

"Okay," Laurel admitted. "Got me there. This is too strange."

"So where's this guy at?"

"Just Google it and see."

"I only Google after about six drinks."

Laurel shook her head, chuckling. "You really should try using your computer once in a while. They're actually useful." She pulled up the Google screen and located their address. "See? Ten seconds, and presto! Special Investigations, Inc."

"Shit. That's almost an hour from here. Call and see if he's there. Otherwise track down his home address."

"We'll need to hit Annabelle's first."

"You know, I hope your ass gets fat. Where the hell do you put all the crap we buy from there?"

Laurel grabbed at her breasts. "Boobs, baby. You should eat more cream puffs."

There was snickering from nearby cubicles. Jackie rolled her eyes and got up. "Let's go, you bitch. You're buying."

"Don't I always?"

"Fuck you," Jackie grumbled, walking away. She never won these things.

The call to Nick Anderson's office let him know they were to be expected. It was located on the barest outskirts of what could properly be called "greater Chicago." It was virtual farmland, carved out in places with wealthier subdivisions.

"More villains need to live out this way," Laurel said. "It's lovely out here."

Jackie gave her a wry look. "Have we passed a single coffeehouse in the past twenty minutes?"

"You've had enough caffeine for the day, young lady. Besides, I could see you living out here. Look!" She pointed at a large white farmhouse, complete with blue shuttered windows, a picket fence, and an ancient tractor with a FOR SALE sign leaning against its front grill. "That place is beautiful."

"And what would I do with a place like that?" Place for a bed, her piano, a fridge, and a bathroom was everything she needed. The rest was just wasted space.

"You could raise three or four kids in a place like that and still have space. A nice, strong guy to throw the hay bales around." She grinned at Jackie. "Anyway. I'm just saying—"

"Three or four kids? Are you insane? I can barely take care of my goddamn cat."

"Actually," Laurel said with all seriousness, "I can see it pretty goddamn clearly."

Jackie stared at her for a second. Was this one of those prescient moments? *God, please, no,* she thought. "You know as well as I do, Laur. I'd be a horrible mother."

"You'd be a great mom." The clipped, forceful tone of her voice had Jackie leaning up against the door. It was that "I know better than you, so shut the fuck up" voice. Sadly, the damn witch was usually right.

"I really hate that tone of voice."

"You just hate that I'm right." Laurel crossed her arms over her chest and stared straight ahead at the road, a smug smile on her face.

Jackie grumbled and shook her head. "Bitch. I'm getting a new partner."

"No, you're not."

"Shut up!"

Laurel laughed but said nothing more.

Special Investigations, Inc. was a very unassuming place. A simple, one-story, brick office building with a small paved parking lot stood in a small strip of older shops in a blip of population along the highway. The downtown was one of those more recently renovated sorts that gave the buildings much of their old-world charm. Cracks in the parking lot were sprouting dandelions and grass, but across the street wafted the heavenly aroma of a doughnut shop.

Laurel pointed at what Jackie's nose had immediately sniffed out when they got out of the car. "Bet there's lattes in there. Everyone makes them now."

"On our way out," she replied. Walking up to the door, Jackie noticed the name of an attorney on the door above Nick Anderson's. The attorney's name was twice as big.

"Not big on advertising, is he?"

"Yeah. Low-profile type." She failed at hiding the sarcasm.

Jackie opened the door and stepped inside, finding a short hallway down the middle of the building dividing Special Investigations from the attorney. The door to the office was unlocked, so she opened it up and found herself in a typical reception office. A variety of Western-themed paintings adorned the walls, which were painted a cool and soothing blue. The furniture was worn but well made with soft, brown leathers and dark wood stain. Next to a colorful bouquet of flowers on the spacious desk was a cute thirtysomething. She could have been passing herself off as Santa's girlfriend with the bright red, tailored suit. Jackie could tell by the way she studied them that the woman was no airhead.

The woman smiled, friendly but still cautious. "Good morning, and welcome to Special Investigations. How may I help you?"

Jackie laid her badge down on the desk. "FBI. I'm Agent Rutledge, and this is Agent Carpenter. I believe Mr. Anderson is expecting us."

The woman picked up the badge and gave it a thorough look before nodding once and handing it back with the same friendly smile. Not a single flinch of worry or concern crossed her face.

"Might I inform him as to what this is about?" The voice was polite in that almost saccharine way that told you a person was not terribly fond of your presence.

"If you could just inform him we're here to see him," Jackie said, trying to mimic the same sweet tone. Behind her, Laurel walked around the room studying the paintings.

The woman shrugged, watching Laurel's casual perusal as she did. "Very well. One moment." She called, and the sound of a phone ringing in the back room could be heard. "Mr. Anderson? There are two women here from the FBI to see you. Yes, the badges look legit." She glanced at each of them for a moment. "Yes, that's right. Okay. You're welcome."

Jackie frowned at the knowing little smile the woman gave them. There had been a strong tone of familiarity in her voice. Either she and Mr. Anderson went back a long ways, or they were intimate. The deep voice on the other end had been slow but too quiet to make out any of the words.

"If you'd like to have a seat, he said he'd be just a moment."

"Thanks," Laurel said and sat down in one of the leather chairs.

Jackie turned to give her a look but stopped when she saw Laurel's grim face. Her mouth was pulled taught, her eyes squinting with concentration. With her back to the secretary, Jackie gave Laurel a quizzical look. *What's going on?* Laurel didn't notice, so Jackie turned back to the woman.

"Actually, could we bother you for something to drink?"

The opportunity to get up and do something appeared to relieve the secretary. "Sure. No problem." The loose-fitting red skirt swished back and forth as she hurried down the short hall to the partial kitchen inset into the wall. "There's fresh coffee," she called back at them.

"Great for me," Jackie replied. "Water for Agent Carpenter." She leaned over Laurel, lowering her voice to barely above a whisper. "What? You sense something?"

The frown relaxed a bit while one hand played idly at the crystal around her neck. "I think I just felt a ghost."

Jackie arched an eyebrow. "You sure?"

She nodded. "Yeah. Gone now, but it was here when we walked in, and the same feeling from the scene is here. It's like ghost central."

That was the last thing Jackie wanted to hear. She avoided asking herself if it could get any weirder. "You okay for this?

"Yeah, just a little unexpected is all. I'll be okay."

"Agents, here's your coffee and water."

Jackie nearly jumped out of her skin. The woman had made no sound coming up behind them and now wore a curiously innocent expression on her face. She would have put her month's check on the fact that the secretary was far from that. Jackie gave her a halfhearted smile. "Thanks."

"I hope it's not too strong. I watered it down just a bit. Mr. Anderson likes his coffee to hold spoons upright."

"It's fine." Could not fault the guy for that, at least.

He came out then, holding his own steaming mug, brown hair cropped short and laying close to his scalp, and with brilliant, gleaming hazel-brown eyes. Jackie found herself staring and finally blinked away. It was the same look from the video. Nobody's eyes were naturally that color. He had on rough, leather, square-toed boots; faded blue jeans; and a long-sleeved, navy-blue T-shirt. Not a dress-up kind of guy, but he was fit, lean muscle through and through. He looked a bit older than his forty years. It was the slight crow's-feet around the eyes, Jackie decided. The rest of his face was smooth, if a bit unshaven.

"Good morning, agents," he said and nodded to each of them. "I'm Nick Anderson. How can I help you?"

No sign of nervousness in the voice. He appeared relaxed. Jackie took a sip of her coffee. "We'd like to ask you a few questions regarding Archibold Lane."

His eyes widened a hair. "This a case I'm involved with? The name isn't familiar."

Like hell. Jackie shrugged. "Perhaps. We'd just like to talk to you for a few minutes and settle some questions for us. It won't take long." *Or it could take all day, depending on how you answer, cowboy.*

"Sure," he said, waving them toward the back. "Come on back. Cynthia? No calls, please."

"No problem, Mr. Anderson."

Nick Anderson's office was quiet and clean, but not compulsively so. There were a lot of Western motif knick-knacks around, dominated by a saddle mounted to the wall behind his desk. Either the guy had some real Western blood in him, or he was really over-the-top on the whole cowboy image thing. She had a hard time imagining it as a selling point for a PI.

Laurel picked an old craftsman-style leather chair in the corner, as far away from him as she could get, avoiding the more comfortable-looking, overstuffed chenille chairs in front of the desk. Jackie wondered but said nothing. She decided to stand before the desk between the two chairs, close enough to show him she was not threatened.

Nick stopped before sitting down in his own chair. "Please sit, Ms. . . . ?"

"Agent Rutledge, and thanks, but I'll stand for now, Mr. Anderson." She wished Laurel had remained standing as well, but she merely sat in the chair, ramrod straight, clutching the case folder tightly in her hand. Ghost feeling must have been stronger in the office.

He sat down and leaned back, sipping at his coffee. "Okay. Suit yourself. What sort of questions did you have for me then?"

"Can you tell us where you were last night from roughly midnight until dawn?"

"Sleeping mostly. I was up around five thirty to go for a swim."

Jackie bit off the sarcastic bark of laughter. "At five thirty AM? What pool is open at that time of day?"

He apparently found her annoyance amusing. "It's quiet then and a pleasant way to begin the day when I have a case to think about. It helps clear my head."

She found her mouth inching into a matching grin, her eyes locked on to his. What was it about them? They had a fire all their own. Or was it just a trick of the light?

Jackie snapped her gaze away from Nick's, focusing instead on his mouth. Tricky little shit. This guy was smooth. She would have to see if he could be ruffled up a bit. "You happen to have any witnesses to corroborate this, Mr. Anderson?"

"Only if someone was hiding out at my lake."

"Bit cold in the morning to jump into a lake, don't you think?"

"More of an oversize pond, but I find it refreshing, and I've a high tolerance for the cold."

The smile on his face once again had the corner of Jackie's mouth quivering upward. A quick glance showed her that Laurel was riveted by this man. She sat unmoving, her pen poised on the blank notepad. What the hell was she seeing? Jackie wished she could have a word with her.

"So after the swim to clear your head, you did what?"

"Showered, ate, came into work around eight."

"Were you here all day?" *Come on, cowboy. Lie to me. Go ahead.*

He shook his head once. "No. I left from about nine until one."

"Doing?" The effort at sounding casual with the question did not fall well on Mr. Anderson. He leaned forward in his chair, placing the now empty coffee cup on the desk.

"Agent Rutledge," he said calmly, "I was at your crime scene today. I was driving through the area and spotted the circus going on in the park. I was curious, so I stopped to see what it was all about. I ran into Agent Carpenter there when she was about to pass out, and then I decided to leave shortly after. I'd heard and seen enough to know more or less what happened."

"What did happen, Mr. Anderson?" Jackie suppressed the urge to wipe the smile off his face, though, admittedly, it was the urge to smile along with him that got under her skin more than anything else. If she got the chance, she would have to ask him how he did that.

"Some sociopath exsanguinated a young boy and stuck him under a tree." There was a note of anger there now, a hard edge to his voice.

"Agent Carpenter? Would you show Mr. Anderson our piece of evidence, please?" When no reply came, Jackie turned and cleared her throat. Christ! What was wrong with Laurel?

"Oh. Sorry." Laurel flipped open the file folder and pulled out the sealed penny, handing it to Jackie with an apologetic smile.

Jackie frowned and plucked it from her fingertips, giving her a "What the hell?" stare. Laurel smiled apologetically, settling back into the chair. She spun back to face Nick and set the coin down on the desk. "Does this look familiar to you at all, Mr. Anderson?"

Something washed over his face, gone as quickly as it appeared. Surprise? Fear? Jackie could not be sure what. He picked up the coin and studied it intently for a moment, turning it over with large, steady hands. The eyes, which so often gave suspects away, narrowed just a hair. Without their gaze focusing on her, Jackie watched them, but everything about his demeanor remained unruffled and calm.

"It's a penny."

Nice deduction, Sherlock. She snatched the penny out of his hand. "Yes, a rather rare and very valuable penny. You know nothing of it?"

"Should I, Agent Rutledge? Was this found on the boy?"

Jackie handed it back to Laurel, who returned it to the folder. They were not going to get anywhere with the penny. That much was obvious. "Mr. Anderson, what exactly is it that you investigate? Special Investigations is a rather vague name."

He paused. For the first time, he looked just a bit unsure about how to respond, and Jackie felt a twang of satisfaction run through her. He looked over at Laurel, and Jackie wondered why Laurel's opinion would make any difference to him.

"Ghosts, Agent Rutledge. Most folk come to me about ghosts."

Jackie blinked a couple times in disbelief. She heard Laurel suck in her breath. That had not been the answer she expected, but given Laurel's response, it certainly made some sense. "Seriously? Why does the CEO of a multimillion-dollar medical company spend his time investigating ghosts?"

The bright hazel eyes caught hers again, and Jackie glared

back. He certainly looked to be telling the truth, as bizarre as it sounded. "It's something of a calling, I suppose."

For about two seconds, it made perfect sense, but then Jackie shifted her eyes away, and the ridiculousness of it all rushed back. "So you expect me to believe a man of your means spends his time being a ghost hunter?"

He leaned back in his chair, the leather creaking against his weight. "Why would I make up something like that, Agent Rutledge? I figured the FBI would have already known that. The fact is, I stopped at the park because I sensed a ghost in the area. Likely the boy's. They will linger at a scene sometimes."

"No," Laurel said, her voice barely above a whisper.

Jackie turned to look at her. "No?"

"No," she repeated, standing up and walking up next to Jackie. "It wasn't the boy's ghost."

Nick looked over at her, a genuinely curious look on his face now. "Do you know whose it was, Agent Carpenter?"

"No, but I sense it here, and it's very close. In this building, I believe."

"Ah," he said, nodding. "You're a medium then. I'd guessed as much."

She shrugged. "Yes and no. I can sense spirits though, and something really strong is very close by. Do you know what it is?"

At that moment, the office door swung open, and a very pretty, dark-haired woman wearing black wraparound sunglasses poked her head inside.

"Nick! There are feds snooping—" She stopped, seeing the two of them at last, and grinned sheepishly. "Oh. Seems the feds are already here."

Jackie could hear a definite note of tension in Mr. Anderson's voice now. "Shel, this is Agent Rutledge and Carpenter. This is my business partner, Shelby Fontaine."

The grin got wider, and she stepped into the room. "Hi." She thrust out her hand at Jackie, who took it reluctantly. The skin was very cool and smooth. Her lips were painted a brilliant, gleaming red, and the hair was pulled back into a French-style braid. Her eyes were a crystalline blue, like tropical ocean water glittering in the sun. It took Jackie a second to realize they had the same unnatural shine to them as Nick Anderson. What the fuck? Was it some special PI mind trick? Jackie decided she didn't like this woman with the model looks and the freaky eyes.

When Laurel took the hand, the friendly smile on her face dissolved like sugar in water. The blood-red nails of Shelby Fontaine's hand gripped Laurel's firmly, but certainly not so tight to create the gasp of shock that burst from Laurel's mouth. The color sank out of her body as though someone had pulled a plug.

"Sweet mother," she whispered, staggering away from Shelby's now limp hand. After a second she regained her balance, looking decidedly green, and then bolted for the door. A moment later, the bathroom door in the hall slammed shut, but it did not entirely muffle the sounds of vomiting.

Jackie struggled to close her mouth, which had mindlessly dropped open. What was going on?

Shelby offered a nervous laugh. "I say something wrong?"

Chapter 8

Nick rubbed a hand over his face after Agent Rutledge left to check on Agent Carpenter, slamming the door behind her. Shelby still stood there, hand frozen in the same place, looking back over her shoulder down the hall. If Shelby's actions had not made the situation completely screwed, he would have found the expression on her face priceless. It took quite a bit to stun Shelby Fontaine.

"Came in the back door, didn't you?"

His voice snapped her mind back in to focus. "Yeah. I um . . . parked out back when I saw the feds." She looked back again, rubbing absently at her hand. "What the fuck just happened?"

"Agent Carpenter is a medium," he said with a wry smile.

"Oh. Shit. You mentioned her before, didn't you?"

Nick nodded and sat back down. The agents would be back in soon, no doubt about that. "Just in passing." He lowered his voice then, to make sure the agents could not hear. "She was at the scene, could sense me in the crowd, but didn't know what to make of it."

Shelby snorted. "Big surprise there. Bet I just scared the living crap out of her."

"Probably."

"They know anything?"

"Just that I was at the scene. I don't want them to know anything yet. Okay?"

"Nick—"

"Not yet, Shel," he said, adamant. The agents could not get involved at this point. It would be far too dangerous for them, especially with a medium to clue them into what they were up against. The trick of course would be to maintain a position he would not be forced to lie from, and with a little luck this would be over before they even realized what was happening. He would not lie to them. They were law, after all, and that was at least one code he had not broken over the course of a century and a half.

"Fine, you stubborn shit." She mumbled the last word and moved out of the way as the agents came back into the room.

Agent Carpenter had a cup of tea in her hand, likely the quick work of Cynthia. Smart woman. It had not even occurred to him to offer anything.

"Everything okay, Agent Carpenter? There's some stomach flu going around. I hope you haven't caught it." It was lame, but Nick felt sorry for her and wanted to say something consoling. It was, however, the wrong thing to say, by the look on Agent Rutledge's face. Her eyes had narrowed, and her hands were now thrust in her pockets. She knew quite well it wasn't the flu.

Agent Rutledge's voice tipped on the fine edge of anger. "Do you sense any ghosts around here now, Mr. Anderson?"

"This building has a couple of them that show up now and again."

Her mouth drew down into a thin line. "Do you sense any of them *now*?"

This woman was going to be trouble. The sort that would not go away once she sniffed something wrong, and her partner throwing up had put a foul scent in her brain to be sure. "One of them was around earlier, but nothing now. No." It was the truth, for the most part.

Agent Rutledge glanced back at her partner and then at Shelby. "Want to tell me what happened with your father in 1970, Mr. Anderson?"

Stoic as he could render himself, Nick nearly grimaced at Shelby's wide-eyed reaction to the question, which likely didn't go unnoticed. "I was three years old then, Agent Rutledge."

"Agent Carpenter, can I have that newspaper clipping, please?"

Nick found a familiar news article slapped down on the desk before him. "Ah. Well, my sordid family history is now brought to light." Out of the corner of his eye, Nick watched Shelby roll her eyes. What a lovely situation this was turning into.

"So you know your father was involved in a case that bears a striking resemblance to this one, Mr. Anderson?"

Nick steeled himself. *Show nothing. This is a solid story I've told a thousand times.* "From what I read about it, the method does bare some similarities."

"You never talked to your father about what happened?"

"My father left just before my fourth birthday. I never saw him again." His hearing picked up the nearly silent snort of air from Shelby. He gave her a quick, hard stare, but she only sat there with her arms folded across her chest, one eyebrow arched up at him. It was a necessary lie. The feds would not handle the truth very well and would likely throw his ass in jail.

"Anyone told you, Mr. Anderson, that you are the spitting image of your father?"

"On occasion." This time Shelby's noise of annoyance was clearly audible, and Agent Rutledge whirled around on her.

"Something here bothering you, Ms. Fontaine?"

"Nothing a swift kick in the head won't solve," she said, her ruby lips spreading into a large, not-so-amused grin. "Sorry. I have my own issues with the cowboy here."

Agent Rutledge said nothing for a moment, looking first at Nick and then back at Shelby. He could tell the agent was stifling some angry reply. He got the impression the fuse on this woman was a bit on the short side.

"Why do I get the feeling I'm getting the shit end of the stick here?"

"Beg your pardon?" Nick said.

"Something's missing here," she said, voice lowered. "I don't think you're being entirely truthful with me, Mr. Anderson. My partner here throws up because she senses something is off . . . *way* off in this place, and yet you act like it's just any other day, like ghosts are just a usual occurrence with you."

"They are, Agent Rutledge."

"Damn—" She cut herself off and snatched up the article from the desk. "I don't buy it. You know, it might be to your advantage to cooperate just a little more. The situation here is serious."

Nick nodded. He felt a little sorry for her, but the truth would just unravel that knot of anger, and nothing would get solved now. She would be back. It was just a matter of time.

"I understand your concern. The murder of a child is about as serious as it gets, and under the circumstances, I would've been checking me out as well, but I assure you, I had nothing to do with that boy's murder."

The hands came out of their pockets and perched on her hips now. "Why do I find no reassurance in that, Mr. Anderson?"

Shelby chuckled, and when Agent Rutledge faced her again, Agent Carpenter finally stood up. "You know, Jackie, it might behoove us to interview Ms. Fontaine and the secretary separately now. Their perspectives on things might even it all out."

Ah, cooler heads at last. Nick smiled. He decided he liked the medium. The stable one of the group. They did the good-cop–bad-cop thing pretty well, he had to admit. He managed to wipe off the smile before Agent Rutledge turned back to face him.

"Yeah, maybe you're right. Mr. Anderson, would you mind leaving us with Ms. Fontaine and your secretary for a few minutes? It won't take long. I promise." The last word dripped acid on the floor.

Nick got to his feet, all too happy to dissipate some of the tension coiled in the air. "I'll get Cynthia and let you have at them. I'm sure they'll cooperate to their fullest abilities." He nodded slightly and stepped around the desk, walking out of the room without looking back.

"Mr. Anderson?" Laurel said, stopping him in the doorway. "I have one more question first."

He gave her the friendly smile, hoping she would not come much closer than she already was. "Sure."

"You said you help people with ghost problems, more or less."

He nodded. "Yes, I did."

"How is it exactly that you do that?" She moved over next to Agent Rutledge now, who visibly relaxed when she stopped next to her.

"Difficult to say," Nick answered. "Being a medium, you should understand the complexities involved in trying to define any sort of psychic ability."

"Are you psychic, Mr. Anderson?"

From most, Nick would have caught the subtle sarcasm behind the question, but she was utterly serious.

He paused. "I would say no. It's just something I can do."

She turned and looked hesitantly over at Shelby, who leaned against her chair. "And you, Ms. Fontaine?"

Shelby smiled—the mischievous smile this time, the flirty "you're kinda cute" smile he had loved so many years ago. "What about me, Ms. Carpenter?"

"Can we cut the coy bullshit?" Jackie snapped. "Just answer the goddamn question."

Shelby frowned and sighed at Jackie. "Mr. Anderson and I . . ." She looked over at Nick for a moment, the smile not quite fading away. "We share the ability."

Agent Carpenter's eyes widened. "That's very interesting, and rather unusual."

Shelby shrugged. "We're an unusual group."

Nick wanted to laugh at that but refrained. It did not even approach the truth. Agent Carpenter looked hard at him, with that probing look he knew went beyond ordinary senses. There was little he could do about that. He leaned against the door frame, waiting for her response.

"Thank you, Mr. Anderson. Your cooperation is appreciated. Just a few minutes with your employees here, and we should be done. For now."

"I'll just get some coffee and wait for you all out here. I hope you can catch the guy. Truly, I do."

Cynthia walked up now, and Nick would not be surprised if she had been standing in the hallway the entire time listening in. "They have a few questions for you, Cyn. Holler if there's a problem."

She nodded, mouth set firm. He knew she would not be put off by them, but the nerves were still there. "I will."

Nick started to step around her, but Agent Carpenter stepped up to the door. "Thanks again, Mr. Anderson. We're sorry to have interrupted your day like this."

He sensed what she wanted even before her hand began to extend, and he gave her a fleeting smile before ducking around Cynthia and heading for the coffeepot. *Not yet, Ms. Carpenter. You and I both know what you want to find out, and now is not a good time.*

Chapter 9

After a fruitless twenty minutes' worth of questioning that had Jackie ready to arrest the lot of them, she drove them back toward the city. Evening traffic had congested the roadways, but, thankfully, she and Laurel were going in the opposite direction. Some semblance of proper color had finally returned to Laurel's face.

"You sure you're okay?"

Laurel nodded again. "I'm fine, really. It just threw me for a loop, is all. Totally unexpected. I'm not even sure how to describe it."

"You don't have to," she said. "The barfing spoke volumes."

Laurel gave her a halfhearted laugh. "Sorry about that. Not good for the image, I know."

"Screw the image. I was worried I'd have to call nine-one-one."

"I'll be okay, Jackie. A little sleep, and I'll be good to go."

"I'll take you home."

Laurel nodded, and they drove in silence for a few moments.

"So what does it mean? That it's so overwhelming as to make you sick?"

"I honestly have no clue," Laurel said. "Normally, when I try to contact the other side, it takes a lot of concentration and effort to just get a peep out of the spirit world. But when I touched Ms. Fontaine, it was like someone kicked open the door and bowled me over."

"Then this whole ghost-hunting thing they claim? It's not just a front or scam for something?"

She shrugged. "I wouldn't go that far, but I would say there's a whole truckload of psychic power in that office back there. If anyone could claim to be able to track down ghosts, that girl could do it."

"What about Anderson?"

"Maybe. I tried to shake his hand before we left, but he avoided touching me like I had the plague."

"Yeah, I noticed. Why would he want to avoid that?"

"Keep his power a secret? I don't know. That kind of thing gets out to the public, and he'd have the tabloids all over him."

Jackie nodded. "True enough. The bastard was avoiding everything though. He was doing his damnedest to appease us and get us the hell out."

"Worked pretty well, too," Laurel said with a chuckle. "We don't have much more than what we came with. Very . . . persuasive man."

Jackie jumped on the gas and sped around a slower-moving car before cutting back in and braking for a sharp turn onto the freeway ramp. "It's those fucking eyes. I want to know what kind of trick he was pulling to do that."

"I'd guess it has something to do with that power they have, or maybe it's just because he was kinda hot."

Jackie snorted. "Did you see the saddle above his desk? Damn cowboy wannabes. I can't stand them. This case is heading right into the Twilight Zone, isn't it?"

"I'm pretty sure they know something they aren't telling us, and the cowboy schtick was real, guarantee it."

"Ha! Pretty sure? I'll bet you a box of Annabelle's finest that they are hip deep in this shit. Anderson had some connection to that penny, I'm positive. Maybe Denny or Hauser can dig up something on that. I don't like cowboys."

Laurel sighed and sank back farther into the seat. "Maybe. We don't have much to go on with them. The connection to that old murder case is flimsy. And you do too like cowboys. Haven't you seen, like, every Eastwood Western ever made?"

"We work with flimsy all the time, Laur. Flimsy Bullshit Investigations. That's us. I want to find out what he knows though. He knows something and doesn't want to say. If there's no direct involvement, why not tell us? Whom or what are they protecting?"

Her eyes were closed. "All good questions, grasshopper. You must meditate upon them and seek enlightenment."

"Who's Grasshopper?"

Laurel smiled. "Never mind. Just get me home. I really need to sleep this off, and admit it—you have a disturbing attraction to cowboys."

She laughed. "Eastwood kicked ass and, like any good man, didn't talk much."

"Mr. Anderson didn't say much either, smart-ass."

After dropping Laurel off at her cute little bungalow house, Jackie headed back downtown and pulled into Marly's, a local bar not far from headquarters, frequented by much of the building's staff. A shot or two would chill her nerves and set her mind on track to see if any of the pieces were fitting together in a way she hadn't noticed yet.

In her usual booth in the corner at one end of the bar, Jackie picked up the last fry from her basket and swirled it around in the dregs of the remaining ketchup. The crowd at Marly's had hit the dinnertime peak. It was noisy, dim, and bustling, and she wished her timing had been better. She liked it far better when the place was half empty and you could hear the jukebox. Billie Holiday was singing, and only every third word could be heard.

More importantly, you could run a tab with Marly, and he didn't believe water had a place in his bar other than for washing dishes. The drinks were strong. Jackie washed down her last fry with the last of her beer, setting the pint glass next to the pair of empty shot glasses Shelly had brought earlier. Shelly was a smart waitress. She never let more than two empties sit on your table. After a while you tended to forget exactly how many you had drank. Jackie could not remember. Six shots? Or was it just four? If it had been six, she would have to wait a bit before leaving. Sadly, the warmth of the tequila had not worked its wonders in untangling the day's events, leaving her muddled and annoyed.

Across the room—through the tangled web of eaters, those meandering with drinks from the bar to their table, and a light haze of smoke in the dim lighting—some of the FBI guys were gathered at a table. Jackie had watched them come in, and, fortunately, they had not noticed her. She had moved to the other side of her booth so her back was more to them. The last thing she wanted was to get called over and asked about the case or to sit and listen to them comment on the body parts of every woman walking to the bar. Besides, Pernetti had joined them, and she just could not stand the prick. How did his wife put up with him? He was a pig with a capital *P*.

Worse, the nagging feeling about this case was not getting burned away with the wave of alcohol. Ghosts, psychics, and twelve-year-olds getting drained of blood had her stomach crawling. They'd had one case five years earlier where Jackie had witnessed enough to make her believe Laurel's psychic weirdness was not bullshit. The case would not have been solved without her, and nothing brought about feelings of ineffectualness like the supernatural. There were no rules, no structure, no FBI training on handling that kind of strange, and this one was strange enough to freak Laurel out. Jackie hoped to hell it was just a normal psycho siphoning off people's blood.

The image of Archie would not go away. She could see the boy running away from his fighting and screaming parents, wanting something he could never have there. It struck far deeper than Jackie wanted to admit, and the tequila was failing to trickle down that far.

Where the hell was Shelly? She wanted one more for the road, and the girl had obviously decided she had had enough. The ticket lay facedown on the edge of the table. The bitch had slipped it in at some point in the last twenty minutes. Damn stealth waitress.

Jackie picked up the check and made her way to the bar. Definitely needed one more for the road. Maybe she would just walk back over to headquarters and go through that info on the cowboy again.

"Hey, Jack!" Marly said with a welcoming grin. His burly hands moved with deceptive grace as they dried one pint glass after another and put them under the bar counter. "'Bout time you came up and said hello. Why you hiding out in the corner over there?"

She shrugged. "New case. Ugly one. Just mulling over shit, you know how it is. It's going to frustrate me, I can tell already." *Fucking cowboy is going to be a pain in the ass.*

"Christ, Jack. Frustrated already?" Pernetti's voice cut in like a mouthful of castor oil.

Goddamn, Pernetti. Did the guy ever know when to shut up? She turned toward his table, which sat off the other corner of the bar. "When's the last time you weren't frustrated, Pernetti?" The other three at the table chuckled at Pernetti, who gave her a "is that all you got?" look and looked at her for more. They knew there would be more from Jackie Rutledge. "Not counting Charlene down in shipping."

That garnered a few outright laughs and good-natured heckling. Pernetti's shiny crown of a forehead flushed a lovely shade of pink. His affair with the shipping clerk was common knowledge, except perhaps to his wife.

Pernetti then sat back in his chair, waving off the barb. "Have a couple more drinks, Jack. That should ease the frustration."

Jackie stepped back from the bar and faced Pernetti. At that moment, Shelly walked by, a trayful of food in her hands.

"Careful, hon. Leave the prick alone."

Jackie frowned at Shelly's back as the waitress walked off into the crowd, tray held high. *Leave him alone? He's the asshole who started it, and now the fucker is accusing me of drinking too much? I'll carefully plant my steel-toed boot up his ass.* Jackie pushed through the bar crowd, ignoring the beer that spilled over her arm and the ensuing swearing from the girl she had bumped into.

At the guys' table, Jackie stopped, staring at Pernetti's dome of a head, glowing with perspiration under the overhanging lamp. He was a bowling ball on legs. "A dozen drinks wouldn't drown out the frustration of your presence here, Pernetti. Is it just me in particular, or are you a shit head around everyone?"

Gamble laughed, slapping Pernetti on the shoulder. "Think it's you, Jack. Must be love."

Jackie pointed a finger at him. "Shut up, Gamble. I wasn't talking to you." Something in her tone made him wisely clam up. She continued before Pernetti could get his comeback out. "You think nobody heard you fucking Charlene in the storage room? I think the security guys passed the tape around, or maybe that was the one of her sucking you off in the delivery van down at the loading dock. You and the wife should get some popcorn and have a movie night, Pernetti."

The laughter at the table had gone quiet with her diatribe. The venom in her voice told them she was far past the joking-around stage. Pernetti's head had gone from pink to a rosy red.

"Okay, fuck you, Rutledge. You want to tell the whole bar?"

"Sure, P," she said, turning to face the room. "That's a fabulous idea. You can tell them about how much I drink, and I'll tell them about how you're a philandering office slut who will fuck anything—"

Pernetti's hand whipped across the table, faster than she would have figured he could move his lumbering body, and shoved her back. "Watch it, Jack. I'm not going to put up with your bullshit."

"Or what, P? You going to take it out on a woman?" Jackie laughed. She felt on a roll now, nice and pissed. Five years she had been putting up with this pig. She suspected he was one of those types who took everything home and dumped it on his wife. The fucker had pictures of his kids on his desk, but not the wife. She had heard him call her a bitch to the other guys. *Yeah,* Jackie thought. *Bring it on, numbnut.* "According to Charlene, you ain't got enough dick to take it out on me anyway."

Pernetti scrambled to his feet, his face a wonderful rose red. Jackie grinned at him and shifted her right foot back just a bit for balance. She knew his type. Set them off, and it was all blind, dumb rage. There were actually a few similarities between him and a stepfather who only crept out of the hole in her mind while she slept. Her thought trailed off at Pernetti's retort.

He leaned over the table at her, hands slapping hard down on the surface, mouth twisting into a spiteful sneer.

"What you need dick for, Jack? You got the dykey little witch to lick your boot heels for—"

Jackie's hand flashed out and slapped Pernetti across the face. He didn't deserve anything more than a good bitch slap. If he pressed it though, Jackie was prepared to bust his crooked, oft-busted nose. At that moment, however, the ring and buzz of her cell went off in her pocket. Pernetti appeared too flummoxed to respond, holding one hand to his face in disbelief.

"Nice one, Jack," Gamble said, pushing away from the table. He was smart enough to see some shit was about to hit the fan. "Maybe we should just get everyone outside so we can cool our heads."

Jackie gave him an icy look and pulled out her phone while Pernetti tried to scramble out from behind the table. Everyone else had wisely picked up their drink but Pernetti, who sent his spilling across the table when he hit it trying to move around to Jackie. She flipped open the phone, noticing Laurel's number on the screen, and keyed the TALK button, all the while enjoying his clumsy attempt to get around to her. What was he going to do, throw a punch?

"Rutledge," she said into the cell just as, to her surprise, Pernetti did indeed throw a punch. Jackie instinctively leaned back, bringing her hand across to block, and his fist connected rather solidly with her phone, snapping the lid off and sending it to the floor. "You stupid fucker!"

Jackie returned fire, her small hands flashing out with blinding speed, even if they did not pack much punch. Pernetti's mouth erupted with blood, and he quickly lost his balance in the puddle of beer he found himself standing in. There was no time to celebrate the glorious image, as a long arm snaked out from Pernetti and he grabbed her shirt. Jackie found herself tumbling down to the floor along with him.

"Damnit, Jackie!" It was Marly's voice screaming at her from the bar.

"Fucking bitch," Pernetti hissed at her through his split lip.

She scrambled to her feet, turning to smile at Marly. "Sorry, Mar. He had it coming though. You heard him, didn't you?"

"Then take it outside, for Christ's sake. You going to clean up that mess?"

Pernetti was getting slowly to his feet, one hand gingerly touching his lower lip. The crowd, which had been swarming in, began to dissipate back to their normal places just as quickly. What could she do? Jackie shrugged, a pained smile on her face. "Sorry. Really. He just . . . you know . . ." She sighed and bent down to pick up her busted phone, hoping Laurel wasn't trying to reach her about anything important.

Gamble had a hold of Pernetti now, helping him back to his feet. "You're a fucking psycho, Rutledge," Pernetti said.

He was embarrassed more than anything. Sally was already walking up with a mop in her hand, and Jackie fished in her wallet for a twenty. "Sorry, Sal." She sounded like a broken record. It was time to get out.

Sally snatched the twenty from Jackie's hand before it had even been offered. "Go home, Jack."

The crowd cheered her on as she walked by the bar, and Jackie felt embarrassed now. Okay, it had been a stupid thing to do. Likely, she would be hearing something from Belgerman the following day. No way would word of this not spread. Marly just glared at her, and she had no nerve for trying to smooth things over. He would forget about it in a day or two. He always did. Her hope now was that there was a kind and beneficent god who would keep Laurel from driving over to see what the hell was going on.

Jackie stepped out into the setting sun, squinting at Laurel, who had stopped and crossed her arms over her chest. The hard, thin line of her mouth said it all. Man, God could be a prick.

Chapter 10

"I tried calling you." Laurel's voice was taut as a guitar string. Her hair was damp with a sprinkling rain.

Jackie winced. When was the last time she had heard that tone of voice? Laurel so seldom got mad at anything she could not even remember. Rummaging through her purse, she pulled out the broken remains of her cell phone. "Pernetti took a dislike to it for some reason."

"Some reason?" Laurel's hands came to rest on her hips, balled up into fists. "Do I want to go in and ask Marly what happened?"

"Um, no." Jackie smiled nervously at her. "I had good reason though. Pernetti—"

"Fuck Pernetti," she snapped back, leaning in close. "How many drinks have you had, Jackie?" She did not wait for an answer and spun on her heel, marching back to her car.

Jackie hurried after her. Unlike the anger that Pernetti's comments inspired, Laurel's reaction had the opposite effect on Jackie. Her stomach instantly knotted up in fear. *Fuck Pernetti? Christ, she really is pissed.* "I only had a couple. He called you a—"

"A couple?" She paused, her hand on the door handle of

her blue Beetle. "You had only two drinks?" Jackie's silence only appeared to inspire her anger. "Don't even know, do you? Did you hit him, Jack?" The feeble smile was all the reply she needed. "Damnit! You can get suspended for that shit, Jackie." She got in and slammed the door before Jackie could stumble out any kind of reply.

Jackie got into the passenger's seat, staring at Laurel in something close to shock. Her partner, best friend in the world, clenched the steering wheel so hard her knuckles were white. Where had this all come from?

"Pernetti started it, Laur. He called you a boot-licking, dykey witch."

Laurel took a deep breath and stared at Jackie for a moment. When she spoke, her voice was trembling. "I don't give a shit about anything Pernetti says, and you know it."

"Well," Jackie replied, trying to sound indignant, "if you had been there, you would've been pissed, too."

"No!" She pounded her hands against the steering wheel. "Pernetti can be a prick for the rest of our lives, for all I care. His behavior is not the problem."

"Oh," she said. "Well, I don't like him."

"You don't like men, period."

"What?"

"Men, Jackie. You got a big issue with them, and I understand why, but I'm tired of seeing it drag you down into this . . . this place you're in."

"What place is that?" Jackie's hand absently went to her stomach, which churned away with a fear that bordered on panic. "What are you talking about?"

"Am I stupid, Jack? Do I look blind?"

"No. You're one of the smartest people I know."

"I know what happened to you. I know why you've got this thing. Why every guy is the biggest asshole in the world. Not all guys are like that, mind you, but it drives you, and that makes you strong in some ways. I admire that drive." She smiled faintly.

"Thanks."

"No, shut up. Let me finish while I still have the nerve."

Jackie leaned away from her, against the door, watching her. "Okay."

"Okay. First thing, why did you fight Pernetti? No, don't answer," Laurel said quickly, holding up a finger to her. "I'll tell you, because I'll bet I already know. He made a quip about what or how much you were drinking." Jackie's sheepish silence answered the question. "How about the guy this weekend? The lifeguard. What was his name?"

What the hell was his name? That whole night was a foggy blank. She had not even known when he left her apartment. "Does it matter?"

"Would you have had any interest at all if you weren't plastered off your ass?"

Jackie looked down at her lap. No. She would not have given him the time of day. "Okay, so I got a little drunk and fucked a stranger. I'm not the first woman to do that, you know."

"Jackie Rutledge," Laurel said, pointing a shaking finger at her. "You don't fuck anyone unless you're so shit faced you don't even know your own name."

"Hey! That's not . . ." Jackie faded to silence again. It was true.

"See! Not a one. I've been with you for eight years, Jackie. You're my partner, and I care about you more than anyone." Her hand reached out and pulled Jackie's hand off her stomach and held it in her own. "Look at me, please."

For a moment she could not bear it, but Jackie finally forced herself to look into the teary eyes of her friend. Jackie squirmed in her seat. "What?"

"They aren't all your stepfather. There are a few good ones out there."

She tried to grin. "That might be debatable."

"Cut the shit! Quit hating yourself, hon. Forgive your mother for being weak and stop being scared you are just like her. You aren't. Trust me."

Anger billowed up inside. "I don't hate myself! And what's with all the psychobabble? All I did was smack Pernetti—"

"Because you're half drunk! Why? To mull over the case? Bullshit! You don't need six fucking shots of tequila to mull over anything."

"I didn't say—"

"Quit talking, Jack!" Laurel released her steel grip on Jackie's hand and stabbed a finger at her again. "This isn't about today or punching Pernetti. This is just the final straw, and I've got to say something before it drives me insane and makes me hate you."

Jesus Christ. The ghost shit had really done a number on her. Clearly, she had to get something off her chest, so Jackie stayed silent and waited.

"I don't want to hate you. I want . . ." She paused, gathering herself, and heaved a sigh. "Damnit, Jackie. You need to figure this out. I don't want to cover your ass anymore on this stuff."

Jackie shrugged. "Okay. Then don't. You don't need to do that. I'm a big girl, you know."

Laughter half dissolved into tears. "That's just the thing. You're still that little girl inside who is terrified she'll become her mother, and no amount of alcohol is going to hide that fear, Jackie. It'll never go away until you face it down."

"I, um . . ." What could she say to those tears? Everything inside turned to a quivering, gelatinous mess. Part of her wanted to lash out, tell Laurel to fuck off for being so presumptuous, but the problem was, she was right. "I will."

"When, Jackie? When cirrhosis sets in? When you're

eighty years old and lonely and bitter and realize you're going to die never having loved a single person in your life because you were too afraid to let them see who you are?"

"I don't drink that much," she said defensively.

"Only when you want to be with a guy. Because you're too afraid they'll see your mother in you."

Tears welled up in Jackie's eyes. "That's not true."

Laurel squeezed her hand, tears spilling down her own cheeks. "It is, and it's ruining you, Jackie. You have to deal with this somehow."

"I can deal with it fine." The words did not even sound truthful to herself, and she wiped at the tear that threatened to spill. "I do just fine."

"You ever want to love? You ever want a real, honest relationship?"

"Of course," Jackie said with a laugh. They had to stop talking now, or she was going to burst into tears, and with her luck, the guys would all come walking through the parking lot just then.

"Then do me a favor."

"What?"

"Next time you want to be with a guy, no drinking. Can you do that?"

What a stupid question. But deep down Jackie was not sure. She tried to imagine taking a guy home for the night, completely sober, completely herself. Christ. Jackie took a deep breath, trying to calm her nerves. "I . . . Yeah, I think so."

"Good," Laurel said, seemingly satisfied for the moment. She reached into her purse and pulled out a tissue. "Here. Scary thought, isn't it?"

"What's that?"

"Letting someone see who you really are. Inside."

Jackie swallowed the lump in her throat and just nodded,

wiping at the tears that ran down her cheeks now. She felt twelve years old all of a sudden.

"You're a good person, Jackie. Amazing, really. You've got nothing to be afraid of in that regard."

The tears kept coming, and Jackie nodded dumbly again. Laurel knew what she was afraid of, far more clearly than she had been willing to admit, obviously. Jackie could see the image of her mother now, floating peacefully, smiling. Sad how the only time she could recall her smile was in death. Her body began to shake now, overwhelmed by the dam of emotion that crumbled within.

"I don't want to end up like her," she said, stuttering through the sobs that welled up. "I can't. I just can't."

Laurel's arms came around Jackie then, holding her tightly. "I know, hon. You won't. Trust me, you won't."

"How can you know?"

"I just do, okay."

For some reason, that was enough. It was the soothing, motherly tone, perhaps. Or maybe she was just being psychic. Whatever it was, Jackie didn't care. The release felt good, and she held Laurel for a long moment, savoring the brief feeling of security it brought. When the sobs had finally stopped wracking her, Jackie let go. "Thanks, Laur."

"Welcome," she said with a little laugh, "and I'm sorry for being a bitch. I had to say something for my own sanity's sake. I've been ready to strangle you for a while now."

Jackie chuckled at the thought and sagged back in the seat. She felt exhausted all of a sudden, beyond tired. "No. I had it coming, I think. I mean, you're my only real friend, for fuck's sake. If you can't stand me, who else am I going to turn to?"

Laurel looked at her hard for a long moment. "Some things need to change, that's for sure. For one, you can quit defending me against the dykey-witch insults."

"Hey, now! I won't put up with homophobic bullshit from anyone."

She gave Jackie a hesitant smile. "Even if the accusation is true?"

"What?" Laurel's words did not sink in right away, dawning on her slowly as Laurel watched her with a steady, expectant gaze. "You're saying you're a dykey witch." Laurel nodded at Jackie, whose eyes suddenly went wide. "But . . . Laur! You aren't . . . I mean, how can you be? Jesus fucking Christ!" She reached over and slugged Laurel in the arm. "How come you've never told me? Oh, my God."

It was Laurel's turn to slump back in her seat. "I'm sorry, Jackie. Honestly, I thought you knew."

"Pernetti knows?" It was quickly becoming apparent that Jackie might be the only person in the bureau who did not know.

She winced at Jackie's embarrassment. "I think most everyone does. They're just afraid to make any remarks about it in your presence."

"Damn straight," she said, "or rather . . . um . . . Fuck, Laur." Her mind just could not get around the idea. How could she have not known? "Am I that self-absorbed?"

"Oh, no," Laurel said, laying a hand on Jackie's arm, who abruptly pulled it away from her touch. "I didn't want it to interfere with anything." She looked down at Jackie's arm with a resigned sadness. "I'm sorry."

Wow. A couple shots of tequila sounded really damn good now. "Well, I'm in no position to say a damn thing, am I?" She laughed at the irony. "I don't even know what to think right now. I can't. I'm half wasted and tired as hell. But I'm okay with it. Being gay, I mean. I'm more shocked at myself, I think."

Laurel nodded. "It's okay. This is good though, us talking about all this. We've needed to get some things out in the open. For once, I guess we can thank Pernetti for being an asshole."

Jackie laughed. "I'm just not sure what to do with it all."

"Nothing." Laurel started up the car. "Go take a hot bath. Sleep. Figure out what you're going to say to Belgerman tomorrow about all this."

"Shit. That's not going to be fun."

"Nope, and I hope it's not as bad as it could be. Did you at least figure out anything more on the case?"

"No." Jackie wadded the tissue up in her fist. "We'll keep looking into Mr. Anderson and his company. There's something there. We just need to find it."

"Okay. First thing in the morning then."

She heaved a sigh, trying to let the rest of the tension dissipate. "I'm glad you finally came out."

Laurel laughed. "Me, too, and don't worry, I won't be trying to stick my tongue down your throat."

Jackie laughed along with her but didn't reply. She had not even considered that option, and now the image refused to leave her alone. Great, just what she needed.

Chapter 11

Jackie waved at Laurel as she drove away, having refused to let Jackie drive home herself. Up above, a dark shadow leaped down from the kitchen windowsill and vanished. Bickerstaff was hungry. The rain began to splatter with greater insistence upon Jackie's face. A proper ending to a dismal day. Fishing the keys from her pocket, Jackie unlocked the street side door and walked up to the hall where four apartments had been carved out of the warehouse space above the shops below. From behind the front right door, the cat's plaintive meows could be heard.

As any cat worth its weight would do, Bickerstaff tangled himself up in Jackie's legs when she stepped in, fumbling for the light switch. The cat nimbly dodged around her stumbling feet and continued to rub up against her legs.

"Christ, Bickers. Is my baby hungry?" She picked up the purring, orange mound of fur and then slid the dead bolt in place. After dumping a can of food in his bowl and adding a bit of milk on the side, Jackie kicked off her shoes in the living room and proceeded to start water for a bath. If anything, a good, hot soak would wash away the stress of the past few hours. Dropping in a handful of bath beads, she stripped out of her clothes, making most of them land in the hamper, and went back to fill a glass from a half-empty bottle of chilled merlot.

She gulped down half of it with a note of defiance. "I do not drink that much, do I, Bickers?" The cat peered at her from his bowl, licking his lips, oblivious to her mood. He blinked once and went back to his dinner. "Yeah, well, what the fuck do you know, damn cat."

Back in the bathroom, Jackie stared at herself in the mirror, imagining how her face might look if it were all sallow and deflated, drained of blood. Better, perhaps, given her current state of self worth. For a brief moment, the reflection of the water in the tub rippled, and the all too familiar face of her mother floated there, white as bone, eyes milky and blank. Wisps of hair undulated around her face, a dark halo of death.

Jackie blinked and turned away. "Goddamnit."

She hesitated before climbing into the now full and steaming tub, making sure the image was not going to haunt her again. For a second, she contemplated draining it and running a shower, but she forced the unease aside. It had been years since she'd given into the feeling, and damned if she was going to do it now. With a ginger first step, Jackie climbed in and slid down into the soothing heat with a groan. The image of the boy still lingered, however.

The question kept creeping in and around every other thought. Why would someone drain the blood from a body? Why a kid? That was even more disturbing. What kind of pathology produced such a desire? And why place the victim sitting against a tree in a park? Was there a message there? More than likely there was, but it could mean almost anything. The Wisconsin woman had been found sprawled in an alley. Jackie made a mental note to take a deeper look at that case tomorrow.

Then there was Nick Anderson and his crew. Jackie

could not get an angle from which to view him clearly. Who was he, really? What kind of rich CEO spent his time being a PI dealing in ghosts? It was so far-fetched it had to be a scam of some kind—a cover, perhaps. What did they know? How involved was he? Could he be the killer or know who the killer was? If he did know the killer, why not say? She would nail him for obstruction, if that was the case. And then there was Laurel's whole take on them.

God, Laurel. She reached over and grabbed the glass of wine from the tubside table and finished it off. The warmth did little to relax the tightness in her throat. The case evaporated into the steam, burned away by Laurel's accusations and full-on assault. Jackie could never recall seeing her so upset. She was always the calm, cool, and collected one. But, worse, that anger had been directed at her. She had caused that pain.

The equilibrium of the universe had just been knocked off its axis. Was it really possible for her to live out her entire life and never find love? Love did not come up on the radar much these days, but if the need arose, guys were certainly willing and able. But, really, there was no love involved there at all. They were always willing to take advantage. When was the last time she had slept with someone sober? Surely, there was at least one? Jackie dredged through the muck of her memories and could find nothing.

Laurel was right. She could only fuck drunk. "I'm the biggest fucking loser."

A couple strands of hair floated in the water before her face, and Jackie had the sudden panicked feeling that her mother was creeping around in the water just below the surface. She swung over the side of the tub in a mad scramble and flopped onto the bathroom rug.

Bickers, wondering what the hell was going on, poked his head through the door to stare, mocking in straight-faced silence.

"Get out!" Jackie kicked the door closed on him and climbed back to her feet. "Son of a bitch."

After drying off and throwing on her robe, Jackie searched the fridge for something to eat and found a two-day-old carton of fried rice from Ho Mei's down the street. Giving her defiance a break, Jackie poured a glass of orange juice and carried her sad excuse for dinner out to the living room.

One half of the space had a couch and chair squeezed uncomfortably close to a forty-inch television mounted to the wall. The other half of the room was taken up by a Steinway, its finish dulled over the years from neglect. There were books stacked on one side and a bowl of kibble on the other for Bickerstaff, who promptly joined Jackie when she sat down and set her dinner on the bench next to her. He gave a disappointed look at the crumbs in his bowl and decided that licking himself would be the preferred course of action.

"Are you making me watch that on purpose, you perv?" He paused long enough to give her a look that indicated only real cats licked their balls and went back to work. "Just trying to make me jealous, aren't you?" She reached up and ruffled his ears, and Bickerstaff moved out of the way with obvious annoyance, settling farther back on the piano top. With a firm stretch and pop of her knuckles, Jackie consumed a large spoonful of the rice and settled in to play some Mozart.

It had become a case-starting tradition several years earlier, recommended by Laurel when she had become particularly stumped on a case. "It's your meditation, your grounding place, Jackie. Playing clears your mind. Give it a try and see if it helps." It had taken three hours, but the puzzle pieces had rearranged themselves into a more logical order, and a new path to pursue had opened up, leading to a break in the case.

An hour later, nothing was coming to her. Her mind was still too unsettled, constantly losing its track, disrupted by Laurel's tirade against her. She would have to come to grips with it soon. Somehow.

Instead she decided to go to her bedroom and see if she could make use of her laptop and find out more information on Nick Anderson. She wanted to find out more details about that case involving his father. Her gut, knotted as it was, knew that its ties were more than coincidental.

Thirty minutes later, drink and exhaustion had Jackie falling asleep to an episode of *Castle* Laurel had e-mailed to her.

Chapter 12

Cornelius Drake sat in the comfort of his Rolls while a light rain whispered sedately against the roof. It had been forty-five minutes, but he was in no hurry. He jotted some notes in a leather-bound journal perched on his lap, pausing every few moments to tap his chin with the tip of his pen. The upcoming sermon this week would be on the Lord's vengeance. God was all about putting down those who defied his will. Drake could appreciate that in a deity, not to mention that that sort of rhetoric got his congregation swimming around in guilt.

Guilt made human beings so utterly malleable, and they so often performed actions that infused them with it. They lived and breathed the choking dust of their guilty consciences. You could count on people to pull around guilt's weight until their dying breath. Nicholas Anderson dragged around that ball and chain with stubborn pride, and Drake had used it against him time and again. Some things never changed.

Drake hit the intercom button. "Wendall? What secret guilt do you carry around with you? Surely, you have some?"

There was a long silence before his crackling voice came

back. "I suppose pilfering your Scotch from the cellar, sir. Good stuff is hard to come by on my salary."

Drake laughed. "Will you be seeking penance to absolve yourself of this sin?"

"Not likely, sir," Wendall said. "God himself can't distill such sweet nectar."

"Indeed. I suppose some prices are worth paying."

"That they are, sir. That they are."

Bernard arrived a moment later, stepping through the wall of the car and seating himself across from Drake. "Boy's recital is finally over. Christ, that was awful stuff. Kid deserves to die on that alone."

"Now, now, Bernard. We all have our passions."

"Just sayin', sir. Hope the next one is into something quiet, like knitting."

Drake smiled. "Nothing so simple as that, my friend." He put his journal into a slot in the door. "Go keep the riff-raff away, my boy. They shall be here soon."

"Aye, sir." Bernard slipped away through the trunk and walked back into the rows of parked cars.

People were filing out of the high school, parents with their children, many carrying their cases filled with violins and trombones. Some paused to put up their umbrellas, while others, not so wise as to have planned ahead, held programs or purses or coats over their heads and made their way quickly out toward their cars. The Morelands, due to circumstances beyond their control, had been running late and had parked at the fringes of the lot, pulling their car onto the edges of the football field. Moments after they had hurried away, violin case banging at the boy's side, Drake had pulled in next to their Honda Accord and patiently awaited their return.

Drake watched them approach in the side view mirror, saw the mother hesitate at the sight of a dark blue Rolls-Royce parked next to their car before continuing forward.

He opened his door and stepped out when she was between the cars.

"Ah, Mrs. Moreland!" Drake's thin lips split into a toothy smile. He popped open the umbrella. "Wonderful recital this evening. Your son, Adam, was particularly good."

The boy stopped directly behind her, and Mrs. Moreland's brief turn of annoyance melted into confusion. "Oh. Hello. Thank you. Adam did very well tonight, I think, didn't you, sweetie?"

Adam shrugged. "Sure, Mom. We could've been better."

"Always room for improvement, isn't that right, Adam?" Drake stood before his open door, allowing no possible way around. "Even the masters look for ways to play better."

"Yeah. I guess that's true," he said.

"Pardon me, but do we know you?" She was trying to smile and cover her irritation as the rain continued to fall. The music program held over her head provided little relief. "Do your children go to school here?"

"We met briefly," Drake said, his grin fading. He drew the glasses down to the end of his nose. "I realized your boy here was a perfect match."

Her free hand came to her mouth, covering the gasp. Adam dropped his violin case on the grass. "A match for what?" she whispered.

"He looks just like an old friend's son, if you can believe that." He motioned at Adam, who quickly pushed his way around his mother. "Come, let me have a closer look at you."

"I . . . I don't know," she began, but faltered, her mouth moving in silence like a gaping fish.

"Hush, Mrs. Moreland. Everything is just fine. No worries at all." She nodded, and Drake turned back to Adam, reaching up to take his chin in his hand. "Indeed. The bone structure is very similar. The eyes are the same. And I shall not have to dye your hair. Wonderful. Wouldn't you say,

J. N. Duncan

Mrs. Moreland?" They both nodded. "Adam, look me in the eye, son, and tell me if you don't see the key to your life's dreams within them."

Adam stared, head cocked slightly to one side, like a dog who has heard a peculiar sound. "I think I do."

"Of course you do." He patted him on the shoulder. "They are dreams of death and quiet and peace of mind."

"I really hate music," he said.

Drake's mouth quirked up at the corner. "I know. Parents always believe they know best, do they not?"

He nodded. "She's a real bitch about it sometimes."

"Why don't you get in out of the rain, my boy? You can leave that wretched violin outside."

"Yeah, cool. Thanks." He stepped into the darkness of the car.

Drake stepped forward and placed his hand on Mrs. Moreland's wet cheek. "I shall be taking your boy here, Mrs. Moreland. Perfectly safe, I assure you. You will think nothing of it. He shall be well taken care of."

She nodded. "I'll just head home then. Will you be bringing him by the house later?"

"You are very tired, Mrs. Moreland. Those lovely eyes are completely stressed. You need to sleep. You can worry about your boy in the morning."

"Okay. I'll worry in the morning."

He folded up the umbrella and laid it down inside the car, taking both of her cheeks in his hands. "And you shall worry a lot when you find his bed empty. You will be sure your precious boy has come to great harm, that he may in fact be dead."

She stared into the glowing, soulless orbs. "But he'll be with you."

"He will be dead, and you will know who did it, but the image shall elude you, like chasing a dandelion upon the wind."

"Oh." The rain running down her cheeks looked like tears. "I won't remember?"

Drake shook his head. "I am afraid not, my dear. You will only know that if you had not made him play music, he might still be alive. Now go, rest. Sleep the sleep of the dead, Mrs. Moreland."

He stepped into the Rolls and pulled the door closed so she could walk by. She drove away without looking back.

Adam sat in the seat, staring straight ahead. "Your eyes are full of death."

He clasped the boy's knee with his hand. "You will be fine, son. Death is not the end."

"You're going to kill me."

Drake grabbed Adam's chin and turned his head to face him. "Does it look so terrible in there, Adam?"

"It looks cold."

"Indeed. Indeed, it is very cold. You shall make new friends though. You shall see."

"And what then?"

"Hmmm? What then?" Drake sat back in the seat, giving Adam a sidelong glance. "Well, then you truly shall die." When Adam merely nodded and continued to stare ahead, Drake pushed the intercom button. "Take us away from here, Wendall. Perhaps later you may have a glass of Scotch with me."

Wendall looked back at the one-way glass dividing them, a smile upon his lined face. "That would be lovely, sir."

Chapter 13

The afternoon had provided little more than a draining of his gas tank. Nick sat in his darkening office, considering what possible preparations they could make and wondering how he was going to keep the FBI out of this until the end. He had no answers. Until Drake made his presence felt again, there was little for them to do other than search the city and hope they got lucky. It would be soon. Given the current state of law enforcement, the timeline would be condensed, a couple days at most between kills. So it was no surprise when Nick felt the familiar pang of the other side, pulling at him like a spaceship drifting too close to a black hole.

Cornelius was drawing upon the energy of the dead, which meant he was feeding on someone. The feeling had been so faint with the boy Nick had been unable to zero in on it. He had not even been sure of the feeling until he saw the body under the tree. This time, he was leaving little doubt. Somewhere within a few miles, Cornelius Drake fed on another victim, daring Nick to find him. He reached to pick up the phone and call Shelby, only to have it ring as he grabbed it.

"Yeah?"

"Shelby's on the line, Nick." Cynthia patched her through without waiting for his answer.

The rumbling roar of her BMW motorcycle made it nearly impossible to hear. "Say that again, Shel. I can't hear you."

"North of downtown!" Her voice filled his head, full of excitement and anger. "I can't tell if the fucker is west or east of the river though. A bit of the real stuff, Nick, I'd find him within the hour."

"No," he replied emphatically. "I'm on my way up now. Just keep trying to zero in on him." She had promised no more blood, and Nick knew the disadvantage it put them in, but it just was not an option, not anymore.

"Nick . . ."

"No blood!" he repeated and slammed down the phone.

Out in the hall, he grabbed a bottle of synthetic from the fridge and gulped it down in one long, bitter draught. Cynthia was standing beside her desk when he came out into the main room.

"It's him, isn't it?" There was a hint of fear in her voice.

"Yes," he said matter-of-factly. He placed a reassuring hand on her shoulder. "If anything is going down, I'll call. Keep the doors locked and don't leave for any reason until I come back."

"Is that really necessary?"

"Just in case, Cyn. I'm not taking any chances. We have no idea what he's up to yet."

She nodded. "Okay."

"Thanks." He gave a brief nod and headed out the door.

Thirty minutes later, Nick had his Jeep on the north side and was wishing he had driven the Porsche in to work. The feeling was definitely stronger, but without the spike of energy real blood would give, they would have to get damn close to home in on him. Drake was teasing them, and Nick clenched the steering wheel in frustration as he dodged through traffic, trying to get a better sense of where Drake was feeding. It had been an hour now, which gave them another half hour to forty minutes tops. If anything, Cornelius could be counted on to be consistent.

Shelby called in again, and Nick could hear the distinctive squeal of tires and the blaring of horns in the background. The woman was hell on wheels, enough to scare the shit out of the best NASCAR had to offer. He tried to keep the image of her getting plowed by a CTA bus out of his head. Damn woman!

"I'm east of the river, beginning to think he might be southwest of here."

"Okay. I just crossed the river at Chicago. I'll head west from here and then south," Nick said. "Head north of me a couple miles and then come over and head down. Maybe we'll get lucky."

"We need blood, not luck," she snarled in his ear and clicked off.

As the minutes ticked by, Nick knew she was right. The odds were slim, and someone was dying, but there would be no bloodshed to find him. *It's wrong,* Nick told himself, like he had been telling himself for years, but the temptation was there, and just the thought made his mouth begin to salivate. Drake, on the other hand, was at that very moment quenching his thirst, draining the life of some poor soul, burning with the cold fire of the power of death. Nick had no clue how he would deal with Drake even if he did find him. Would bullets stop him? Enough of them might. Even the power of the other side can only heal so fast. With blood though . . .

Shelby interrupted the tormenting thoughts with another call. "West!" she shouted. "He's west of me. Your side of the river." Her engine was loud in the background, revved up high.

"Slow down, Shel. You will kill—" He stopped when the phone went dead again.

She was a good two miles north of his location. West of

her could mean anything up to three or four miles. Six to eight square miles of city. Twenty minutes. Nick dug a Rolaids out of his pocket and popped two. Frustration was simmering away in his gut like a rancid witch's brew. They would not find him. Not yet. It was all just part of the game, but one Nick could not afford to stop playing, because somewhere out there, another person was almost dead, and if Drake stuck to his routine, a fifteen-year-old young man had just about succumbed to a decades-long plot of revenge.

Nick veered east and headed for the freeway. The eerie call of death had started to fade. Reluctantly, he punched in Shelby's number. "Go home, Shel. He's done for now."

"I could have had blood in five minutes, Nick." Her voice was choking up. Nick swore silently to himself. "I could've tracked him, goddamn you!"

He didn't bother saying good-bye and dropped the cell on the seat beside him. He knew she would not go home, not yet. She would ride around the rest of the evening, hoping to pick up the scent, something beyond that usual faint whiff of foulness one smelled when another one of them was within twenty-odd miles of you. She would yell more at him later, cursing his weakness, demanding he have the courage to drink, to be like Drake. But he could not. It was a promise he refused to break. It was the only one he had left, and God help him if he defiled Gwen's memory for the sake of revenge.

Pulling into his garage, Nick got out and watched the rain whip across the driveway until the door had closed. He felt tired, beyond even the thirst for blood. The synthetic would give him his energy back, but this tired went beyond bone deep and sapped at his soul. He closed his eyes for a moment and took a deep breath.

"I'm sorry, hon. I just can't do it," he whispered.

Chapter 14

For the first time in six months, Nick sat on his back deck watching the sun burn its way through the morning shroud of fog, a handrolled cigarette burning down between his fingers. He could no longer remember the number of times he had quit smoking. At this point, it really didn't matter. He took a long drag off the sweet tobacco and flicked the remainder out into the wet grass.

"Enjoy it while you can, Sheriff."

Down the gentle slope of his backyard, a whiter, more solid shape of fog shifted and danced across the still waters of a reed-encircled pond, taking on a more recognizable shape as it approached the house. Nick picked up the cold cup of blood-spiked coffee sitting on the small table next to the lounge chair and winced down the cold dregs. Hot or cold, it always tasted like shit. The familiar, overall-clad form walked up through the rail and stopped next to him on the deck.

"Morning, Reg."

He grinned at Nick, an indifferent sort of twist of his mouth that Reggie had whether the news was good or bad. The dead had a slightly skewed sense of humor when it came to the living. "Mornin', boss. Good a time as any to take up smokin' again."

Nick gave him a hint of a smile. "I suppose. Things went as planned?"

Reggie held out a fist so intensely white it looked nearly corporeal and dropped something into Nick's hand. "I'm guessin' so."

"Ah, thanks." Nick turned the small square of clear plastic around in his hand a couple times before finally holding it up for a better look. "You know, I hadn't even realized Drake had this. I thought it gone when I burned the cabin down."

He nodded slowly. "How would you've known, boss? We owe that bastard something big."

Nick studied the penny, the year 1862 standing out clear as the day he had bought it for his son those many decades ago. "The prick has had it all this time. Joshua never even had the chance to put it with his collection."

"Do you suppose Drake has other things?"

Nick figured as much. He nodded at Reggie, rage bubbling up in his throat so acidic he was afraid he might spit fire if he spoke at that moment. He slid the coin into his pocket and closed his eyes, taking in a deep, cool draught of air. A poor kid was dead, unfortunate to have a passing resemblance to another boy dead for 144 years. Who else in Chicago resembled his dead family? Who was about to find themselves on the wrong end of a twisted vampire's vengeance? The familiar game was afoot, and Nick did not feel ready to play. Where to begin? The chance for saving the next victim was already gone.

"Did you find anything else?"

The never-ending smile stretched a hair. "Little evidence that I saw other than the coin."

"Anything from the police?"

"No. They seem to be washing their hands of it."

Reggie's hands disappeared into the pockets of the overalls. "The blond woman is going to be trouble."

"The medium?"

Reggie nodded.

"Yeah, no doubt about that. She knows we're not what we seem."

Laughter bubbled up out of Reggie—a soft, maniacal cackle. "Oh, I spooked her good this morning. She's a keen one though. Had to get the penny from their evidence room. Her house is warded something fierce against spirits. I'd have set off alarms all over if I'd tried. She could tell when I picked it up though. Had to practically cross back over to avoid being seen."

Nick shrugged. "Doesn't matter now. We'll be hearing from them again soon, I expect. They'll be gathering more intel on me, and after showing me the penny yesterday, that Agent Rutledge is going to be all over us. We'll be lucky to avoid their involvement in this."

Reggie gave him a wry, sad smile. "That didn't go too well the last time, boss."

"Agreed," Nick said. "We may have little choice in the matter, however, if they try to pin anything on me or drag my ass in."

"They have no evidence yet."

"Circumstantial. I was at the scene. They know I'm connected somehow, and technology is going to be to our disadvantage now. They can find out things too fast these days."

"It's a strange world. Some days it's good to be dead."

Nick almost laughed. "Let's not get ahead of ourselves just yet. I'll call Shel and Cyn to let them know to expect another visit from the feds. Things are going to get complicated real quick, I'm afraid."

"I'll be around if you need me, boss."

He motioned with the penny to his old friend. "Thanks, Reg. As always, it's much appreciated."

"We're going to take him down this time, Mr. Anderson. You'll see."

Nick watched him dissipate into the air. "Yes, we certainly will, Reg."

It was going to be a lovely day. He got up from the chair, hands going into his pockets, and rubbed at the plastic case between his fingers. Unwanted memories stirred like the wisps of fog down on the pond, ghostly tendrils rising up from the murk below.

Chapter 15

It was still dark when the phone rang. Jackie startled awake, still propped against the pillows, and watched her laptop slide off the burgundy comforter to the floor. Bickerstaff, who was perched on the end of the bed below her feet, looked down at the computer and then back at her. He appeared to have been waiting for that precise moment all night and now had a very catlike smirk upon his face. She kicked at him from beneath the covers while reaching for the phone on the nightstand and then watched him indignantly jump to the floor. The number was Laurel's.

"Hey, it's six thirty in the morning. Think I'm bringing you a custard doughnut now?" It was not much of a threat, but with sleep still fogging her brain, it was all she could come up with.

"Get your tiny little butt down here, and I'll take two of Annabelle's custardy delights, thank you very much."

Jackie sat up, one hand rubbing at the sleep in her eyes. It was against the laws of nature to sound that functional before the sun came up. "Okay, I'm up, more or less. What's going on?"

Laurel's voice rose in pitch, a clear sign she was excited

by something. "We had a little visitor in the evidence room this morning."

Little visitor? "What, like a gremlin or something?"

"Someone stole our little twenty-five-K penny."

That got Jackie to her feet. "You're joking. How the hell did someone break into the evidence room?"

"Because they weren't really here," she said. Jackie could hear the smirk in her voice.

"Damnit, Laur. You telling me a ghost ran off with evidence?"

Her voice snapped back. "Looks that way."

"Okay, okay. Sorry." Jackie sighed and stared up at the ceiling. "I believe you. I just hate when supernatural shit gets involved. No standards for this kind of thing."

"Makes life interesting. Coming in now?"

"Yeah. Let me throw clothes on. I'll grab a bite on the way. Wait. My car is still downtown."

"I got Denny to take it back for you."

Jackie listened for but could find no hint of annoyance in Laurel's voice. "Thanks."

"Which means Annabelle's. Don't forget."

A morning sheen of fog put a damper on an already shitty start to the day as Jackie drove into downtown, sipping on Annabelle's Mississippi Mud coffee. How could someone break into the evidence room of the FBI building without getting busted? Security was tighter than Pernetti's ass. A ghost could get in there, but, then, how did it get out with evidence in hand? Did they even have hands? How the hell did you deal with an evidence-stealing ghost?

Jackie sipped and muttered all the way to the FBI offices, stewing in the elevator as she rode up to the third floor where the evidence room was located. Laurel greeted her at the elevator door, hand extended in anticipation at the white bag Jackie held.

"Boy, someone's excited this morning."

Laurel snatched the bag and snagged one of the chocolate-frosted, custard-filled doughnuts. "Mmmm. Oh, that's so good. I've been jonesing for one of those all morning."

"How long have you been down here?" Jackie handed her the other coffee and tossed the carrier over to a nearby garbage can.

"Five-thirty or so." She shrugged and happily bit down on the doughnut, wiping at the custard that squirted out around her mouth and licking her finger clean.

"Christ, Laur. What for? And can I have my chocolate croissant, please? You're hogging the bag." Laurel gave a sheepish grin and handed the bag back, and Jackie smirked. "Thanks." She reached in and pulled out the croissant, crumpling up the bag. Her second shot at the waste can missed horribly. "So. What have you got, Sherlock?"

Laurel walked over and placed the bag in the can before heading down the hall. "There's not much to see, really. I was having a hard time sleeping last night."

"Archie?" Jackie guessed. The image of a bloodless child tended to stick in your brain, and Laurel had a harder time tuning out that kind of stuff. Sometimes Jackie would not even let her inspect the victim if it was too messed up.

She nodded. "Among other things. Anyway I decided to come in and go over the evidence again, see if anything popped up for me before the morning meeting."

"I was hoping to dig into that murder case with Anderson's dad some more."

"Okay, but first I want you to check this out." She opened the door to the evidence room and led Jackie inside.

There were two men inside snooping around. The closest, a middle-aged man with a thinning, brown buzz cut and soft pouting lips, stood up when they entered the room. He had on the uniform of building security.

He looked up at them. "We got nothing, Laurel. Hey, there, Jack."

"Figured," Laurel said.

Jackie had to glance at his name tag before she recalled who he was. She had said hello to him how many times coming into the building? Sad, very sad. "Hi, Walt."

"Don't know what to tell you guys. Video is blank. Nobody went in or out other than you, Laurel."

"No signs of tampering?" Jackie asked.

Walt shook his head. "Not that I can tell, but we'll give it to the geeks and see if they can find anything."

Laurel walked them over to the box containing evidence for the case. "I checked it back in when I came up this morning."

Jackie looked through the handful of plastic bags in the box. Nothing in the room looked disturbed. Whoever had intruded had known what they were looking for and gone directly to it. "Too fucking weird. What could be so important about a penny to warrant the risk of breaking into FBI headquarters? Walt, let us know if anything turns up on that surveillance video."

"Will do," he said.

"Thanks. Laurel, let's go. I want to check out Anderson's history some more."

She sighed with obvious annoyance, but Jackie ignored her and walked out. There had to be a more logical explanation than a ghost walking out with the penny. If the videotapes showed a plastic-covered penny floating off down the hall, she would reconsider.

Back at their cubby holes that somehow were considered offices by the management, Laurel plopped down in her chair across the aisle from Jackie's desk and picked up the cup of tea there. "You think someone snuck in there, don't you?"

"I just like real possibilities better, and I didn't want to go all supernatural with Walt right there."

Laurel shook her head. "Yeah . . . well, fine."

"So how does a damn ghost pick up a penny and walk out of an office building? Wouldn't someone have seen something?"

"Hardly anyone was here, but you're right that it doesn't make a lot of sense. All I know is I felt the presence really strongly for about two minutes, but by the time I'd narrowed down where it was coming from, it had gone."

"Any ideas on how we deal with an evidence-stealing ghost?"

"At the moment, no." Laurel's brow wrinkled. "I'm not sure what to make about a lot of things on this case."

"So, fine then. What do we do?"

Together they said, "Stick with what you do know."

"Which means we focus on Anderson and see what we can find out about Fontaine and the rest of his business. Hauser needs to get here. He'd do this in half the time."

"He might have looked into it already. He likes weird cases like this."

"He just wants into my pants. He'd be interested in any case we have."

Laurel laughed. "You could do worse."

"Ew. No. Can you imagine the flack I'd get around here?"

"I'd have to hide your gun."

Jackie grinned. "There would be much bloodshed."

"Hey, Jack." Belgerman stopped between them, his tie already pulled loose from his shirt. "Can we talk for a minute?" He didn't wait for an answer and kept walking.

Jackie winced. "Fuck. Does he always come in this early?"

"Sometimes," Laurel replied, "but not very often."

"Great. This day has turned to shit, and it's not even eight AM yet."

"Sorry," Laurel whispered to her as Jackie got up and walked down the hallway toward Belgerman's office.

Jackie closed the door to the office. He said nothing, leaning against the edge of his desk, hands folded with quiet calm in his lap. She thrust her hands in her pockets to keep them from fidgeting and felt the saliva evaporate from her mouth. His walls at least were reasonably thick. Someone walking by at the right time, however, would hear. With her luck, it would be Pernetti.

"You're a fucking idiot sometimes, Jackie."

Yep. Not happy at all. The look he gave her said far more than the words. If she felt any smaller she would be able slink out under the door. Out the large picture window behind his balding head, a low bank of gray clouds slid by. A light rain was beginning to fall, beading on the glass. It offered little to distract Jackie from the stern, livid, and fatherly gaze Belgerman leveled at her.

"Yes, sir."

"Don't give me the 'yes, sir' bullshit. What the hell were you thinking? Punching a fellow agent?"

"Yes, sir. I know, but, sir, he's—"

"An asshole?" he replied with little surprise. "Even he will tell you that, Jack."

Jackie felt a warm flush creeping into her cheeks. *Great. Just great. He's going to suspend me this time, I know it, and Laurel won't be bailing me out of this one.* There were no excuses. "I see that, sir. I lost my cool. I apologize."

"And you will apologize to him, too, after I'm done with you." He pushed away from his desk and walked around to the window. "What are you going to do next, Jack? It's embarrassing as hell and makes us look like a bunch of goddamn, punch-happy Neanderthals to the public." He pointed at the paper on the corner of his fastidiously clean desk. "Made the paper, even. I guess there was a reporter sitting in there having drinks when you went off."

Jackie cringed. Could it get any worse? "It won't happen again, sir."

Belgerman gave her a pained smile. "Damnit, Jackie. At least be truthful about yourself to me. It'll happen again. You get into shit like this all the time, Jack. It's your nature. You're pissed at the world. I get that. It's part of what makes you good at what you do, but keep it out of the fucking papers. I can deal with the Pernettis of the world. I've put up with you for almost ten years now, and I'm still alive." He finally relaxed a bit, leaning forward again, placing his hands on the desk. "I get paid this shitty salary to make sure you nitwits get along and still catch the bad guys, but don't go out of your way to make it worse for me. I don't need the ulcer."

Jackie stared down at the gray carpeted floor. "Yes, sir."

"You say 'sir' one more time, and I'm sending you home for the rest of the week. I'm not your father."

She shifted her weight back and forth from one foot to the other. "I had some . . . personal issues I was dealing with last night. I think it's all squared away now."

He looked skeptical. "You sure?"

No, not at all, actually, but hell if I'm going home. "Yeah. Had a little heart-to-heart with Laurel about everything. I think I'm good."

"Good. You should listen to her more. She's the most stable agent in this office."

Apparently, I don't listen to her close enough. "Can I ask you something, off the record?"

Belgerman smirked. "This conversation never existed unless you decide to go beat up more agents."

"Did you know that Laurel is . . . um . . . actually, never mind. I'll apologize to Pernetti first chance I get."

He contemplated her in silence for a moment. "Okay. I'd appreciate that. It won't change his mind about you, of course, but you'll have put forth the effort at least."

"Thank you . . . John. And I'm sorry. Really. I never want to embarrass you or the organization." Jackie got up and shuffled back toward the door. "I'll just go get ready for the meeting now."

"Jack?" he said, freezing her at the door.

"Yes, sir?"

"Get this anger thing dealt with, whatever it is. It's going to force you out early if you let it, and it's been eating at you for a long time."

"I'll be fine. I just need to deal with the Pernettis of the world a bit better."

"You need to deal with yourself." The tone had an edge to it, a bit of fatherly anger. "Next time I won't be giving you an option."

Jackie nodded. "Understood, sir." She knew he was serious. Next time she would be suspended or, worse, forced to go to the damn shrink. "I'll just go get ready for the meeting."

Laurel waited impatiently at her desk when she walked back. "Here. He chewed you out good, didn't he?"

Jackie stuffed half a croissant in her mouth and plopped down in her desk chair. "Wasn't so bad."

"Your face is still red."

"Christ. Okay, it wasn't great, but I'll live. I just have to eat some crow for Pernetti."

"Ugh. Sorry," she said, making a face. "Beats getting suspended though."

"Barely."

Laurel chuckled. "Okay, two things before we prepare for the morning meeting on this case." She clicked on her computer monitor and turned it toward Jackie. "First thing is I had a little visitor last night at my house."

Visitor. With anyone else that might mean the local stray cat. "Great. Am I guessing correctly that you don't mean the living sort?"

She smiled. "Yes. Something wanted into my house

pretty bad, but the spells I have in place kept it out. It left in a pretty shitty mood."

"Was this the same one you felt before at Anderson's?" If they had some kind of vengeful spirit running around, that would be bad news. They had actually experienced that type on a case a few years earlier.

"No, but it wasn't around long enough for me to chat with. I'm not sure what it means, but I don't like it. I'm beginning to suspect this case has multiple parties involved. Anyway, this other thing is even more interesting. Look at this."

Another headline from an old newspaper clipping was displayed upon Laurel's screen. "Bayou Blood Drinker? Should I know this one? Is this the same case we looked at earlier?" The name didn't ring a bell at all for her, but then Jackie recognized the man in the photo, or at least it looked like him. "Nick Anderson?"

"Nicholas Rembrandt, actually. Hauser sent it over to us."

"What, his grandfather this time?"

"Don't think so."

"Hey! Is that Ms. Fontaine next to him?" Jackie studied the picture closer. It sure looked like her, but they were dressed in very old-fashioned clothing.

"Look at the year, Jackie."

It took a moment for her to find it. "What the fuck? 1934?"

Laurel nodded. "Yeah, I know. Freaky, isn't it?"

She studied the picture but was hard-pressed to find anything different in the appearances of this Nicholas character and the current Nick Anderson. Could three generations look that much alike? Unlikely. It dawned on Jackie then, why Laurel looked so excited by the article. "You think it's the same guy, don't you?"

She nodded. "Could be. Maybe the geek squad can figure it out for us."

"You realize that would make Nick Anderson around a hundred years old."

"Or older," she added. "I'll bet you that's Shelby Fontaine there, too."

"That's nuts, Laur. They wouldn't be—"

"Human. I know. I think they're vampires."

Jackie nearly snorted coffee out of her nose, coughing hard for a moment until she could regain her composure. "Can we let the geeks look at this before we jump to any conclusions like that? Vampires. That's fucking crazy. There's no such thing."

"You don't know that, and I sent an e-mail to Hauser. He's on his way in now to do an analysis of the pictures."

"We need a detailed workup on this shit. I don't want to go into the meeting and claim we're after a vampire. I've been embarrassed enough for one day, thank you very much. Maybe we should get some tails on Anderson and Fontaine and see what they're up to. I don't want to confront Anderson with this without some kind of empirical proof."

"Can I ask Ms. Fontaine?"

It took Jackie a second to get the vague sound of interest in her voice. "Wait a sec. You think . . ." She paused and rolled her chair over to speak quieter. "You think she's hot, don't you?"

Pink crept into Laurel's cheeks. "No. Well, okay, kinda."

Jackie didn't know what to say. This was utterly new territory between them. "That's . . . Laur, she's a suspect. You can't be interested."

"Hey, interest does not mean I'm going to do anything about it. Give me a little credit."

She heaved a sigh of relief. "Okay, fine. That's . . . fine. You really think she's that hot?"

Laurel nodded. "Oh, yeah. Drool worthy."

"Man, this is weird." She waved off Laurel's look of concern. "No, I'm good with it. It'll be good. We can talk about your sex life instead of mine for a change."

She laughed at Jackie. "I'll have to have some first."

Silence fell between them. Jackie wasn't quite sure how to respond to that. "Speaking of awkward conversations, where's Pernetti at? I need to go humiliate myself."

"Called off."

"Great. We going to be ready for this meeting?"

"Not now. We need Hauser's analysis."

"Okay, I'll talk to John and see about bumping the meeting then. Short notice, but—"

"Jack?" Belgerman had come out of his office.

Butterflies leaped back into Jackie's stomach. "What's up?"

"Let's get the team together this afternoon. I've got Emily to give us preliminary autopsy results on the boy. She'll see you in thirty minutes."

Jackie let out her held breath. "Will do. Thanks." She turned to Laurel. "Let Hauser know to e-mail us the second he finds anything else. We need to go."

The coroner, one Dr. Emily Liyang, a tiny, fortyish Chinese woman with a rope of spun, black silk hanging to her waist in a simple ponytail, greeted them when they arrived. Belgerman pulled a fair bit of weight with her and could call in the occasional favor. Jackie had never heard what he had done to garner such a benefit, but it had proven beneficial on more than one occasion. Emily was hardly what one typically expected of a coroner, but then, Jackie knew she was not what one thought of as an FBI agent. That shared background had given them no small amount of mutual respect toward one another in the few times they had needed to speak.

"My two favorite feds," Emily said, smiling. "Haven't seen you two in a while, and now you bring me this boy. You owe me a drink."

"Anytime, Emily," Laurel piped in before Jackie could respond. "Glad you could get to it so fast. This one is bad."

"Yeah, I noticed. Your boss man called me this morning and asked in his friendly 'I'm FBI, so do as I say' sort of way to please expedite this case." She opened up a folder that had been sitting on top of some others on her spacious, compulsively neat desk, and began to remove some photos. "I finished the prelim an hour ago, but I won't have a tox report until this afternoon at the earliest. Did you want to see the body?"

Jackie shook her head. "Unless you think we need to. We had our own look yesterday."

Dr. Liyang gave an absent shrug. "Not really. I have all the info here. No reason to subject you to that again." She smiled at Laurel this time, fully aware of her weaker stomach. They had gone out for drinks a couple years back to celebrate the capture of a serial rapist, and Emily had sent Laurel to the bathroom with an increasingly graphic description of some of the bodies that had come through her office. Jackie had listened with half a curious ear. She found forensics intriguing but had no desire for the work. Slapping the handcuffs on the bad guys was far more rewarding.

The photos laid out on the desk showed Archie in the various stages of autopsy, taken from a variety of angles. "Pretty straightforward, at least from the initial investigation. See here?" she said, pointing at the first picture. "The boy was bound with zip ties. You can tell by the unique marks. They go all the way around, wrists and ankles, so I'm guessing he was laid out on a table or the ground. Little evidence of struggle, and just a few bruises you might find on any typical twelve-year-old.

Jackie studied the pictures, leaning over the desk along with Laurel, looking for signs of anything they might have missed from the day before. *I was a lot more banged up than that at twelve years old,* she thought, rubbing at the dull ache that appeared in her own wrists as she studied the pictures. All he'd wanted was to get away, and he'd stepped into the arms of a killer. Jackie suppressed a shudder and continued to follow Dr. Liyang's summary.

"Puncture wound here on the left arm is where the blood was drained out of him. Everything indicates he had been dead a good ten hours before you found him. No signs of sexual abuse. There were a few fibers we lifted off him that we'll analyze, but other than that, he was pretty clean. I think he may have been washed, but this is the one intriguing thing I found." She tapped at Archie's head in a close-up picture of his face from the eyebrows up to the hairline.

Jackie noticed right away. Without the close-up, it had not been obvious before. "He colored his hair."

Emily smiled at them. "Sure, if he was a zombie."

Laurel's mouth formed an *O* of understanding. "He was already dead when this happened."

"Yep. At least I'm almost positive. I'll know definitely by tomorrow and let you know, but it seems your killer wanted him to have different hair."

"Was it cut, too?" Jackie wondered.

"The clothing will be gone over later today. If we find any evidence of that, I'll call you, Jack."

"Thanks. Why would a perp want to do that?"

Dr. Liyang shrugged. "That's what you girls get paid the big bucks for."

Driving back to headquarters, they continued to discuss that question. Jackie sped in and around traffic, absently maintaining the speed she knew would allow her to make all the lights through that part of town.

"Could be a fetish thing," Laurel suggested. One hand clutched tightly on the door handle, while the other was braced against the armrest in the middle between them. "Sweet mother, Jackie! Knock it off already."

She backed off the pedal and was forced to brake for the next light. "Damnit. What's the matter?"

"Quit driving like you're taking your expectant wife to the hospital."

Jackie looked at her, imagining that soft belly expanded to the size of a basketball. Laurel's body was built for babies. The smile vanished when she realized Laurel would likely never have one.

"I would race you to the hospital, though, if you were about to pop one out."

Laurel shook her head and waved at the window. "Just drive normal, please." There was silence for moment, and she continued. "You don't think it was a fetish thing though, do you?"

Jackie shook her head. "No. It fits too much with the whole neat-arrangement-in-the-park scene. I think that boy was put there like he was on purpose. Someone went to some trouble to prop him up there and have him look a certain way."

"Okay, I can go with that," Laurel said. "But who and why?"

"No clue." She drummed her fingers along the steering wheel. "Care to bet any money that Nick Anderson has an idea why?"

"Not really," she said. "I think I'd lose that bet."

"You would," Jackie agreed. "Right now, I want to have a little sit-down with the geeks and see what else they've dug up. I want some proof we aren't dealing with a recurring case of serial murders involving a hundred-year-old man."

"He makes a good case for dating older men."

Jackie glared at her and then rolled her eyes. "Oh, yeah. That, and drinking blood. That's right up at the top of my list, too."

Chapter 16

They found Hauser at his desk, the computer screens turned into a bank of old photos and newspaper clippings. He had pictures loaded up on three of them, two of which Jackie recognized. They were the old newspaper clippings Laurel had showed her earlier. He spun around in his chair to greet them when Jackie knocked once.

"Hey! How are Chicago's loveliest agents today?" He gave them a devilish smile.

Jackie thrust her hands into her pockets. "Hungry."

"Got half a chicken-salad sandwich here you can have," he said, and when it got no response, the grin faded, and he continued. "Okay, sourpuss, look here. This is some weird-ass shit I've found. These are the two clippings you've already seen, the first from 1970, the other from 1934." He wheeled his chair over by the screens and pointed. "You can see the similarities in them, might even say they look like the same guy."

"They're thirty-six years apart though," Jackie said. She had a sinking feeling she already knew where Hauser was heading with this.

"Yeah, I know. How could it be the same guy, right?" He

pointed at the next screen. "Here's another photo, thirty-six years before those."

It was a yearbook photo from Princeton University. The name listed beneath it was Nicholas Rembrandt. The image looked slightly younger than Nick Anderson, but not by much. The skin was smoother, without the crinkle in the corners of his eyes, and he wore small, round glasses, just enough to cover the eye, but the bright glaze on them was still evident, even in a black-and-white photo.

Jackie leaned over and scanned the page. "Hauser, this pic is one hundred and eight years old."

He grinned with the evil glee of a thirteen-year-old who has uncovered his dad's secret stash of porn. "Yeah, pretty freaky, huh?"

"You telling me it's the same guy? Please tell me you aren't."

Hauser nodded. "Had Platt take the scans and analyze them. 'Puter is ninety-eight point seven percent sure the guy in all these photos is the same guy. It is statistically impossible that relatives could look that closely alike."

"Great."

"Oh, it gets better," he said, chuckling. He switched the third screen over to another picture. "Look at this one."

Laurel leaned in with her to get a close look. "Sheriff Nicholas R. Anderson and family. Is this the real guy here?"

"So says the great god of circuitry," he said.

Jackie glanced at the article, which spoke of welcoming the new sheriff to the area and looking forward to his services and ability to keep the area protected. It was from some place in Wyoming Jackie had never heard of before. They looked like a typical Old West family: father, two teen sons, a young daughter, wife, and someone who looked to be a grandmother. "This is impossible, Hauser."

"You'd think."

"It's him," Laurel added, sounding far more sure of herself than Jackie wanted.

"Laur?" Jackie said skeptically. "This would make Nick Anderson, like . . ."

"One hundred seventy-six years old," Hauser replied.

"There has to be some other reason for this." Jackie's mind could not wrap around the implications. There were none that fit her view of the world. It just didn't work.

Hauser laughed. "Told you it was creepy. The guy should be dead."

She looked over at Laurel and remembered what she had said about holding his hand. The guy had felt like he was dead. Laurel was still studying the photos, looking back and forth between them. "What about her?" She pointed at the image of what looked like Shelby Fontaine.

He shrugged. "Don't know. Haven't run her. You want me to?"

Laurel nodded. "Yes, please."

"Laur?" Jackie said again. "What are you thinking here?" She was going to have to put some trust in her opinion on this because she could make no sense of it.

After a few seconds, Laurel finally stood up straight. "Not sure yet. I think I need to go talk with someone about this."

"Someone?"

"A witch friend of mine," she said with a faint smile.

"Cool," Hauser said.

Jackie frowned at him. Witches. This case was going in completely the wrong direction. "Wish we could just arrest the prick."

They both snickered at her. Hauser turned back and pulled up the information he had been working on. "You're such a ballbuster, Jack. Glad I'm not married to you."

Laurel slapped him on top of the head. "Be nice."

"Anything else, Hauser?" Jackie snapped back.

"Yeah. Another couple news articles during that same

year as the Princeton pic. Seems our crotchety old man was involved in another serial murder case. Five people killed, and he could never be tied to it, but was a person of interest apparently."

Now that was interesting. "And the first one?"

"No murder case, but his career came to an end a few months after that photo was taken. Big shoot-out with some local outlaw. His family was killed, and he quit."

"Interesting," Jackie said. "There are five family members in the photo here."

Hauser shrugged, smiling. "Very interesting."

Five. They were all fives. "All these things are thirty-six years apart?"

"Freaky, isn't it? Like some bizarre repeating murder spree."

Laurel tugged absently at her ponytail. "I wonder what significance the thirty-six years has?"

"Oh," Hauser answered, "that might be a simple one. Anderson was thirty-six years old when his family was killed."

"How old were the family members?" Jackie wondered.

"Um, give me a sec and I'll see if I can find out." He began clicking through screens with his mouse faster than Jackie could read what he was pulling up.

"You don't suppose," Laurel said, finger twirling at her ponytail, "that Anderson or someone related to him is repeating the death of his family?"

The thought had just occurred to Jackie as well. "It's awfully suspicious, if you ask me."

"Here we go," Hauser cut in. "Boys were twelve and fifteen, girl was eight, wife thirty-one, and Anderson's grandmother seventy-five."

"Twelve," Jackie and Laurel said together.

Jackie poked Hauser in the shoulder. "Run the other cases. I want as many of the vic's ages that you can find."

She felt her mind beginning to spin in helpless futility.

The scenario they were considering was insanity. "Okay, this is more than I can digest. I want to get a tail on Anderson and Fontaine. Hauser, can we prove these are all the same guy? A judge would laugh this out of court."

"Haven't turned up any kind of paper trail yet to prove anything. We'll keep digging. This stuff has been easy to find so far. He's not going far out of his way to hide his past, just altering things a bit so nobody makes any obvious connections."

"Well, who would believe that shit?" Jackie shook her head. "I can't believe it."

He laughed. "I know. It's like he's cloning himself, or . . . or he's a fucking vampire! That would be so cool."

Jackie shook her head. "Shut up, Hauser. This is about as far from cool as it gets. Laur, we need to get Gamble on organizing tails, see if Belgerman will okay a phone tap. There has to be some way to get Anderson to implicate himself or whomever it is he knows is doing this."

"Why not just ask him?" Laurel offered. "Show him what we have? Maybe he'll see the game is up and cave in."

"He's too cool for that. If it's someone else, he doesn't want us to know, for some reason. We need something to entice or threaten him with. He needs to want to talk."

"Most killers want to talk," Laurel said.

"Did you get the impression he wanted to? Or that he was baiting us to find out what a genius he is?"

"No, which is why I'm leaning toward some other killer he doesn't want to talk about."

"Exactly. So how do we sucker him into blabbing or leading us to the real culprit?"

Laurel shrugged. "We have a stolen penny, and we have information about his past."

"The penny." Jackie walked to the doorway. "Hauser, send everything you've found by five today. I want to go over everything we've got tonight." She motioned to Laurel. "Come on. I'm so hungry I can't think, and we need a plan."

Chapter 17

The afternoon skies bore down on Nick like a gloomy gray stone. A steady, windswept drizzle coated the city in a glossy sheen. Not that bright blue skies would have made the task any easier. Drake had been frustratingly hard to pinpoint. The tingling sense of awareness of the other side would pop up but then fade a few minutes later. It was something Nick could not understand. The feeling should have been more constant, even if Cornelius was driving around. The fleetingness of it made no sense, and Nick found himself growing more irritated as the day wore on. They were being played with, and there was little they could do except keep playing the game.

Drake would be taking his next victim soon. After the first it had been days between victims, but now, knowing full well how quickly law enforcement could work, Nick figured he would be lucky if it was more than a day or two. Drake would want him to get a good whiff, too—offer up a little extra inspiration and maybe do something to link him even more closely to the murders. Jackie Rutledge would be all over him then. He'd be lucky if he didn't get arrested—but then, that would ruin the game. Cornelius would not want that, so he was counting on Nick's ability to avoid incarceration. Nick had entertained the thought of turning himself in just to break things up, to see what Drake would do, but who was to say he would not just march right into the jail and slaughter everyone, including himself for not playing by the rules. If anything, the man had proven he did not like his life to be interfered with.

He found himself thinking more about what might happen to Jackie Rutledge if she got too close to things. Technology made it so difficult now to circumvent investigations. The odds were growing stronger by the hour that he would be brought in on suspicion. If they found reason to get a warrant to search his house, shit would really hit the fan. The woman was close to the point of pulling him in just for breathing funny.

Nick crept along, barely holding the speed limit while he let his mind wander, catching the occasional whiff of a ghost, potent enough to still be lingering in the world of the living, but missing that peculiar, bittersweet stench of the other side. Shelby was right, of course. The FBI could make this search easier. Whatever Drake had up his sleeve, it was confounding their senses. They were no closer to him now than earlier. Of course, a little blood would go a long way toward evening the odds. No matter how much the thought lingered though, Nick could not bring himself to call Drake's bluff on that account. Promises had been made, ones that would damn him to hell regardless if he broke them.

Then Nick caught the familiar whoosh of the door to Deadworld opening up, a faint but persistent echo in his mind, like the caw of a crow stuck in an endless loop. Drake was feeding again, and it had not even been twenty-four hours.

Turning north up Western Avenue, Nick gunned his engine and began to weave through traffic, ignoring the blaring horns. It was up near the area Shelby had been searching in. The soft, singsong lilt of her voice spoke into his ear.

"Hi! Shel here, and, no, I'm not. Just leave me a—" Nick grumbled and clicked the cell shut. What the hell was she doing?

Five minutes later, he tried her again with similar results. "Damnit, Shel! Where are you?" A thousand hopeless, gut-clenching scenarios tumbled through his head while he began to zero in on the source. He was close, a few blocks, perhaps. Then, mysteriously, the feeling faded away to the usual dim whisper.

This time, her voice rang loud and clear. "Hey, babe."

"Where in Christ's name were you? I had him for a minute. I'm on Western, heading north."

"I was ignoring all the calls to flash my boobs," she said, laughing loudly.

Funny. He was years removed from feeling any jealousy over her. "You could take this just a little more seriously."

"Oh, fucking lighten up, Nick. We're closing in. He's close."

She was evading. Being a sheriff and a PI did give you certain advantages at times. What would she need to be evasive for? "You weren't actually flashing your breasts at anyone, were you?"

"Aw, could my Nick be—" She cut off for a moment, her voice replaced by the screaming roar of her motorcycle's engine and the screeching of tires. "Out of the way, dipshit!"

Nick pulled to a stop in front of a Starbucks. Coffee sounded good now, and he could use a break. "Where are you going in such a hurry? You're going to kill yourself, powers or not."

She laughed again, the sound almost giddy. "Just cruising,

sweetie. Clearing my head. Besides, I need to lose this tail again. These feds suck."

The tail had been a constant since noon. It did not take much to lose them, but it wasn't long before they picked either of them up again. It hit Nick abruptly then, like a punch in the gut. Sweetie. She had not called him that in thirty years.

Anger and fear swept through him like wildfire. "Damnit, Shel. Tell me you didn't just drink. Tell me that feeling I just had five minutes ago was Drake and not you drinking from someone." There was no answer, just the changing of gears on her bike. "Shelby! Answer me, goddamn you!"

The BMW screeched to a halt in his ear, and the roar of the engine quieted to a dull rumble. The sarcasm stung Nick like a wasp. "Drink what, Nick?"

Nick slapped a hand over his face in disbelief. "You did. Sweet mother of God, you drank blood."

Shelby was silent for a moment. When she spoke, her voice was more subdued. "I didn't kill anyone, Nick."

"Like that makes a fuck—" He stopped himself, taking a deep breath. The anger would do no good. Shelby would enjoy the fight, more than likely. "That doesn't make a difference, and you know it."

An exasperated sigh whispered in his ear. "So what, Nick? You realize the position we're in now, don't you? One down, four to go, and then it's you, babe. We're no closer than we've ever been."

True, but still wrong. "You promised me, Shel. No more blood." *We swore upon the graves of our loved ones. Swore never again to be so corrupt and evil.*

"Yeah, I did. It was thirty fucking years ago, when it didn't really matter." Her voice grew steadily louder in his ear. "But it matters now, and we need all the goddamn help we can get. Besides, he deserved it, Nick. Don't worry, he'll live. We won't if we don't do something."

"There are other things—"

"What things!" she yelled in his ear, years of frustration and rage bursting out of her so loudly it made his ear ring. "We aren't doing anything, and you are shuffling your weary ass up to the firing line just so you can feel better about getting shot. Well, fuck that! Fuck that, Nick. I'm not doing it. My senses are pumping now, and, oh, does it feel good. So I'm going to hunt a while, babe. Okay? You're lucky I don't give Agent Rutledge a call and have her join me. Later."

The phone went silent, and Nick hurled it against the opposite door. She was right and wrong at the same time. Moral ambiguity was such a pain in the ass. Nick forgot his coffee and gunned his car back into traffic. Somehow she had gotten over the ethical hump and broken her promise. It didn't mean as much to her. How could it? Nick swore. He could almost hear the blood that had been singing in Shelby's veins, pushing open the door and letting the delightfully abhorrent rush come pouring through. Damn her.

The thought of blood would not leave his mind. It would be so easy to give in, but it would make him once again into that same monster Drake was.

On the passenger-side floor, his cell rang, interrupting the troubling thoughts. Nick was forced to pull into the parking lot of the Riverview Plaza so he could stop and pick up the phone. The number didn't indicate who was calling.

"Anderson."

"Agent Rutledge, Mr. Anderson. Am I bothering you?" Her tone was decidedly calm.

"Just running some errands, Agent Rutledge. How can I help you?"

"Everything okay there, Mr. Anderson? You sound a little annoyed."

Nick took a deep breath. She picked up cues well. "Frustrating day is all."

"I hear you there," she said, sounding a little too pleased. "I had something come up today I was wanting to ask you about."

Nick put the car into park and sagged back into his seat. "Ask away."

"That penny we showed you before—you remember the one?"

"Of course."

"Well, it was stolen this morning from our evidence room."

"That's unfortunate," he said. "And, no, I'm not sure how or why that would have happened. If that's what you were wondering."

"Oh, no," she replied, not taking the bait. "We have some strong leads on that account. I wanted to ask you though if you had thought of anything relevant in this matter, you know, that might help us pinpoint our culprit. We have some suspicions, but it would help us out if you might offer some information that would narrow it down for us."

Where was she heading with this? Could they really know already? No, he assured himself. He would be handcuffed in an interrogation room right now if that was the case. She was fishing. "I was perfectly honest with you before, Agent Rutledge. I have no additional information for you in that regard."

"Hmmm, okay," came her simple reply. "I wanted to double-check before we head out to look into these leads. Thank you for your time."

"Anytime. Feel free to call again if you have any further questions."

This time her reply had a tinge of anger. "Oh, we will. Don't worry."

Nick clicked off his phone and put it back in his pocket.

At least he knew they didn't have him on that yet. They were trying, however, and it was only a matter of time. One thing was certain. Their presence was not going away any time soon. He put the car into gear and pulled back out onto the street. A block behind, he caught sight of the brown sedan as it pulled out of a gas station and began to follow.

Chapter 18

The door to Jackie's apartment swung open, and Laurel stepped in, plastic shopping bags dangling from her hands.

Jackie looked away from the oversize corkboard mounted on her living room wall where all the pictures Hauser had found were tacked up with multicolored push-pins. "What's that? You cooking us dinner?"

"It's stuff for your pathetic excuse of a kitchen," she said. "You can't live off day-old Chinese food, you know."

"Why not? I like Chinese food." Grocery shopping rarely ever made it on the to-do list.

Laurel shook her head. "You're an embarrassment to independent women everywhere. College dorm rooms are better stocked."

"Peh!" Jackie waved her off. "Coffee, wine, and chicken fried rice. What more could a girl need?"

"Oh, how about some fruit? Vegetables? Maybe a little dairy once in a while?"

"There are veggies in the rice, and I get milk in every latte."

Laurel put the bags down on the counter and began to unload the food. "Your body is going to hate you. You can't catch bad guys on such a shitty diet."

"Hasn't been a problem so far," Jackie said with a smile. "Besides, you bring all that healthy crap over a couple times a month, so it's all good."

"Only if you eat it."

She shrugged and looked back to the board. "I eat some of it."

"Uh-huh," Laurel replied. "So, your nutrient-deprived brain figure out anything new for us to work with?"

"Not really." Jackie sighed and put her hands on her hips. "Other than being completely weirded out by the whole prospect of dealing with someone who drinks blood to stay alive, I haven't figured out anything. Nothing that makes sense anyway. I'd like a motive that doesn't involve a century-long serial-murder spree by the undead, and I'm just not finding one."

Laurel wrinkled her nose at a Chinese food carton as she dropped it in the garbage. "You ruling out the penny?"

"No. I don't know. We tracked Anderson and Fontaine around a four-square-mile area north of downtown all afternoon and got nothing. They didn't stop to talk to anyone. Anderson's phone calls were to Ms. Fontaine and work. That's it."

"He could figure we're baiting him."

"Or even if the penny is relevant to the case, it has nothing to do with what is motivating our killer." Jackie tapped at the sequence of pictures detailing the murders. "It's in these murders somewhere. We don't have every last detail on them, but our intel indicates we've had someone killing off a group of five people every thirty-six years since Anderson's family was killed."

"This would make the fifth time it's happened, too." Laurel began to rinse off a tomato and bell pepper in the sink. "The numbers are significant."

Jackie stared at the old picture of Nick and his family, the classic sheriff's star pinned to the breast of his shirt.

"Maybe he just snapped when his family died and has been reliving the murders over and over again."

"And only do it every thirty-six years?" Laurel chopped the vegetables on a cutting board. "That is some serious self-restraint for someone who's snapped."

"Yeah, I know. Very atypical pattern," Jackie said, "but a pattern nonetheless. If this holds to form, we should have another victim very soon. Could be another child."

"We don't have enough to bring him in."

"Fuck, I'm not even sure it *is* him. The vibe is all wrong." Jackie stepped away and sat down on the piano bench. "Or maybe he's just snowing us. I can't get a read on him at all."

"He's one hundred seventy-six years old," Laurel said. "He's had a lot of practice. You want blue cheese or Italian?"

"What?"

"Dressing. What kind of dressing you want?"

"God. You made us salad?"

Laurel laughed. "Shut up. It's your monthly intake of vegetables."

"It's lame is what it is. Blue cheese." Jackie took the bowl of salad without further complaint, however, and set it on top of the piano. Laurel set hers there as well and remained standing, looking across to the picture-strewn board. "We need another angle."

"Who killed Anderson's family?"

"No info there," Jackie said. "Hadn't been caught when the article was written."

Laurel chewed thoughtfully on a chunk of tomato. "So, you think Anderson quit being a sheriff to go after whomever it was?"

"That would be my guess." Jackie gave in and picked up the salad, forking in a blue-cheese-slathered chunk of lettuce. "I would."

"Okay, what if he still is?"

"Still?" She looked at the board, trying to figure what Laurel might be seeing. "Chasing a ghost? Can ghosts murder people?"

"Not that I'm aware of," Laurel said. "I was thinking more like—"

"Split personality!" Jackie stood up and pointed at Nick with her fork. "He kills them as Jekyll and then tries to catch the family killer with Hyde."

"Actually," Laurel said, nodding, "that might work. Psychotic break when his family was murdered, can't find the killer, so makes it up himself in order to get revenge. Need evidence from him at a crime scene to have a shot at that one though."

"Need to prove that penny was his somehow."

"Which will be a bit difficult, given it was stolen," Laurel added.

"By a ghost that you felt out at his office."

"And we'll prove this how?"

Jackie threw up her hands. "How the fuck would I know? You're the ghost person, Laur. How do we deal with ghosts?"

She shrugged. "You don't *deal* with them. You're lucky if you can interact with them at all."

"Well, that helps." Jackie sat back down. "Maybe the ghost gave it back to Anderson?"

"Maybe," Laurel agreed. "We can't get a search warrant based on that though. You know no judge will accept anything supernatural. We need something concrete to link that penny to him."

"Yeah, yeah. Technicalities."

Laurel chuckled. "Don't even think about going to look. Anderson won't let you."

"He will if he doesn't have it or knows we won't find it."

"Hmmm. Does the Hyde know what the Jekyll is doing?"

"I know, it's a stretch." Jackie shook her head in frustration and dug back into the salad.

"Not so much. It's a wild theory, but it works if things fall into place."

"I prefer not to wait for someone else to die in order to find out."

"All we can do is watch him and wait, Jackie. If he makes a move, we'll be there."

"And if we're wrong, another child might be dead."

"I know," Laurel said. "We can only work with what we have, and we don't have enough."

Jackie slapped her hand down on the piano keys, creating a harsh jangle of notes. "Then we need to find it. What the hell are we missing? I'll bet it's right here in front of us."

"We'll find it. We always do." Laurel laid a hand down on the keys by Jackie's. "Play something. It always helps you think."

"I'm not in the mood."

"Okay, then eat the salad. You've eaten crap all day."

Jackie straightened up and laid her hands upon the keys. "You're a pain in the ass. Any requests?"

"Nope," Laurel said. "Just something soothing."

Jackie flexed her fingers, popping a couple knuckles, and thought for a moment on her choice. She played for no one, except on occasion for Laurel when she insisted. Everyone else brought out the nerves, and the embarrassment of screwing up was so not worth it.

The notes for Brahms's *Lullaby* rose out of the Steinway like a soft breeze, drifting with ease around the room. Laurel smiled and closed her eyes, elbows resting on top of the piano, her chin in her hands. Jackie's teacher had told her she had a very light touch upon the keys—"quiet grace," she had called it. At the time, Jackie had not cared. Learning to play had been the important thing, carrying out her mother's wish to have her learn. The song was one of

Laurel's favorites and not overly complicated to play, so it was often a choice when she was over. On more than one occasion it had put her to sleep.

Frustration melted away while Jackie's fingers roamed over the keys. Her head cleared, but no revelations were forthcoming. The missing piece still lay out there in the ether somewhere.

Laurel sighed when the last of the notes faded away to silence. "I love you when you play—I mean, *it*—I love *it* when you play. Sorry, Freudian slip there." She gave her a sheepish smile.

Jackie smiled back, utterly unsure of what to say. The words, the thought, had been lingering in the back of her mind since Laurel had admitted her sexuality. Jackie had conveniently stashed the thought back into the recesses of her brain, but now here it was, front and center.

"I know what you meant," she said. "You're my one and only fan." Did that come out right? No. It didn't sound right at all. "What I meant was . . . uh . . . I meant . . ."

Laurel stood up straight and laughed. "Sorry. Awkward moment. I know it's something that needed to be said at some point, but this isn't exactly what I'd been thinking. It's just been on my mind a lot since yesterday, and I wanted to get it out there and . . . you know, clear the air. I don't want it to make things weird between us."

Jackie shook her head. "No weirdness. I'm fine with it, Laur. Really. You're my best friend and partner. You've saved my butt more times than I can remember. So how could I not be fine with practically anything you do or say?"

She wrung her hands together. "I know. It's just this is kinda different." Her shoulders slumped and her face flushed. "I didn't want you worrying I'd try to stick my tongue down your throat or something."

"Laur!" Jackie had finally managed to get it out of her

head from before, and now it was back. "I'm truly not worried about you doing that. Really."

"Sorry. Sorry! Shit." Her hands covered her mouth in shock. "I didn't mean to. I take it back. Pretend I never said it."

Jackie rolled her eyes and shook her head. "Not going to happen. Look, can we just shelve this for now? Please? I know this is, um, not how it's supposed to work. I get that. Maybe it'll change things, and maybe it won't, but not now. We've got a case to figure out, and it'll never happen with this stuff hovering around us. If there's more you want to talk about, we will. I promise. Okay?"

She nodded. "Okay."

Jackie sighed. *Please just let this go for now.* "All good, right?"

She nodded again. "Right."

Jackie's phone buzzed on top of the piano. Where had that call been two minutes ago? She picked it up. "Rutledge."

"Hey, Jack, it's Gamble. I'm going home. Peterson is taking over for me out here at Anderson's, but I think he's done for the night. Last I checked, he was sitting by his fireplace reading a book."

"Figured as much," she said. "Anything with Fontaine?"

"Um, no, but we lost track of her an hour or so ago and haven't picked her back up yet. Apparently, she used to race motorcycles, and nobody can keep up with her."

"Great. Thanks. Have them check in if anything comes up."

"Will do," he replied. "Anything on your end?"

"Besides huge amounts of frustration and lack of evidence? No."

"Ouch. Sorry. I'll see you in the morning."

"Later." Jackie clicked off and set the phone down. "Back to the board. Let's go through it all again."

Laurel walked around to the wall. "Did I hear him say Ms. Fontaine raced motorcycles?"

"Yeah, and I'll bet she can swing from branches with her whip and call upon the feline forces of Chicago to assist her."

Laurel made an amused "mmm" sound, which Jackie wisely chose to ignore. "Let's just focus on dead people and vampires for now. Much safer topics."

Chapter 19

"Where is he, Reg?" The echo of gunfire was still ringing in Nick's head, but the dream had been wiped away by the abrupt, cold brush of Reggie's hand through his shoulder.

"Floor of the vault of the Woodbridge Federal Credit Union." There was a tinge of sadness to his voice this time. "Got him laid out on a pile of pennies, boss."

Damn. Drake was really going to rub it in this time around. "Any law enforcement there yet?" Nick turned and glanced at the bedside clock. It read 8:26 AM.

"Got called about five minutes ago, I'd guess."

So much for an advance investigation of the scene. "Okay, see what you can find, but get out of there before Agent Carpenter shows up. I don't want any more suspicions tossed our way now."

Reggie rolled his eyes and shook his head. "Little late for that, if you ask me, but I'm on it. What are they looking for out here? They aren't being very subtle."

"Playing out the penny angle, I believe. Agent Rutledge wanted to see if I'd take some bait."

"They would be more useful *with* us, boss, but I guess you already know that."

Nick held up his hand. "I know, Reg. I can't risk any more lives on this."

He shrugged. "They get paid to take these risks. Should let them earn their paycheck, boss. They have resources and manpower."

"It's not something they are prepared to handle," he said.

Reggie snorted. "Hell, Sheriff, it's not something we're prepared to handle."

"True enough." Nick dropped his hand. "I've enough blood on my hands already."

He nodded. "Understood. They may give you no choice, you know."

"We'll cross that bridge when we come to it. For now, see what you can come up with. I'm tired of us chasing our tails in the dark."

"Will do, boss." Reggie waved. "Check in later."

"Hey," Nick said quickly, stopping him halfway through the wall of his bedroom. "How are you holding up? I know this has got to be hard."

He shrugged, a wry smile crossing his face. "It's draining me, but we're near the end. Either way, I'm good." He turned and vanished beyond the wall.

Nick could feel his presence glide away and then vanish through that doorway to the world of the dead.

"Either way," Nick muttered, rubbing his hands over his face. "Either way, Reggie."

Sleep had been spotty the night before, worried as he was about Shelby, who had continued her search until after three AM. He could tell her to abandon the search, but it was pointless now. The victim had died hours ago, and Drake would be found only if he wanted to be. The bastard had an incredible knack for staying just out of reach. With a twinge of guilt, Nick found himself wondering more about what Drake might have left behind than whom he had killed. It would indicate who the next victim might be, more specific perhaps than a simple penny had been.

Nick took the time to make a decent breakfast of ham, eggs, grits, and toast and sipped on a full cup of espresso. Next to the plate, Joshua's penny stared mockingly up at him. It had been the last one collected, picked up on the day the new pennies had arrived at the bank. Three days before Cornelius had come sauntering into town on his brightly painted wagon. The image of Josh, grinning ear to ear as he held it up to the sun, glinting in the light, marveling at its shiny newness, was remarkably clear and painful. Funny how all the years didn't dull memories such as those.

Finally, Nick picked up the penny, put his dishes in the dishwasher, and marched upstairs, opening the narrow door that led into the loft space over the garage. There resided the past Nick could never let go of, the memorabilia of days long gone, painstakingly arranged to provide the sharpest reminder of what had been taken from him all those decades ago. In a handmade binder, painted and decorated with stamps and postcards pasted on by Joshua with the help of his mother, Gwen, Nick turned to the last page, and in the last spot—which had remained empty these 144 years—Nick carefully slid the penny into its rightful place.

Straining his senses, Nick could almost hear their voices if he remained perfectly calm and still. His heart pounded now in his chest, and he sniffed away a tear that threatened to spill. In moments like these, Nick wanted nothing more than to just lie down and let that doorway draw him through to the end.

"Goddamn you, Cornelius. Damn you to hell." He slammed the book shut and marched out of the room.

Chapter 20

There was another victim.

At least the call came while they were on their way downtown, allowing them to avoid some traffic and head toward the bank.

Jackie glanced at the GPS system in the dashboard after Laurel put in the address. "This bank is close to Special Investigations, isn't it?"

Laurel nodded. "About six blocks."

"Coincidence?"

"Doubt it."

"Anderson isn't dumb enough to dump the body right by his place of work," Jackie said.

"Unless he has good reason to put it there."

Jackie pulled her five-shot venti on ice from the cup holder and took a long draught. She needed it after last night's endlessly frustrating picking through of Nick's story. The key piece of information still eluded them.

She could see the flash of blue and red before they even arrived at the scene. Television vans were parked along the street. A small crowd had gathered on the sidewalk along the bank's parking lot.

"Or someone is trying very hard to make Anderson look

like a suspect," Jackie said. She had gone to bed last night with that thought, based on a question Laurel had given. Who else could be involved and why? As much as she wanted to hold on to the idea that Nick Anderson might be a split personality, a far more disturbing notion waited in the wings. The original killer was still following Nick Anderson around.

"You didn't want to entertain that idea last night," Laurel said.

Jackie shrugged and swung their car up into the bank parking lot behind the flashing lights of several police cars. "Because I have no clue how we'll find out who that is if Anderson won't tell us."

"I still think we should just ask him. Our info didn't indicate who killed his family. They were never caught."

"And for some reason, the bastard doesn't want to clue us in." She closed her eyes and took a deep breath before opening the car door. "Look at this mess. It's sad that the TV crews are out here before we are."

She closed her door and leaned on the roof, looking out at the crowd, a very different look on her face. The skin between her eyebrows crinkled down in concentration. She turned and leaned back against the car a few seconds later. "He's not here. I don't think anyway."

Jackie walked off toward the bank. "Figured. Let's go have a look."

Inside the bank, the officer in charge of the scene was actually someone Jackie knew. He was a detective from their violent crimes task force, a lean, tall black man with facial features sharp enough to hurt yourself on. She had slept with him a few years back after hooking up in a hotel bar during some law-enforcement conference. He had abs you could springboard off of.

"Detective Morgan," Jackie said, shaking his hand. "Good to see someone familiar on the scene. This is craziness."

"Cluster fuck is more like," he said, frowning. "Some bozo ran down the street screaming his goddamn head off. This a fed case now?

"Think so. You got someone drained of blood?"

"In the vault there. It's all yours, Jackie girl. I hate these freaked cases."

She waved him off. "Coward. You have the guy who went screaming down the street?"

"Yeah, somewhere. I'll make sure he sticks around."

"Thanks. You're on the task force, Morgan, so we'll be seeing you later today I expect. Let's go have a look, Agent Carpenter."

In the middle of the vault floor, thousands of pennies had been poured into a large pile. On top of it, a young man lay in coffinlike repose, feet crossed at the ankles, hands folded over his chest. He looked peaceful. The gentle smile on his face gave her the uneasy feeling that he was glad to be dead. Jackie knelt down next to the pile, surveying the body. Her finger trembled slightly as it pointed at the body's hands.

"Care to take a guess at how old our vic is here?"

Laurel nodded. "Fifteen."

She had no doubts now. Two down and three to go, which meant that soon a little eight-year-old girl was going to fall into the hands of this monster.

"Look, Laur. Same ligature marks on the wrists. Zip ties."

"Yeah," she said, her voice hoarse and quiet. "Same sense of evil, too."

The forensics team was coming in then, the toolboxes in hand. Jackie stood up and nodded to Mike Leavy, who led their group of micro snoopers. "Mike, you let me know if you find anything odd on the body."

"Like?"

"No clue. Last vic had a collectible penny under him. Just keep an eye out, okay?"

"Sure thing, Jack. You okay?"

She shook her head. "Not particularly. This case is really starting to get on my nerves."

He gave her a grim smile and went to work. Jackie led Laurel out of the vault. No reason to be in there until they were done, and the feeling Laurel had was wigging her out, as evidenced by the heavy sigh she gave upon passing the threshold. Jackie touched Laurel lightly on the elbow as she stopped. "You okay?"

"Yeah. I'll be fine. This guy is just really bad, Jackie. It's going to get worse, you know."

Words of encouragement. "Then we better hurry up and catch this fucker." She turned and looked at the vault door, going over the frame and edges of the large metal door. There was not a scratch or ding on it. "Hey, Morgan!" she shouted across the lobby at him. He had moved over by the main door, likely hoping to sneak out. Jackie pointed up at the video camera.

"It's clean," he replied. "Not a thing on it."

"Security company?"

"On my to-do list," he said with a humorless grin.

"I'll track that down later, Jackie," Laurel said.

"I want a report on what you got before you bail on me, Morgan."

He nodded and went back to talking to one of his officers who had popped his head in through the door. Jackie looked around in thought, trying to think how someone could have gotten into the vault without causing any damage. "Someone had to have let him in."

Laurel agreed. "Sure looks that way."

"Or gave our perp the code."

"That could be, or maybe they work here."

"We'll check them all out, but that is way too obvious for this." Jackie stared at Laurel, noticing the little crinkle in her forehead had never gone away. She was still stressing. "What else?"

"Huh?"

"You have another theory. I can tell by that look, and it's probably one of those shitty ghost theories that I'm going to hate."

Laurel gave her a hesitant smile. "Probably."

"Jack? Got something here," Mike's voice called out from the vault.

Inside the vault, Mike sat crouched on the balls of his feet next to the victim. In his hand he had a pair of large tweezers, which grasped a card-sized object.

"What is it?"

He held it up for her. "Looks like a tarot card to me."

"Oh, really?" Suddenly interested, Laurel leaned over Jackie's shoulder to look. Her gasp hissed in Jackie's ear. "Wow. I think I know what that is."

"Yeah? Mike, you get that bagged up for us? I think I'd like to show it to someone."

"Sure. Let me dust it and log it in, and it's all yours."

A few minutes later, Jackie held the sealed card out to Laurel. "You okay to be touching this? In case it's . . . evil or whatever? I don't want you puking on my shoes."

Laurel grabbed the card, turning it over in her hands. "I'm prepared for it this time, thank you very much." She squinted, holding the card close to her face. "I think this is handpainted. If it's an original, this thing is worth a lot of money. I have a printed version of this deck at home. They're . . . There is something odd with this."

"Odd like what?"

Laurel held the card squarely between her hands, the edges digging into her palms, and closed her eyes for a moment. "It's got that thing's presence all over it, but there is something else, something . . ." She sighed. "I don't know. It's really faint."

They walked out a few minutes later, after forensics had

finished and found nothing else out of the ordinary. Jackie had begun to wonder. "Did it feel like Mr. Anderson again?"

"Could be."

"I think we need to go have a little heart-to-heart with Nick Anderson and company."

"Good idea. I think we should see them again, too."

Jackie took out her phone and called up Gamble. "Hey, Gamble. You back out at Anderson's?"

"Oh, yeah. He's out at the ranch here, Ma," he said in a horrible Texas drawl. "You comin' out?"

"Yeah, bonehead. We'll be out in a bit."

"Sweet. I want to see the inside of this place."

There were details to go over at the scene, but Jackie felt positive there would be little to gain from it, and she was itching to talk to Nick. The crew could handle things, question the employees, and finish gathering what little evidence she knew there would be. This guy was squeaky clean and operating with methods they could not get their minds around. Worse, he was working fast, which meant there was no more time to waste. So, after delegating tasks, they were on the road to Nick's.

They crested a hill and found Gamble's car parked across from a sprawling ranch-style log house, and Jackie slid to a stop next to him. "Keep an eye on things out here, Gamble. I want to know if anything goes on while we're in there."

"Aw, come on. I want to see inside."

She smiled and rolled the window back up, ignoring the bird he flipped her as she pulled across into Nick Anderson's driveway. She stopped next to a slick-looking BMW motorcycle. A thick growth of oak and maple lined the edge of the garage and ran down the side of the house to the back. The grassy mound of the front yard sloped down around the opposite side and faded into a field of long grasses and wildflowers. Out beyond the field was another dense copse of trees. The house itself was one of those custom log-cabin deals and spread out in a long, angled line. Jackie guessed four to five thousand feet easy.

Laurel whistled. "I want to live here. This is awesome."

"Come on," Jackie said. "And quit drooling. Feds don't drool."

"You can honestly tell me you wouldn't give just about anything to live out here in a place like this?"

She shook her head. "Nope."

"You are such a liar."

Jackie spread her arms. "What the hell would I do with a place like this? It would take all damn day to vacuum the stupid thing. Who wants to spend their weekend doing that?"

"Can't you see yourself sitting on the back porch, sucking down lattes, watching the sun set?"

Jackie stopped at the front door, eyeing the rainbow of stained-glass windows lining either side. "I'll bet you it's a bachelor's cesspool inside."

"Five bucks says one look inside and you'd live out here in a second, minus the possible serial killer, of course."

"Oh, of course." Jackie rolled her eyes. "Make it a Starbucks with a cinnamon roll, and you're on."

"Done!" she said, far too cocky for her own good.

The door opened before Jackie could hit the doorbell, and Nick Anderson stood in the doorway, his eyes raised in mock surprise. "Hello, Agent Carpenter, Agent Rutledge." He offered them a faint, welcoming smile and stepped back to let them inside. He wore faded blue jeans and a Northwestern University sweatshirt. His feet were covered in bright white socks. He watched them coolly with those same, unnaturally bright eyes.

Jackie paused for a moment. "You expecting us, Mr. Anderson?" The lack of nerves bothered her. Most people got nervous around federal agents regardless of their guilt or innocence. They tried too hard to be cool. Nick Anderson looked relaxed, unworried.

He gave her a little shrug. "After seeing this morning's news, I figured there was a good chance."

"We have a few more questions for you, if you don't mind. As you expected, I'm sure," she added and stepped past him into the foyer.

"Anything I can do to help."

The foyer opened up to the second floor. A landing led to what appeared to be an office of some kind. Skylights let the sun pour through onto a slate floor. A large grandfather clock quietly chimed the quarter hour on one side. Beneath the landing, two large archways led into the main living space, and Jackie could see the wall of windows beyond, surrounding an enormous stone fireplace made of river rock. No fire blazed away in it now, but she could well imagine. Unfortunately, the place was immaculately clean.

Laurel nudged by her with a smile and stepped into the living room. Jackie followed. Starbucks was going to be on her after all.

Chapter 21

Laurel stood before a painting of an Old West town churned into a muddy swamp by a powerful storm. "You have a knack for painting, Mr. Anderson, and an apparent fondness for the Old West."

He gave her a nod of thanks. "A fascinating part of our history, in my opinion. Would either of you care for coffee or tea?"

Laurel smiled. "Tea, thank you. Agent Rutledge prefers coffee."

Jackie frowned. She was not in the mood to be taking anything except information from Nick Anderson today. Her thought was quickly lost, however, as her eyes roamed the expansive, light-filled living room, which opened on to the other side of the loft area. It was a very warm room, stained a rich, reddish brown in the trim and a similar tone in the solid, craftsman furnishings. There was a certain modern, Western flair to the decor in his home, surrounding you in earth tones and natural materials and accented with wood and brass. For owning a company worth millions, the wealth was very understated. The sunken area before the huge river-rock fireplace had a charm and coziness all its own. Jackie ignored the pang of jealousy. Who wouldn't like to curl up in front of that fire?

"Do you like any flavors in your cappuccino, Agent Rutledge?" he called over to her. "I'm not partial to them myself, but I've a cupboard full of the stuff if you have a preference."

Jackie glanced over at the kitchen. Nick was working before a restaurant-style espresso machine. "No. I really don't need the coffee. I just need some questions answered."

"Have a seat then. I'll have these ready in a minute. Shel, did you want one, too?"

"Nope. I'm good, thanks."

Jackie spun on her heel and found Shelby Fontaine standing in the far corner by the archway leading out to the foyer. The far side of the living room had a pool table, and she stood by it in black jeans, a black T-shirt with the Pink Panther emblazoned on the pocket, bare feet, and sunglasses. She had a bottle of beer in one hand and raised it toward Jackie with a smile.

"Good morning, agents."

"A little bright in here for you, Ms. Fontaine?" Jackie failed to hide the sarcasm.

"No, just a little hungover," she replied with a little laugh.

"Are you available for a few questions, Ms. Fontaine?" Laurel said.

The smile got a little bigger when she turned toward Laurel who sat now by the fireplace. "Anytime." She slinked her way over to the U-shaped configuration of overstuffed couch cushions in front of the fireplace. A round glass table sat in the middle of them, a twelve-inch bronze statue of a cowboy rearing up on his horse in the center. Shelby flopped down across from Laurel like a big, lazy cat and put her bare feet with their bright red toenails up on the table.

There was something unnerving about the woman that

Jackie could not put her finger on it. Maybe it was just Laurel's "touch of death" vibe that put her on edge, but something was telling her that Shelby Fontaine was not the "diva poser Angelina wannabe" that she appeared to be. So why the front? They needed to get her alone.

Jackie reluctantly moved down to the seating area and stood next to Laurel, who gave her a faint "thank you" smile. Cordial cop just went against Jackie's grain. She wanted to be able to pace around while she questioned Nick, point fingers, and look down on the suspect. It was a far better position to be in than this "over for coffee" setup in which she now found herself.

The sounds of frothing milk finished, and Nick walked over, carrying a tray with steaming mugs on it, and set it on the table next to the cowboy statuette. A smooth, white froth topped two of the bowl-sized cups, while a third had the string of a teabag dangling down the side. A small white teapot sat next to it. Jackie almost smirked. The cowboy was serving tea. How cute. It was a nice suck-up move. He seated himself on the empty couch, closer to her than to Shelby. What sort of odd relationship did these two have? The image of the old newspaper clipping popped into Jackie's head then, the story of a pissed-off Shelby Fontaine decking one Nicholas Rembrandt on the courthouse steps.

Jackie picked up her coffee and took a sip. The black liquid beneath the deceptively docile-looking foam was pure venom. It was coffee concentrate, distilled smoky heaven. The bastard.

"Is it too strong for you, Agent Rutledge?"

There was no hint of a smile there, but Jackie could sense it lurking in the background. "No. It's fine."

There was a quiet chortle from Shelby, who said nothing and sipped on her beer.

"So what can we answer for you today?" he asked. "I'm

assuming you know where I've been the past twenty-four hours, given the constant surveillance we've been under."

So this was how it was going to be. Smart-ass. Jackie took a deep breath, her gaze lifting upward to see the other side of the open, upstairs room. Nestled behind the rail was the unmistakable mass of a piano. He played piano, too? What else could this man do?

"Are you familiar with the Woodbridge Federal Credit Union?"

Nick nodded. "I do my banking there."

That figured. "Does the name Adam Moreland ring any bells?"

"Can I assume that's the boy who got killed?"

There was the slightest hint of something there in his voice. Sadness perhaps? Remorse? "Yes, Mr. Anderson. He was drained of blood just like the other boy, laid out on a pile of pennies in the bank vault."

He simply nodded at her, his mouth drawing just a bit tauter. It was a momentary expression, quickly covered by a drink from his coffee mug. Shelby sat up, suddenly interested in what Jackie had to say. A tap from Laurel had Jackie turning to find the tarot card in the little baggie. Jackie kept her face expressionless and took the evidence from Laurel's hand.

"We did find this interesting piece of evidence, Mr. Anderson."

He leaned forward to look. "Oh? What is it?"

The tone of his voice held genuine curiosity now, and Jackie wondered why that might be. She handed the baggie to him, her gaze zeroing in on his face, watching for any changes in expression. He plucked it from her fingers, holding it up and turning it around to examine both sides. Shelby leaned forward to see, and unlike Nick's steady, nonplussed stare, her perfectly plucked eyebrows arched high in surprise over the top of her sunglasses.

"Interesting," he said. "It's a tarot card."

"Yes. A very old, handpainted tarot card. Forensics still needs to get us an accurate date, but, assuming it's not a fake, we're guessing it's roughly a hundred and forty years old." It was pure conjecture, but Jackie wanted to play the hunch anyway. Still, he was frustratingly blank. The man must have been made of stone.

Shelby, on the other hand, did not run so cold. Her mouth had quirked into a half smile. "Roughly? Are you an expert on antique tarot cards, Agent Rutledge?"

"I am," Laurel chimed in. "I have a set similar to this at home. I collect them, and this style dates from Civil War times, more or less. It's a valuable collector's item."

"I see," Shelby said. She turned toward Nick for an instant, and the smile looked decidedly smug before she took another drink from the bottle of beer.

Nick's look of stone disappeared for a second, transforming into a flash of annoyance. Jackie caught the exchange out of the corner of her eye, and that was all she needed.

"Is it familiar to you, Mr. Anderson?"

He smiled and handed it back to her. "Please. Call me Nick."

"Fine, Nick." Her voice took on a harder edge. "Do you recognize the tarot card?"

"Not specifically, no."

"So you don't know anything at all about this specific hundred-and-forty-year-old tarot card?"

He stared at her then, holding her gaze, with those bizarrely bright, hazel-brown eyes. Jackie forced herself to hold it, pushing down the impulse to look away from the penetrating look. It was a Laurel look, one of those peering-into-your-soul sorts of looks that made your stomach squirm up into knots. Finally, he blinked away the contact.

"No. I'm sorry, but I don't."

Bullshit. Bull . . . fucking . . . shit. "I think you're lying to me, Nick."

"Beg your pardon?"

"You're lying—not telling me the truth, hiding something. I'll bet you know exactly what this is," she said, waving the card at him, "or know what it means in relation to this murder investigation." She took a long drink from her coffee and set it down on the table before getting to her feet. She needed to pace. "I have a little hunch, Nick."

"Okay." The cool facade had a trace of hesitancy in it.

"I think you probably know something about that penny we found on the first victim. Hell, maybe it's even yours, but, oddly, it's missing from evidence now. I don't suppose if we got a search warrant that we'd find that penny of yours tucked away in a drawer here somewhere?"

Shelby leaned back on her couch, one arm behind her head while she sipped on the beer. There was a pleased grin on that gleaming, red mouth. Jackie wondered for a moment why she would be pleased by this turn of events. Did she want Nick to get nailed, perhaps?

"I told you, Agent Rutledge, I'm not—"

She waved him off. "Something is very wrong with this case. My bullshit meter is redlining, and it just about shorts out pointed at you, Nick." Jackie stepped by Laurel and walked around behind the couches, circling behind Nick. She wanted to push his defenses. "And, Ms. Fontaine, why do you find this so amusing?"

She grinned. "I'm just have fun watching Nick squirm. Not many women can do that to him."

Jackie stopped in her tracks. She didn't appreciate the tone. "I'm only after the truth here, Ms. Fontaine. Squirming is not the issue. I have two dead boys with the blood drained out of them, and if for some reason you all have information pertaining to my investigation, I'd suggest you share, because, trust me, I'm this close to hauling you both in for obstruction." Laurel gave her one of those "calm down" looks, but Jackie ignored it. A pleasant conversation was not what was needed for this. She needed to dig under that thick skin of his, and being nice had gotten them nowhere.

Nick turned on the couch to face her better. "Agent Rutledge, I appreciate your dedication and zeal in going after guys like this."

She leaned toward him, hands on the back of the couch. "But?" The stare came again, his mouth drawn into a tight, firm line. She wanted to tell him to stop, but it was the wrong time for weakness. "But what, Mr. Anderson?"

He shook his head. "You're just looking at the wrong guy for answers, that's all."

Shelby actually rolled her eyes at his comment, and Jackie leaned down closer to him, no more than a couple feet away. There was a razor-thin scar that ran from his temple down along the jawline to his chin.

"You protecting someone, Mr. Anderson? Shelby, perhaps?" It was a shot in the dark, more to provoke a reaction, but the bemused smile was not what she had expected.

"No, Agent Rutledge. I am not protecting anyone. Trust me. I would be more than happy for you to catch this killer."

"I trust you about as far as I can throw you." Shelby snorted, and Jackie had finally had enough of her amused silence. "What about you, Ms. Fontaine? Someone here knows more than they're saying, and all you've been doing since we got here is give Nick every condescending response in the book." Jackie was starting to think that arresting them might be a good idea regardless, but she was not on good enough terms with Belgerman at the moment to afford any kind of screw up.

"I just work here," Shelby said with mock innocence. "Nick tells me to say something, I say it. If he doesn't, I don't."

"Bullshit. What exactly is the nature of your relationship with Mr. Anderson?"

Again, the careless shrug. "I work for him."

When she was not more forthcoming, Jackie stood up straight, hands on her hips. "Do I look stupid, Ms. Fontaine? How about the non-pat answer, just to humor me?"

"I'm not fucking him, if that's what you mean."

Jackie threw up her hands in disgust. "I really should just arrest you both."

Nick said, without looking at her, "That would waste all our time, Ms. Rutledge."

"Gee, you think? I don't know what your game is here, Nick, or you, for that matter, Ms. Fontaine, but it's damn obvious to me that you know something. You're either hiding something, or—far handier for me—you are both involved, and given that I've got two dead boys on my hands and don't want a third, I'd say that arresting you is looking like a good option here."

"I assure you," he said. "You'll find no direct evidence—"

"Direct?" That was it. The evasive bullshit had to end. "That's the problem here. Things are just vague enough to keep us guessing. Is that what you want, Mr. Anderson? People are dying here. Kids. Are. Dying. Either you're directly involved, or you know who is doing this. And, frankly, I'm fucking sick of your evading everything we ask. Why are you protecting this monster? Or are you in league with him somehow? Is that it?"

"I'm in league with no one, Ms. Rutledge." He took another drink from his coffee and set it down on the table. "I'm protecting you."

Not the answer she'd been expecting. Jackie took a step back. "What? So you do know who the killer is?"

"You, the FBI, and anyone else who tries to get involved. You won't catch this monster. You can't."

"Presumptuous bastard." She gritted her teeth, resisting the urge to punch him.

"Jackie," Laurel said quietly.

"Nope." She waved a finger at Laurel. "Not calming down this time." The finger drifted back over and stabbed at Nick. "How dare you, Mr. Anderson, if that is what your real fucking name is. You don't presume anything about us. It's my . . . our job to catch killers like this. We are far more capable, with more resources than you'll ever have, to nail monsters like this. How could—" She paused, fists now clenched at her sides. God, it would feel so good to deck the prick. "Who is it, Nick?"

"You read the file from 1970?" He leaned back in the cushions, an arm flung along one of the pillows, showing little regard for her tirade. "Two FBI agents were killed by him then. You get involved, the same thing will happen."

She wanted to scream. "That was thirty-six years ago! We are far more—"

"Doesn't matter," he said with a shake of his head. "You aren't equipped to handle him."

Jackie reached out and grabbed his arm, fingers digging into firm flesh. "Don't you dare tell me what I'm not equipped to handle. You don't have that right. Now tell me who the fuck it is!"

Nick looked down at her hand for a moment, unflinching before meeting her gaze once again. "He's a ghost."

"A ghost." The anger dissipated like so many dandelions upon the wind. "You're serious. A ghost is draining the blood from the children of Chicago?"

Shelby leaned forward, elbows resting on her knees, chin in her hands. She, too, appeared interested in this news or what Jackie's reaction to it was going to be.

Nick cleared his throat. "Not literally. Whomever he's possessing is doing it."

"The ghost of the man who killed your family, Mr. Anderson?" Laurel had leaned forward as well at his words, but she looked decidedly perplexed by the news.

"Great-great-great-grandfather's family," Nick said. "It's been hounding my family for generations."

Laurel clasped her hands together. Her voice was thoughtful. "So the man in all the photos we have, who looks so much like you it's uncanny, are your relatives?"

Nick didn't hesitate. "Yes. It's a blood feud that this spirit refuses to let go of. So you have to understand, Ms. Rutledge. You are chasing after something you can't catch."

"If it's possessing a body, we can catch the body," Jackie said. Her mind churned through the information. It still didn't sit right with her, but where to pick at it eluded her. "Does this jibe for you, Agent Carpenter?"

Laurel sighed and leaned back into the couch. "I don't know. Maybe. It's possible, I guess."

Jackie wanted to throw up her hands in disgust. Now was not the time to be wishy-washy, but what else could she do? This was not her area of expertise, and for the life of her, she could not get a good read on Nick Anderson. If he had been effusive to this point, however, what was to say he wasn't being so now?

"What's the tarot card tell us then, Nick? You know all about the history of this case apparently. What's it mean?"

He looked at each of them for a moment, lingering the longest on Shelby, whose curious arched brow spoke volumes. Jackie needed to get her alone, and the sooner the better.

"Likely, it means someone resembling Gwendolyn will be next," he said.

"The wife is next?" Jackie asked.

"So it would indicate," he said.

She crossed her arms over her chest. Why did she feel like she was being led around by the nose? "So a thirty-something brunette woman will be the next target."

He nodded. "More than likely."

Yeah, that narrowed it down. "Anything else, Nick?

You know, something we might find useful in catching this guy?"

Nick shrugged. "I wish I had something more for you. Shelby and I have been trying to track him down. We've sensed him a couple times, but not strong enough to pinpoint."

"You can track him?"

"As you recall," he said with a faint smile, "we can sense spirits. When he's fairly close or in the process of possessing someone, we get a feeling, but it's sometimes like tracking down a light in the fog. You don't actually see it until you're right on top of it."

Jackie looked over at Laurel, who nodded in agreement. Okay, so maybe that wasn't bullshit. God, she hated the supernatural. Why couldn't ghosts stay where they belonged? "This what you've been doing, driving aimlessly around the city? Sniffing out the ghost?"

"Yes, ma'am, it is."

Her lips puckered, holding in the retort. Ma'am? Really? Jackie couldn't recall anyone ever referring to her that way. Sadly, she could not discern any condescension in his voice. It almost made it worse that the word was genuine.

"I'll want locations of every place you've sensed this guy and when."

"It won't help you—"

"You know what, Nick?" She'd had it with him. "Quit telling me what we can and can't do. Not one more word. If you do, I'm arresting you for obstruction. Answer my fucking questions. It's pretty simple. Let us do our job and quit trying to be a hero."

The relaxed line of his mouth tightened. "As you wish. Ms. Fontaine and I will continue our search, however."

She wanted to say no but thought better of it. If there was any truth to what he said, it might be they would be the only ones who could find the perp. "Fine. You will inform us the second you detect him. You will let us know when you are searching and when you stop. You will also let our agents continue to follow you and quit trying to lose them."

Shelby grinned at Jackie, who returned it with a hard stare. *You're next, Croft girl. We'll see how much you're grinning later.*

"That's agreeable," Nick replied.

Jackie shook her head. "Really. Well, thank you, Mr. Anderson. I'm glad you've decided to work with us. Understand you are civilians here, involved in a federal murder investigation. We aren't partners. Do as you're told. Stay out of the way when you're told and, for fuck's sake, quit trying to hide everything. All you do is turn my suspicions on you, which I still am, by the way. Your story doesn't ring right with me. If and when I find out you're bullshitting me, your cozy log cabin here will become a concrete cell."

"Understood," Nick said. There was the hint of a smile at the corner of his mouth.

Jackie and Laurel gathered what little information Nick had to give and prepared to leave. He walked them to the door, quiet and polite, holding it open for them as they walked out. Laurel stopped on the threshold and smiled at him.

"Thank you for your time, Mr. Anderson. We appreciate your cooperation." He merely nodded, but she reached out and shook his hand before he could move. Her gaze held his for a moment, while both of her hands clasped his. Jackie noticed the hesitation before he replied, the smile he forced upon his mouth.

"Let me know if there's anything else. You have my number."

Laurel nodded, and Jackie stepped aside when Laurel quickly moved out of the house. The ashen look said it all. *God, no hurling on the guy's front porch. Please.* Nick did not look surprised at all by Laurel's response.

"We'll be in touch, Mr. Anderson."

He nodded. "I know."

Jackie turned on her heel and left without looking back. In the car, Laurel stuck her head down between her legs and sucked in deep breaths. Jackie laid a comforting hand on her back. "He felt just like Ms. Fontaine did, didn't he?"

Laurel nodded. "Yeah. Sorry."

"Don't be. Did you buy everything in there?"

She sat back up, heaving a big sigh. "Sweet mother, it's so strong. Some of it. I don't buy the great-grandfather bit though. I'm convinced he's the same guy."

Jackie agreed and pulled out onto the road. "So this blood-feud thing is really a personal attack on Anderson."

"Think so. Unless of course your split-personality theory is true. It still could be, you know."

"Maybe. That leaves a lot to be explained though."

Laurel nodded. "It does."

"I want to go back to the bank," Jackie said. "I want to know how the hell the thief got into the vault. What was so strong back there?"

"Nick Anderson."

"Worse than Fontaine?"

"Yes, but different. He felt . . . more dead." She laughed nervously. "That makes no sense, I know.

"You're right, it doesn't."

"I don't know how to adequately explain it, Jackie. It's like they're dead. If I closed my eyes and touched either one of them, I'd swear I was touching someone who just died."

A shiver went down Jackie's spine. "You don't need to explain more. Really. When you figure it out tell me, but until—"

Her cell phone rang, and she put it to her ear. "Rutledge."

"Agent Rutledge, it's Shelby Fontaine." Her voice was hushed and hurried.

"Yes?"

"We need to talk. Can you come to my apartment around four?"

"Sure. What's this about?"

Jackie heard her sigh in background. "Everything. I'm tired of Nick's bullshit. You need the whole story."

About fucking time! "We can meet now, Ms. Fontaine. I'm just down the road."

"No," she said. "Meet me at four. I'm off to hunt. He'll be getting the next one soon. Oh. Say hi to Agent Carpenter for me." The connection abruptly ended.

Jackie stared at the silent phone. "Fuck. I don't think I like her."

Laurel laughed. "I do."

"She could be a killer."

"Doesn't mean she can't be likeable."

"What's to like? She's a little diva wannabe."

"She's hot and rides a motorcycle."

Jackie grimaced. "She could be possessed by some evil fricking ghost, for all we know."

Laurel sagged back in her seat. "Thanks. Ruin my image, why don't you?"

Jackie felt bad. She had never once heard Laurel comment on someone else's looks. She had always been so . . . nonsexual about everyone. "Sorry. Just weird to hear you talk about someone like that, but it's fine. I comment on cute asses. So can you."

She was quiet for a long, thoughtful moment. "Thanks, and don't be sorry. Not your fault I've never told you any of this."

More silence followed, and Jackie felt like squirming in her seat. "So, *Matrix* girl is your type?"

Laurel shrugged. "More or less. She's cocky, fit, sarcastic, can kick ass, and is obviously loyal to those she cares about. She's passionate about things and doesn't give you any bullshit. There's a soft side there, too. I think."

"Jesus Christ. Did you two have a date while I was gone? How do you know all that? She hasn't said more than three sentences."

"Skills," she replied with a knowing grin.

"Oh, bullshit." Jackie laughed. "She just makes you wet."

She nodded. "That, too."

"God! I don't need to know this."

Laurel pouted at her. "You're just jealous."

"She gets cleared, you can jump all over her. Until then, hands off."

"Same goes for you and cowboy."

"What! Oh, don't even go there."

"He's just your type, Jackie, but he's a suspect, so I understand."

"You understand nothing," she said. "I wouldn't touch Nick Anderson with a ten-foot pole even if he was so clean he squeaked."

"Yes, you would."

Jackie felt her face flush. "Fuck you. Being friends with you sucks sometimes."

Laurel smiled—that friendly, warm, no-worries smile that always made Jackie feel better. "Want me to stop being friends then?"

Jackie snorted. "Nah. I'll take my chances."

"Good. Because you couldn't get rid of me if you tried."

Chapter 22

The vault at the bank turned up more questions than answers. Like everything else with the case, nobody seemed clear about anything. From what they could tell, the body had just materialized inside the vault. The employees were as clueless as they were upset. So, having wasted a bulk of the day, they drove to Shelby Fontaine's apartment, situated inside a renovated industrial warehouse with converted lofts. She apparently had money to burn as well.

"Are you fidgeting?" Jackie let her fist drop to her side and brought the Starbucks cup up to her lips. She glanced at the number on the door of Shelby Fontaine's apartment and back at Laurel.

"No," she said firmly. A bit too firmly to be believed. "I'm fine."

"You were fidgeting," Jackie replied, unsure if she should be amused or worried. "Because of the whole ghost thing?"

Laurel shrugged. "Yeah. I'm just stressing on this case, that's all. You know, chasing after people who may already be dead." She smiled at Jackie, but Jackie didn't buy it.

"You said earlier that you didn't think they were actually dead—just felt that way."

"I know, sounds crazy."

"Yeah, it's fruitcake crazy. Not supposed to be chasing after vampires. We aren't supposed to do that kind of shit, but here we are."

Laurel merely smiled back and nodded.

"You sure you're okay?"

Laurel reached over and pounded briskly on the door. "I'm fine, damnit. Focus on the case."

The door opened almost immediately, so fast that Jackie wondered if Shelby had been listening on the other side. "Agents Carpenter and Rutledge. Please come in."

Said the spider to the flies. Jackie pushed down her nagging annoyance at the woman. It was her job to be somewhat objective, and it was more than the facade she always had going on. She got the feeling the woman was far more dangerous than she appeared. The information they had indicated little, other than that Hauser figured she had to be over one hundred years old. She had done a lot of things in her various incarnations, but nothing obviously illegal beyond some traffic violations and disturbing the peace.

Shelby wore knee-length black spandex and a University of Illinois T-shirt. A pale blue towel was draped around her neck, her wet hair pulled back into a ponytail.

"This a good time?" Laurel said.

Jackie wanted to smack her. Did it matter? She gave Laurel a stern glance and crossed the threshold. "Thanks. I'm glad you decided to speak with us, Ms. Fontaine. Your boss has been less than forthcoming."

She laughed—a deep, throaty sound leaving no doubt about her amusement. "Nick has it down to an art, Agent Rutledge. He would prefer to tell you absolutely nothing or just enough to make you go away."

The inside of Shelby's apartment was an interesting contrast of old Chicago warehouse loft and Victorian England. The furnishings were all antiques, in pristine condition by the look of things, but Jackie was far from an expert on furniture. The place would be featured in some home magazine. The kitchen was partially enclosed on one side of the large space, with a bedroom loft above it. An enormous four-poster bed swathed in gauzy curtains shrouded the area in a cloudy haze. Above them, a large glass chandelier illuminated the space. Outside, Chicago's wind whipped a light rain against the great wall of windows.

Shelby grabbed a gray sweatshirt off one of the sofas and walked toward the kitchen. "Anything to drink? I've got tea and water, but no coffee. Sorry, Agent Rutledge." She flashed a charming smile over her shoulder at Jackie.

What the hell was that for? "Thanks. I'm sure I'll manage."

"Tea," Laurel said, clearing her throat. "Tea is fine."

"Earl Grey?"

"Um, yes. That'd be nice."

Jackie turned to Laurel, a questioning eyebrow cocked up, but Laurel refused to look at her, instead sitting down on one of the pretty little sofas with its frilly throw pillows. Preferring to walk, Jackie kept slowly perusing the space, stopping to idly check on a Tiffany lamp or an old painting on the wall.

A few moments later, Shelby came out with a tray holding a lavishly painted tea set with a pot and two cups. It certainly struck an interesting contrast to the BMW-biker-chick motif she walked around with. Jackie didn't give her time to stop serving. She was tired of waiting.

"Look, Ms. Fontaine," Jackie said. "The tea is nice and all, but you said you had the whole story for us."

Shelby dropped a cube of sugar into Laurel's tea and handed the cup to her, her hand lingering on Laurel's for just a moment longer than necessary. Laurel's faint smile faltered for a second, but Shelby's flashing teeth and full, lush lips brought it back. "Patience, Jackie. When you've been around as long as I have and lived with Nick Anderson, you learn to have some."

Jackie took a deep breath. "Look, Ms. Fontaine. I don't know how seriously you take this situation, but I do. I've got blood-drained children. I've got a suspect and his business partner slash former lover slash fiancé slash whatever, who aren't really what they appear to be. You and Mr. Anderson have given us nothing but bullshit from the outset, and one or both of you have been lying about this whole thing from the beginning. You tell me that you're out hunting because there will be a next victim soon. Excuse me if I'm a little short on patience today."

Shelby grinned at Jackie, and without turning back to face Laurel, said, "Is she always such a hard-ass?"

Laurel paused, assessing her reply. "Pretty much."

"Explains why Nick finds her so appealing."

Laurel nearly spit her tea back into her cup, and Jackie found herself momentarily speechless.

"What?" Jackie said.

"Appealing," Shelby repeated, smirking at Jackie. "He likes you, Agent Rutledge. Your hard edges suit him."

Jackie avoided glancing at Laurel, who she was sure had some smarmy look on her face. "You would think he'd be a bit more cooperative if he liked me, Ms. Fontaine. I hardly think there is any interest there."

"If I'm going to help you, Agent Rutledge, you can start by calling me Shelby. I hate Ms. Fontaine. Makes me sound like a third-grade teacher."

Jackie shrugged. "Fine. Shelby. So what's the real story?"

Shelby took a deep breath and drank down the rest of her tea. Jackie studied her, wondering if she might be preparing the next round of lies or if indeed she meant to help. After she set down the teacup, Shelby looked up directly at her, those eyes glowing even brighter than Nick's had.

Laurel's words about them being dead ran through her head, and Jackie looked away.

"First off, I'll tell you that Nick has been silent in an effort to protect you, Agent Rutledge."

"I don't need protecting," she said. "This is my job, Shelby. Not his."

"Not just you. Laurel, too. Anyone not personally involved in this."

Laurel inched forward toward Shelby, her hands steepled under her chin as if she were in prayer, attention riveted.

Jackie wondered what she could be doing. Maybe it was some kind of psychic thing. "Except we *are* involved. What makes this ghost so bad? He sounds much like any other psycho we've dealt with before."

She gave Jackie a wry smile. "For one, he's a vampire, not a ghost."

Jackie ignored the sharp inhalation of breath from Laurel, who glanced up at her with a moment of "I told you so" fear.

"The FBI is pretty adept at handling even the worst cases. Drinking blood doesn't come close to topping our list of worst-case scenarios."

"That's the least of your concerns," she said.

"Well, why don't you tell us what we should be concerned about then? It's about time we got some real information out of you two."

Shelby took a sip from her tea and then got up to walk around. "The man's name is Cornelius Drake. At least, that's the name he's been going by. I don't know what his real name is."

The name didn't ring any bells for Jackie. "Okay, we'll check that out."

"Like I said," she continued, "he's a vampire, meaning he needs to consume blood to stay alive. Without an adequate supply, he'd be as dead as the day he should've died."

Shelby's explanation lost her. "What do you mean that he should've died?"

Shelby continued pacing, making her way over toward the kitchen. "Some time in the past—who knows when—Cornelius Drake should have died. Something happened that was going to end his life, but he was able, through consuming blood, to draw upon the life force held within that blood to keep himself in the world of the living."

"And how the hell did he do that?"

Shelby opened her refrigerator and reached inside. She came out with a metallic bottle in her hand. "I don't know. Someone must have showed him."

Jackie couldn't help but be skeptical. The whole thing sounded so absurd. "That's handy. Here, drink this and you'll live forever?"

"It's a bit more complicated than that," she said. "You have to want it. You need a certain force of will for it to work. At least, I think so."

Laurel's voice, shaky and quiet, spoke up. "So that means you and Nick?"

Shelby nodded with a little shrug of a shoulder. "Yes. We're vampires, too."

Jackie could tell by Laurel's expression that there was no disagreement. Lovely. The whole far-fucking-fetched story was true. "This Drake guy show you how?"

She shook her head. "Showed Nick. Nick showed me."

"Wait. What?" Jackie stared incredulously at the metallic bottle being offered to her by Shelby. "Nick turned you into a vampire? What's this?"

"Yes, he did. And that," she said, "is the worst-tasting shit you will ever drink."

"What is it?"

"Synthetic blood."

Jackie nearly dropped the bottle. "Blood? This is what you drink?"

She nodded. "Yep. Developed by Nick and his brainiacs over at Bloodwork Industries."

Jackie handed the bottle off to Laurel, who looked far more intrigued by it than she was. The notion of bottled blood creeped her out. "I see."

"Why did Nick turn—or, um, show—you how to be a vampire?" Laurel asked, turning the bottle over in her hands.

At that, Shelby gave a sardonic little laugh. "Because he couldn't let me die."

"Care to explain?" Jackie said.

"Drake had shot me," she replied. "This was back in 1934. My guts were practically on the floor, and I was going to die. Nick couldn't bear to let Drake win, so he did what he thought was his only option."

Jackie tried to consider if she would want to stay alive if the option were to consume blood to keep living. No. Not a chance in hell. "Why would he do that to you?"

She smiled at Jackie, wistful and knowing. "Love can make you do strange things."

"That it can," Laurel whispered.

Jackie gave Laurel a sidelong glance, who turned her gaze quickly away and then held up her teacup. "Can I have a bit more, please?"

Shelby flowed around the couch with the smooth grace of a dancer. "Certainly."

A knot formed in Jackie's gut. What was up with Laurel? She was being no use at all with this. "All insanity aside, why not come forward with this? No laws have been broken. Law enforcement is far different now than in 1970."

"I promised Nick a long time ago that I would never expose him or what was going on. The decision was his to make."

"It's getting people killed is what it's doing," Jackie stated. "You've obviously had no luck stopping him to this point."

"Agent Rutledge . . . Laurel." Shelby turned and gave a sweet little smile to Laurel. "You need our help. We need yours. Nick has a lot of blood on his hands and would rather this played itself out without any additional casualties."

"Chivalrous of him," Jackie said. "It's obstruction, too. I should have him arrested."

The smile on Shelby's face vanished. "You can't arrest him. At least, not yet."

"I didn't say I was, but I—"

"No." Shelby shook her head. "Drake will come after him no matter where he is. You won't be able to stop him."

Jackie avoided rolling her eyes. Cocky bitch. But her earnestness gave Jackie pause. "Why is this guy so dangerous that even the FBI can't handle him?"

Shelby's smile was more of a wince. "He can do things we don't quite understand. He has power that goes beyond just drinking some blood. Trust me, I know."

No. Jackie was pretty sure she didn't want to know about that, but what choice did she have? They needed information. "Give me an example."

"He can travel in ways that make him untrackable. We'll sense him someplace, and then, just like that, he'll be gone. That's just an annoyance, though, compared to the real power we have, which is this kind of hypnotic control over people."

"Hypnosis?" Not a trick Jackie had ever had any faith in, but she knew of its possible effects. "So all that movie crap is true?"

She laughed, a bubbling, lively sound that filled the room. "God, no. I love garlic. Crucifixes don't burn my flesh, and I don't sleep in a coffin. The sun, however, does bother me."

"So the whole bright-eyes thing? That's an effect of being a vampire?" Under other circumstances, Jackie would have laughed at this line of questioning. Even working with

Laurel, who had spoken to a ghost or two in her lifetime, would not have taken her into the realm of vampires.

"Oh, these," Shelby said, her fingers touching the skin beside her eyes. "They're contacts."

"I knew it!" Jackie had pegged something right about them at least.

"You don't want to see the real thing."

"Perhaps I do," Jackie said with a defiant tilt of her head.

"Then maybe you'd like to spend the rest of the afternoon polishing my mahogany bedposts?"

"What?"

"It's what I could have you doing if I caught you in my gaze long enough."

"Seriously." Jackie didn't believe it. A look at Laurel, though, said otherwise. She half expected her to get up and go polishing. Was Shelby working some kind of vampire voodoo on her now?

"Yep." Shelby nodded. "Unless it's something that might get you killed. I can bend your will only so far."

"I see." Okay, she didn't really. Jackie was half tempted to take Shelby up on that bet but thought better of it. "And Drake does this to his victims?"

"Yes. Only, there is no resisting him. You can't say no."

"I find that hard to believe," she said. "You telling me this guy could make me just walk off a cliff to my death or pull out my gun and shoot myself in the head?"

"Basically, yes. Maybe not directly, but his power is such that he would give you a compelling reason to believe that walking off that cliff or shooting yourself in the head was the most appealing option available to you."

All right, then. That notion set Jackie's nerves on edge. "This why Nick is trying to keep everyone else out?"

"Yes. He knows that if you encounter him, the result will likely mean your death."

Laurel sat up straight now. "Then how does he plan to stop him?"

"That's the infuriating thing about Nick Anderson," she said, her voice showing the first real signs of anger Jackie had heard. "I don't think he's planning on stopping him at all."

"Wait." Jackie held up her hand. "Hold on. He's trying to keep us away from a murderer he isn't trying to stop?"

"Oh, he'll try," she said. "Nick is alive today because he promised to try to stop him, but he's sure he can't. He's just playing this game out until its inevitable conclusion, which with three more deaths will come to its horrible, mindless end."

"What end is that?"

"Drake is going to kill Nick."

"Ah." Things were falling into place now. The history was making some twisted sort of sense. Jackie walked over and sat down next to Laurel. "Maybe you should give us your whole story, from the beginning."

She laughed again. "You have a few hours?"

Jackie leaned back and folded her hands over her stomach. "Yeah. Yeah, we do."

Chapter 23

Only an hour later, Jackie leaned back in the safety and privacy of her Durango and ran her fingers through her hair. She closed her eyes, waiting, hoping for things to settle, come together, and get off the tabloid pages.

"You okay?" Laurel said and then laughed nervously. "I couldn't tell if you were going to laugh her out of the room or slap her upside the head."

Jackie dropped her hands to her lap. "I wanted to smack you a couple times. What the hell was going on in there? It was like watching a supernatural episode of *The Dating Game*."

She looked at Jackie for only a second and then looked outside, at her hands, and at anywhere but near Jackie's face. "Sorry. It . . . I was just . . . um . . ." Her face scrunched up, trying to unscramble whatever jumble of words were running through her head.

The pink flush of embarrassment brought a smirk to Jackie's mouth. She had never seen Laurel in this state before. It had always been the other way around. "It wasn't very subtle, you know. She touched you every chance she got."

Laurel sighed. "Pretty obvious, huh?"

"I should arrest her just on principle, flirting with an FBI agent in the middle of an interview."

Laurel came halfheartedly to Shelby's defense. "I don't think she was trying to disrupt our questioning."

"I think Ms. Fontaine is the sort of woman who does what she wants, when she wants, and doesn't give a rat's ass what anyone else thinks about it."

Laurel gave her a meager nod and shrug of agreement.

"That's . . . You like that sort of . . . Shit! I should have slapped her upside the head."

"I could have dissuaded her if I'd wanted to, Jackie. You don't have to protect me from that."

"I know," Jackie said, flustered. "It's just that . . . um . . . just, I've never seen you do this before. Like, ever."

"I should have been more professional. I'm sorry."

"Well," she started. Laurel was right, of course, but why now of all times? "Yeah, you should have, but maybe it helped loosen her up, too. She was nervous." Despite the incredulity of the story, Jackie could not free up her mind from their interaction. "She's really that irresistable?"

Laurel nodded. "Oh, yeah, and then some, but it's more than that. She's . . . powerful is the only word I can think of. But it's more than that."

Jackie started up the Durango finally and got them back on the road. "Is it because she claims she's a vampire?"

"No. Well, I guess that has something to do with it." She laughed. "Crazy, isn't it?"

Who was Jackie to say? She could hardly make any claims to know anything about healthy relationships, but one fact remained, nonetheless. "You can't pursue this right now, you know."

Laurel leaned back against the seat with a heavy sigh. "I know. I have a tendency to fall for women I can't have. It's a curse."

Jackie watched the road in silence, the words sinking in. "Okay, I guess we're going to have this conversation now."

She sat quietly in her seat, eyes closed for a moment. "I was in love with you, Jackie." There was a mixture of anger and regret in her voice. "And, yes, I know it was dumb and irrational, but you were what I wanted, simple as that, and despite the advice of several therapists, I could not let you go. You needed me as much as I needed you."

Jackie stared straight ahead. What could she say to that? What did she want to say? This was virgin territory, beyond her realm of experience. Was there a *Dummies* book for this kind of shit? And, of course, what she *did* say sounded completely inane and absurd to her ears. "When did you get over me?"

"About an hour ago."

The light they were stopped at turned green, but Jackie's feet were frozen. She stared over at her best friend. "I wish I'd known."

Laurel laughed at Jackie, perhaps a little too bitterly. "Why? Would it have made things better? Would you have sat there with me in the seat next to you, feeling comfortable knowing I was in love with you? That I dreamed of making love to you?"

Jackie squirmed in her seat, and someone behind honked. She put the portable siren out on the roof and rolled the window back up. "I don't know how I would have felt, Laur. I didn't get the chance, and maybe you're right. Fuck, you probably are right. I'd have been weirded out. But I'm your best friend, and doing good by you matters more to me than anything. I'd have dealt with it."

Tears fell, rolling down Laurel's cheeks. "That's good to know. Thank you. And you're right. I should have trusted you would deal with it."

Silence followed, and Jackie let her foot off the brake and continued on toward downtown. Finally, she said, "No.

You're right. I'm a fuckup when it comes to relationships. If you'd told me, I'd have screwed things up between us somehow. Or, worse, gotten drunk and slept with you."

Laurel laughed at that. "The thought has crossed my mind a time or two."

The tension eased, and Jackie smiled at her friend. This was all good. They would figure it out and move on. Things would get back to normal. She would find someone to love who would feel the same way. "I wouldn't even know if I should be top or bottom."

"Oh," she replied with a knowing grin. "You'd be top, Jackie, believe me."

The laughter rolled out of her now. "True enough, I guess. This is just the weirdest conversation. Will I get to hear all the sordid details of your sexual escapades?"

"Slut. You're just as curious what a vampire will do in bed as I am."

"What? No! Christ, no. You and biker girl go have fun . . . after the case is over with." Who was she kidding? She would want to know everything. "I'll expect a lengthy and detailed report."

"You might regret that choice, Agent Rutledge."

Jackie grinned and shook her head. "Undoubtedly."

Back at headquarters, Jackie dropped off the sample of synthetic blood to be analyzed and found that Belgerman, for better or worse, was still in the office. He had likely read Hauser's data by now and was waiting impatiently for an update. There would be a meeting of the violent-crimes task force in the morning, and he would want something clear and concise to give them.

Yeah, good luck with that one. Jackie flopped down into her desk chair while Laurel seated herself in hers. "We need to let Belgerman know that all this crazy shit is real. He won't be happy."

"The team needs to know what we're dealing with," Laurel said.

"We don't even know what we're dealing with. Ms. Fontaine wasn't exactly full of details on that end."

"I know. The next one will be an adult female though, according to what Shelby said."

"Thirty-one, brunette," Jackie said. "That doesn't narrow it down a whole lot. Likely a couple million of those in the Chicago area alone."

"Maybe that tarot card had more of a clue in it than just which family member this guy was going to kill next?"

"Could be. Give it to Hauser and see what the geeks can come up with." Jackie pushed away from her desk. "Let's go fill Belgerman in."

They found him in the conference room, the case notes spread out across the large cherry tabletop. A map on the wall had several pushpins inserted, marking all relevant points of interest. Next to it, a dry-erase board highlighted the basic information discovered thus far.

He motioned Jackie and Laurel to the chairs and then walked over and closed the door. "One of you want to clue me in on this?" He tapped Hauser's report on the table. "I can see you've got something, and that means I like what I saw in these pages even less."

Jackie glanced over at Laurel. "You tell him. This is your area, not mine."

Laurel gave her a sardonic smile. "Thanks. Sir, in my opinion, we're after something supernatural."

He plopped back down in his chair and rubbed a hand over his tired face. "Yeah, I suspected as much. Is it Nick Anderson?"

Laurel shrugged. "Maybe, but if I were to guess, I'd say no. He hasn't been very forthcoming on his side of things, but we got Shelby Fontaine to share some information with us that sheds some light on this case."

"If it's true," Jackie added.

"Yes," she said. "It's a pretty big 'if' to swallow."

Belgerman motioned for her to continue. "No suspense, please. Just tell me, Laurel. I've heard this kind of stuff from you before, so as weird as it may be, I trust your opinion on anything that smacks of otherworldly."

"Thank you, sir," she said, smiling. "But this is beyond even what I've encountered or know about. Our killer does indeed seem to be some sort of vampire who draws blood from his victims to sustain his life, and for what else, we have no idea. He is killing in retribution for the death of his wife and son at the hands of Nick Anderson."

"So, the stories Hauser dug up?"

"We think they are true, sir."

"So, Nick Anderson and Shelby Fontaine?"

Laurel winced at her own reply. "Vampires, too, sir."

"Lovely. Can we keep this out of the papers? It'll be a fucking circus if it gets out that we're after a real vampire."

"Yes, sir," Jackie said. "I have every intention of doing just that."

"Good," he said, standing up and patting her on the shoulder. "'Cause if it leaks, you are the spokesperson on this one."

"You're too kind," Jackie said. "We'll keep it quiet. I just hope the rest of the team can, once this comes up."

"They have no choice," Belgerman said. "See if Anderson will come in tomorrow, and let's see what he has to say. The rumors flying around this case are giving me a migraine. I want everyone informed."

"Sir, he wants us as far away from him as possible."

"Then find a way to convince him, Jack. You're good at that sort of thing." He got up and walked to the door. "We need a way to track this thing down. Right now we're just driving in circles waiting for him to kill someone again."

"We realize, sir." He was clearly frustrated. John Belgerman didn't take to being clueless very well. "I'll convince him to come in, one way or another."

"We'll change the task-force meeting until after lunch, two PM. Gives you a little more time. If you have to, bring Anderson in on suspicion. I don't care how weak it is." Belgerman gave them a curt nod and closed the door.

Jackie cleared her throat. "Well, that went fairly well, all things considered."

"Think you can actually get Nick to come in?"

She shrugged. "If not, we'll get Fontaine down here. She likes to talk. I'm not sure Anderson will say much if I force him to come down here."

"I'll talk to her in the morning and let her know," Laurel said, sounding more cavalier than she needed to.

Jackie bit off her reply. "Get that card down to Hauser, and let's go get food. Any luck, maybe Nick and Shelby will find that damn light in the fog, and we can get some traction on this psycho."

Burgers and chili fries were the highlight of the evening. Jackie was watching the White Sox lose, and Nick did not answer his phone, so she could only leave a message. If he refused to call back, she would ring him first thing in the morning. Shelby thankfully agreed to come around whether Nick did or not, and agreed in such a way as to make Laurel blush.

Jackie dragged the last of her fries through the dregs of chili in the basket. "This is going to be a lot of fun, you know."

"Shut up." Laurel reached for her soda and nearly knocked it over. "I deserve a break."

"You do," Jackie agreed with a grin. "Still going to be fun as hell. I never get to give you shit over anything."

"And there's nothing to give me shit over." She took a long gulp from her glass. "Not yet."

Jackie laughed. "Will be if Shelby has anything to say on it. I don't think she's the sort to have patience when it comes to something she wants." Jackie pointed her half-chewed fry at Laurel. "And did you see that bed? Right out of a fucking movie."

The pink in Laurel's cheeks turned crimson. "Fuck you. I hate you."

Jackie popped the last fry into her mouth and giggled. "So much fun."

A phone-call update from Gamble indicated nothing new. Nick and Shelby were still combing the same general area of town, but with no leads of their own, all the FBI could do was follow. The geeks apparently had come up with nothing recent on Drake.

"So what do we do now?" Laurel wondered.

"Wait," Jackie replied. "Drake needs to make a move. We're just grasping at straws."

"It's almost nine now."

"Yeah, I know. I'll take you home. I'm going to go through everything for the task-force meeting tomorrow. Maybe someone will have a brilliant idea."

"He might take someone tonight."

Jackie grabbed her leather coat. "And unless we hear from our local vampires, there won't be a damn thing we can do about it."

Chapter 24

In the dark hours of the morning, Jackie's phone brought her out of a bathtub full of blood, where two boys continuously dipped their hands into the thick liquid and insisted she drink.

"Do you want to live forever?" they asked in droning unison over and over.

In the doorway, her mother stared in blank-eyed silence, slashed wrists dripping into a dark red stain at her feet.

Jackie sat up in bed, kicking at the covers, and Bickerstaff complained with a disgruntled meow, jumping down to floor with a thud. The glowing numbers on her bedside clock read 4:12 AM.

"Jesus fucking . . ." Jackie grabbed the phone off its stand. The readout told her it was Laurel. "Hey."

"Sorry, Jackie," she said in a hushed voice. "I've got a little visitor here right now."

She sat bolt upright, panic gripping her gut. "What? You okay?"

"Shhh. It's okay. It's the good sort," Laurel said.

Sleep was depriving Jackie's brain of coherent thought. "Good sort of what? What are you talking about?"

"There's a presence here in my room. Right now."

Presence. Goddamn ghosts. "Why are you calling me at this horrid hour then?"

"You remember the tarot card I gave to Hauser before we left last night?"

"Yeah. What about it?"

"It's sitting here on my desk." Her voice was filled with quiet awe and something darker. Fear?

Jackie thought of the mysterious, vanishing penny. "You sure it's the same one?"

"Of course!" She was irritated. "It turned up in my tarot deck."

The fog still shrouded Jackie's brain. "You're losing me."

"I was doing a reading for myself," she replied. "I couldn't sleep. I shuffled my deck, and it was the first card I turned up."

Okay. Weird, but given what had been going on, Jackie no longer found it out of the ordinary. "This couldn't wait until morning?"

"It keeps turning up as the top card, Jackie. The inverted empress. I've shuffled this deck a dozen times now, and it's the first card every time. Always inverted."

"Why is that important?"

"It can mean impending danger, possible death."

Some things Jackie could just give no credence to, and tarot reading was one of them. "Give me the punch line, Laur. I'm too tired to think."

"It's a message, Jackie. Someone is trying to tell me we're in serious trouble."

Jackie rubbed at her face with her free hand. Was she really up at four AM for this? "We're always in danger with cases like this. For Christ's sake, we're chasing after vampires."

"I know, but this is serious," she said, adamant. "The dead don't talk like this unless it's very important."

"Who would be sending us this kind of message?"

"I don't know. She's desperate though, and . . ."

There was silence, long enough that Jackie began to worry. "Laur?"

"Shit. It's gone now. She's gone."

Thank God. "So we need to be extra careful now, I take it?"

Laurel sighed. "Jackie, this is bad. Bad, bad, bad. You need to stop chasing this guy. Nick was right."

Had she heard that right? What the fuck? "Are you on crack? Did you just hear what you said?"

"I know Goddess-be-damned well what I just said, you stubborn girl!" Anger raged in Jackie's ear. "We need to turn this case over. Give it to someone else. You can't keep chasing this guy, Jackie. Please."

Holy shit. She was totally serious. "Laur . . . It's just . . . It's a tarot card, for crying out loud. I can't bail on a case over a bad tarot reading."

The voice on the other end was teary. "It's real, damn you. This is serious."

"Okay, it's serious." Jackie tried to be soothing. She knew Laurel's sense for this stuff could not be discounted. If there was trouble coming, she was probably right. "I can't just blow this off to someone else though. He's killing kids. He has to be stopped."

"I know that! Let someone else stop him. He's going to kill you!"

Jackie pulled the phone away from her ear and stared at it in disbelief. What had gotten into Laurel? "I'll be extra careful, okay? Are you all right? You want me to come over?"

There was a pause and then a sigh on the other end. "No. I'm fine, Jackie. Go back to sleep. I'll see you in the morning."

"I'll be careful, Laurel. I'm not blowing this off. I know it's serious," she said.

"I know. Get some rest. I'm sorry I freaked."

"I understand. You get some rest—"

"Night, Jackie."

The phone clicked off before she could reply. Jackie held the phone for a long moment before setting it back in its stand. No point in sleeping now. Her nerves were sufficiently frazzled. A shower and a pot of coffee were in order so she could go over the case notes for the task-force meeting later in the day and maybe figure out how in hell to get Nick Anderson to come in to talk.

If there was any doubt over Laurel's annoyance, Jackie found herself driving into headquarters by herself. She decided to make peace by stopping at Annabelle's and getting Laurel's favorite custard-filled, chocolate-covered doughnut. Jackie got her usual chocolate croissant and latte with two extra shots.

She found Laurel at her desk going over the case file. "I brought you a doughnut."

Laurel took the bag and peeked inside. "Yum! Thanks."

"Any more ghostly visits?"

"Nope," she said. "I gave the card back to Hauser this morning."

Jackie nodded. "Okay. I'll be extra careful, Laur. I mean it."

Laurel looked up at her and smiled. "I know. You better. I know you can't bail on a case, Jackie. I'm sorry I mentioned it. The whole thing stressed me out."

"You've never been wrong with this shit before. I'll keep my guard up." She meant it, too. Laurel's intuitions and spiritual connections had never panned out false. The FBI hadn't hired her without cause, so Jackie knew better than to just brush it off. If Laurel said shit was going to hit the fan, they were due for something.

"Thank you," Laurel said. She took out the doughnut and sank her teeth into it. "Mmmm. Perfect. Think you can get Nick to come in today?"

Jackie sat down in her chair. "I will. Somehow. I wonder if Shelby has told him she spilled the beans yet?"

"Think that will help? He'll probably be pissed." She waved Jackie off, the half-eaten doughnut in her hand. "No, not pissed. More like mildly annoyed. I don't think that man gets pissed."

"I don't think he cares enough anymore to get pissed about anything," Jackie said.

"No, he cares. I think he cares a lot actually. Remember what Shelby said though. You're dealing with a man who believes he has lost already."

Jackie sipped at her coffee. "After a century of this shit, I think I would, too."

"You'd have gotten yourself killed by now," Laurel stated.

"Is that a compliment or an insult?"

She laughed. "Both."

Jackie took out her phone and looked up Nick's number. "Might as well get this over with now."

"Have fun with that," Laurel said.

She stuck out her tongue while the phone rang.

"Good morning, Agent Rutledge. How can I help you this morning?" The dark timbre of his voice was smooth and calm.

No need for pleasantries. "You can help me by coming in this afternoon to talk to our task force about this case and what we're actually up against."

The silence lasted so long Jackie thought the connection had been lost.

"You spoke with Shelby last night."

"Yes, and, fortunately for us, she was far more forth-coming than you've been, Mr. Anderson." Jackie forced her tone to remain neutral. "We need the story, Nick. We need to know everything that's going on. We need to know exactly how we can confront this . . . thing."

His sigh whispered in her ear. "You don't know what you're getting into, Agent Rutledge. Even if you do, it won't help."

Jackie bit her lip and shook her fist at the phone. She took a deep breath. "Just let us do our jobs. We need your help as much you need ours, Nick. Help us get this guy."

Again he was silent. "What time is this meeting?"

Yes! Thank God. "Two PM today at our headquarters. You know—"

"I know where it is," he said. "I want to talk with you beforehand first."

"We're talking now, Mr. Anderson."

"No. In person, away from the office."

Jackie hesitated. "Why?"

"I want to show you something so you will more fully understand everything before I say anything to the rest of your agents."

Jackie didn't like the sound of that. Laurel, who had been listening intently, picked up her ringing phone.

"Is that really necessary, Nick? You can't just do that here?"

"No," he said. "How about we meet for lunch? It won't take very long."

Jackie rolled her eyes. This wasn't going to go her way. "Fine. Where and when?"

"Do you know Ernesto's? Italian place out by—"

"No, but I'll find it. What time?"

"Noon will work?"

"Yeah. Noon is fine. I'll see you there." Jackie clicked off and thrust the phone back into her pocket.

Laurel still spoke on her phone. "Really?" She giggled like a young girl. "That sounds like fun. I've never ridden on a motorcycle before." She laughed then, covering her eyes with her free hand. "No, no. That's just fine. I'll see you there. Thank you."

Laurel closed the phone with a sheepish grin, and Jackie watched in disbelief as her cheeks turned the slightest shade of pink. "Holy shit. You're blushing again?"

"Shut up!" Laurel snapped back, even more embarrassed. "I'm meeting Shelby for lunch. She wants to show me something. She agreed to come to the meeting."

"What?" Jackie wondered, already suspicious. She trusted Shelby about as far as she could throw her, and considering the woman could probably kick her ass, that was not very far.

"She didn't say," Laurel answered cryptically. "Just that only I would be able to understand."

"Yeah, right. I have a pretty good idea what she wants to show you."

"Jealous?"

"Hardly," Jackie said a little more quickly than she would have liked. "I don't trust her. I wonder if those two were together? Nick just asked to show me something as well."

"She wants to help us, Jackie."

"I don't like this, whatever it is. Maybe we should all meet together."

Laurel laughed. "You *are* jealous." She stood up and kissed Jackie on the cheek. "It's so cute."

Jackie didn't quite know how to respond. "You better call me as soon as you're done. I want to know what she has to say."

"Yes, Mother."

"I mean it, damnit." It was sad. She almost did feel like a mother at the moment. "Seriously. You need to be careful with her."

"And you don't?"

"I can handle the Nicks of the world," she said. "Shelby Fontaine is a whole other animal."

"Jackie, I don't think there are any other Nicks of the world."

"You know what I mean. Watch yourself is all I'm saying. I'm still not convinced they aren't trying to put us off the trail somehow."

Laurel's grin faded to a gentle smile. "Don't worry, I will. I think you can trust them."

"And we both know where I stand on that," she snapped back. "I'm going to let Belgerman know what we're doing just in case some shit goes down we're not expecting."

"Quit being paranoid."

Jackie got up, pointing a finger at Laurel. "It's my job."

Her voice followed Jackie down the corridor. "And you do it so well."

Chapter 25

Ernesto's was a quaint little restaurant tucked into the middle of a row of 1920s brick storefronts. One of those local eateries that had likely been in the neighborhood for forty or fifty years, where the owners knew 90 percent of the people who came in to eat. Not the sort of place one would expect a wealthy, blood-drinking PI to frequent, but, then, what was expected from them? Jackie stared in through the front glass window for a moment, seeing only her tousle-haired reflection. Rain pattered on the awning overhead and dripped behind her onto the sidewalk. The dull, gray backdrop matched her complexion all too well. She had looked better.

And I am worried about this because? She shook her head and stepped into cool darkness, surrounded immediately by the soft sounds of Italian opera. Old black-and-white photos from Italy and Sicily decorated the walls, and pristine white tablecloths dotted the landscape before her. It was not so neighborhood as Jackie had suspected. It was more the romantic-dinner-for-two kind of eatery. For a moment, she pondered spinning on her heel and walking back to her car.

"Ah! You must be the lady Mr. Nick is having lunch with, yes?"

A thick-mustached, portly Italian man with a graying fringe of hair ringing his head stepped out of the kitchen area, clasping his hands together like he was entirely too happy see her. Mr. Nick? So he was a regular.

"Yes, I'm supposed to meet him here." Old Mr. Ernesto looked far too under the impression of this being some kind of date.

"Excellent, excellent! Follow me, please," he said with a wave of his hand. He dropped back in step with Jackie. "Mr. Nick did not say you were so beautiful a lady. The man needs a good woman." He flashed a big, mischievous grin at her and winked.

Lovely. Uncle Guido was friends with the vampire.

At the far back end of the restaurant, next to an open pair of French doors that stepped out onto a small patio with a few more tables, sat Nick Anderson, a faint smile on his face as they approached.

"Hello, Agent Rutledge," he said, standing up as Ernesto brought her to the table. Even with the glare from the doors, his eyes had that soft, eerie glow about them.

"Mr. Anderson," Jackie said, nodding curtly and seating herself in the chair Ernesto had pulled out for her.

Nick seated himself. "Two espressos please, Ernesto."

"Right away, Mr. Nick." He gave a quick bow and walked briskly away.

Jackie stared at his implacable mouth in order to avoid his eyes. It looked soft, relaxed. No annoyance or tension there. She realized hers was drawn tight. "I didn't ask for coffee."

"You didn't want any?" The question was stated simply enough, but that slight quirk at the corner of his mouth flared with sarcasm. "You strike me as a die-hard coffee person, Ms. Rutledge."

"Are we done with the small talk now?" she snipped back.

Nick sat up, folding his hands on the table. "Sure. We can get right to it then."

"Great. Let's," Jackie began, meeting his eerie gaze for at least a second and a half. She got interrupted, however, by the bubbly voice of the waitress bringing their coffee.

Nick smiled at the woman, something Jackie could not recall his mouth ever doing to this point, and for just a moment, the tired, stern man vanished into something warm and caring. "Thank you, Mia. It's good to see you."

"You've not been here in months, Nicholas," she said in a motherly tone. "And you bring this lovely woman with you, whom you've not even been polite enough to introduce to me."

Nick chuckled softly. "It's a business lunch, Mia. Have no fear. If I bring a date, I'll call you personally ahead of time so you can make all the necessary preparations."

"Bah," she said, waving him off. "Ernesto foolishly implied otherwise. So sad. Perhaps you can make it both, eh?" She winked at Nick and gave Jackie the same mischievous grin Ernesto had.

Jackie gave a halfhearted smile in return. "Really, it's just business."

She leaned over and laid a conspiratorial hand on Jackie's shoulder. "He's a good man," she whispered. "Very good catch, and I see the way he looks at you. He likes you." With a little squeeze, Mia stood back up and turned to Nick. "So, Nicholas. What shall you two be having today?"

"Honestly," Jackie said, "I'm not really hungry."

"Surprise us, Mia. Something . . ." Nick looked back at Jackie for a moment, studying her intently. "Something seafood, I think."

Jackie watched Mia walk away, still trying to process the

interchange that had just taken place. "What was that? They talk like you own the place."

"I do," he replied, obviously pleased that something had come up she was unaware of.

"Seriously. You own an Italian restaurant?" Why had it not shown up in their profile of him? "And what was the deal there with Mama Mia?"

"I bought the place from Ernesto's father about eighteen years ago. He was a friend of mine and about to lose the place, so I helped him out."

"And that other bullshit?" Jackie demanded. "You set them up for all that just to amuse me?"

The humorous smirk faded. "No, Ms. Rutledge. Mia is the motherly sort, and it's her way of showing she cares, that's all. I'll apologize if you were offended by the implications."

Heat rose up in her cheeks. Shit, shit, shit. Embarrassment was the last thing she needed. "No, no. That's fine. I just don't want you getting any ideas from them, that's all."

"I don't date, so you're safe."

"Is that because you're old enough to be most women's great-great-great-grandfather?"

He paused for a second, espresso cup poised at his lips, and then nodded. "So you believe the evidence now?"

"To be honest, I'm still on the fence about what I believe." She flicked her gaze back up to his and found him watching her, unblinking. "And would you quit with the staring already? It's fucking rude."

He sat back, surprised at himself. "Oh. I apologize. It's habit, watching for subtle changes of behavior and inflection. Easier to see what is going on with a person."

"And what is going on with me, Mr. PI?"

The stare came back, and Jackie forced herself to defiantly return the look, feeling her guts begin to squirm like a bucket of angry worms. "This case is stressing you out beyond what you're used to, but you also have personal matters that are making this case even more difficult."

Jackie bit off her retort. She wanted him to come back with her to the office, not start a fight. "That's some awfully big assumptions just from looking."

Nick shrugged. "Lots of practice."

"There's more to it than that." She picked up the espresso cup and downed the strong, bittersweet liquid in one gulp to hide her shaking hand. She wished Laurel was with her now to help her navigate this supernatural no-man's land she found herself in. She was supposed to be the cool one under fire. "Tell me, Nick. How often do you drink that fake-blood shit your company makes?"

The relaxed mouth creased into annoyance. "What else did Shelby tell you?"

"Enough."

"And there's nothing I can say to convince you to stay away, is there, Jackie?"

The personal note sent a pang through her. Was that a jab? A dare? A warning? "Not in my nature to just let a case slide, Mr. Anderson. Especially when kids are being murdered."

"Even if it gets you or your partner killed?"

Jackie folded her arms on the table and leaned toward him. "That a threat, Nick?"

He started to say something and then apparently thought better of it. "No. I just don't believe you, Ms. Carpenter, or the FBI are prepared to deal with this killer."

"It's not your place to make those kinds of presumptions. It's our case now. Cooperate or get out of the way. I'd prefer to do it without tossing your ass in jail. Unless, of course, it's supposed to be there."

Mia returned at that moment, a curious expression on her face, her tray loaded with salads and a fresh loaf of bread.

A subtle look from Nick was all it took to send her away without a word. "I've been chasing this guy for a long time. You honestly don't have any idea what you're up against."

"Why don't you show me then, Nick? Come in and show the team," she demanded, finally fed up with his martyr routine. "You think it's even possible for me to just let the case go? It freaking you out 'cause I'm a girl? That rub your old-school sheriff sense of justice the wrong way? This is a federal case now. You need to leave it alone unless we say otherwise. If we need your assistance in tracking him down, then fine, but if I find you interfering in our case whatsoever, I will throw you in jail faster than you can blink. Can I make it any plainer to you?" She really wanted to reach over and shake him, slap him upside the head, but part of her was afraid of what he might be able to do.

Nick sighed and took a bite of his salad, chewing in silence. When he swallowed and drank down some water, he finally answered. "If you get too close to him, if your partner is able to home in on him or track him down, and you threaten to disrupt his plans, he'll kill you and anyone else who gets in his way."

"Then explain it to me. Tell me what we're up against. What can Cornelius Drake do that makes him so unstoppable, because he surely isn't going to just sweep in and suck all of us dry, now, is he? Is he going to hypnotize us all? Let us do our job, damnit. Catching killers is what I'm good at."

"And I don't doubt that for a moment," he said, sounding surprisingly sincere, "but I don't want your blood on my hands if you die trying to get this guy."

Guilt. Jackie sensed it was a major theme for Nick. His past overflowed with dead bodies. "That's sweet, really, but you've had your chances with this guy and not been able to catch him. Things have changed a lot in the past . . . decades."

"Technology can't really contend with this," he countered.

"Guys like you, you mean?"

He paused so long she thought he might not answer. "Yes, Ms. Rutledge, guys like me."

"I could have you locked up in a psyche ward for an admission like that, you know."

"And you will never find Drake, and he may just kill a bunch of you to get to me."

"What is he, the Terminator?"

Nick's smile held no amusement. "Worse in some ways. Look, if I show you something, will you seriously reconsider pursuing this guy?"

"Going to show me your fangs, Nick?" She wiped at the smear of butter at the corner of her mouth and tossed the napkin on the table. "I won't agree to anything. I'll consider anything you have to say or show me that is pertinent to the case. If this doesn't change my mind, will you come in this afternoon to speak with our task force?"

"Spoken like a true lawman."

"What?"

"Nothing," he said, bemused. He reached into the coat lying on the chair beside him and pulled out a small case. "I'll agree to those terms."

"What is that?"

He held it out to her. "A contact-lens case."

Ah, so the freaky eyes were fake after all. "I knew you must be wearing something," she said while he removed one, and then the other lens, putting them into the solution-filled cups. "Let me tell you, those contacts give you messed-up eyes, Nick. They weird people out, but what's this got . . ."

Her sentence trailed off as Nick looked up and met her gaze, crystal-blue eyes, deep and glowing with no iris at all. They were just solid, pulsing blue, within which murky gray tendrils swirled around.

"Look," he said, a finger pointing up at his eyes. "Look in here and tell me what you see."

"What the fuck?" They were downright disturbing and oddly compelling. How could he have no iris?

"Please, Jackie. If you want to understand the danger you're in, just look. It won't hurt. Trust me."

She leaned forward, staring at him, and there was something in there, moving, ebbing, and pulsing like a heartbeat. The beat began to fill her head, soothing, calming. Fear washed away in the cool, blue waters of his eyes, so deep one could easily drown in them, sinking away into dark and blissful nothing. Part of her realized what was happening. The word *hypnosis* ricocheted around in the far recesses of her brain, but she could not latch on to it. The thought swam away in the cool flood of his gaze. Jackie sagged back in her chair. "That's messed up."

"What is? Me? You? This case?"

His eyes looked right into her—cold, intense water that filled up every part of her, seeping into her bones, into the deepest parts of her soul. The layers of her just washed away, exposed by that pulsing blue light, until even those bottom layers of muck that Jackie avoided treading in were exposed to his willful stare. He could see it all, and Jackie offered it up to him with eager hands, unable to hold back. Some part of her screamed, filled with terror that he could just reach in and open that Pandora's Box of nightmares, blood, and death, that releasing its contents could consume them, destroy them in the blink of an eye. The other part of her was sure he held the answers to all her needs, that he could simply cleanse her soul of the blight upon it with a wave of his hands.

He did nothing, however. He acted as little more than a tourist on safari in unknown lands. There was no judgment, no accusations, no blame, just the sense of knowing. He had opened a door into her most private self, or, worse, Jackie had opened it and invited him right in, like a best friend perfectly at ease knowing all the good and the bad.

"Everything is messed up," she said, aware of the words, but unaware of where they were coming from. "This case is freaking me out; my partner, Laurel, just came out of the closet, we had a big fight because . . . I . . . I drink too much. I fuck guys I can't even remember the next day. Hell, I don't even like men very much."

"Why is that, Jackie? They treat you badly in the past? Are you having feelings for Laurel?" His voice held the deepest sincerity, a father's concern for his daughter, or one lover for another.

"Laurel?" She laughed, and the words just kept bubbling up out of her, unbidden. "No. I love her to death but, well, no. She was in love with me, and it makes me sad I have been so oblivious to it, like she is this whole different person I didn't even realize. Guys, on the other hand." She waved a finger at Nick. "I'll tell you some horror stories there. Can't trust them for shit. They all secretly hate women, you know? Think they are dumber, less than human. They killed her, just beat her down until she gave in, and felt like she didn't even deserve to live anymore."

"Ah, I see. Your mother?"

Jackie sniffed and took a breath. "Yes, my mother. Fucking stepdad tortured her. Sucked the life out of her until there was nothing but an empty shell, too useless to do anything except crawl into the tub and die." She wiped at the tear that spilled down her cheek. "I didn't do a fucking thing. He just walked away and never looked back."

"I'm not like that though, Jackie. I'm one of the good guys. I have a great deal of respect for you. I'd never hurt you."

The tears kept falling. The aware part of her psyche, buried under that pulsing blue light, finally threw up her hands in disgust. "I know. You are a good man, but you'd never want a stone-cold bitch like me. God, I'm crying. I'm sorry."

Nick reached out and took her hands in his. "No, crying is just fine. You probably need to shed a few tears." Jackie nodded at him and blinked at the faucet that had turned on inside her head somewhere. "Maybe after lunch we can go back to my place. I'm sure I could think of ways to make you feel better about yourself."

She nodded. Yeah, that sounded like a wonderful plan. That lean, swimmer's body curled up around her, hands roaming over her in a long, sweet caress. Heat began to swim through her body. "I'd like that, Nick, but you're a suspect still. Really, we should wait."

"For what, Jackie? Do you really think I'm a suspect? Can't you tell I'm one of the good ones? I'd like the chance to show you."

She nodded. "Okay. I'd like to be with you, Nick. I need it."

"Jackie, look out the doors there, onto the deck."

"Huh?"

"Look out into the sunshine. Look now."

Jackie turned and stared out beyond the French doors, staring blissfully at nothing. Then a cool breeze came wafting in, blowing right through her like she was nothing more than a gauzy, billowing curtain. Nick's presence pulled out, leaving a painful, hollow emptiness inside. She looked back to find Nick putting the contacts back into his eyes, and the reality of what had just happened hit her like a brick to the head.

"You . . . you . . ." she spluttered, fighting against the anger constricting her throat, at the utter, mortifying embarrassment that flushed into her face. "What the fuck did you do?"

Nick let out a deep breath. "If I had been Drake, you would've come back to my place, and you'd be dead." He leaned forward, hands splayed out on the tablecloth, his voice a sharp whisper. "I'm sorry. I didn't expect you to be quite so forthcoming, but do you see now, Jackie? How easy it is to have your will just swept away? And Drake is far more powerful than I. He's been feeding and has the power of the dead on his side."

She heard his words, but Jackie still floundered around in her head over what had come out of her mouth. How could she have said all that? To a complete stranger! She turned and looked out the window, unable to face Nick. "You had no right to do that. It was . . ."

"A violation? Emotional rape?" Nick answered, and Jackie could only nod in agreement. "I apologize. Truly. I did not really expect anything so personal, but I had little choice left other than showing you what you are up against. I need you to believe just how dangerous this is. He is not your typical gun-wielding psychopath."

"You've made your point," she said in a shaky voice, wiping away the tears that stained her cheeks. Yet it changed nothing. It couldn't. "But I'm still on this case, and now I've got even more incentive to get him. Nobody should be allowed to do this kind of . . . thing." His hand lightly touched her arm, and Jackie found herself pulling reflexively away.

"I'm sorry, Jackie. Honestly."

She waved him off, more angry at herself for being so easily drawn in, so utterly defenseless against whatever it was he had done to her. "No. Yes, that's fine. No, actually," she said, slapping her hands down on the table, "it's not fine. You didn't have to go crawling around in there to make your point. You could have stopped."

Nick leaned back against the seat. "That's the thing though, Jackie. I didn't do any crawling. I merely prompted. I didn't make you say any of that. You needed to see what Drake is capable of. If I had stopped, I don't think you would have really understood how defenseless you are against him."

Defenseless. The word squirmed in her gut like a ravenous

worm. "That's . . . that's not for you . . ." Jackie stopped and took a drink of water. It took tremendous force of will to keep her hand from shaking. "You had no business digging . . . around in there."

He closed his eyes for a moment and then leaned forward again, elbows on the table, hands folded together. "There was no digging, Jackie. This power, it just drops all the barriers. I wouldn't . . . I'm not like that."

"Like what? Not like all the other goddamn vampires out there?"

He winced. "No. I don't use this curse to take advantage of anyone. It's not a power meant for the living."

Laurel's words echoed in her head. *They felt like they were dead*. How did you stop someone who could just turn your brain to mush with a single look? Nick could just as easily have asked for her gun, and Jackie knew without a doubt she would have handed it to him without thinking twice. For the first time, some serious doubt began to creep into her head.

"Is there any way to avoid being affected by it?"

"Don't look him in the eye."

Jackie rolled hers, shaking her head. "Yeah, no shit, but I mean—"

"Other than Shelby and I, no. Not that I've ever seen."

Figured. "You need to promise me to never, ever do that again." She had no way of knowing how much he had seen, what sort of crazy bitch he must have thought she was. Part of her wanted to ask, but Jackie didn't really want to know the answers either.

He nodded. "You have my word. For the record though, I didn't see—"

"No." She held up a hand to him. "Don't. I told you to show me, and I believe you now, but it doesn't change anything. There's still a killer out there, and it's my job to stop him."

The smile he gave had a measure of sadness. "I expected as much. You know more about us than any cop before. I hope it helps."

Her cell phone rang, and Jackie flinched at the sudden noise. *And you know more about me than anyone has a right to.* "Rutledge."

"We got an interesting call a few minutes ago about your vampire."

"A break, I hope?" *My vampire. This case is going to mark me for the rest of my life.*

"Maybe. County General just called. Apparently, they have a victim in their emergency room who claims a woman attacked him and drank his blood."

"Shit. Thanks. We'll check it out." Jackie clicked off and dialed Laurel's number. A goddamn woman. That could mean only one person. Shelby Fontaine. Laurel's phone went to voice mail, and Jackie reached for her jacket just as Mia brought out two steaming plates full of seafood pasta. "Come on. You're coming with me, Nick."

"Where are we going?"

"Hospital. Apparently, a woman attacked someone and drank his blood, and Laurel is out with Shelby somewhere not answering her phone." Laurel's angry voice echoed in her head. *Let someone else stop him. He's going to kill you!* The jaws of panic began to gnaw on her gut.

"Ah," was all he said and grabbed his own jacket.

"If anything has happened to her, your ass is mine, Anderson."

"Nicholas?" Mia stood with the two plates in her hands, a look of chagrin and confusion on her face.

"Sorry, Mia," Nick said and stood to kiss her on the cheek. "I'll explain later."

Jackie headed for the door without looking back.

Chapter 26

Nick stepped into an empty patient room at the end of the hall, the first available spot away from Jackie, who was asking a lot of implicating questions at the moment with Shelby's victim. He knew it would turn to trouble. Blood always did. Shelby's phone rang half a dozen times again before going to voice mail.

"Shel, you better watch your ass if you get this message before you're being checked into the county jail, and have Ms. Carpenter call Jackie so I can get her foot out of my ass. You're really pissing me off now with whatever the hell it is you're trying to pull. I showed her a while ago. She believes, but she isn't going to stop. I've got no choice but to try to use their help, and no thanks to you, I'm guessing. Just watch yourself, please." The last thing he wanted was for Shelby to get shot up, but she had blood in her for the moment, which would help her out if shit hit the fan.

He dialed the office, and Cyn picked up on the first ring. "Hey, Cyn, has Shel checked in with you?"

"Hi, Nick. Nope, haven't heard a word. Reggie let me know earlier that the ghosts were out and about over there where you've been hunting. Everything okay? You sound stressed."

"I'm at County General at the moment."

"What?" Her voice jumped an octave. "You okay? Did you get hurt? You didn't find—"

"Whoa, slow down. I'm fine for now, but I might be spending a night in jail here if Shelby doesn't make her whereabouts known pretty quick."

"Jail?" Cyn sounded more worried about that than any trip to the hospital. "Should I be calling Dewey?"

"Wouldn't hurt. Just in case I need him."

"Okay, I'll do that now. Be careful, Nick. That FBI woman has a lot of dark energy around her."

"Yeah, I kind of figured that one out. Take care, Cyn."

Drawing Jackie in had shown him that clearly enough. Something awful had happened to her in the past that still tormented her. Scary thing was she had peeled open like a ripe banana, putty in his hands. The tough exterior was all that was keeping that woman together. She was a survivor, and Nick certainly related to that. More so, she was terrified of people seeing what she was like underneath, and Nick knew all too well what that was like. He had been living a veiled existence for over a century now, and he knew the effects it had on one's soul.

Nick took a deep breath and exhaled slowly, letting that doorway to the other side open just a crack, and winced at the sharp, icy wind that sucked at him. "Reggie! Get over here. Now, please." It didn't matter how loudly or softly he called. Reggie always heard.

A moment later, Reggie dropped out of the ceiling. "Hey, boss. Something's going down. I've felt Drake, and he's got ghosts freaking out all over the place."

"Ghosts. Why are they worried about him?"

Reggie shrugged. "Don't know. It's like fish darting

away from rocks dropping in the pond. I had a bead on him, but when the boss calls . . ."

"Damn. My luck, of course. Okay, get back out there and see if you can find him. If you see Shelby, let her know the cops may be out in force to get her unless she shows her face real soon."

"They worried about her and that agent girl?"

"You've seen them?"

Reggie smiled. "Yeah, Shelby was flying out of town with her clutched on to the back of the cycle. Took her up to that park north of town that looks out on the lake, can't think of the name."

"You followed them?"

"Hey, easy for me, and I was, you know, curious." He laughed. "I wouldn't worry too much 'bout them, boss, if you know what I mean."

Nick ran a hand through his bristled, short hair. "Christ. What is she thinking?"

Reggie gave Nick a wistful smile. "How'd you feel about finding someone who realized what you were and didn't run screaming in the other direction? Or is it the girl-girl thing that's crimpin' your dick?"

Nick glared at Reggie's ghostly right hand. "Reg! You know Shelby and I—"

"Nick Anderson!" It was Jackie's voice, yelling for him outside the room.

"See ya, boss. Got things to do." Reggie vanished into the floor before Nick could reply.

Jackie stormed in a moment later. "What the hell are you doing? I heard Shelby's name. Who were you talking to?"

"Just a call to the office, Ms. Rutledge."

She walked right up to him, her finger stabbing him in the chest. "Where is Shelby? What is she doing with Laurel?"

Nick stepped back, raising his hands defensively. "Honestly, I don't know."

"She sucked three pints of blood out of that guy in there. Sliced him open with a razor and bled him out." Jackie's trembling hand hovered over the grip of her Glock. "She's the killer, isn't she, Nick? Isn't she!"

"No," he said, keeping his voice calm. "She's not." Nick decided against informing her that her partner might be making out with her new number-one suspect.

"You knew she did this, didn't you?" Nick's silence appeared to confirm her suspicion. "You are so fucking under arrest." Her voice shook with terrified rage. "If she's done anything to Laurel, so help me, I will bleed you out myself."

Nick raised his hands behind his head, keeping a careful eye on the hand that now clenched around the holstered pistol. It looked like nobody would be catching Drake today.

Chapter 27

"We're back!" Shelby yelled at Laurel over the rumble of her motorcycle.

Laurel peeled herself away from Shelby's back and looked around. Her car was there in front of them, parked across from the Jade Dragon, where Shelby had picked up Chinese for their lunch. She licked her windblown lips, still tasting the faint sting of the chili peppers that had been in Shelby's food and hot upon her tongue.

The icy-cold wind of the dead had still not left her bones. Shelby had let down her guard and let Laurel see, let her be witness to what Shelby was, a woman sitting on the border between life and death, drawing energy from the blood of others to keep herself on this side of the doorway, able to draw upon the spiritual energy of the dead lingering on the other side. Shocking did not even approach how Laurel felt at the discovery, though it came pretty close to the feeling of Shelby's lips on her own after the fact. She felt sixteen at the moment, returning from her first real date. It was completely absurd, and though she was still overwhelmed by the events, a certain giddy elation kept her body tingling.

"Damn. I was just beginning to enjoy the ride." Laurel swung her leg over and stepped off the back of the BMW.

"You can ride with me any time you like, Laurel." Shelby grinned and pulled Laurel's purse out of the storage compartment. "It was nice having your arms around me." She handed the purse over to her. "Here."

Laurel felt the warmth rush to her cheeks yet again. Shelby had no qualms about saying exactly what was on her mind, a refreshing and certainly attractive attribute, especially when it was her that appeared to be occupying Shelby's mind. "Thanks. It's been an . . . enlightening trip, to say the least."

"I was worried you'd freak and want to arrest me on the spot."

"Oh, no," Laurel said, shaking her head. "I knew all along you had nothing to do with killing those boys. "Your aura is all wrong for it."

Shelby reached out and took her hand. "What is my aura telling you now?"

Laurel swallowed hard, embarrassed that she was actually embarrassed. Okay, she had not been on a date in forever, but still. The woman's touch sent goose bumps down her spine. "It's telling me that maybe there's another meeting in store for us. Soon."

She squeezed Laurel's hand and laughed. "God, I certainly hope so. I haven't wanted someone so bad in years." Shelby leaned over and kissed her quickly and then sat back on her motorcycle, zipping the leather jacket up to her neck. "It'll happen. I can promise you that, but I need to get back out there. I can sense that fucker Drake in the area. It's weird that he keeps fading in and out like this, but we'll track him down. He wants us to find him, after all."

"Call us if you do," Laurel insisted. "Don't take him on by yourself."

"Worried about me?"

Again her cheeks began to flame. "You need to quit embarrassing me every two minutes."

"It's cute as hell though." Shelby revved the engine and flicked on her blinker. "You telling Jackie what happened?"

"Yeah, I need to."

"Will she believe you? Will she understand?"

Laurel shrugged. "Believe me, yes, even if she doesn't understand it. What about Nick? Can you convince him to cooperate and help us?"

"I'll talk to him again, but I don't know. Part of me thinks he wants Drake to take him down."

The thought sobered Laurel up in a hurry. "That's no good."

"Nope. He's tired and full of guilt. Can't blame him too much, really, but he can't give up now. I think we might actually have a shot at Drake."

"I hope so," Laurel said.

"I know so," Shelby said with a heartless smile. "He wants us to." With that she gunned the BMW and roared off into traffic, taking the next corner nearly horizontal to the ground.

"Wow," Laurel whispered, feeling the trailing cold tails of ghosts whip by her as Shelby vanished around the corner. The feeling lingered, however—cold and malignant.

Laurel turned and felt around, using her sense to home in on the spirit. It was near, a block or two at the most. Why had she not felt it earlier? There was something oddly familiar about it as well. Shouldering her purse, Laurel began walking down the sidewalk.

A cold wind picked up the closer she got to whatever it was. Whispering along with it, dark and unkind, came a voice. "Laurrrelll."

It hit her then, why this spirit felt familiar. It had been the same one outside her window a couple days earlier, the one that had tried to claw its way through her protective charms. What was it doing over here?

The cell phone buzzed in her purse, reminding her she

had yet to check in with Jackie. She could wait a few more minutes. She wanted to find this ghost before it stepped back into the world of the dead. Deadworld. Shelby had spoke as if it were a place you could go visit, like Holland or Bermuda. Shelby. The cool fingers on Laurel's face had certainly not left her feeling cool. She grinned at herself, feeling light and a bit crazy. She might have a date with a vampire. What a strange world.

"Laurrrelll."

There. A mini market across the street. She was sure of it now. Laurel waited for traffic to clear and hurried across to the corner store, its windows plastered with ads and posters for lotto tickets, cigarettes, beer, and other assorted healthy ways to spend one's money.

Bells tinkled overhead when she opened the door and walked inside, looking much like any other inner-city mini mart one might walk into, crammed to the gills with over-priced convenience and an assortment of cheap, imported knickknacks. A young woman stood idly by the till, smoking a cigarette. The ghost was somewhere in the back.

Stepping around an end cap on the far side of the store, Laurel was surprised to see a materialized apparition, vaporous and not wholly formed, but definitely recognizable as a man. She studied him for a moment, but nothing about his features looked familiar.

"Hello?" she said quietly. "I can hear you. What do you want?"

It shimmered, a malevolent grin spreading across its face before it began to glow and stretch into smoky tendrils. Through this dim haze, darkness yawned open in the corner, and to Laurel's amazement, an impeccably dressed man stepped through, wearing a dark blue suit with a crimson tie. His hair was short, graying, and combed straight back with a bit of a wave. It was thin enough on top that you could see his scalp peeking through in places. Your average fiftysomething executive. He smiled, but it was one of those humorless things that corporate types learned to plaster on their faces when meeting with clients or the competition.

And his gray, irisless eyes glowed like bright, hot coals.

"Good day to you, Ms. Carpenter. So good of you to come."

Panic tried to claw its way out of her brain, but the signal to run had been short-circuited. Those eyes knew why. They knew everything. Deep, soulless eyes that gazed with the power of the Goddess herself, peeling away every last vestige of defense, exposing and revealing every horrible and hidden secret. There was no judgment in there, just the ambivalent acceptance that came from all things dead.

She absently fumbled in her purse for the cell phone, finding only the thin, painted empress card, and managed to squeak out three words. "And you are?"

"Drake, my dear, lovely woman. Cornelius Drake." His smile stretched wider, revealing all his yellowing smoker's teeth, and he stretched out a hand toward her. "Come. My car is out front. Let's take a drive, shall we?"

Laurel extended her hand, watching it as if it were someone else's, getting wrapped in the cold fingers of the grim reaper himself. His grip was comforting, reassuring, and—much like Shelby—Laurel knew she would do anything for him.

In their wake, the old empress card tumbled to the ground from Laurel's other hand, its warning unheeded.

Chapter 28

Once again Jackie stood in the entry of Nick Anderson's house. He had given her the keys without even asking. She wanted to say a jail cell had made him cooperative, but he had given them to her as they'd walked into the FBI building.

"Go look," he had said. "Save you the effort of getting a warrant."

She had snatched the keys from his hand without reply and left him cooling his stubborn ass in a holding cell. Gamble and a handful of others were searching Shelby's house. She didn't expect them to find anything. If there was something to find, Jackie figured Nick's place would be where they would find it.

Nick had said something about Shelby wanting blood to help find Drake, but the rest of the conversation was a blurred-out wash of noise. Anger and fear had been churning through Jackie so furiously that nothing Nick had to say mattered. The fact that Shelby had attacked someone for blood, and Laurel had gone off with her, was enough. Now, in the quiet of Nick's house, reason had crept back into Jackie's senses. Laurel had likely just turned off her phone and forgot, but it was still unlike her, and the fact that

Shelby did not answer either was worrisome. What if they had gone off on her motorcycle and crashed? They could both be dead in a ravine somewhere.

Jackie tried calling Laurel again for the twentieth time and clicked off when the voice mail began. "Damnit, Laur. You're pissing me off."

"What was that, Jack?" Agent Pederson stood in front of her, looking into the living room.

"Nothing. Just annoyed at Laurel."

"Probably just got her phone off. I'm sure she's okay."

"Yeah, I'm sure you're right." Jackie didn't sound very convincing. "Take Warren and Smith down to the bedroom wing there. Summit, we'll start upstairs in the loft."

"Sounds good," he said and marched up the steps two at a time.

The curving staircase opened onto a loft space that looked down on the entry on one side and the living room on the other. The roof peaked overhead, letting in light through a series of skylights. A wide hallway extended out in one direction over the bedroom wing, lined floor to ceiling with bookshelves. He had a small bookstore's worth of books. At the opposite end she could see a pair of over-stuffed leather chairs, a table and lamp between them. The loft area itself had a large desk with a computer monitor perched on one corner. The rest of the room drew most of Jackie's attention, however. There, in all its gleaming black glory, was a baby grand. A Steinway. It looked far more impressive up close than it had from the living room floor.

"Son of a bitch." Did it have to be a nicer, better-kept version of her own?

"Find something, Jack?"

"No, keep looking. Check the desk. I'll look in the library."

Jackie walked the length of the hall, looking for anything out of the ordinary, but for all intents and purposes it appeared to be just what it was. There were books on all manner of subjects, even an entire section devoted to the supernatural. Somebody else was going to get to catalog everything if it came to that.

"Storage area over the garage here, Jack!" Summit called down to her. "You want me to get the picks and open it?"

Jackie wandered back toward the loft. "Just break the fucking thing open."

"It's dead bolted."

"Interesting. Get the picks then."

Five minutes later, Summit had the storage door open. The men downstairs had turned up nothing of interest to that point. Jackie flicked on the light switch next to the door, and the interior flooded with light, revealing what Jackie could think of as only a museum.

Summit whistled. "Wow. What the hell is this?"

She stepped in, careful not to disturb anything. A life-size painting of a woman was mounted to the wall at the far end, some twenty-five feet away. A display case had rows of quilts neatly stacked inside. Next to it was an old rocking chair, draped with one of the quilts and stacked up with dolls—the old, handstuffed Raggedy Ann kind. There was an old flip-top desk, and Jackie saw when she walked up that the top had been changed to glass, turned into a display case, which covered a neatly arranged assortment of coins inside plastic sleeves.

"The little fucker," Jackie muttered under her breath and opened the case. She grabbed the penny sitting in the last spot in the last row of the collection.

"Hey," Summit exclaimed. "Is that the penny stolen from the evidence room?"

"I think so." It would be interesting to hear Nick explain that one away.

"What is all this shit, you think?"

Jackie put the penny in her pocket and kept looking around. Though a museum had been the first thought that had come to mind, she realized now, as she approached the painting at the far end, what it really was. "Memories," she said.

Nick Anderson had built a shrine to his dead family.

A framed piece of newsprint on the wall caught Jackie's eye. The title, written on a small placard beneath the old news clipping, read, GWEN AND THE KIDS, FIRST DAY ON THE JOB, APRIL 1862. It was the photo Hauser had pulled up on his screen. There were a couple more old photos of the family. On top of a small curio stand by the painting was a small wooden box with tarot cards inside. Carefully, Jackie fanned through them. They were all in the same style as the one they had found, and—sure enough—the one they had was not in there.

The nervous pang of fear returned in full force. Jackie could not shake the feeling that Laurel was in serious danger. What if the freak-out about Jackie needing to be careful had really been intended for Laurel? What if her little visitor had been trying to tell her that she specifically was in danger? She gathered up the box, knocking over one of the photos, which she noticed had the names and ages of the family on the back. The realization hit her, a sucker punch to the gut, leaving her momentarily breathless. Gwen and Laurel were both thirty-one. How had she missed that?

"Summit," she said, motioning to everything in the room. "Pictures. I want pictures of everything in here. I've got to head back now."

He gave her a perplexed look. "We just got here."

"Just do it, Summit. I'm going." She pushed passed him and leaped down the stairs three at a time.

Chapter 29

Five minutes from downtown, her cell rang, and Jackie snatched up the phone. She recognized the number, but it had not been the one she was expecting. Clenching it so tightly her hand shook, Jackie flipped it open, her voice barely above a growl. "Where is she, Shelby? Where is Laurel?"

"Jackie, listen," Shelby's voice came back, sounding winded. "I don't have her."

"So help me, you bitch, if you've hurt one hair on her head . . ." She blindly ran a red light, swerving around oncoming traffic and narrowly avoiding causing an accident. Her fear and frustration boiled over. "Get out of the fucking way!"

"Listen to me, Jackie. It wasn't me. Drake has her."

"Liar!" she yelled into the phone. "We've talked to your last vic in the hospital. We found the penny, the tarot deck. You've been covering for each—"

"Penny? What the hell are you talking about?" She sounded truly dumbfounded.

"Don't be stupid. You know exactly what I'm talking about. This whole Drake thing is a front for your own twisted little vampire games. I want to know where she is,

Shelby. It'll be much worse for you if I have to track you down."

There was a bark of sarcastic laughter in her ear. "Would you just listen to me for two fucking seconds? Drake is—"

"No!" she screamed into the phone, fed up with the stalling and angry she was not getting the reply she wanted. Why couldn't Shelby have just said Laurel was fine and on her way back? Why did the worst case have to be what came out of her mouth? Jackie did not want to believe. "You listen. You'll bring her back right now before I hunt you down and blow your bloodsucking head clean off." Her voice cracked at the end as Jackie fought back the tears of fear and terror.

"Silence!" Shelby snapped back, and Jackie could almost feel her mouth being held shut. The feeling startled her back to some sense of reality. "We don't have time to waste. He's somewhere within a mile or two of West Central and Pine, likely in a blue Rolls. I dropped her off at the Jade Dragon two hours ago, and some chick at a mini mart saw her walk out with a man in a blue suit, Jackie, so pull your damn head out and call out your cavalry. And get Nick. I need him out here before it's too late."

Too late. Jackie stared blankly at the phone until horns began blaring at her to notice the green light. "Shelby?" The cell answered her with silence. "Fuck. Laurel. Be wrong. Please be wrong." She called downtown and got Belgerman to scramble the men into action. Local enforcement would be notified. She didn't trust Shelby, but the risk of disbelief far outweighed throwing money away on a manhunt that wasn't there.

"What about Nick Anderson?" John asked her. "Should he help?"

Shelby's words echoed again in her head. She could not ignore the request if there was any chance at all he could or would help. "Yeah, get him ready to go. I'll take him over to where Ms. Fontaine said Drake's likely location is."

"Jack?"

"What, sir? I'm nearly there now."

"You good for this?"

"Good for what?" She hit the parking-garage drive too hard and bumped her head against the roof of the car. "Ow! Fuckin' A!"

"You in the right frame of mind to be leading this now?"

She slid into an empty parking space too fast to avoid crumpling the bumper against the concrete barricade. "Shit. Sir, with all due respect, unless I'm dead, don't take me off this." How could he dare think it?

"Not off the case, just off this. You are too close on this one, Jack. Laurel is more than just a fellow agent."

"You worried I'll go ballistic on whoever grabbed her?"

"I'm concerned your judgment may not be optimal, Jackie. Give me a fucking break. You know as well as I what the deal is here."

Jackie took a deep breath and let it out. She knew, but if something happened, it was her responsibility. It had to be. "I have to take this, sir. You want me off, you can take my badge."

"That's what I thought you'd say," he said, not bothering to hide his annoyance. "Fine, just don't make me regret the decision."

Up at Nick's cell, Jackie had security release the bolt. She opened the door and found him lying peacefully on the small bed that occupied one wall. He actually looked pale. "Come with me. Shelby insists we need you to get Laurel back."

"Ms. Rutledge," he said, his voice sounding strained. "I won't be much use to you unless you get me some of the synthetic I'm sure you have down in a lab being analyzed as we speak. I'm about two hours past due."

"What? Why?" She tossed his things at him and turned around. "Never mind, I don't want to know. I'll find it. Get ready."

On occasion, being known as a ballbuster had distinct advantages. Jackie marched into the lab room and demanded to know where the synthetic blood was. She took a bottle and marched right back out. One raised finger of warning was all it took.

Nick downed the contents in a few seconds, wincing as he finished it off. "Okay. One minute and I'll be ready. How do you know he has her?"

"Shelby called—said some girl in a mini mart saw her walking out with an older man in a blue suit. They got into a Rolls-Royce and drove away."

He nodded. "That sounds like him."

"It's him," Jackie said back and grabbed his arm. "Let's go. She's been gone nearly three hours now."

"We have any leads?"

"Ms. Fontaine said West Central and Pine."

"Ah. We've been driving around him the whole time."

Encouraging words. She led him down to the garage, feeling his presence next to her the entire time. The irrational fear that he would grab her and bite into her neck would not go away, and for a four-floor ride, the elevator sure ran out of air fast. Apparently, she had not completely forgotten about the incident in the restaurant. So much for wishful thinking.

She stepped away from him quickly when the doors opened and walked to the car. He remained thankfully silent, but once on the road, Jackie felt his oppressive form taking up all the clean, breathable air in the car. She was forced to roll down a window on the graying evening. Rain was coming off the plains, the air thick with the smell of moisture. Finally, Jackie could no longer tolerate the silence.

"What's the deal with the room over your garage?" She

reached into her pocket and pulled out the penny. "This look familiar?"

He continued in silence, staring at the penny, his face unreadable as always. "Memories, Ms. Rutledge. So I don't ever forget."

"You believe you'd forget your own family?" Sometimes Jackie wished she could forget hers. "Given what happened, I find that hard to believe."

"Never forgotten," he replied, his voice quiet. "A hundred and forty years tends to dull everything."

She glanced at him, avoiding his curious stare. Yeah, in a perverse sort of way, that made sense. He wanted to keep the pain fresh in his mind. He didn't want to lose his edge for catching Drake. "And the penny? I'm really curious how you managed to get it out of our evidence room."

"Reggie," he said, the hint of a smile on his weary face.

"Who?" Why had this name not come up before?

"He's a ghost, Ms. Rutledge. One of my former associates from long ago who stuck around to help me out. He's good for . . . special projects."

"You lead a very strange life, Nick." Her cell rang again before he could reply. It was Shelby.

"Can you call off the damn cops? I'll never get a solid bead on him if I have to keep sidestepping the law."

"It'll take a while to filter down to them, Shelby."

"Just do it, please. How close are you?"

They were crossing over the river now. "Not far."

"Okay, I'm south of Central and Pine, and the feeling is getting weaker. So head north. Nick with you?"

"Yeah, you need to talk to him?"

"Nope, just call if he gets a hit on him."

Shelby hung up, and Jackie called in to have the cops quit looking for her. North of Central and Pine did not narrow things down much.

"Anything?" Nick wondered.

"North of Central and Pine."

"Okay, we aren't far. Slow down a bit so I can concentrate. A bit of luck, and we'll triangulate somewhere nearby."

"You can feel Drake around here?"

He nodded. "Yes. When he's ripe with blood, he's difficult to miss, but he's been harder to pinpoint this time. Keeps fading in and out. I haven't figured out what he's doing yet."

Ripe with blood. "Can you tell if he's fed on Laurel?

"He hasn't yet."

Oh, thank God. Laurel was a smart cookie though. If anyone could deal with something like Drake, it would be Laur. She knew all about that supernatural shit. "Did you know Laurel is thirty-one?"

"I'd have guessed as much now," he replied, leaning back in the seat and closing his eyes. For all Jackie could tell, he was going to sleep. She checked in on her phone, but nobody had come across anything. Shelby had been spotted, though the story of her leaping over moving cars stretched the limits of believability.

"How much stronger are you when you drink real blood?" Morbid curiosity kept her brain churning and helped to keep it from preoccupying itself with Laurel.

His head turned, a softly glowing eye shielded by heavy lids. "Much. The strength of ten men probably. The mind-control thing is even more easily done, and control over the body is such that you can make your skin knit itself up from wounds, mend bones, and the like. The power of the dead, Ms. Rutledge, is not human. It's an otherworldly thing."

Hard as it was for her, Jackie kept the car at the posted speed limit of thirty-five miles per hour. Her stomach was nothing more than a squirming bucket of worms now, every minute leading closer to a fate so incomprehensible her mind refused to acknowledge it.

Chapter 30

Reality snapped back like a broken rubber band for Laurel when Drake let her go at last. She had not been oblivious to him and had in fact been aware of his every action. The ride in the Rolls had not been long. She even knew where they were but had missed the exact address. The decaying sign over the doors had said FITZSIMMONS FURNISHINGS. It was a warehouse, or used to be at some point in time. The windows had been boarded up, and most of the inside was scattered with refuse, clutter, and fallen ceiling tiles. Three floors up, the entire floor had been converted into a living space. Of sorts.

Upon entering the room, nothing had been visible other than the stainless-steel table in the center of the room. A dangling fluorescent lamp illuminated it and provided the only light in the cavernous room.

"Please, Ms. Carpenter. Have a seat upon the table."

The slight British accent might have had charm under other circumstances, but now, feeling trapped within her own body, she could only think of Hannibal Lecter. She obeyed like a mindless zombie and sat on the edge of the table, noticing the raised lip around the edges and the hole in the corner. She had seen tables like these numerous times in the past, generally in unfavorable conditions. A cadaver's table.

On one side of the table, a chenille-covered lounge chair and ottoman, floor lamp, and side table. On the table were several books and a newspaper. Dimly, she had awareness of there being more to the space. There were other aspects, more furnishings, but they were barely noticeable in the glare of the overhead light, and her eyes had no will of their own to wander and take in the surroundings.

She watched him move around the room, into and out of the central light, removing his jacket and draping it carefully over the back of the lounge chair, then disappearing into darkness until she heard the unmistakable tinkling of ice cubes. He returned with a drink in hand. His tie had been removed, and the top two buttons of his crisp, white shirt were unbuttoned. He seated himself in the lounge chair and sipped down the martini, reading through some of the newspaper. With no sense of time to speak of, Laurel could only guess how long she sat there unmoving before he finished off the martini and laid the paper back down.

Drake pulled her cell phone from his pocket and held it up. "Fourteen calls now, Ms. Carpenter. You appear to be a rather popular woman. Why is that, I wonder?"

Laurel had nothing to say, as he had given her no permission to speak. *I can't die like this, not buried inside my own body.*

Fourteen calls meant Jackie was wondering why she hadn't called to check in and would wrongfully suspect Shelby of taking her. They would be focusing on the wrong person.

Drake sighed with exasperation. "I suppose I should strap you down so we can have a proper conversation. Don't you agree?"

"Yes," Laurel replied, unable to keep her lips from forming the words.

He leaned down and opened a drawer beneath the table, and Laurel soon found her wrists zip-tied to the edges of the table. Her legs from the knees down still dangled over the end. "Well, then, there we go. We may speak freely now."

And like that, the impenetrable weight upon her mind lifted, and Laurel could control herself once again. "You're going to kill me." She was surprised at the finality in her voice.

He stood next to the table, looking down on her much like a wolf looks at a fawn with a broken leg. "I'm going to drain the blood out of you, sucking the precious life force from it until you leave this world of the living and enter that of the dead. It is more a transition, really, but not one I highly recommend." He smiled, and the charm may have been there in his lips, but the eyes ruined it completely. No charm was possible from glowing, irisless eyes. "It is wretchedly cold over there, and most of the fellows are a bit of a bore. I'm afraid you will not find it much to your liking."

The bastard was a talker at least. That much went in her favor. There was little other advantage she had at her disposal, however. The straps would only get tighter if she pulled on them. Time would prove to be her only ally. She needed it badly. "You aren't exactly what I'd imagined from a . . . um . . ."

"Vampire, Ms. Carpenter?" He laughed softly. "Such an amusing twist of the reality, but in essence, yes, I am one of the very same, and it is not so much like the stories portray. Both more and less, as it turns out."

"You are both living and dead at the same time," she said. Shelby had shown her that much. She wondered if Shelby was out there now, cruising the streets on that death trap on wheels looking for her. Jackie would be. Two hours of no contact would be about her limit, if she guessed her friend correctly. Her patience and paranoia would have met head to head by now.

"Why, yes, indeed I am, Ms. Carpenter. How very astute of you. Your ability serves you well. I wonder," he said, leaning over her, his face next to hers. Laurel turned away from those enthralling eyes. She could not bear the notion of that mindless enslavement again. His breath sucked in next to her ear, a deep inhalation. "I wonder if your blood is any richer because of it?"

A shiver went down Laurel's spine. Not a question she hoped to have answered any time soon. "Why did you choose me, Mr. Drake?" She had to keep him talking, soothe his ego, and let him think she found him intriguing. At least that was what she had been told to do when one found themselves in the hands of a kidnapper.

He bent down below the table again, opening drawers. "You fit the bill, Ms. Carpenter, ordinary as that might sound. I saw you at the park that first day and noticed you bore a reasonable resemblance to Nick's dead wife. The fact that you were involved with the case has made it sweetly ironic, wouldn't you say? Ah, here we go." He stood back up clutching a variety of items. "But as you likely have deduced by now, your hair color is all wrong."

"So the dye was to make the boy resemble one of Nick's children."

"Yes," he said. "Now then, let's get you tilted up so I can get at you a bit easier."

The head end of the table dropped down, and Laurel found herself down at knee level staring up at Drake. From beneath the table somewhere he had pulled out a snaking cord with a showerhead on the end of it. He was going to dye her hair right there.

"I don't really make a good brunette, Mr. Drake."

He smiled, and from her angle it looked like a twisted frown. "Nonsense. You'll be lovely. Besides, we must do something to pass the time. Your friends aren't close enough yet."

"You want them to find you?"

"But of course, my dear," he replied, spraying her hair down with warm water. The unusual care with which he took going about dying her hair made Laurel's skin crawl. "I had thought you smart FBI types would have deciphered this game Nicholas and I have been playing. You have all the evidence you need, or are they too dense to believe in such a plan? But then again, the man does so dread involving others. Far more entertaining this way, really, I must say. Back in '70 it was far more interesting. You fellows got rather close at one point. I dare say killing you will up the stakes a bit."

With his hands covered in plastic gloves, Drake began to massage the coloring into Laurel's hair.

Laurel could not get the morgue pictures of the boy out of her head now, close-ups of the dead skin colored with dye. "Why do all this though? Why didn't you just kill him after you killed his family?"

"Suffering, Ms. Carpenter. One's enemies do not suffer if they are dead, and besides, when you cannot die, one needs some way to pass the time." He chuckled and continued working the dye into her hair. "You know, you really have gorgeous hair. Your best trait, I must say."

"Thanks." Laurel could not tell if he was being serious or merely playing her.

"Ms. Fontaine seems to like it. The little cunt has good taste."

The breath caught in Laurel's throat. He'd seen them together? How was that possible? It was the first time she had heard anything close to animosity coming out of his mouth. "You don't like her."

He gave her a faint smile. "In her way, she is more cold-hearted and vicious than I, but not to you. No, no. She's sweet on you, Ms. Carpenter. *That* she made rather plain to see. So your death will be doubly delicious, I must say. Two birds with one stone, or so the saying goes."

"How did you know?" She did not need to know, but it would keep the conversation going, and she was admittedly curious.

"I have my little helpers, just like Nicholas," he said.

Laurel realized then. The ghost that stole the penny. The ghost she saw just prior to Drake showing up. He had help from the other side.

He pulled her hair out straight over the edge of the table and let it hang down before proceeding to rinse most of the dye from her hair. His fingers were gentle upon her scalp.

"Now then, I suppose that will have to do. Not quite the right color, but we don't have much time. Your Ms. Fontaine has a bit of blood in her and will be closing in sooner than I wish."

He came back up from under the table yet again, this time holding a bowl filled with items she could not see. Only a strand of rubber tubing jutted out from the top. "Now what?"

"I'm going to hook us up in a moment, Ms. Carpenter." He set the bowl down on the table and began to roll up his sleeves. "But first, a proper bit of scenery needs to be dealt with if you're going to be Nicholas's Gwendolyn. Look, Ms. Carpenter. Look here," he said and leaned over her with a soft smile on his thin lips.

She tried to turn away, squeezing her eyes tightly closed. That feeling of being trapped inside oneself was almost more than she could stand. "No."

A hand slapped her face, snapping it back the other direction. Laurel gasped and winced, tasting blood in her mouth. "You will look, Ms. Carpenter, or I shall remove your eyelids with a razor and make your final moments in this world most unpleasant."

Tears began to slowly trickle out of the corners of her eyes. "I'm not ready to die."

"I'm not killing you yet, my dear. We have about half an hour, I'd say, possibly forty-five minutes. Now then, look here. This next part's not really as difficult as all that, and you will be far more relaxed under my influence.

"How can you be so sure of that?" She looked at him as he asked the question and felt herself at once drawn in and shut out at the same time.

"I can feel them coming, Ms. Carpenter. They are closing in, eager to save their friend. It shall be close, painstakingly even, if I do say so myself. Now then, let's get those pants off. I buggered Gwen before I killed her, and you shall have the same privilege. We can't be leaving out any of the important details, now, can we?" The slight quirk of a smile held nothing but menace this time.

Laurel wanted to scream, but her body no longer belonged to her mind. Everything had become disconnected. Her only choice was to sit back and watch or let herself sink deeper, further out of his reach. He could abuse her body, but in the end, at least he could not touch her soul.

She sank into darkness, Drake's deadpan accent fading away, finding quiet and solitude. Years of practicing deep meditation allowed her to find that place with ease. In this state, away from Drake's prying presence, she could reach out. The spirit world was within her reach if she could only achieve a deep enough state of relaxation.

Shelby. If anyone could hear her cry, it would be Shelby. There was a connection between Drake, Nick, and Shelby, a link amongst the dead, but maybe Laurel could hear it. Her abilities did not lean in that direction, but what could it hurt? She had nothing left to lose.

Laurel thought of the sign over the door, with its flowing script and large FF that abbreviated Fitzsimmons Furnishings, and called for Shelby as somewhere above, in the world of flesh and blood, she gave hers willingly, and it began to siphon away.

Chapter 31

"He's started!" The unmistakable voice of Shelby yelled into Nick's cell so loudly Jackie could hear it from the driver's seat. The words sent a chill through her.

"Started? Started what, Nick?"

Nick raised a hand to silence her so he could hear, and Jackie wheeled over to the curb—screeched to a halt. Nick bounced off the side of the door as the front tire hit and rolled up onto the curb.

"You tell where?" he asked Shelby, keeping his hand up to Jackie. A moment later he nodded. "Okay, yeah, I'm getting it, too, now."

Jackie swatted the hand aside. "What's he started, Nick?" Panic clawed through her, a tiger ready to devour the last vestiges of rationality and sanity she might have. "Tell me, goddamnit!"

"Head up Steele," he told Jackie. "We're at one hundred sixty-fifth, I think, so we'll start moving up. It can't be too far."

"Nick, I swear to God, if—"

"He's begun drawing her blood, Ms. Rutledge."

"No! Fuck, no!" she screamed at him, punching him in the shoulder. "It's been only three hours. It's too soon."

Jackie pounded her fists against the steering wheel. "This isn't happening. This isn't fucking happening."

The cool, firm grip of his hand on her arm jarred Jackie out of it. "Can you drive?"

"What?"

"Are you okay to drive? We need to keep moving. We're in the right area now. It's just a matter of narrowing it down."

"Of course I can fucking drive."

"Slowly," Nick added. "I can't sense as well if I'm worried you're going to plow us into a telephone pole."

She nodded and pulled them back out into the street, light flashing, creeping along at twenty-five miles per hour. Nick did little more than tell her to turn left or right, his hands braced on the dashboard, eyes closed. Jackie gripped the wheel, knuckles white, her mind slowly unraveling as the minutes on the dashboard clock ticked by. Forty-two minutes, excruciatingly slow moments of her life, pulled out like fingernails. *Hang in there, Laur. We're coming. Soon. Just a bit longer. Keep him talking.*

The words were no good, however. Jackie's mind had the image of a red tube dangling from Laurel's arm, with some grotesque, fanged monster sucking on it like a kid's favorite milkshake. "Are we any closer? I'm going to lose my mind here, Nick. Hurry the fuck up."

He had an earphone hooked up and was in constant contact with Shelby, who apparently was running on foot. "Okay," he said. "Head up Steele then. We'll come over on one-seventy-eighth. Careful, Shel." He turned to Jackie. "We're close. Be ready for anything, Ms. Rutledge." He sat back in the seat now and pulled the plug out of his ear. "Left here on one-seventy-eighth. He's somewhere between us. Two blocks at the most."

"Shit," Jackie answered, fumbling at her phone to call down to headquarters. "We're near one-seventy-eighth and

Steele. Look for my car. Suspect is currently in this vicinity, and victim is in jeopardy. I repeat, victim in jeopardy." She clicked the phone shut. "You sure about this, Nick?"

"I can feel him. He's close but difficult to pinpoint exactly. I'm hoping Shelby gets a stronger hit than I do." On cue, Shelby's voice was an excited, inaudible yell coming out of the earpiece. "Fitz what?"

Jackie knew in that moment exactly where he was talking about, a block and a half ahead on their left. She had purchased a couch there when she first got her apartment. "Fitzsimmons," she said and gunned the engine.

Leaning on the horn, Jackie sped through the next intersection, this time not fortunate enough to avoid causing an accident as a Ford Explorer swerved to avoid her and sideswiped a taxi coming the other way before sliding into a pair of parked cars.

As they approached the building, the first drops of rain began to fall from a darkening sky. Jackie didn't bother with a parking space and flew over the curb, sliding up to the main entrance to the warehouse. At the same time, something dark bolted across the street, coming at them with uncanny speed. She reached for her gun, but Nick's hand stopped her.

"Shelby," he said in one of those startling commanding voices that came from somewhere not quite living.

Jackie watched in disbelief as Shelby came sprinting up, faster than a human had any business running, and launched herself through the door. The twin metal doors erupted inward in a shower of glass and twisted metal.

"Holy shit," Jackie muttered and bolted after her, gun drawn. Nick jumped and slid over the hood in one smooth motion, following up the steps closely behind.

Inside, the entryway was cloaked in darkness, except for the fading gray light coming in through the doorway. Shelby stood in the middle, her heavy breath quickly slowing. She

held a 9mm Beretta in her hand. "Up," she said simply.
"Where's the stairwell at?"

Right on cue, as if the heavens might actually be interested in their events, the sky belched forth a flash of lightning, and across the blowing, stirred-up refuse, a sign on the
wall next to the elevator read STAIRS. Jackie pointed her
Glock at the sign and followed behind Shelby. The agent
part of her brain screamed for backup. They were rushing a
lethally dangerous serial killer—an agent with two civilians,
one of them armed. To be sure, there was more than one
violation there. Rational agent Jackie Rutledge had been
run over, however, by the stampeding fear and panic monster who guided her with sole, focused purpose. Laurel was
dying. If she failed, it would all be over.

Up the stairs three at a time, Jackie kept wondering
about blood. How much could you lose before you died?
Were you just plain fucked after a certain point, or could
transfusions save you?

"Jackie, be careful," Nick said in a quiet rush from
behind. "He'll run, but he might try to take you or Shelby
out along the way."

She heard Nick say something behind her, but Jackie
was not in a frame of mind to listen to him. Her heartbeat
thumped in her ears, racing along at a frantic pace. Her
hands were so eager to find Laurel, to assure she was alive,
that they trembled. Holding the gun up in both hands and
swinging around the third-floor doorjamb, Jackie aimed
down a hall into darkness, the tipping of the gun bouncing
around like an angry bee in a jar. There were no doors to
be seen.

"Shit," Shelby said in whisper. "She's up here somewhere." She darted down the hall to the left. "Go around the
other way. Look for a door into the middle."

Nick took off before Jackie could even react and was

around the opposite corner before she could barely get going.

Before she was even halfway down the next section of hall leading around to the other side of the building, Shelby's voice boomed across the whole floor. "Drake!" A quick burst of four gunshots followed.

And then there was laughter. Dark, rich, and utterly humorless.

"No." Jackie ran as hard as she could, careening off the wall as she rounded the far corner. The hall was a gigantic square surrounding a room in the middle. The only door in had been on the opposite side. She watched Nick dart in without hesitation, and she quickly followed into singularly illuminated darkness.

The silence was all wrong. No running footsteps, no cries of "here he comes" or "look out." Jackie swung her Glock back and forth, sweeping the room, but she could see nothing other than the center fluorescent light. "Where? Where is he?"

"Smiley fucker just stepped across, Nick. Just opened up a door and walked right through." Shelby's hands went up to her head then, the Beretta lying across the top. She began to walk toward the light. "Oh, goddamnit. Laurel."

Jackie had noticed it upon entering the room, but her brain only just now let her really see the body that lay on the steel table in the middle of the room. Dark hair cascaded down over the side, along with a limp arm. The hair was all wrong. That could not be her. It wasn't her! A momentary wave of relief washed over Jackie, and she walked forward to see, to verify the possibility that this was a big mistake. She watched Shelby pick the arm up and lay it gently by the body's side.

"I'm sorry, Jackie." The voice was Nick's, coming from behind. He knew before Jackie got close enough to verify.

Thirty feet away, Jackie stopped, gun dropping to her

side. Nick was right. She could see it in the features of the face. Drake had colored her hair. "She's dead?" Her voice was soft, quiet, sounding like a young girl.

"A little blood, Nick. If you'd been on blood we would have been here sooner." Shelby held up her hand and stomped toward him. "Five fucking minutes. Five!"

"Wouldn't have mattered, Shel. He would have killed her anyway."

"Maybe," she said, and from behind her, Jackie heard the unmistakable thump of someone getting slugged in the gut, the grunt and coughing rush of air. "Maybe not."

Jackie finally made her feet move, shuffling forward. She vaguely heard Nick drop to his knees in the fading background. The world narrowed the closer she came, as if she were approaching a precipice, beyond which lay nothing. The body lay upon the steel, clothed only from the waste up, her lower half covered in a familiar-looking quilt. On the left calf, Laurel's familiar blue-and-green fairy no longer danced with a magical life of its own. Her face was serene, eyes closed, one corner of her mouth turned just the slightest bit up into a smile.

Rage. There should have been screaming rage, hurling furniture, the need for a straightjacket, but Jackie only stared, and the gun slowly slipped from her numb fingertips and fell to the floor. Her mouthed worked. There were words somewhere, something she wanted to say, but nothing worked. There under the bright fluorescent bulb, the world had died and now lay broken at her feet.

She took Laurel's cold fingers in her hand and held them, wanting to say good-bye, but for the life of her, Jackie could not force the words out of her mouth. Instead the words built up and finally spilled down her cheeks. Somewhere in the background, the chaos of sound marking the rest of the FBI entered the room, as well as Shelby's voice, far closer—next to her, even.

"Jackie. Come on, we should move out of their way."

She shook her head, violently enough to fling tears off around her. She wanted to get those words out, whatever they were. Had to. Jackie squeezed Laurel's hand in hers, hoping that even in death she might give the same strength and inspiration she gave off in life, but there was only failure.

"I'm sorry," she whispered. "I'm so sorry, Laur." Her knees buckled, and Jackie sagged against the table. The rest of the words vanished into tearful nonsense, buried under the bubbling gasps of sobs that, once started, didn't want to stop.

Jackie clutched on to Laurel's body, her head pressed to the unmoving chest, and wailed.

Chapter 32

Nick sat on the hood of Jackie's car watching the FBI help Shelby into the backseat of one of their cars. Her usually petulant mouth had drawn out into a thin, angry line. The flashing red and blue lights did little to accentuate the puffy eyes. They were taking her in on the assault, but he knew better. It would not stick. They just wanted a chance to get her downtown for questioning. Part of that anger was directed at him, the rest at Drake, and the tears were for Laurel Carpenter.

He said nothing to anyone, having been told to wait, which he reluctantly did. They had some questions, of course, beyond the usual documentation. The look from Jackie's boss had held a thousand of them. So Nick sat and nursed the sore ribs where Shelby had sucker punched him. He had dropped like a stone on that one—had not seen it coming. Nearly had him puking on the floor, but felt like it anyway after watching Jackie fall apart. They had to drag her off Laurel's body and she had fought to keep them from taking her away until somebody had knocked her up with some sedative. At that point, Nick had walked out and down to the street.

Guilt stung Nick down to the quick. It always came back

to blood in the end, and, once again, the lack thereof had cost another life. Damn it all. He had warned them, but, then, who was going to reasonably listen to stories of vampires and a century-old tale of vengeance? Would it have even mattered? Something had happened. Drake had power Nick had never seen, an ability he did not realize they could do. The man had crossed over.

He could walk among the dead if he so desired, but why would anyone want to? The living and dead were separated for a reason. More to the point, there were dead over there Nick was not sure he wanted to see. Who was he kidding? He desperately wanted to see them, and was terrified they would not want to see him. Without precious blood, however, the game was over.

The FBI could be dealt with, however. Once Jackie got her feet back on the ground, there would be some rather awkward explaining to do. They would all be pissed. One of their own had been killed. He could hardly tell them it was a bad idea to go after this guy. All he could do now was minimize the damage, get to the end as quickly as possible, and try to save them any more grief on his part.

Nick rubbed his face with his hands and let out a long, weary breath. A cigarette and a whiskey sounded damn fine at the moment. *Ah, Gwen! I'm not going to hold up my end of the bargain after all.* When he looked up, the blanket-clad figure of Jackie came out of the building, her boss's arm wrapped around her shoulder. Her eyes, swollen and dark as the churning, raining sky overhead, looked straight ahead, unmoving. She looked smaller, Nick thought, as if Laurel's death had carved some of the flesh from her bones, and those wide, staring eyes made her look sixteen.

The sight grew unbearable for Nick, and he got up to take a walk—and ran right into one of the agents.

"Mr. Anderson," he said, not sounding at all pleased to be chatting with him.

"Yeah?"

"Don't be going anywhere. You can ride downtown with me. We'll want an official report from you on what happened here, and any other information you might find . . . useful to tell us."

"All right," Nick said. "I'll need a ride back later to get my car."

"If and when you go, I'll bring you back for the car," he replied. "Don't talk to the reporters, please. You might find it better just to wait in my car over there." He pointed to one angled into the curb behind where Jackie had been shut away.

It occurred to Nick then that they would want the same information out of Jackie Rutledge, and she was in no condition to do anything. "You aren't taking her downtown, are you? She may need a hospital."

"Let us worry about our own, Mr. Anderson. Agent Rutledge is as tough as they come, but that was her friend in there that got killed. Believe me, she'll want to get after the fucker as soon as possible."

Nick had a feeling that might not be true. She looked broken, and not in a "patch it up and send it back out" sort of way. He had seen it many times over the years, and been there, too. A lot of times you did not come back from that kind of injury. The wounds never closed. A pang of sympathy went out to her. "I'll just wait in your car until you're ready."

He nodded. "Good idea."

Nick crossed the street, pausing long enough to let the other FBI car pull away from the curb. The shrouded head of Jackie leaned against the window, and for a brief moment, Nick thought he saw recognition in those eyes, but what feeling lay in that blank stare, he could not fathom. He held the gaze for that instant and gave her the one solace he had at his disposal. Sleep. He mouthed the word to her, drawing what bit of power he could to impart the suggestion, but had no idea if it held before the car sped away.

An hour later, Nick found himself seated in a conference room surrounded by a dozen FBI agents, none of whom had welcoming expressions upon their faces. It was a somber and angry room. Belgerman, the head of the Chicago division, stood at the head of the table, pouring himself some coffee into a Styrofoam cup.

"Coffee, Mr. Anderson?"

"Sure, thanks," Nick said with a nod. "You might as well call me Nick. I have a feeling this isn't the last meeting we'll be having." He picked up the second cup of coffee. "I'm really very sorry for your loss. I liked Ms. Carpenter. She was . . . gifted."

Belgerman cut off someone's reply with a raised finger. "Keep the comments to yourself, Pernetti. Everyone here is hurting with the loss of Agent Carpenter, but you will all measure your responses here tonight with respect. Am I clear?"

The silence was agreement enough. Nick decided he liked John Belgerman. He was his kind of guy—caring, demanding, and no bullshit.

"Mr. Anderson here has agreed to give us the rundown on what happened tonight, and any other extenuating and unusual circumstances involving this case. Every word, and I do mean literally every word spoken in this room, now stays in this room. We appreciate your help, Nick." He offered him a faint smile, and Nick took it for what it was worth: "You cooperate with us, and we'll get along just fine. You owe us."

"I don't know exactly what information you have on things," Nick began. "I don't know exactly what you know about me or Ms. Fontaine, or who it is you're dealing with—"

"We have a fair bit of unusual and conflicting information, Mr. Anderson," John cut in. "Why don't you just tell us your side of this case. It may fill in some of the holes we have."

Nick looked around the table at the faces staring at him. He had experienced tougher rooms, but this one had a thick cloud of suspicion and doubt floating in the air. "All I ask is that you keep an open mind to what I'm going to say. If anyone has a question, feel free to interrupt." Their silence appeared to be an invitation to speak. "In Wyoming, back in 1862, a traveling preacher by the name of Cornelius Drake came into my jurisdiction. I was a sheriff back then." To his surprise, they had nothing to say on that, and so Nick continued, telling his story for the second time in several days.

Before he got out of the 1860s, John interrupted him. "Let me get this straight, Mr. Anderson. You turned yourself into a vampire so you could come after this guy, even though you knew if you failed to get him, another twenty people's blood would be on your hands, plus whoever might go after him as well, and possibly innocent bystanders who just got in the way?"

Nick grimaced. "Put that way, it sounds like a poor choice."

"True," John agreed. "Very poor, but I would have probably done the same. He killed your family. I'm sorry to hear that, Mr. Anderson. Please continue."

An hour later, he had caught them up to that evening's events. "We arrived, and Drake stepped through to the other side. Ms. Carpenter was dead at that point."

"Stepped through what?" someone asked.

Nick shrugged, as he was not exactly sure himself. "A door, portal, I don't know exactly how to describe it. I honestly didn't realize he could do it until I saw it happen. It explains why we've had such a difficult time tracking him."

A guy with a large shiny forehead leaned forward on the table. "So you're saying this murderer is lounging around with ghosts or spirits or whatever and will just pop back over when he feels like it?"

"I'm assuming so," Nick said. "It's not something I can do, so I can't explain it or understand it. I just know it's what he's doing now."

"Can you tell where he'll come back?" another asked.

Nick shook his head. "Unlikely."

"Well, that's fucked," the agent said.

"Any clue who the prick is going after next?" It was Pernetti this time, and Nick realized now that maybe this group was not so skeptical after all. Perhaps they actually believed him. "You said it's people who look like your family he is killing."

"My grandmother," Nick answered. "Seventy-five-year-old quilt maker. She made handcrafted rag dolls as well."

"We have a picture of her, I believe," John added.

Pernetti frowned. "Not much to go on."

Nick agreed. "I know. Our main hope will be in tracking him down before he can kill again."

"And you can do that?" John said.

"With Ms. Fontaine's help. It just takes time. We can sense each other, Mr. Belgerman, and the more blood he's had, the easier he is to find." Nick downed the rest of his cold coffee in one gulp. Killing him would be an entirely different matter.

"Can we keep him from just stepping through one of those doors again?" Gamble wondered.

"I don't know," Nick admitted, his voice dry and harsh. It was a tough pill to swallow. Drake had figured out how to cross over and back at will. Nick had thought it a one-way trip, but, apparently, he was wrong. Yet without real blood in his veins, how could Nick realize any of those possibilities? He needed to get out of there soon. The emotional constraint was beginning to fray his nerves. "I think you need to get rid of the notion of catching this man," Nick said quietly through gritted teeth. "You'll need to try to kill him."

Gamble leaned back in his chair, letting out a pent-up breath. "Why do I get the feeling you think that's easier said than done?"

"Because it will be," Nick replied. "I'm not even sure we can anymore." It was the sad and depressing truth.

Chapter 33

The miniature grandfather clock atop Jackie's bookcase rang a single chime, signaling her that it was now 3:30 AM. The bottle of tequila sitting on the piano stood three-quarters empty, while the bottle of sleeping pills prescribed by Matilda Erikson, the FBI's shrink, sat next to it un-opened. Tillie had filled the prescription and given them to Jackie without even asking if she wanted them.

"You won't be able to sleep," Tillie had said. "Take them. You need the break." She had held Jackie's hands, still trembling with the chill of death, in her own, warm with life. "And call me if things get bad."

Jackie knew what that meant. If she thought about swallowing a bullet, she should call and let Tillie talk her out of it. The Glock lay on her nightstand, now, too far away to make it even worth the effort. Everything was too much effort now. The effort to live required some amount of force of will that Jackie hardly felt like holding on to.

The thing was, Jackie had no desire to sleep. She did not need a break, nor deserve one. She had let down her best friend when she'd needed her the most. Her fingers played out parts of Mozart's *Requiem* on the piano, missing keys every few notes and then starting over. At one point, she tried to play a Carly Simon song, a favorite of Laurel's, but had broken down eight notes into it, sobbing until her stomach hurt so much she had thrown up half the tequila. Ten minutes or a half an hour later, the tears would begin to run once again, not even aware that she had been thinking anything at all. It was like her body and mind were on two separate grief schedules.

The one person she could turn to in a time like this was no longer around to lean on. The world had become a vastly emptier place. Finally, the bottle dribbled its last few drops onto her tongue, and Jackie hurled it across the room. She could not even be rewarded with the violent shatter of glass, as it hit the thick curtain over her window and fell harmlessly to the carpet below.

About six AM exhaustion finally overcame Jackie, and her body began to tremble. From cold or nerves she could not tell, but once started, it would not stop. She curled up on the couch, clutching a couple throw pillows against her stomach, her breath coming in ragged half sobs.

"Laurel," she stammered. It was the only word that would come out of her mouth, and Jackie kept saying it over and over again until sleep finally overtook her.

Amidst the chimes of the clock and her telephone, Jackie bolted upright from the couch, the vague images of a dream from the night before fading from her brain. "Laur?" Jackie rubbed the sleep from her eyes. One of those eyes was starting to ache horribly, and a vile paste coated her mouth. A drink was in order before she had to run for the bathroom. The dream left the uneasy feeling that Laurel had been talking to her. She had no memory of the words, but Jackie didn't want to hear them, could not stand to hear them.

The clock finished its chiming. Straight-up noon. "Damn," she said and pushed to her feet, groaning. Caller ID told her it was Tillie checking up on her. After several rings it finally went to voice mail. Jackie shuffled into the kitchen and pulled out the carton of orange juice from her fridge. She took a couple huge gulps before putting it back. It was the only thing left to drink other than tap water.

Deciding it was enough effort for the moment, Jackie collapsed back on the couch. She had the day off. Tillie's orders, backed up by Belgerman. Maybe she just wouldn't go back. Thinking of facing Laurel's empty desk at the office brought fresh tears to her eyes. Jackie let them run— all those little things they did at work, the coffees, poking fun at each other's idiosyncrasies, and half the time knowing what the other was going to do or say before they did it.

In the middle of it, Tillie called back again. Jackie knew she would call every fifteen minutes until she got through or decided to come over, which would be far worse. Still, she did little to hide her annoyance at the interruption. "What, Dr. Erikson? I'm fine. I'm still here."

"No, you aren't, but good. I'm glad you're still here." Her voice had that insane parental calmness to it, where no matter how irate you got or how many fits you threw, the tone never changed.

"If I say I'm fine, I'm fine, goddamnit. Don't be telling me how to fucking feel, Tillie. You don't get paid enough for that." The vitriol flew out of her mouth before she even realized it was coming. "Christ. Sorry. My head hurts, and, no, I'm not doing fine. It's a shitty day."

"Would you like to come in later this afternoon, Jackie? Or I could come by this evening if you pre—"

"No."

"You sure?"

"I'm in no mood for talking about anything right now. I've got the day off. I'm going up to the local pub and getting shit faced, drowning my sorrows, and all that kind of bullshit. I'll see you back in the office, I'm sure. Bye, Dr.

Erikson." Jackie clicked off and turned off the power on the phone. No more calls. No more anything right now.

Jackie got up, found her wallet and keys, put on her sandals, grabbed her jacket and headed down the street to her local pub. Fortunately, Tarnigan's lay four blocks east of her apartment, because Jackie realized halfway there that she was still pretty drunk. The couple strange looks she got confirmed the fact that she at least looked that way.

Sam—the fat, balding, fiftyish bartender—gave her a wide-eyed look when she sat down at the bar. Sam was reliable. He wouldn't chat unless you wanted to chat, and he didn't care how drunk you got, as long as you didn't drive away from his pub.

"Christ, Jack. You look like you got run over."

She nodded and tapped the counter with three fingers. Having made it in and down on a stool, Jackie found what little courage she had mustered to get out the door and down there melted away with Sam's worried look. The tears lay like some fathomless lake behind her puffy, bloodshot eyes, and she knew if she spoke then, the dam would crumble, and that would be that. But, true to form, he said nothing else and poured Jackie three shots.

In quick succession, Jackie downed the fiery shots, propped her cheek on her hand, and stared up at the Cubs game on the television. The alcohol warmed her gut but did little to touch the chill around her heart. She began to play out scenarios from the day before, running through them in her head over and over, but Nick's words always came out at the end. *He would have killed her anyway.*

Jackie wiped at her eyes. "Sam! Three more. Please." The last came out a bit choked, and she pressed her lips together, forcing the surging tide behind her burning eyeballs at bay.

He poured one shot and set the bottle down. "You let me know when you need a ride home."

She nodded. "Thanks." *Oh, by the way, Sam, some vampire killed Laurel last night. Can you believe it?* She couldn't, did not want to, but had woken up to Laurel's absence. It had been no freakish nightmare. *How am I going to do it, Laur? How will I do this without you?* It seemed such an inane and yet impossible question. The hollow sensation on her right side, where Laurel had always walked when they went anywhere together, felt like a vacuous hole where she had been torn away from her flesh. Part of her was missing now, taken away along with Laurel.

How did people do this? Jackie wondered with despair. How did they move on when half their soul had been ripped away? Her impulse was to just lay her head down on the bar and weep, but Jackie refused to make a spectacle of herself. A little more alcohol, and she would not remember any of tonight regardless, at which point she knew she could just let everything out. Sam would call her a cab. He could just pitch her into the river, for all it mattered.

"Rough day?"

Jackie's blurred vision sharpened on the man who sat down on the stool next to her. Navy suit, red tie, little hint of shadow across his cheeks, and a handsome wave of reddish brown hair kept just longer than business norm. "And you care because?"

He shrugged and smiled, blue eyes glancing down at the array of shot glasses and near-empty tequila bottle. "I didn't say I cared. I just asked if you were having a rough day."

Jackie eyed him, far too gone to judge if he was as good-looking as the dozen shots made him appear, but he hit the right note regardless. Oblivion. The guy could fuck her right into oblivion. Just the cure for a soul suffering too much awareness. "Someone died."

Sam put a beer in front of the man, giving her a quizzical look, but she ignored him. The man put down a five, which Sam quickly swiped up, and the man's mouth quirked up in one corner. "People die every day. You'd be dead of alcohol poisoning if that was your modus operandi."

Hmmm, not a bad thought, really. Worse ways to go. "Sometimes it's just the wrong one."

He nodded, a sage expression on his face, and sipped his beer. "Yeah, always wrong for someone, and for them . . ." He raised his beer. "To better days. My name's Scott, by the way."

Better days. Jackie could not see how that might be possible any longer. "Jack. Most folks just call me Jack." She downed another shot, hardly even feeling its warmth anymore.

"Nice to meet you, Jack. Are you in mourning? I'm sorry to intrude, if that's the case."

She thought about it for a moment, her sloggy brain taking longer than it should to formulate opinions on much of anything. "Nope. Just lamenting life in general. I needed cheering up, so I walked down here to bother Sam."

"Ah, I see. Well, Sam here does look like the cheerful type."

"Be careful with her," Sam quipped. "She bites."

"Most encouraging news I've had all day." Scott smiled and turned back to Jackie. "Do you bite, Jack?"

"Only if provoked." The words came out slightly slurred. That last shot had been the tipping point. She poured another, knowing from habit how this downward slide would progress.

"And what, may I ask, provokes a woman like yourself?"

"Smart-ass guys in suits, for one."

Scott laughed. "Your lucky day. Fortunately, my ass is quite intelligent, and the suit's Armani, for what it's worth."

She snorted. "Nothing. You always take advantage of drunken women, Scott?"

He eyed her for a moment, and Jackie knew he was

thinking for just a second if she was being serious or flip, but the tequila should have given that one away without any thought at all. "Every chance I can get. Twice on Sundays."

Yeah, he would do just fine. Jackie smiled at his lame humor and downed one more shot before getting off the stool. "Guess it's your lucky day—" she started and then tripped over the leg of the stool before Mr. Suit could catch her. "Well. Shit. Pay the man, Scottie, and walk me home. I need something cute to lean on."

He put a fifty on the bar and took Jackie's arm. "Mom always said my MBA would come in handy."

"Oh, a funny man! My mother was too stupid to even spell MBA." She leaned against him and managed something halfway between laughter and tears. She just wanted him to hurry and up and get her home—fill that empty pit that had swallowed a dozen shots of tequila and still left her feeling hollow. The mortar that kept her bricks in place had liquefied, drained away on a steel table in an abandoned warehouse, and one by one the bricks were tumbling down into the hole.

Walking home on the arm of another handsome, unknown man, Jackie smiled grimly at the thought of one more broken promise.

Chapter 34

"Here," Shelby said, handing Nick one of his handrolled cigarettes. "Take it, damnit. I know you want one."

He let out a huff and took it from her, plucking a match from the container sitting on the counter. With a quick pop of his thumbnail, it crackled to life, and Nick took a long drag on the harsh, sweet tobacco. He watched Shelby light one for herself, something he had not seen her do in years, and then take a long draught off her third beer. She rarely had more than two drinks, but it had little apparent effect on her as she paced around the kitchen and out to the living room to stare through the huge panes of glass at the steady rain that buried Illinois in a sea of gloom.

"And fucking eat something, would you?" She pointed at the burger he had made but had not touched. Hers had been gone in two minutes. "This 'woe is me' thing is pissing me off."

Nick picked up the burger and took a bite, and admittedly it tasted damn good. His stomach had been rumbling since the previous night but he had not had the inclination to eat. Not to mention, Shelby was probably right. Maybe there was a little punishment going on. "Sorry. This thing has me in a poor mood."

She took another deep drag on the cigarette and then put it out, blowing a long stream of blue smoke out toward Nick's face. "Yeah, it has me worried, too, but I was out there all night trying to find the prick while you moped around out here and brooded on the possibilities. You know, Nick," she began with a shake of her head and paced off toward the windows again, "there was a time when the little people got stepped on, you stepped up and made it your business to mete out a little justice. I loved that about you. You stood up for what was right, even if it meant risking your life."

Her words stung. "I still do, Shel. You know that."

"Then what are you doing, babe?" She spun around, sloshing beer out onto the floor. "Drake is out there killing people, and you're acting like you can't really do anything about it."

"Can I? Can you?" he added, pointing a finger. "Even with blood, do you honestly think you have a chance against him now?" Frustration, anger, impotence—all began roiling over inside Nick. "If we both had blood, would it make any difference at all? You saw the same thing I did, Shel. Drake opened a doorway and just stepped right through to the other side. We can't defend against that. If he's got that much control over it, he could probably just open a door here and take us out while we slept."

"Why hasn't he then? Huh? Why?" She stomped across the room at him and stabbed a finger hard into his chest. "You just want an excuse not to fail yet again, knowing that if you blow it this time, you die. You're taking the coward's way out, Nicholas."

He reached up to slap her but caught himself at the last moment. His heart pounded against the tip of her finger, angry and embarrassed. Shelby looked at him, her face flushed with indignation, her mouth as petulant as ever.

She stared at him and then finally drew back, smiling. "Had your chance there, hon. For a second there, you could have had me."

"I could never hit you, Shel, even if I wanted to."

"You know, sometimes control is the last thing you need to exercise."

"What is that supposed to mean?

She rolled her eyes. "Christ, you're such a guy some-times. It means go with your gut and your heart. Fly in the face of the odds. Do it because it's far more glorious to go out with your guns blazing, even if you know you're dead. You let Drake beat the life out of you, Nick. You let him grind you down, and now you're letting him gloat over it."

She had been walking in a slow circle around the dining room table, clenching and unclenching her fists. Now she stopped and looked hard at him, with something of sympathy perhaps in her eyes. Nick was wincing before the words even came out of her mouth.

"You think Gwen would be happy if you just gave up and crossed over? Because, really, that's what you're doing. You gave up back in '70. I just didn't realize until now."

The words sat Nick back down on the bar stool. Shelby could just as easily have sucker-punched him in the gut. "That's not a fair thing to say."

She shrugged. "Truth is still the truth. Don't dishonor her memory by just walking off into the fucking sunset."

Nick gritted his teeth. Now he really did want to hit her. "You know what?"

"Hit me if you want to. I can certainly take it. Maybe it'll even make you feel better. Hell, hit me hard enough, maybe I'll be inspired to give back a little." She gave him one of her mock, impish grins. "But, really, you blew your chance the last time. We could have been fucking like bunnies for old time's sake right here on the table if you'd followed through the first time."

"That's not what I want," he said, the anger dissipating. Painful as it was to hear, she was right. He could never face Gwen on the other side, if she still lingered there for him. Maybe she had made peace with it after all these years and moved on, but he doubted it. No, she would be there, and the notion of greeting her as a failure terrified him beyond measure.

Shelby laughed. "Liar. You'd just feel too guilty over it anyway. Better you direct that energy at someone who really needs it."

"What, Agent Rutledge again? You need to get over yourself with that, Shel. I feel bad for her. She took everything . . . hard."

Shelby patted him on the cheek. "The fact that you even think that is what I meant confirms it. And I know she took it hard. I sent Reg to keep an eye on her."

"You did?"

"Did you see her?"

"Well, yeah, but nobody takes the death of a partner very well." He had lost his share, but in light of his family going down before his eyes, the impact got diffused a bit.

"You know, for being one hundred and eighty years old, and fairly enlightened by most standards, you can be denser than rock sometimes." Shelby chuckled and went to the fridge for another beer. "She didn't just take it hard. It crushed her, Nick. I saw the look in her eyes, or lack thereof, I should say. The poor girl's life force just snuffed out like a candle in the wind."

It was a feeling he could relate to far too well. There had been some pretty rough low spots in his life. "You think she could be suicidal?"

Shelby wrapped her finger around the bottle cap and

pulled it off, taking another long draught of beer. "Maybe. Doesn't hurt to be safe. Besides, I'm thinking Laurel may try to contact her."

"Why so soon?"

"Because she's strong, Nick, and she has seen the other side. She's not afraid of it, or at least she's not so over-whelmed by the Deadworld to need much time to get used to things there."

"You don't think she'll move on?"

Her bark of laughter was sharp and held a hint of jeal-ousy. "As long as Jackie is alive, Laurel is one of the linger-ing dead, and she's familiar with things, Nick. She'll figure out how to get around soon enough, and before long, Jackie will get contacted. I just hope she's stable when it happens, because . . . well, it might be bad."

"Were the two of them intimate?"

"Hardly. Agent Rutledge is more afraid of intimacy than she is of goddamned Drake."

"Oh." The statement baffled Nick. "You don't even know her."

"You could see it easily enough if you knew how to look," Shelby said. "Regardless, Jackie had more than love for Laurel. I think they were more married than most mar-ried couples, if you know what I mean."

Nick nodded. He did. "Jackie feels like half a person now."

Shelby shook her head. "No, she feels like a nonperson now because she's afraid to look at the half that's left and find there's nothing there."

Nick finished off his beer and shook his head. "So weren't you a little worried about how she might take you and Laurel?"

Shelby put the beer down on the counter and crossed her arms over her chest. "What is that supposed to mean?"

"Means Reggie told me you two were having a moment before Drake kidnapped her, that's all. I don't mind, really, but what were you thinking, getting involved with her in the middle of this case?"

"Reggie!" Shelby stomped her foot. "The little shit. I'll wring his neck."

"You couldn't wait?" The point was moot now, but the chance to poke back at her even just a little was too hard to pass up.

"Unlike you, cowboy," Shelby replied, her hands bracing against the counter as she leaned toward him, "I like being with someone more than every few decades. And don't give me the 'no one could understand' bullshit either. You could have had Cynthia any time you wanted. The woman utterly adores you and sure as hell knows you aren't quite there in the reality department."

"She's my secretary—"

"Oh, for fuck's sake, Nick! You wouldn't be the first guy to bang his secretary."

Nick's eyes widened. The thought that Shelby actually felt bad for his lack of relationships had never really occurred to him. "That's not the point."

"Okay, sorry." She ran her fingers through her hair and heaved a sigh. "I'm frustrated and pissed off and sad."

"Yep, me, too, Shel. Me, too."

"Bad time?" Reggie's form seeped up out of the floor and stopped in the center of the table.

"You!" Shelby pointed an accusatory finger. "You need to quit spying on me."

Reggie chuckled. "You're far more fun than the boss here, Miss Shelby."

She dropped the finger. "Why are you here?"

"That FBI girl you wanted me to, you know, spy on, might be in a spot of trouble."

"Drake?" A tremor of panic rumbled in Nick's gut. It couldn't be. Jackie would not fit any family member's profile.

"Oh, no. That devil seems to be busy bouncing between here and the beyond. Your agent seems to have gotten herself a bit drunk and taken a man home with her."

"Why is this any of our concern?" Nick wondered. "She probably is just looking for some comfort after losing her friend."

Reggie winced and shook his head. "Maybe, but I don't think so, boss. Not the way she's talking."

"Talking how, Reg?" Shelby said, sounding worried.

"Well," he said, scratching his stubbly chin in thought, "that dead agent keeps trying to contact her, and I think it's about driven her crazy."

"Shit!" Shelby ran for her coat on the living room sofa. "Let's go, Nick. I'll meet you there."

Nick marched purposefully toward the garage. "I'll drive, Shel. You're on your fourth beer, and I don't want you on the death bike when you're buzzed."

"I'm not buzzed, you old ninny."

"Just get in the car," he snapped back. When she arched an eyebrow at him, he eased off. "Please." She rolled her eyes, walked up to the car, and got in. "Thank you." He turned back to the door. "Where does she live, Reg?"

He drifted out and gave them an address. Nick slammed the door shut and gunned the engine, backing out just clear of the rising automatic door. Jamming the brakes, he spun the wheel halfway down the driveway and had them heading out onto the road. He ignored the fact that Shelby had refused to buckle up. She gave him an amused smirk.

"What? Don't tell me I'm going too fast."

"No, just reminds me of why I was in love with you once upon a time."

"My driving reminds you of that?"

"No, you dolt," she said, laughing. "You racing after the damsel in distress, or maybe it's the thought of some strange guy between her legs."

Nick stared at her in disbelief. "Were you such a bitch when I met you?"

"Worse." The thought amused her, but she turned and looked out at the scenery racing by the window for a minute before continuing. "I do love you, Nick. You know that?"

"Should I even try to answer that?"

"Not *in* love. I have no desire to dive between your sheets anymore, but I do love you. Always will. You're a good soul, babe. I just wanted to make sure I told you that before . . . well, before shit hits the fan and you go all martyr on me and get killed."

Ouch. "I don't plan on just getting killed, you know. I could have done that years ago."

"Then why didn't you?"

The question momentarily stumped Nick. Why hadn't he just given up, even after four failures and so many deaths? It wasn't clear enough that he couldn't do it? Or was it that he hoped Drake would slip up just once so he could nail him? "Hope, I suppose."

"Exactly—hope that you can somehow figure out a way to get him, or hope that he fucks up along the way, and hope that one day this might all be over so you can live your life again."

"That's . . ." . . . *So true,* Nick thought sadly. *I've been waiting 144 years to live again.* "Sounds a bit pathetic when you put it that way."

"Only if you lose, babe, and until that fucking door slams shut on you, there's still a chance. You used to say there was a way around or through everything if you were patient and kept your eyes open."

"I've been patient for a long time, Shel."

"And is it going to hurt anything for you to kick some ass for a few more days? If not for me, then do it for Gwendolyn."

He winced. "Must you use her every time you want to make a point?"

She shrugged. "Works, don't it?"

"Yeah," Nick said, heaving a sigh as he smoked the tires up a freeway on-ramp. "Sadly, it does."

Chapter 35

Blood. For a moment, Jackie thought she smelled blood, but then Scott grabbed her wrist and spun her around, yanking her into his embrace. One hand clenched into the short, unwashed hair at the back of her head and pulled on it so his mouth could have easy access to hers. The top of the piano pressed into her back while she bit at his lip. He eased off for a moment and then bit back, twice as hard. When he pulled away, Jackie could taste blood.

She licked her lip. "It's a good start."

He bent her over the top of the piano, laying his bulk against hers until she lay flat on the cool wood surface, her feet not even touching the floor. His hands pinned hers over her head. "Exactly how bent are you, Jack?"

One hand slid up beneath her shirt, finding a small, bra-less breast. Jackie smirked until his fingers found a nipple and pinched hard. Alcohol numbed it for the most part, but she still sucked in her breath at the brief, piercing pain. An image of her mother, hands bound to the headboard of her stepfather's bed, flashed in her mind. It was not the fact that her mother had been tied up that had unnerved her nearly twenty years ago, but the reddened welts across the backs of her mother's legs from the nightstick in Carl's hand, and the wild, rage-filled eyes that had turned on her when the bedroom door had squeaked in her hand.

"Live and learn, you stupid little bitch!" he had yelled at Jackie with the slightly slurred speech of a twelve-pack, tempered with a quarter ounce of coke. "Someday," he said, snapping the nightstick across the back of her mother's legs, as she did little more than sob into the pillow, "you'll grow up and be just like her."

Her mother had picked up her head, turning for a moment so she could speak. "Go, baby. Just . . . go." Her face had been swollen and smeared red with blood.

"Truly fucking bent," Jackie said, her voice barely coherent. "Bedroom . . . now," she demanded, pushing at his chest but too drunk to move him at all. "Cuffs are there."

"My kind of girl," Scott said with a grin and pulled her back to her feet. "I think I need to visit Tarnigan's more often."

"Don't worry," Jackie replied, shuffling toward the bedroom hall. "I'm the biggest slut there, hands down. I'll sleep with anyone."

Scott laughed. "You should really try to make this more difficult."

Jackie paused and looked over her shoulder at him. "You should quit being so nice."

"Okay," he said, nodding and grabbing her arm in a vise-like grip. "I can get into this game. You just say stop if it gets too much for you, Jack."

Laughter bubbled out of her. "You aren't man enough to take it that far, Scottie."

Inside the bedroom door, Bickers hissed at him and darted out between their legs into the safety of the kitchen. Scott then pushed Jackie to the bed and began unbuttoning his shirt. Halfway down, he stopped.

"What the hell? Is that a gun?"

Jackie rolled to her side, gazed over at the dresser, and laughed. "Oh, shit. I shoulda put that away."

"You a cop or something?"

Something. The days of agenting are over. I can't do it without her, Jackie lamented, pulling at her shirt but getting stuck with it halfway off her head. *I'm no good without her, and I couldn't fucking save her. What fucking good am I now?*

"Not anymore," she muttered, struggling out of her shirt and kicking off her sweats.

Scott walked over and picked up the holstered gun and the cuffs next to them. "Nice." He jingled them at her. "I believe, Ms. Slut, that you are under arrest for lewd and lascivious conduct."

"You'll never take me alive, copper," she cried but only managed to roll over toward the other side of the bed before one cuff latched around her wrist.

Scott laughed at her. "You can't fucking walk, much less get away, but I think that counts for evading arrest as well." He pulled her toward the headboard, and Jackie hardly felt the metal digging into her wrist. "Maybe a few lashes with the belt will put you back in line."

"Jackie."

She pulled on the cuffs until the metal dug into flesh. "Take more than a lousy belt to hurt me, bucko, and it's Jack, not Jackie."

"Jackie." She heard the soft, faint voice again.

Jackie turned back to glare at him, her heart in her throat. Fuck, he sounded just like Laurel for a second. "It's Jack."

Scott shrugged. "Got some ID, bitch?" His belt whipped across her backside from left to right. "No? How many violations is that now, four?" He brought the belt down across the other cheek, and Jackie flinched, the burn of pain washing through her. "Or was it five?"

"Just don't call me Jackie."

Hands reached around her, digging into the flesh of her breasts, and Jackie could feel the hardness of him pressed against her ass. His mouth whispered close to her ear. "I'll call you whatever I like."

"Jackie, please."

She turned, looking toward the other side of the room. "Laurel?" *My God, I'm losing my fucking mind.* The belt stung her again.

"Jackie, stop." The voice was quiet but insistent.

Jackie gritted her teeth, yanking on the cuffs while the belt came down again and again. *She's going to haunt me to my grave.* "I'm sorry," she said. "I tried."

"Think that's good enough, you stupid slut?" Scott sneered, getting into his role.

"Enough, Jackie."

Jackie squeezed tears out through clenched eyes. "You can't do this to me. Please," she said, beginning to sob. "I wasn't good enough. I wasn't." She could hear the sound of the nightstick rising up from the past, thudding against flesh, tearing away humanity with each bruising strike.

"Let me show you what you're good for," Scott said, and Jackie felt her knees pushed out wide as he pushed himself into her.

"Jackie," Laurel's voice said, very faint this time.

She gasped for air, stuttering through the now hysterical crying that had overtaken her. "Harder!" she yelled. "Come on . . . Carl. Is that . . . all you've got?"

"Carl? Who the hell is Carl?"

"Make it bleed . . . you fucking prick. Where's your fucking nightstick?"

"Huh? You okay, Jack?"

"Go ahead!" she screamed, yanking on the cuffs, bucking against Scott, whose momentum was waning. "Where's your fucking nightstick now? You want to shove it up my cunt? Or . . . or . . . or tear into my ass? Make me bleed, you motherfucker. Come on!" Control vanished. Screaming, crying, fucking—it didn't matter. Nothing touched the pain that was eating her from the inside out.

"Whoa, I think we just passed my stopping point."

She felt him pull out of her, and suddenly she was an empty void once more. "No! No, no, Carl, please. I know you want to. You said I'd end up just like her, and you were right. You were! Please, please don't stop."

"Jesus Christ! Your wrists are bleeding all over the place. You crazy bitch."

Jackie bucked her body, yanking twice on the cuffs until the piece of wooden lattice in her headboard broke under the stress. She flung herself around, catching Scott flush across the side of his face. Blood burst from his mouth, and he fell sideways, crying out. She fell on him, too drunk to actually lunge, and began punching, awkward two-barreled swings of connected fists.

"Fuck! You psycho." He shoved her back onto the bed. "What is the—" He stopped and raised up his hands. Jackie had pulled her Glock free of the holster he had slung over his shoulder. "Hey! Take it easy, Jack."

She pushed away from him, backing toward the head of the bed, the gun shaking in her hand. "You killed her," she said in a tremulous voice, full of pain and anger.

"What? I didn't kill anyone," he said, clambering off the bed, hands still held in the air.

"She killed herself because of you, Carl, you . . . you sadistic . . . little shit."

"Carl?" His voice was growing shaky. "Who the hell are you talking about? I'm not Carl."

Jackie wiped away the tears with the back of her hand, smearing blood across her cheek. Her eyes were wild and staring, focused on nothing. "Twenty years! I've waited. . . ." She took the gun in both hands now, but the shaking continued. "Hunted you for twenty . . . goddamn . . . years!" Her voice rose to a shriek.

A hand reached in through the door at that moment, grabbing Scott by the hair and yanking him off his feet, into the hall.

"Jackie!" Shelby's voice boomed through the room like a thunderclap.

For a moment, Jackie's breath stopped. Then her body swayed uneasily before giving way, and she sat back on the edge of the bed.

She blinked, looking like a lost child caught in the rain. "Laur? You're okay?"

Shelby stepped into the room toward the bed. "Aw, baby. Here, give me the gun."

The Glock came free of Jackie's hands with ease, and Shelby set it on the dresser. She sat down next to Jackie and put an arm around her. "Jackie? Sweetie, look at me. It's Shelby."

She stared at Shelby for a moment, reaching up to touch her dark hair. "Shelby? But Laur. I heard her. I . . . I can smell her perfume."

Out in the hall, Scott's ranting voice was being met by Nick's very calm tone. "Mister, I suggest you leave now while I still have my patience."

"I'm calling the fucking cops. Who are you people?"

His voice betrayed nothing. "Did you hurt her?"

"Listen, buddy—"

There was the sound of flesh slapping flesh, and Scott cried out. "The last thing we are is buddies. I asked you a question. Did you hurt her?"

"Jesus Christ, the crazy bitch wanted me to hit her, thought I was some dude named Carl." There was a quick crack of sound, followed by the unmistakable thump of a body hitting the wall. "Fuck! You broke my nose, you cocksucker."

Nick poked his head in and, seeing it was safe enough, grabbed Scott's clothes off the floor.

"You all right?" he asked Shelby.

She nodded. "Yeah, go take care of that." Nick nodded and walked back down the hall. Shelby turned back to Jackie. "It's all right now. Everything's going to be okay. Are you hurt?"

Jackie pointed toward the open door. "Carl. It was . . . Where's Laur?"

"She's gone, hon. Laurel's dead, remember?"

Jackie stared at Shelby, recognition creeping back in. "Oh." Her head came down against Shelby's breast, her body beginning to shake. "I let her die. I let her die."

Shelby stroked Jackie's hair while the tears soaked into her shirt. "No, baby, you did no such thing."

Chapter 36

"She has a piano, Nick," Shelby said, giving him a little smirk. "I wonder if she's any good?"

"I don't know. Why don't you wake her up and see if she'll play something for us?"

She ignored him and began to play something, her touch soft upon the keys. Nick had always found her playing quiet and sad, which held considerable appeal to his general state of being. The remains of Indian takeout were still scattered on the coffee table, and Nick picked absently at them, unsure about what to think or do with himself. Shelby had slept on the same couch for three hours earlier in the evening, but he had not been able to. It was not his bed, and no amount of wrangling or shifting around could make it comfortable enough.

Shelby had insisted on staying, and her reasons were sound. Jackie likely wasn't safe by herself. He had seen nervous breakdowns before, and been on the edge himself more than once in his lifetime, so he could not say no. Despite the uncomfortable nature of hanging out in a near stranger's house while that stranger slept, Nick wanted to stay. He felt part of the responsibility lay on his shoulders.

More lives ruined on his account—on his failure to get the job done.

As if she were listening to his thoughts, Shelby asked while she continued to play, "Still beating yourself up over this, aren't you?"

He declined to answer. "I want to know how we're going to deal with a guy who can cross over and back at will."

"Blood, babe. Lots of blood."

The answer he did not want to face, and yet there seemed no other way except blind, dumb luck. He picked at the cold chicken curry for a minute before putting it back down. He was too tired to think clearly, and several hours of staring down the hall at Jackie's bedroom door had helped little. The image of her naked body, rivulets of blood trailing down her arms, had burned into his brain. Shelby had bandaged her wrists and given her a little extra incentive to sleep. They would be lucky if she was awake before morning. For some reason, John Belgerman had been all right with them keeping an eye on her. Nick was not sure he would have trusted himself if the roles were reversed.

The piano went quiet. "Got it all figured out yet?"

He rubbed his hands over his face. "No. I haven't."

"Let me know when you do, okay? I'd like to get Drake soon."

Nick sighed, annoyed with her flip attitude. "And I'd like it if you stopped being a bitch and cut me a little slack." Wrong thing to say. He knew it as soon as the words left his mouth, but he had grown tired of her constant prodding over the course of the evening.

Shelby spun around on the bench and glared at him. "I've not even begun being a bitch to you, Nick, so get over yourself. And as far as slack goes," she said, pausing long enough to grab the half-empty glass of wine on top of the piano and drain it, "I've been cutting you slack for far too long. You don't deserve any. The dead don't give a shit whether you have any slack or not. They want justice, and they deserve it."

He stood up, pointing a finger at her to mark his words. "That's hardly fair, and you know it. You don't think I want justice?"

She got up and marched over to the couch, standing right up in his face, stabbing her own finger at his chest. "I think you want whatever will free you from the guilt on your overburdened conscience. You aren't a sheriff anymore, cowboy. Quit trying to act like all those rules still apply."

"I don't think—"

"Yes, you do!" she yelled back. She tried to take a drink from her empty glass and slammed it down on the end table in frustration. "Shit. I want a cigarette now. Being around you drives me—"

"There's some in the kitchen." It was Jackie, her voice rough and quiet. "I'd like one, too."

"Hey," Shelby said, turning soft and friendly in a heartbeat. "How you feeling, Jackie?"

"Terrible in every way imaginable." She looked it, too, huddled in the bedroom doorway, clutching at the robe wrapped around her. She eyed them suspiciously. "Why are you here?"

"Aspirin?" Shelby wondered, heading for the kitchen.

"By the sink. Cigs are on the fridge. I could really use a drink."

Shelby gave Jackie a disarming smile. "Coffee, juice, or water?"

"Coffee, I guess." She walked out, surveying the remnants of dinner, and stepped around the coffee table to sit on the end of the couch opposite where Nick stood, watching in silence. She curled her feet under herself, crossing her arms over her chest, watching Nick and Shelby with puffy, bloodshot eyes. A moment later, Bickerstaff appeared, hopping into her lap, and the tension abruptly melted away as she let her arms enfold the great mass of orange fur.

This was not a situation 176 years of living gave much familiarity with. Nick could only shift back and forth on his feet uncomfortably.

"Why are you here?" Jackie asked again, her fingers absently stroking the cat.

"We wanted to make sure you got through the night okay," Shelby said. "After yesterday, we thought it best you didn't wake up alone."

Her face flushed a bit at that, and she looked at Nick for a brief second before glancing away. "Thanks, but you didn't have to do that. I . . . It was a rough day, that's all. Did anyone call?"

"The FBI knows we're here," Nick answered. "I talked to Belgerman. He seemed okay with us being here to offer any help that might be needed."

Jackie only nodded, saying nothing, and they avoided looking at each other in silence for a few moments. Shelby appeared to be taking her sweet time making coffee and finding cigarettes. Nick guessed she was doing it on purpose. He had to wonder if Jackie even remembered much of the day before. Peering into her bedroom had provided a strong enough indication of alcohol that he knew she had been drunk off her rocker. Any luck, and the memories would be vague at best.

The sad thing was, he found himself wondering about just what the hell had happened. This went beyond being distraught over the loss of a friend. There was a wound here that went far deeper, and Nick struggled with the feeling of connection he found himself having. The words that came out of his mouth next defied the laws of tact or intelligence.

"Do you remember much about what happened last night?" The heat rising in her face as it turned away from him was all the answer he needed.

After a moment, she looked back at him, her eyes suddenly calculating. "How did you know to come over here when you did? That wasn't coincidence, was it?"

Nick had not prepared himself for answering that question yet. She was in no state of mind to hear that sort of discussion. "Well, not exactly, no."

"Nick," Shelby said with venomous warning in her voice. "Quit being an ass." She came in and set a tray down on the coffee table with a plate full of crackers, a glass of cranberry juice, and three cups of coffee. She had a cigarette in her mouth, lit it, and handed it over to Jackie before lighting one for herself. "Why don't you tell Jackie your story."

"Which story is that?"

She handed him the cup of coffee. "Your story. The whole thing. Besides, if you don't, I will."

"That's cheating," he said, mustering what little defense he could. "I don't think she . . ." The look Shelby gave him said enough. "Fine. I'll tell her."

"The whole thing," she insisted. "Jackie deserves no less."

Nick shrugged. "Still don't think this is the most appropriate moment for this."

"Nick."

"Fine! The whole damn thing it is."

"Oh, goody," Shelby said, a childish grin on her face. She plopped down on the couch next to Jackie, who watched them both with a curious gaze. "This is good. Trust me. Nick tells one hell of a story."

"Funny," he said. "You're real funny." He took a long sip from the coffee cup. "This may take a while."

Jackie shrugged. "It's two AM, and you should have told me this from the start."

Nick winced at the barb. In retrospect she was right. Maybe it would have changed things.

Four AM chimed on the clock before he finished. Nick left out little. He didn't want to. Part of him wanted to tell the story to someone who might not believe, might think he was utterly crazy, or worse, condemn him for his sins. The guilty conscience wanted that, wanted confirmation that what he had done was wrong, that everything he had done or tried to do had been a horrible, bloody mistake. He stopped the story when he got to Laurel. There was no need to bring that up now, and Jackie's glassy-eyed look told him the wounds were far too fresh to endure any discussion of it.

"And that's pretty much how it is," Nick said, unsure how to finish. "No closer than I was a century ago."

"Forever the optimist," Shelby quipped. "So, Jackie, did that leave any stones unturned for you?"

She looked at each of them in silence, sipping at her cold coffee. "You realize how insane all this sounds. Even when we figured it had to be you involved in those old cases, I still could not quite believe it. Only . . . Laur really believed it."

Shelby laid a comforting hand on Jackie's leg. "She had a gift."

Jackie looked for a moment like tears would fall, but she took a deep breath, and the moment passed. "How exactly did you get turned into a vampire? You explained how it works, why blood is needed, but . . . did Drake just open a vein and make you drink or something?"

Nick stared at her. That was the last question he expected her to have, and the last one he wanted to answer. Thankfully, Jackie opted out by waving him off.

"Never mind. That's just too weird a question. I don't really need to know."

"Nick?" Shelby said, a rough edge to her voice.

"What?"

"I know that look."

Shit. The woman had keener senses than a bloodhound. "What look are you referring to?"

"Relief," she replied, turning now to face him, her mouth drawn into a hard line. "You don't want to tell her. Funny thing is, you never really explained that to me either."

Damn the woman! "If it's all the same, I'd rather not. It's really not that important in the scheme of things."

"Nicholas Anderson! You'd better fucking tell me."

Jackie shifted up against the arm of the couch, trying to back away. "It's okay," she said. "Really. It's not important."

Shelby turned and patted her leg. "Yes. It is. Hon, you don't know Nick. He wanted to tell you, but he won't if he thinks it's too painful for you . . . or him." She glared back at Nick now, eyes alight with anger. "He won't hardly lie about anything, but he'll certainly refrain from telling you the truth. So spit it out, Mr. Anderson. I don't give a shit how much the truth makes you squirm."

"Now you're just being a . . ." He stopped himself. She was right, of course, damn her, but could he tell them? Some things were rightfully kept in the dark.

"Bitch? You can say it. I'm going to be a bitch until you can stop being a prick by continuing to hide the truth."

"I'm not hiding anything."

"Bullshit, Nick!"

He wanted to slap her now, make her shut up, but then all that would have done was give him a bloodied nose or lip in response. There would be no denying her, now that she had sniffed out something suspicious.

Jackie began to uncurl her legs. "You know, I can just step out for a minute."

"No." Shelby reached back and pushed Jackie back to the cushions. "Don't you move an inch. You deserve to know every goddamn thing, and so you will."

Nick slowly exhaled, trying to let the tension roll out of him, but it did no good. Instead he began to pace across the living room behind the sofa instead, needing to move. He could not stand still and say the words. "All right. Drake showed me what to do, what I *had* to do to become this . . . what I am, but I didn't drink his blood to turn. He merely gave me a taste. No. That would have been far too easy for him."

Shelby leaned on the back of the couch, watching Nick, thinking and remembering. He realized she would put the pieces together quickly enough. Jackie might not—she wasn't familiar enough with the story—but he was wrong. Jackie opened her mouth to speak even as Shelby's eyes grew wide with shock.

"It was Gwendolyn," Jackie said matter-of-factly, as though it was just another point of interest in the case. "You said she was the last one to die."

Shelby's mouth was open, but it took her a moment to form any words. "Fuck, Nick. You drank Gwen's blood to turn yourself?" Her cheeks were flushing red, and Nick couldn't tell if it was anger for what he had done or the fact he had never told her.

But it was out there now. The grand albatross of shame had flown and landed in the middle of Jackie's living room. Nick turned away, unable to look at them any longer. "Yeah," he whispered. "I drank her blood." He suddenly felt weak in the knees and light-headed and had to sit himself down on the piano bench.

Shelby was up and moving around, stopping every couple seconds to stare at him. "This! This . . . this is the thing, the 'something I will never tell anyone.'" Nick nodded, and she rolled her head in dismay. "God, Nick. What gave you the right to keep that a secret from me? How could you?"

He tried to speak, but his heart had lodged somewhere up in his throat. He should have told her. She should have been the one person he could trust with the horrible deed, but in the end, he had been unable to let go of it, shackled as it was to his soul. He swallowed several times, trying to get some amount of moisture back in his mouth.

"Gwen did," he answered.

She stopped, throwing up her hands. "What?

"Gwen gave me the right. She told me to do it." The image regurgitated itself from the bowels of his brain, fresh as the day it had happened on that day, 144 years ago. Nick clenched his hands into fists to try to keep them from trembling.

"'Do it,' she said. I refused at first. I thought it better to die with her there, but she wouldn't let me." He looked up at Shelby now, his voice loud and shaky. "She said, 'You will do it.' Her voice was so strong for someone with her blood running out onto the floor. She held my hand so hard it actually hurt." He smiled at the memory. Yes, Gwen had been strong, the strongest women he had ever known. "She said, 'You will do this thing and get him for us, Nicholas.'" His voice began to falter now, the words coming out one at a time. "'Get him for everyone he's killed, because . . .'" He stopped for moment, wiping at the tear that finally spilled, a single drop filled with more than a century's worth of sorrow and suffering. "'Because you're the god-damn sheriff.'"

He said the last word, stabbing his finger out at Shelby, much like Gwendolyn had done then, and got up off the bench, feeling the need to move then, before he completely broke down. He walked over to the sliding glass door, looking up at the dark skies that spit rain down on the window, thinking of all the times he had wanted to shed tears for that moment but had refused himself the right.

"Nick . . ." Shelby said, her tone consolatory.

He raised a hand to silence her. "She said . . . 'If you love me, you will do it.'" Nick reached out and touched the drops running down the outside of the window, feeling the tears that now burned down his cheeks.

A moment later, Shelby's hand was on his shoulder. "Goddamnit, babe. You should've told me this a long time ago. You didn't need to carry that around all this time."

He nodded, unable to speak for a moment. Finally, he said, "Sorry."

She slugged him in the shoulder. "If that's for refusing to tell me all these years, then fine, I'll accept. Otherwise, you have nothing to be sorry for, hon." She reached up and turned Nick's face toward hers, and there was a tear running down her cheek as well. "Even the sheriff can be human."

Chapter 37

If you love me. Jackie watched them in silence, Shelby's hand caressing the square line of Nick's jaw, wiping at the tears on his face. The image was hard to comprehend, but she understood. If Carl had been there with a knife in her back, telling her that if she drank her mother's blood, she would have the chance at revenge, she would not have thought twice about it. The thought made her stomach squirm. Maybe she would have chickened out in the end. Watching Nick now had her wondering if she could have stomached the consequences of such an act.

Nick looked different to her now. Everything about him and how he had been made some kind of sense. He wanted justice, even if he had to sacrifice everything to get it, but now she realized just how difficult that was. How could he have known what would happen once that decision was made? Would it have mattered? No, Jackie figured, it would not. He would endure until justice was achieved or die trying. She appreciated that and realized maybe they were more alike than she had thought. Laurel had been right. Jackie sighed and sipped more of her cold coffee.

Shelby stepped away from Nick and pointed at the piano. "Play something, babe. Don't argue with me, just do it."

He glanced over at Jackie, but she could not tell what the look meant, and he gave a helpless shrug and walked back over to the piano bench. Suddenly, Jackie felt self-conscious, remembering the perfect, beautiful baby grand he had sitting in his loft. Hers was likely horribly out of tune in comparison.

"Come on, Jackie. Shower. You look like hell," Shelby said with a smile, motioning at her to get up. "And Nick could use a few minutes, I think."

She glanced over at Nick, who sat staring at the keys. She really wanted nothing more than to hear him play. Shelby waved at her again, more insistent this time, and Jackie finally struggled to her feet, noticing for the first time since waking up that her body hurt. "Okay, you're right, a shower will feel good."

To her surprise, Shelby followed her in and closed the door. Before Jackie could ask what she was doing in there with her, she slid her pants down and sat heavily on the toilet, sighing with obvious relief. "Christ! I never saw that coming. Only a guy could sit on something like that for so long."

Jackie nodded, not exactly comfortable standing there watching the strange, headstrong woman pee in the toilet. She had to admit, though, that Shelby was growing on her. The woman was confident, knew what she wanted, and seemed utterly capable of getting it. She also drank blood. "Yeah, I suppose so."

Notes from the piano began to roll down the hall toward them like a sad wash of fog, seeping into every surface. The music plucked on Jackie's heartstrings with a haunting finesse. God, he really was good.

Shelby looked at the door and frowned. "He never had a name for that piece, but now I think it must be *Ode to Gwen* or something equally sentimental."

"It's very sad," Jackie said.

She nodded. "Yep. That's our Nick, far too maudlin for his own good." She flushed and stood back up. "Okay, shower. Now. I want to go get breakfast soon."

Jackie turned and caught her reflection in the mirror. Shit! She had been sitting out there with them all this time looking like this? More disturbing were the bandages around her wrists. They made her look like a suicide patient. "Are you taking one with me or something?"

Shelby offered a sly smile. "Did you want me to?"

"Um." Jackie gulped. Okay, wrong question. "No, not really."

"Okay then," she replied, laughing. "Get in there and take one. And scrub with something foofy. You still smell like tequila."

Jackie's face flushed. God, she was worse than a mother. Feeling more than a little self-conscious, Jackie hung her robe up on the hook behind the door and stepped into the shower. The music continued to invade the room, the melancholy notes bringing Laurel to mind more strongly than Jackie felt like coping with.

"Personal question?" she asked, sucking in her breath at the sting of water on her wrists as she unwound the gauze that covered them.

"Sure."

"What's it like having to drink blood to stay alive? Doesn't that bother you?"

The electric shaver clicked on, and Jackie watched Shelby's distorted, half-naked form begin shaving her legs.

It was not a scene she would have imagined possible. "Yeah, but it's a bit like being an addict, I think. You feel horrible for doing it, but it's still wonderful when you do. When the other option is death, you sort of adjust your priorities."

"So it's that good? I just can't wrap my mind around that."

"Well," she said, pausing while she perched the other leg on the toilet seat, "it's kind of beside the point when you need it to live, but it's . . . hmmm. You ever tried heroin?"

"What? God, no."

"Ever had such a strong orgasm you nearly passed out?"

"That's rhetorical, right?"

Shelby laughed. "No, actually. But I'm guessing the answer to that is no, which is too bad. You need better lovers then, hon. Anyway, the effect is the most perversely pleasurable thing imaginable."

"Oh." She washed in silence, her brain now turned to the absurd notion of cumming so hard that it could make you pass out. She wondered if Nick had been the one to do that to Shelby. Was it some kind of vampire thing? Some weird power they had?

"Regardless," Shelby continued, "I wouldn't recommend it. The withdrawal symptoms are a bitch."

"But Nick found a way around it. You don't actually drink real blood anymore."

"Discounting the prick in the hospital? Yeah, but it's a poor substitute. We're far weaker on that shit."

"Isn't that better than having to drink someone's blood?"

"According to Nick, yes."

She sounded bitter. He had said something about them refusing to drink any more blood after he had developed the synthetic. "So you disagree with Nick's abstaining?"

Shelby sighed and turned off the razor. "Nick believes

that being moral is better than being just. He's too pigheaded for his own good sometimes."

Jackie thought about that while the water rinsed the shampoo from her hair. That was a tough call. Still, she wondered if she could live with herself if she needed to act immorally to achieve justice. "Why can't you have both?"

The shower curtain pulled back, and Shelby stuck her head in. "You want to catch Laurel's killer?"

The question churned her gut. "More than anything."

Shelby's face looked grim and sad. "Then it's going to take blood. One way or another. Which is going to leave you with the clearer conscience in the end, Jackie? Morality or justice?"

Jackie realized unequivocally what the answer to that was. "I want to kill the fucker."

Shelby nodded and grabbed a towel. "Exactly. And now you know why Nick just pisses me off."

Jackie turned off the water and grabbed the towel. "He's right, though, for the most part." It occurred to her then just how hard it must be for him to try to balance those two clashing needs. "He thinks he's going to die trying to get Drake, doesn't he?"

"So do I," Shelby stated. "It doesn't stop me from doing what I think needs to be done."

Her tone sent a shiver down Jackie's spine. "That include drinking more blood?" Shelby's look answered the question for her. "Just don't tell me when you do, okay? I don't want to have to arrest you."

She laughed. "Hon, at that point, you won't be able to."

The thought chilled her. "You two scare the shit out of me."

"We're not the ones you need to be scared of, Jackie. We're on your side."

"I know that now." She needed them. She needed to work

with a couple vampires to catch another one. This supernatural shit was too much. The aching loneliness for Laurel's presence suddenly burned inside her. Jackie draped the towel over the curtain rod and put her robe back on. "How am I going to do this, Shelby?" She had not meant to ask the question out loud. Shelby was a virtual stranger, yet she felt some sort of friendship to her already.

Shelby turned and looked at Jackie and immediately stepped over to give her a hug. "You start by getting through today, and, little by little, it will get easier. I miss her, too, and I barely knew her."

Jackie swallowed back the tears that threatened to spill again. "It's like the good half of me is gone now. I'm not even sure how to function anymore."

"Aw, hon. I know the feeling, but you'll rebuild yourself, and you'll never forget the things she brought to your life."

She sniffed against Shelby's shoulder. "Yeah, I know, but . . . I never thought it could hurt this much."

Shelby stepped back, her hands on Jackie's shoulders. "You'll need to be strong, Jackie, if you're going to see her again."

"What?"

"If Laurel crosses over again and tries to contact you, you need to be strong enough to handle that."

"Then . . . last night? It was real?" She had not been imagining it. Laurel's ghost had been trying to talk to her. "Fuck! I completely blew it."

"Quit being so hard on yourself. It's not an easy thing to deal with, and you had other issues."

Jackie turned away. "You must think I'm a total nut job."

"Hardly," she reassured her, "but now is not the time to rehash old shit. That's what therapists are for. The question is will you be able to handle seeing Laurel again when she shows up?"

The thought both exhilarated and terrified her. "You think she will?"

Shelby gave her a confident smile. "Oh, I think it's a matter of when, not if."

God! What the hell would she say? *Sorry about the whole "not saving you" thing? Great to see you, and really sorry you're dead? I wish it had been me?* "I don't know if I could talk to her without turning into a blubbering idiot."

"Blubbering idiot is fine," Shelby said and chuckled. "Just don't pass out or run screaming in the other direction."

"I'll really see her again?" Jackie could hardly believe the possibility.

"Almost guaranteed, but it could be anytime or anywhere. I just want you to be prepared for the possibility."

"Should I look forward to this?" she wondered. "What if Laurel's really pissed off?"

Shelby reached up and grabbed Jackie's deodorant off the shelf containing the few toiletries she had. "Laurel? Pissed? We talking about the same beautiful psychic here?"

"Okay, point taken. She wouldn't be pissed. I think. So what do we do now?"

"Breakfast."

The mere word made her stomach rumble in anticipation. "That sounds good. I'm actually hungry."

Shelby followed her into the bedroom and borrowed a clean T-shirt. It was like having an older sister come by and rummage through her stuff. She watched Shelby slip off the old shirt, exposing a long, thorny rose vine tattooed down her spine. The stem disappeared somewhere between her cheeks. Seeing it reminded Jackie that Laurel had had a big thing for tattoos but never had the nerve to go get herself poked with needles to get one.

"Laurel would have really liked you," she said. In its way,

the statement was about as close as Jackie could get at the moment to admitting her like for Shelby.

Shelby gave her a wistful smile. "She did. I'm sad we didn't have more time."

Jackie heaved a sigh. Everything about Laurel was putting her on the constant verge of tears. "Me, too."

"Come on, hurry up," Shelby said. "You need to keep your mind from brooding, and that means getting back to work."

"Am I strong enough for this?" *Why the hell am I asking her this?* She realized it would have been something to ask Laurel. Stability. Shelby Fontaine was about as rock solid as you could get, even if she did have one foot in the grave. "I feel like I have *loser* stamped on my forehead now."

Shelby turned and crossed her arms over her chest, a very "what the fuck" look on her face. "You catch murderers for a living, Jackie. It doesn't come much tougher than that. You didn't catch them just because of Laurel. Prove it to yourself and to her. Remember, she's dead, but she's not gone."

Jackie pulled on her boots and began to tie them. "You realize how ridiculous that sounds."

"And true nonetheless."

Yes. Disturbingly true. Laurel had tried to contact her and would probably try again. Was it possible to want and dread something so much at the same time?

Back out in the living room, Nick stopped his blissfully melancholy song when they exited the bedroom. "We going somewhere?"

Shelby nodded. "Breakfast. There's a Cracker Barrel down the road."

Nick looked at them both, and Jackie wondered what his thoughts were about this whole debacle. His gaze lingered on hers for a moment, studying her. He shrugged. "All right."

She hated the fact that he was so difficult to read. Maybe

Shelby would show her a trick to looking a vampire in the eye without completely freaking out. They were heading out the door when her cell phone rang. Picking it up, she saw that it came from Gamble. It was awfully early for a wake-up call.

"Hey, Jack," he said with concern. "You functional?"

"More or less. Getting some food and coming in."

"Good to hear, 'cause we've got vic number four here."

Damnit. Cracker Barrel had actually sounded good.

Chapter 38

Shelby left in Nick's car to go get her motorcycle and meet them at the scene. Nick now sat silently in the Durango's passenger seat, looking straight ahead. Jackie could not help but feel he was somehow usurping Laurel's spot in her truck. Maybe it was just the silence. Laurel would not have let things be quiet for so long—she would have had something to say, whether important or inane, to fill the void. Jackie wondered if, in fact, Laurel had come up with things to say because she knew the silence made Jackie uncomfortable. It begged the question of just how much Laurel had done in general to keep things running smoothly, because Jackie now realized she had been walking along the brink for a very long time.

"Nick?" She had to talk about something. Maybe it was a male thing to be comfortable in silence, but she could not handle it any longer.

He didn't bother turning. "What?"

"You bothered about earlier, with all that you . . . you know . . . said? If you—"

"No. Just thinking about things."

"Case related? If it is, you might want to clue me in. I've been known to be helpful on occasion."

His glance finally flicked in her direction. "I was thinking about Drake and what happened at the warehouse."

The subject left her mute for a moment while her stomach knotted. *Shit, okay. I can do this. I have to be able to talk about what happened. It's just a case.* "Okay . . . so what gives?"

Nick turned and looked at her, the brown, luminescent eyes appraising. "I thought it better to avoid talking about that incident just now."

She leaned on the horn at some ignorant motorist who had not seen the flashing light mounted on the roof of her truck. Jackie wondered if perhaps Nick was right, but that was not going to stop her. "Are you trying to coddle me?"

"What? Coddle?" He leaned away from her, a look of surprise on his face. "No. I was just . . ." He stopped, and the corner of his mouth turned up a hair. "Yes. I apologize. I just didn't think it wise."

A McDonald's loomed ahead, and Jackie jumped on the brakes, whipping into the parking lot. She pulled in behind three other cars waiting at the drive-through. "You are working with me on this case, aren't you?"

"Of course," he said. "We agreed—"

"Good. I'll readily admit we need yours and Shelby's help on this case. Vampires—or whatever you are—is beyond our scope. We don't have a fucking clue, okay? But if you're going to assist, that means filling me in on everything and anything that might be pertinent to this case. It's that whole give-and-take of information, formulating plans of attack, and all the other bullshit that goes with it."

"I realize that, Jackie, but, it's just . . . I know everything must be pretty damn raw right now."

Her knuckles went white on the steering wheel as she gripped it in frustration. "You're right. It's raw as hell, and this is really fucking hard right now, but I'll manage. So spare my feelings when other people's lives aren't on the line, okay?" She lowered the window as they reached the speaker. "Egg McMuffin and a large coffee, black. What do you want, Nick?"

"No cash on me," he said.

Jackie rolled her eyes. "Two hash browns, sausage and egg biscuit, another large coffee, black. That's it." She pulled forward, staring straight ahead. God! Five minutes with the man, and he was already annoying the crap out of her. "I think the FBI can front you for some fast-food if you can manage not to treat me like a cracked egg."

She paid for the food and handed Nick his bag and coffee. He gave her a hesitant smile. "Thanks. I'll try not to coddle you anymore."

Admittedly, Jackie knew she wanted nothing more. Anything to protect her from the bottomless hole that had opened in her gut, and the despair and loneliness that gnawed at her insides. She dug the sandwich out of her bag and began to eat before they had pulled back out onto the road. Crap that it was, it tasted damn good.

"I'd appreciate that," she said. "We're both professionals here, and we have a job to do. So let's get to it." At least she sounded confident.

She watched him lay a hash brown between the biscuits with the sausage and take a huge bite. After a moment, he washed it down with coffee. "I was thinking about what Drake did when he left the scene."

Jackie had not even considered that fact in the time since. Drake had just vanished, and at the time, just the fact he had gone was all that mattered. There had been more important things going on. She shoved the images out of her mind. "He just up and vanished. Shelby got off a couple shots on him, didn't she?"

"Too late by then. He'd already stepped through to Deadworld."

"This is bad because?"

"It's bad because I had thought for all this time that you couldn't do that, that crossing over was basically it. Once in Deadworld, you were pretty much dead."

God how she hated that name. Why couldn't he call it something else, like "the other side" or "Ghostland"? "So he can go over and come back whenever he wants to?"

"Apparently."

This did not sound like it would help them much. "Can you go there?"

He shrugged. "Never tried. I think it must require a lot of blood to hold the door open like that."

"Great. Then how can we catch the bastard?"

"That's what I've been trying to figure out. He can do that at will, but I have no idea how we can."

"Lovely."

They reached the scene of victim number four under a cloak of ashen, threatening skies and the whirling flash of lights from a dozen law-enforcement vehicles. Jackie pulled her Durango into the parking lot of the Julietta Marconni Assisted Living Community and turned off the engine. She stared at the bank of blinking lights and yellow strands of crime-scene tape cordoning off the front of the building. Her mouth went dry, and clammy hands worked nervously on the wheel. To her horror, Jackie realized she was afraid to get out of the truck.

Nick opened his door. "You ready, Agent Rutledge?"

Jackie could not make her hands let go of the wheel. She licked her lips and said nothing, her blank stare reflecting the orange, red, and blue flashing lights. She wanted Laurel there with her. Not having her there felt completely and terribly wrong.

Nick's hand came to rest on her shoulder. "You okay, Jackie?"

She shook her head. "No." So much for sucking it up and dealing with your shit.

"Hey," he said, his voice both calm and demanding. "Look at me." When she refused, he gave her shoulder a squeeze. "Jackie, look at me."

Jackie forced her head around, tearing her gaze away from the overwhelming scene in front of her. "What?"

His eyes locked on to hers, and this time she could not look away. That soft glow and intensity held her. "You can do this. You are strong, capable, and more than able to work on your own."

She sighed and let go of the wheel. "I know. It just feels all wrong."

He nodded. "I know, and it will for a while. It's hard, but you can do it. Trust me."

Jackie shivered and sucked in a deep breath. "Goddamn, this sucks. Okay, let's get this over with."

Nick let go of her and stepped out of the truck. Jackie could feel the lingering imprint of his fingers on her shoulder, and she wondered if he had just pulled one of his voodoo mind tricks on her. Did it matter? The paralyzing fear had subsided into the background, and for the moment it was all she needed. She got out and followed Nick toward the chaos.

Inside the front door, Jackie stepped right into Pernetti and his flappy-lipped grin. "Looking good there, Jack."

Before she could open her mouth to reply, Gamble walked up behind him and cuffed the back of his head. "Shut the hell up, Pernetti." Gamble smiled at her, a poorly disguised look of sympathy on his face. "Can't tell you how glad I am you're here, Jack." He thrust out his hand to Nick. "Mr. Anderson. Thanks for coming to help out. We appreciate it."

Nick shook his hand. "Yeah, no problem, Agent Gamble." He looked around the lobby, shaking his head. "I should've guessed. Plain as goddamn day."

Everyone turned to try to follow his gaze. Gamble looked excited for a moment. "What? You see something?"

"This place. I should have thought of it. My company funded this place. It's named after my mother."

Jackie stared at him. "No shit?" She was getting annoyed, as they were all ignoring the fact that she was supposed to be in command of this case.

"Corporate profits put to good use," Nick replied with a wan smile.

She had no energy for a snappy retort. "So we know why he picked this place. Great. Tell me what we've got here, Gamble." Standing around was getting on her nerves.

Gamble waved them forward through the lobby and led them toward a door on the far side. "She's in here. Cleaning crew found her this morning about six. Same as the others, looks like. Scene looks pretty clean, from what I can tell. She's got some kind of rag doll tucked under her arm, which I'm guessing has some kind of tie to Nick."

The room was filled with the faint, sickly sweet scent of death, which had Jackie pausing as she entered the room, the image of Laurel on the stainless-steel table filling her head. There were numerous chairs and tables in the room, most of them filled with what looked like baskets of yarn and sewing needles. There were quilts full of color and detailed with intricate patterns and needlework hanging on the walls.

Nick looked at the elderly woman sitting in a rocking chair in the corner of the room. One arm dangled down, a thin, dark trail of dried blood running from elbow to fingertip. She looked otherwise like she might have slumped over from a stroke or heart attack, if not for the small hole in her arm.

"This some kind of quilting or crocheting class?" Jackie wondered.

"Yep," Gamble said. "All sorts, apparently. They make

the quilts to raise money for community projects. I guess they sell pretty well, from what the director said."

"I have a couple of them myself," Nick added quietly. He reached down and gingerly took the doll from under the woman's arm. "The doll is my daughter's. My mother made several of them for her." His shoulders visibly slumped as he held the doll in his hands. "This one was her favorite. They went everywhere together."

Jackie felt a pang of sympathy for him. He had been forced to relive his own horrors again and again. She had not truly understood the sadistic nature of the vengeance being exacted upon Nick. "She'll be next then, right? Some representation of your daughter?"

He turned and looked at Jackie, nodding once. The look on his face pained her. "Yes, my daughter will be the last, an eight-year-old girl, probably strawberry-blond hair, brown eyes, thin as a cornstalk."

Gamble pulled out a pad of paper and scrawled down some notes. "Shit, Nick. I'm sorry, man. I can't even imagine. We need to get moving. I really want to nail this fucker."

"Okay," Nick said. "What leads do you have on this?"

"Nothing yet. Nobody saw anything. Parking-lot video shows nothing, so he carried her up here from somewhere. I've got some guys checking the grounds—"

Nick shook his head. "They won't find anything. He didn't walk here."

"So he just popped in out of thin air?" Gamble took a step back in disbelief when he realized Nick was being serious. "Christ. This is so fucked up. Jack? You can take over anytime now."

Take over what? She had no idea where to go with what they had any more than he did. How did you deal with a guy who ignored the usual laws of being human? "I'll guess this scene is clean. The doll is the clue, but what we do with it, I have no idea right now. Nick? You think of any connections at all the doll might have?"

The frustration on his face was apparent. "Not off the top of my head, no. It might not have any connection at all."

Shelby stepped into the room then, looking a little wind-blown. Jackie realized the speed with which she had arrived defied reason. "Something to do with doll making, perhaps?"

Gamble snorted. "That would narrow it down to every craft store in the Chicago area, not to mention any community groups that do any of that stuff."

They would never cover those kinds of possibilities within the day or so they likely had. There had to be something though. Standing around waiting for a killer to kidnap a little girl so he could drain her blood was unthinkable. "We have nothing else right now, so at least it's a start. The guys in the Geekroom might be able to make some kind of connection for us." She needed to contact them ASAP to find out if there had been anything new in the past day.

"And," Gamble added, "you need to get downtown and get clearance to be doing this. I went out on a limb getting you over here, Jack. So go sign whatever papers you have to before you put my ass in a sling."

Shit. That meant talking to Tillie. "I will, don't worry. I'm going to want updates every hour, and if we don't have anything definite by five, I'm taking this to the six-o'clock news."

Gamble winced. Shelby smiled in agreement, and Nick looked resigned to the obvious publicity it would make. They had no choice. A public warning just might give whatever little girl Drake had picked out a chance.

"Boss may not like that one too much," Gamble said.

Jackie shrugged. "He'll deal."

The annoying chirp of a cell phone interrupted them, and Nick pulled his out of his pocket, cocking an eyebrow as he looked at the screen. Even before it reached his ear, Jackie heard what sounded a lot like someone throwing up.

"Cynthia?" Nick said, looking worried. "Cyn, you okay?" The sound of shattering glass had him pulling the phone away from his ear. "Shit. We need to leave. Now."

Shelby stepped up to him and grabbed his arm. "What's going on?"

Nick shoved the phone into his pocket and was already moving toward the door. "No idea. Cyn's in trouble."

"Need our help?" Gamble said.

"Maybe," Nick called out over his shoulder. He was already running for the door.

By the time Jackie caught up to them, Shelby was on her BMW. Nick was getting into the driver's side of the Durango. He motioned to her to hurry up. "Give me your keys."

For a second, Jackie hesitated. She'd never handed the keys over to anyone other than Laurel. She didn't trust anyone else to drive her around, but the look of panic on Nick's face pushed the trepidation aside, and she tossed her keys to him before getting into the passenger side.

"Where we going?"

"Not far. Buckle up."

He gunned the engine and didn't even bother backing out. The Durango spun its wheels for a moment and then churned up grass and mud as it sped across the lawn toward the street.

Not far was a twenty-minute ride through hell. They followed Shelby, catching up to and losing her several times as she dodged around traffic, jumped several sidewalks, and occasionally defied the laws of physics. Jackie braced her feet on the floorboard and held on to the handle over the door for dear life. The flashing light on top did little good, as Nick was going far too fast for anyone to notice in time to pull over to the side of the road. For the first time, she realized how Laurel must have felt during the few chases they had been on together. She swore never to take being a passenger for granted again.

Sliding around a corner into a quiet neighborhood of mostly 1930s bungalows, Nick finally eased off the gas as they approached the end of the street. "Call nine-one-one."

Jackie then realized the source of his order, a black plume of smoke rising over the treetops up on their left. She barely got the call through before Nick bounded over the curb and slid to a halt in the front yard of a house in chaos.

"This is FBI Agent Rutledge. We have a house fire at . . . Nick, where are we?"

"Thirteen-fifty Applewood!" he yelled at her. He was already out the door.

Jackie repeated the address and left the phone in the seat of the truck before leaping after him.

Shards of glass were scattered across the front lawn, the remnants of the living room window having been blown out. Flames licked at the sides while a curtain of black smoke whipped upward into the sky. Shelby's motorcycle lay on its side in the grass, and Jackie ran around it, heading for the front door, where Nick shoved Shelby aside and kicked it in off its hinges. He started to move in but immediately turned and ducked when a piece of furniture, an end table by the look of it, bounced off his back and went tumbling into the yard.

Jackie drew her Glock and crouched as she approached the blown-out window, but the haze of smoke made it difficult to see what was going on inside.

"Stay back!" Shelby yelled. "The little fucker is on a rampage."

"Is Cynthia in there?" she wondered.

Nick turned and pointed a finger at her. "Stay here. Don't come in unless I say so." His finger shifted to Shelby.

"You, too!" With that, he assumed a defensive crouch and darted inside.

What the fuck? Since when did the law remain outside while the civilian entered a potentially lethal situation? Shelby looked at Jackie and rolled her eyes in Nick's direction. She didn't need to say anything for Jackie to know what Shelby intended. Jackie returned the nod and ran up next to the door, gun held at the ready. With Shelby's second nod indicating her readiness, they rolled around the edge of the doorway and entered the house.

Smoke clouded the initial view looking from the entry into the living room, but Jackie didn't even have time to react to the box of CDs that came zipping out of the gloom and caught her solidly in the thigh.

"Son of a bitch!" She leaped across the hardwood floor to take cover against the edge of the archway leading into the room. Able to see inside more clearly, the scene froze her in her tracks before she could follow behind the hunched-over form of Nick.

A tornado had spawned in the middle of Cynthia's living room. Every loose item in the room, from vases to books and every possible form of decorative knickknack, whirled about the room with deadly speed. Fire was beginning to take over the ceiling above the front window, and an overstuffed chair beside it was spewing forth dark, acrid smoke.

In the middle of the floor between the window and the fireplace on the far wall, two figures, pale and translucent, were engaged in a fight. It looked like a poorly functioning hologram was playing out the fight scene from a movie. One figure wore a derby hat with a long trench coat and had the smaller, far slighter figure in a choke hold. Jackie watched the smaller one stomp on the arch of the derby man, and he made a silent yelp of pain before letting go. The figure turned, and Jackie's breath froze in her lungs.

It was Laurel. Jackie fired a shot at the man, only to see a cloud of plaster explode from the wall behind him.

"Use that table, Jackie!" Shelby said before diving into a roll across the floor to reach Nick, who knelt on the floor beside the far end of the couch on the other end of the room.

A small table stood behind Jackie in the entry, a pair of flowering plants perched on top. She was not quite sure what Shelby meant until a candlestick whistled by her head and dented the plaster in the wall on the far side of the entry. She quickly holstered the gun and grabbed the table, hoisting it up before her as a shield.

She followed them in, one eye on Laurel, who struggled against the far more powerful man. She blocked his round-house punches, flashing her fist in with quick jabs to the man's face. Where had she learned to fight like that? Something heavy and wooden slammed into the table, nearly wrenching it from her hands, and Jackie was forced to re-focus her attention on Nick, who was struggling to his feet with Cynthia's limp body cradled against his chest. A six-inch metal figurine bounced off his shoulder, and Nick dropped back to a knee, swearing up a storm.

"Get out of here!" he ordered. "Run!"

Shelby grabbed the couch, picking it up from one end, and spun it around at the flying objects, knocking a good many of them to the ground. Nick, hunched over the unconscious body of Cynthia, made a lunging run for the front door. Jackie turned and caught a six-inch-diameter candle, spinning like a Frisbee, in the side of her left knee, dropping her to the floor before she even got the cry of pain out of her mouth. The table shield went tumbling to the floor as her hands went straight to the explosion of agony in her knee.

"Fuck! Shelby—" Her call for help got cut off when a two-inch-thick book jammed itself into her ribs just under her right breast. Another candle, the size of a softball, caught her in the left side just beneath the ribs, and the last of her burning breath escaped her lungs in a whoosh. She blinked back tears, partly from pain, the rest from the smoke, and began to crawl for the door.

"Take her, Shel!" Nick's voice yelled ahead of her. A moment later, he was beside Jackie, his hand digging into her arm.

Jackie felt herself pulled half up off the floor as he dragged her back to the entry. She finally struggled to her feet, shaking loose of his grip. *I can take care of myself, goddamnit.*

Something bounced off Nick's back, and he winced. "Go, damn you."

"I can handle—"

Jackie never completed the sentence, as yet another of Cynthia's candles found its way out of the living room and struck her in the side of the head, sending the world into darkness.

Chapter 39

The firemen were rolling their hoses back up, satisfied that Cynthia's house was safe from smoldering back into flames. Water dripped from the eaves like tears over the gaping wound of the front window, exposing the now hollowed, gutted living room inside, strewn with soggy, smashed debris. At least it was repairable. Cynthia had been wheeled away, still unconscious, but stable. Nick had hoped she would wake enough to offer some explanation, but all he could do now was hypothesize.

Something had come for her. Likely a goon of Drake's. The question was, why? Laurel had come to stop him. How had she known? What was happening on the other side? How? He wondered about Reg. He generally had the beat on anything ghostly going on. It worried Nick that nothing had been heard from Reg for a while now, and his call to him earlier had gone unanswered. Deadworld was becoming the great unknown factor in all this. Drake's trump card. It was all a matter of blood. Nick turned away from the ruins of Cynthia's bungalow, hands thrust in his pockets, and made his way toward the street.

Shelby's motorcycle was gone. She had left almost immediately to check on Cynthia and then head out to look for

Drake. Jackie sat in the front seat of Belgerman's car, parked behind the paramedic's truck. She had refused to go to the hospital, even though the knot on the side of her head likely indicated a mild concussion. She should have been in the damn hospital. Against his better judgment, he approached and squatted down next to her, holding on to the open door for support.

"Not going to the hospital, are you, Agent Rutledge?"

She opened her eyes and lifted the cold pack from the side of her head. "Would you?"

Nick grimaced. "No, but that's beside the point. You might have a concussion."

"And a little eight-year-old girl might be dead by tomorrow if we don't figure out what the fuck to do."

The better part of him knew to just get up and walk away. There was no point arguing with her—stubborn to the bone, which likely accounted for her appeal in a frustrating-beyond-reason kind of way. She would keep going until she collapsed, and in her current condition would likely serve the case little good.

"You aren't going to catch anyone at the moment, Jackie. You need rest. I'm surprised Belgerman hasn't ordered you home."

She stared at him for a moment, mouth working in furious silence. "You done being good samaritan now? Do you feel better that you've checked up on me? If you hadn't been playing the fucking hero, I might have gotten out of there without getting waxed."

"Hero?" He bit back the rest of his retort. No point fanning flames. She was hurt and pissed. "It was a bad situation in there, Jackie. It could have been a lot worse."

"I'm not blind! Christ, I saw what was going on," she snapped back but then sagged into the seat with a groan, putting the pack to her head. "What the fuck was going on in there?"

Nothing like a concussion to batter the bravado down. He just wanted to make sure she was going to take care of herself. She looked so small and fragile now, battered, bruised, and emotionally wrung out. If he had been Belgerman, there was no way he would have let her continue. Beyond the fact that the case was too dangerous, she had lost her partner. He had figured there was mandatory leave when events like that happened, unless of course Belgerman was letting it slide until the case was over. Nick would have to ask him about that. If she could be forced to sit the rest of this out, all the better.

"My guess is Drake sent someone to get Cynthia, and Laurel came to stop him."

Jackie was quiet for so long, Nick thought she had fallen asleep. Finally, she said, "How? Why? I don't get it."

"Neither do I," he said. "I'm going to the hospital after this to check on Cyn. Hopefully, she'll be conscious and be able to shed some light on things."

Jackie nodded. After a moment, a single tear trickled out of a closed, puffy eye, and Nick resisted the urge to reach out and wipe it away. "Laurel's dead, and she's still working the case."

He had not even considered that line. So much for sending Jackie home. She would probably kill the person who tried. "It seems Laurel is trying to help us. I am, too, Jackie. I've been dealing with this kind of thing for a long time. If I tell you to keep back, it's not to play hero—"

She sat up, eyes suddenly alive with indignation. "Are you running the FBI now, Nick? Did Belgerman die and make you boss?"

"Look, Jackie—"

"No! You look." She threw the pack at him, and Nick stumbled back, catching the pack against his shoulder. "You're just a fucking civilian PI. This is my case! You don't give the orders around here, Sheriff." The last came out with a nasty sneer in her voice. "You want to play hero, go . . . just go! Leave me the fuck alone."

Nick stood up. It was time to bail before things got even uglier. "All right. When you've got things situated again, call me. I'll be out looking for Drake."

"Everything okay over here?" Belgerman walked up and stopped behind Nick, his face heavy with worry.

"It's fine," Nick said. "I was just leaving."

Jackie reached out and yanked the car door closed. "Can we get the hell out of here?"

Belgerman cocked an eyebrow at Nick. "Sure. Things appear to be under control here. We need to get that head of yours looked at."

Jackie looked incensed. "The paramedics already—"

"Looked at it and said you should go in to make sure you don't have a concussion or cracked ribs or anything else. So just sit back and relax, Jack. I'm ordering you to have it looked at. Better?"

"Fucking-A. Fine!" She fumed in silence as the window went up.

Belgerman gave her a sarcastic little smile and laid a hand on Nick's shoulder. "Call Gamble and check in with him to see what's going on, if he needs your help with anything. You got his number?"

"Yeah. Thanks."

"Was this Drake's handiwork, Mr. Anderson?" he wondered, waving his arm at the house.

"Looks that way."

"Okay, I think we need to have a little more informative briefing from you on things. Like this afternoon."

Nick agreed. "Tell me when. I'll be there."

"Good. I'll let you know by noon."

Belgerman walked around and opened up the car's door. "Hey, you got a ride back?"

"I can bring Agent Rutledge's vehicle in." He hoped that was all right. He had no other transportation available.

"Just take it to your place and lock it up. We'll send someone out later to pick it up."

"Will do. Thanks."

Jackie was shaking her head, muttering something under her breath, and Nick was glad the window was up so he didn't have to hear. He felt bad for her, and the guilt ate at his insides. He had tried to keep them out of this, tried to keep her away, but there was no denying a woman like Jackie Rutledge. She was like the hunting dog who had found itself in a losing battle with a bear, but once latched on to it, she was not going to let go until either she or the bear was dead.

Nick shook his head and headed for the Durango. The bear was winning.

Chapter 40

Jackie finally turned to look at John after ten minutes of silence in the car. She had feigned sleep in the hopes of quelling any conversation he might have, but now that he was actually saying nothing, the silence was beginning to bother her. He glanced at her once, expressionless, for the most part, and then faced back toward the road. Jackie figured it best not to ask what was on his mind. If it was important, he would tell her.

Five minutes after they left, she had felt a pang of guilt over sniping at Nick. He likely had saved her from more serious injury, even if she could have crawled out of there. She just remembered Laurel, her body gray and transparent in the smoke, fighting the man in the derby hat. Ghosts, both of them. Jackie sighed. She could not recall ever feeling more out of control of a case in her life.

"I'll take a long vacation after we nail this guy, sir. I swear, a month at least. I think it will be over in a few days."

John gave her a smile that was some mixture of sadness and understanding. "You still have to speak with Tillie, Jack. I bend a lot of rules, but not that one."

"We're talking only a few days," Jackie said, trying not to sound desperate. "I'm good for that at least."

"You're good for nothing at the moment, Jack," he replied, annoyance creeping in at last. "You're lucky I didn't force you to stay the night in the hospital for observation. You can go talk to her and then get a few hours sleep, or you can sign a vacation slip now, and I'll see you back in the office next month. Clear enough?"

Jackie humphed and then winced at the pain it caused in her side. "With all due respect, sir, you suck."

"Privilege of being the boss," he said as they pulled into the underground garage. "Now go see Auntie Tillie, and I'll see how you're doing after. I'm going to try to get Mr. Anderson down here to brief us more thoroughly on just what it is we're dealing with. No more special investigators for the supernatural. Everyone is going to deal with it."

Jackie shoved her door open as they came to a stop. "I guess I shouldn't take that personally, should I?"

"Jack, you know what I meant. You're a damn good agent who is hurting bad. Go speak to Tillie. If she gives you the go-ahead, I won't second-guess her."

She got out and slammed the door. There were no words he could soothe her with when it came to speaking to their local shrink. Doing her damnedest to look normal, Jackie favored her leg, limping over to the elevator, and left Belgerman behind.

Seven floors up, Jackie stepped out onto the human-resources floor, an area she saw maybe once or twice a year. An innocuous-sounding part of the floor was entered through a door labeled PERSONNEL SERVICES. Matilda's office was at the end of the hall beyond the small reception area. The carpets were plush and silent, the colors soft and muted. Everything about the damn place screamed calmness. Jackie crossed her arms over her chest, about to tell the fluffy little receptionist she was there to see Aunt Tillie, when Tillie stepped out in the hall and motioned her down the hall.

Jackie eyed the young woman behind the desk. "You beeped her, didn't you?"

She gave Jackie a faint smile. "I was really sorry to hear about Ms. Carpenter. I liked her."

The snarky retort Jackie had been building up died in her mouth. "Yeah, me, too." She limped off down the hall to meet her doom.

Aunt Tillie was sitting down in her soft, plump, cushioned leather chair across from an identical one that Jackie found herself sinking into. She would have stood, just to annoy Tillie, but the knee was killing her, and she had to admit that staying awake was becoming a struggle. The chair could have almost been termed a love seat, perfect for curling up in, and much as she tried to dump the thoughts, sleep kept invading her system in all directions. *A little nap, couple hours, I'll be good for the afternoon.*

"Hello, Jackie," Tillie said, her voice filled with concern. From a tray beside her, she filled a cup with some tea and set it down on the small coffee table between them. Behind her on the other side of the chair was her big, old mahogany desk that everyone secretly wished to kill her for. Nobody in the building—or most of the city, for that matter—had such a lovely, ornate, and perfectly polished desk. The skyline outside the floor-to-ceiling window was a shroud of gray, swirling mist.

"Dr. Erikson."

"Drink," she said. "It will help you relax, and lord knows you look like you could use it."

"I'm fine, really," Jackie said. She didn't even believe herself. Sitting up straighter, she made an effort to smile, but sitting across from the big, motherly woman—in her green cashmere sweater, a pleated khaki skirt, her little gold chain with the charms, and the little pearl earrings—had Jackie's stomach in knots. "Okay, I'm not fine, but I'll live." God, the woman made her want to crawl out of her skin!

"Dear, relax. This is informal. No notes, nothing on record, just a conversation between two grown women."

Jackie contemplated picking up the tea, but feared her shaky hands would make the cup rattle in the saucer. Any more signs of nerves, and, no doubt, Tillie would have her shipped off to the psych ward. "I was ordered here, Dr. Erikson."

"Tillie, please." She sipped on her tea for a moment. "All right, so it isn't a social call, but still. You can let that guard down for two seconds, Jackie. I'm not going to recommend you take time off. Yet."

Just like that? No prodding? No "tell me what's really going on"? She had gotten enough of that from her during her last psychological evaluation. She had dug around in Jackie's past enough to know a good deal about what was really going on, and to this point, Jackie had successfully avoided any direct conversations with her about it. "Seriously? You'll let me finish this case, just like that? No questions? No 'what about Laurel'? Nothing?"

"Jackie," she said, setting down her tea and leaning forward. Her hands were folded together, arms resting on her knees. "Look at me, please."

Jackie had turned away without thinking when Tillie had leaned forward. There was a soft, pitying look about her face that made her stomach squirm, and not so much because she didn't want that sympathetic, trusting gaze falling upon her, but because she realized it made her want to talk. Tillie was worse than the vampires.

"What?" Jackie asked.

"I know you're hurting physically, emotionally, spiritually.

You look beat in more ways than one. If you agree to come back and see me after this is done . . . on a weekly basis . . . I won't tell John you should have a month off at a minimum."

What? Extortion? The kindly, plump mother of the FBI's Chicago office was resorting to extortion? "Why would I agree to that? You know I have no desire to be here."

She leaned back and picked up her tea, sipping at it for a moment. "Because if you don't, dear, I suspect your career in the FBI is over."

There was no threat implied. They both knew what she referred to, and Jackie chewed on her lip, pondering the choice, and suddenly found herself appalled that she could even consider trading justice for Laurel over her own discomfort, pain, and embarrassment. "Fine. It's a deal. I can't believe you're resorting to such low tactics. You're a sneaky bitch when you want to be, Tillie."

She laughed. "You have no idea."

"Why do I get the feeling you've been planning for this moment for years?"

"Oh, but I have," she said, the smile turning sly. "I knew it would come. One day something would come along that would mean more to you than protecting that hurt, twelve-year-old girl locked away in your heart."

Jackie swallowed hard. Damn her. Bitch was doing it on purpose. Didn't matter if she was right. "We done here then?"

Tillie shook her head. "No. I want to know what's happened on this case from your point of view. John filled me in, but I think I find it's lacking some things. I'd like to hear your side."

"Why?"

"Humor me, Jackie. I need it regardless to note your current state of mind so I can file the proper paperwork."

"Are you this big a pain outside the office?"

She just smiled. "Pick up your tea, if you can without spilling, and tell me what's happened."

Jackie took a deep breath. Therapists were the devil, no two ways about it. "I'm not thirsty."

Chapter 41

Nick watched Jackie doze off for the fourth time during his briefing. Gamble kindly kept nudging her, but Nick wished he would just let her be. The case appeared to finally be unnerving the rest of them. It had begun to sink in, the fact they were dealing with something both more and less than human. Nick held out the vague hope that he could set the stage by having Reggie show up, but Reggie remained curiously and disturbingly silent. Even the smart-aleck Pernetti kept his mouth shut.

After sixty minutes of explaining everything he and Shelby could do, what he had seen Drake do over the years, and his own meager efforts to stop him, Nick had the group about as up to speed as he was. They now knew what their capabilities were.

"Thank you, Mr. Anderson," Belgerman said, standing up from his seat. "I'm not sure how much it will help, but we are more informed than we were, which can't hurt."

"If we catch him on this side, can we keep him from crossing back over?" Gamble wondered after leaning against Jackie yet again.

"The crossing over is, like I said, a mystery to me as

well," Nick said. "I've never done it. I intend to do it only one time."

"And what if the only way to catch him is to follow him to wherever the fuck it is he goes?" Pernetti asked.

Nick could only shrug. "I don't know. Let's hope it doesn't come to that. Has any information been dug up on him?"

"No," Gamble answered. "We're trying to trace him through the Rolls and the old furniture store, but it's been nothing but dead ends. Something might break, but it could take days or longer before we find it."

"We probably have less than two," Belgerman added. "So let's get back to it, everyone. Mr. Anderson and Ms. Fontaine are our main links to tracking this guy down right now, so everyone keep an ear out for their call if and when it comes."

It didn't matter. Drake could track them easily enough if he had access to spirits on the other side to do his grunt work. Cynthia at least would be fine—some smoke inhalation, a cracked rib, and some bumps and bruises. He wondered what she had been up to in order to bring down one of Drake's goons. He needed to keep her out of all this. She needed to stay on the sidelines.

Shelby had said little since Cynthia's, but the undercurrents in her voice had told Nick all he needed to know. She would be out for blood at the first opportunity, and Nick knew there would be no stopping her.

"Jackie, go get some sleep. You slept through half the meeting." Belgerman's tone indicated that it was not a suggestion.

She stood up, one hand leaning on the table for support. Nick could see the imperceptible wavering of her body. She would not even be able to stand much longer, much less stay awake. "I'll grab a cot in the break room."

"No," Belgerman said, sounding much like a father. "You'll lay down on a real fucking bed and get five or six hours minimum of sleep. If I hear from you before eight o'-clock tonight, you're fired." He pointed a finger at her, stabbing the air for emphasis. "And take some goddamn meds, for Christ's sake. Being awake does you no good if you're in too much pain to walk."

"It looks worse than it is," Jackie said, limping toward the door.

"Bullshit," Belgerman snapped back. "Gamble, take her home, and you better find someone to post there. She might be a target now, for all we know."

"That's a waste," she retorted. "I don't need a damn babysitter. I just need—"

"Do you know that you aren't a target?"

"Sir, I'm not . . . Okay, fine, I don't know. I can just sleep here anyway."

"People doze here, Jack. They don't rest. You going to push me on this?"

Her shoulders slumped, and she leaned wearily against the doorjamb. "No, sir."

"Good."

Nick offered a pained smile even as he spoke up. "She can stay at my place. I've got extra rooms, and I can hang out there until this evening. If Shelby gets a hit on Drake, you send someone out, and I'll head into town. Drake won't be coming to my place."

"What?" Jackie pushed herself back straight. "I'm not sleeping at your place. That's crazy."

Belgerman's eyes narrowed. "Why is that crazy? Sounds like a reasonably legit plan to me. You aren't staying here, and, honestly, I trust Nick's opinion on this stuff. If he says you'll be safe out there, that's where you should be."

Nick watched Jackie pondering the trap she was in. Her mouth worked in soundless agitation, and the look she gave might have melted lesser men. He knew she didn't want to, but, like it or not, she would be protected at his house, and if he guessed right, she would not want to look chicken by saying she would rather be at home pulling an extra man out of the search for Drake.

She threw up her hands. "Fine. Stupid fucking idea, but fine. I'll get a couple hours in and then come back down to help out. That okay with you two?"

Belgerman nodded. "That's fine. I'll see you back here—"

The door slammed shut behind her as she limped out. Nick let out his breath. Maybe it was an even poorer decision than he'd first thought. "She'll need more than two hours."

"Don't worry, Nick. She'll be fine once you get her out there and in a bed." He chortled at his own wording the moment he finished. "Sorry, didn't mean it quite that way."

Nick gave him a feeble grin. "I wasn't even close to taking it that way. I think she would prefer to strangle me at the moment."

"Probably right," John said with an amused shrug. "Glad she's at your house and not mine. She's on vacation the second this case is done."

She needed that vacation now. Yesterday. Nick could not help wondering to himself if Jackie would even make it to the end of this case. Emotional stress was particularly hard to manage if you were physically hurting. He knew that well enough. "She really needs it."

"Nick," he said, laying a hand on Nick's shoulder. "You're absolutely sure this Drake guy is not going to come anywhere near your place?"

He nodded once. "Trust me, John. He's too close to the end, and he won't risk mucking his plans to come after one little beat-up FBI agent on the off chance I get lucky and get him. She's safe."

"Okay, thanks. This is just a little against protocol, but we don't really have one when it comes to dealing with vampires."

Nick shook his hand and left to track down Jackie. *This is just a little against my protocol as well.*

Chapter 42

A little demon inside Jackie's head continued to jab his pointy little fork at her skull. His cousin lanced her ribs with a shish kebab skewer on every breath, and some torturous little bastard with hot coals and a cheese grater was telling her to keep the knee still or else. Mostly, however, it was the notion of going to sleep at Nick's. Why had she agreed to such a stupid idea? Grief. It had to be the only logical explanation for thinking that napping at the vampire's pad was a good idea.

He stopped at her apartment so she could pick up extra clothing, and grabbing a few things from the bathroom gave Jackie time to actually look at her reflection in a mirror for the first time since the attack at Cynthia's house. "God, I really look like shit." Then again, that was probably a better state of affairs when hanging with a vampire. Maybe the attraction for blood was less if you were unattractive. "Nuts," she muttered and grabbed the small bag with a brush, toothbrush and paste, and deodorant. "I'm completely fucking nuts."

Outside the bathroom, Jackie realized there was a dent in her wall. She could not even recall how it had gotten there. She fed Bickerstaff an extra-large bowl of cat food with some tuna mixed in, scooped his cat box, and marched back out the door with her duffel. The sky was threatening, storm clouds rolling in from the west. There would be rain. All the better, Jackie figured. It suited her mood.

The rain had begun to fall by the time they reached Nick's, and the misty drizzle, along with the fading, late afternoon light, gave the house a warm, inviting look. Fucker. Why couldn't he live in a shitty, two bedroom apartment like every other lowlife private dick?

Fortunately for Nick, he had kept quiet the entire trip out, letting Jackie doze, her head propped against her hand. She had been ready for him to say something, anything remotely tactless, and give her a reason to tell him to fuck off, but he had not. He had known to leave well enough alone. He said nothing until the clunk of the garage door behind them made Jackie jump in her seat.

"I'll take your bag into the spare room and get things situated for you."

Jackie looked at his hand as if he held a cockroach in his palm. "I'll hold on to it, thanks. Just show me the room, and I'll get my couple hours. Then you can turn around and take me back downtown."

He shrugged. "Suit yourself, Jackie, but there is no way you will be back up in two hours."

Opening the door, Jackie stepped out of the car. "It looks a lot worse than it is, believe me. I've been worse off and been just fine." The look Nick gave her, staring at her with those luminous eyes, clearly stated his opinion on her assessment. "Fuck you. I'll be fine. I didn't need to come out here."

He stepped around the car and opened the door into the house for her. "Then why did you?"

"Because . . ." The reason escaped her for a moment, lost on her while she stood in the doorway beneath the arch of Nick's arm. "I had no choice."

"Fair enough. You want anything to drink? Tylenol? I have some with codeine around here you could use."

"Nothing a shot or two of tequila wouldn't fix," Jackie muttered and stepped inside. "I'm fine, thanks. Just show me the damn room."

"Go through the entry and down the hall. Second door on your left."

Jackie made an effort to avoid limping as she proceeded across his house, but gave in after several steps and continued with the limp. Did she really have to prove herself to him? No. It didn't fucking matter what he thought. She just needed to get a little energy back, and then they could get back out and find that bastard Drake. They had to. Some little eight-year-old's life was depending on her to figure things out before it was too late.

The room had more of the same craftsman-style furnishings, a double bed with a heavy head- and footboard, a large leather-covered chair in a corner, and a bookshelf filled with more Old West knickknacks. The man could open a tourist shop with all the shit he had around his house. Jackie tossed her bag on the chair, kicked off her shoes, and sat down heavily on the down comforter covering the bed. The instantaneous relief made her groan. Nick showed up at that precise moment, a bottle of something in his hand.

He had a vague smile on his face. "You still think two hours?"

"I'm setting the alarm on my phone," she snapped back. "I'll be up. Take my fucking phone, and I'll kill you."

Nick put two shot glasses down on the nightstand next to the bed and poured from a bottle of Patrón tequila. "This bed will spit you back out when it's good and ready. I'm guessing four hours minimum. Here," he said, handing her a shot. "It'll take the edge off."

"You know your tequila at least."

He nodded, raising his shot to her. "I've had my share. Here's to reaching the ends we seek and to better days."

Odd thing to toast, but Jackie could argue with neither. "Thanks."

Nick poured one more shot in her glass and headed for the door. "See you when I see you, Jackie. Get some rest." He closed the door behind him.

Jackie stripped down to panties and a T-shirt and pulled back the comforter, revealing burgundy flannel sheets smelling faintly of lilacs. Not exactly the smell she would have associated with Nick Anderson. More of an oak-and-leather kind of guy, she thought, setting the alarm on her cell phone for two hours. Five thirty PM. They could be out of there by six, hit a Burger King on the way in, and be downtown, good to go, by seven.

Slipping beneath the sheets, Jackie moaned with pleasure at the softness enveloping her body. It felt like the bed was wrapping itself around her. "Goddamn," she said and reached over to turn up the volume on her phone. She downed the other shot of tequila and sank back into the feather pillow with a heavy sigh. Jackie slept before the warmth from the shot had faded from her throat.

She woke with a gasp in near darkness, the sounds of someone thrashing in water fading quickly from her foggy brain. She swore and reached over to pick up the phone, its screen glowing faintly in the dark. It read 9:37 PM.

"Son of a bitch!" She sat up and swung her legs out of the bed, feeling a bit light-headed. Leaning up to reach the lamp on the nightstand, Jackie put pressure on her injured knee. For a moment she thought something hard tore itself right off the bone. "Oh, goddamn." An instant later Jackie was on the floor, all her weight shifted to the other side of her body.

The door swung open, and for a horrifying moment Jackie thought Nick was going to rush up to her, her T-shirt hiked up to her breasts, sprawled on the floor. The far slighter and curvier silhouette revealed Shelby.

"Jackie! What happened? You okay?" In one smooth motion, she reached down and scooped Jackie up, depositing her on the bed as if she weighed little more than a rag doll. Her hands were hot against Jackie's skin, and her blue eyes literally were glowing in the dark. "Christ, look at that knee."

Jackie could only shrug. "You have an ACE bandage out here anywhere? I really need to get back downtown."

She smiled and patted Jackie on the cheek. "Sweetie, you shouldn't be going anywhere, though I'm admittedly curious about how Nick got you to agree to come out here."

She felt heat flush to her cheeks. "I was ordered out here! I had no desire to be out here in his bed."

Shelby laughed. "His bed is down the hall, Jackie. Don't worry. You won't be offending me with anything you might do out here. Now lay back for a sec. Let me see what I can do."

Jackie slumped back in the bed. "I didn't mean it like that. I just meant . . . I didn't need to come out here for a fucking nap."

"You need to sleep the rest of the night, Jackie," Shelby said, her fingers brushing with light strokes over and around the injured knee. "Things are getting done. The entire FBI is out combing the city for this guy, and so are half the police. Not that they will find him, but I, on the other hand, am better situated to sniff out the crotchety old fuck."

Something warm and syrupy began to crawl through her knee. The relief was instant. Jackie stared. "What did you just do to me?"

Shelby grinned. "Don't worry. It's just a little vampire voodoo. Against my better judgment, but it should have you up and moving in pretty short order."

"You drank more blood, didn't you?"

"You can tell, huh?" She chuckled and winked at Jackie. "I wish Nick would hurry the hell up. I want to get back out on the street."

"You didn't kill anyone, did you?"

The grin faded for a moment. "I don't kill for blood, Jackie. Ever."

"Good. I don't have to arrest you then."

The front door thumped shut before Shelby could answer her. "About fucking time." She stood up and pointed a finger at Jackie, her eyes electric and pulsing. "Get more rest, hon. You'll be more help tomorrow at full strength instead of half-assing your way around tonight."

Jackie struggled to sit up but found herself wanting more and more to just curl up and go back to sleep in the soft, downy warmth of the bed. "Damnit, Shelby. Don't do that."

Her mouth curled up on one side, a sly, sardonic grin. "It makes me powerful, Jackie. It's like someone turned the volume up on everything, inside and out, and it's a good thing I'm leaving, because you smell good enough to eat, and I'm really hungry." She giggled and skipped out the door as Nick came in, stepping sideways to avoid running into her. "How's Cyn doing?" Shelby asked as she passed him.

Nick looked at Jackie for a moment before glancing back down the hall at Shelby. "Sleeping. She's drugged up pretty good at the moment. I did manage to get out of her that she was trying to contact Reg but found someone else, apparently, who didn't want her snooping around. Laurel tried to rescue her. I think something's happened to Reg on the other side."

"Damn. I hope not," Shelby said. "Reg is a good guy. I'll call you later, babe. I'm hitting the streets."

The front door slammed shut before Nick could reply. Jackie threw the cover back over her legs before he could look at her. She had the feeling he would see whatever it was Shelby had done to her leg. The warm puddle had begun to expand, crawling like warm goo beneath her skin.

"I tried to wake you at six," he said but did not sound terribly apologetic. "You didn't even move, so I figured you would be good until I got back from seeing Cyn. Shelby kept an eye on things."

"Yeah, I see that," Jackie replied. How had Nick ever dealt with a woman like that? Of course, he would have been drinking blood back then, too. "It's important I get back downtown though. I'm the lead on this case."

Nick's mouth creased into a frown. "Can I make a blunt observation without you deciding to bury your fist in my face?"

"I wouldn't . . . What? Fine, I won't."

"I think you are quite aware of the fact that you are not capable to lead this case right now." His mouth worked in silence for a moment, pondering the next words. Jackie decided to keep the "so what" reply to herself until he finished. "Your partner and best friend is dead, and every second you are away from this case is a betrayal to her memory. I know how this works, Jackie. I've been there myself. If you want to help her out the most, stay here and rest and get some strength back."

Jackie stewed on the words. What could she say to that? The bastard was right. Still, it infuriated her that he could assume how she felt about things. "So I'd guess a hundred forty-four years is a long time to be betraying your wife?" She knew the instant she said it that it was uncalled for—spiteful even. The hard, fathomless look from Nick just made it worse. "Sorry. I'm being a bitch. Really. I didn't mean that."

His look softened. "Don't worry about it. You've had about as shitty a couple days as one can have. You deserve to feel bitchy, and I could have easily kept my trap shut. It's not my place to suggest you do anything."

"Thanks, but I should still get back. I can give Gamble a call and have him put my apartment on hourly watch."

Nick ignored her. "It's a bit late, but I'm going to make dinner, and you probably haven't eaten anything since McD's this morning. I'll make some coffee, and the shower is the next door down the hall on the left."

Jackie crossed her arms over her chest. She could just as easily grab a burger on the way in. "You aren't taking me back in, are you?"

"It's safer if you stay, Jackie. Drake won't come here."

"You honestly think he'll come after me?"

"If you interfere with his plans, he'll kill you."

"And you don't want that on your guilty little conscience, do you?"

He gave her a half smile. "Not really, no. So go shower. I'll have food and caffeine by the time you get out." He turned and walked out.

"Stubborn asshole!" she called after him, but he said nothing.

She could just call a cab and tell him to go fuck himself, but real food and coffee sounded wonderful, as did the shower, and Jackie felt a little nervous about going anywhere until the weird, vampire-voodoo thing was done doing whatever it was doing.

The shower turned out to be the size of a walk-in closet with its own steamer built in. Ten minutes of that, and Jackie had nearly turned into a puddle on the slate tile floor. The throbbing headache had reduced itself to a background pulse, her breath caught on only the deepest inhalation, and when she stood up from the stool, she could actually put pressure on the knee. Everything from the waist down felt thick and tingly. Jackie found it oddly pleasant but wondered how it would be if that syrupy warmth kept on going until it filled her head. All she could do was trust Shelby knew what she was doing.

"Because I smell good enough to eat," Jackie mumbled into the towel outside the shower as she dried herself. She laughed at the absurdity of it. Could the world be any more fucked up?

Clean, warm, and dressed in sweats and a T-shirt, Jackie felt nearly human again as her sock-covered feet padded silently into the kitchen. An Italian opera played quietly through hidden speakers, and Nick Anderson stood there in an apron and an oven mitt, shoveling some kind of garlic, cheesy-covered pasta into bowls on the counter. Quart-sized coffee cups sat next to them, steaming away with the black oil of the gods.

"Thought you might've fallen asleep in there," he said.

"That's a cute look for you. Are you generally so domestic?" *Be better without the clothes though.* Jackie blinked away the thought. *God, let's not go there, thank you very much.*

He picked up a basket of garlic bread off the stove top and set it between the plates. "I find cooking is a good stress reliever. Have a seat. Please."

Jackie moved around the counter to the bar stools and sat down. The kitchen, she noticed, looked like it had not ever been used. *Clean as you go. Man like that would be handy to have around.* She picked up the coffee cup and sipped, finding it overwhelmingly strong, with hints of citrus and something almost flowery. "Wow. Where did you get this coffee? It's amazing."

"Starbucks, I believe," he said. "I like it."

She could feel the caffeine flowing through her veins. "You know, you make coffee stronger than anyone I've ever met." *Christ! Why am I being so damn chatty? The ass basically forced me to stay here, and now I'm acting like it's a fucking date.* She poked her fork at the pasta, spearing prosciutto, rotini, and what looked to be roasted pepper, all held together by a white sauce that turned out to be heavily laced with gorgonzola. Her mouth was watering before it even managed to get in her mouth.

Jackie groaned with delight, her stomach rumbling for more, and Nick cracked a smile and sat down next to her. "To your liking, I take it? It's my favorite pasta dish."

She nodded, her mouth already full with the second bite. Not only did it taste like heaven, but every texture caressed her tongue—the slippery softness of the pasta, the smoothness of the gorgonzola cheese—making everything else she had ever eaten pale by comparison. *Men who cook like this do not need to look or smell good, and this guy is all of the above. It's almost better than sex.* "It's not fair to cook food this good."

Nick cracked a smile, or at least half a one, revealing the faint crinkle of lines around his eyes and laugh lines around his mouth. Jackie could picture him, if he actually would ever provide the whole thing, with a wide, toothy smile, full of amusement.

"Easy to make, too." He paused, chewing a mouthful of bread, pointing at her with his fork. "You okay? You're looking a little flush."

Does freaky vampire goo in the veins count? The warm tide had pushed up into her chest now, and she did indeed feel like she was running a low temp, but Jackie shook her head. "Maybe a little, but this is actually the best I've felt since . . . a couple days ago." *Fuck, I can't even say it. Laurel died! Laurel died!* Jackie pulled the coffee cup to her lips to hide her annoyance.

"It gets easier," he said, reading her thoughts. "It never goes away though."

"I don't want it to get easier," she snapped. "I just want her back."

Nick nodded. "Yeah. I wish they were all back."

The words hit Jackie, and she realized again how old

Nick really was. "You can't blame yourself for all their deaths you know. You didn't kill them."

He gave her a wistful smile and took a big drink from his coffee mug. "Does it matter?"

"No point in needlessly torturing yourself, is there?"

"Exactly." He smiled and picked up their bowls. "Still hungry?"

Jackie stared at him, her own annoyance quickly transferred. "Bastard. You set me up for that."

"Maybe, but true nonetheless. It's an easy thing to do when you're in the business of finding justice. Ice cream?" He turned on the sink and began to wash the dishes.

Ice cream. If it's anything double chocolate, I might have to actually be nice to him. "I have a shrink to play mind games with, thank you very much. How about we change the conversation to something less case oriented, and what flavor?"

Nick opened the freezer, reaching for a pint-size container. "Oh, you mean like real people do?" He gave her a snarky half smile. "Why, Ms. Rutledge, that would almost be like we were acquaintances or friends or something." Pulling a spoon out of a drawer, Nick handed both to Jackie. "I keep this around for Shelby. She calls it 'woman's best friend.'"

Triple chocolate. Damn him. "You just keep this around to lure women in, I'll bet." Jackie took a bite and closed her eyes. *Oh, man! Now this is like eating sex.* Shelby's words reverberated in her head once again, but along with them came the image of Nick standing naked in the dark at the edge of his pond. She nearly gagged on the spoon. *What is wrong with me? That blow to the head has fucked with my brain.*

"Shelby is the only woman I keep food around for."

Only woman. He made it sound like she was the only

woman, period. "So what is the deal with you and Shelby anyway?"

Nick set two wineglasses on the counter and spoke as he looked through an assortment of wines in an under-counter rack. "Deal? Are we asking personal questions now?"

"Does it matter?"

He chuckled. "Fair enough. Shelby and I are friends, former lovers, almost-married business partners. Our situation makes us unique, I'd guess you could say. Mostly, we're just friends who are there for each other because nobody else understands—or would want to, for that matter." He poured a white wine into each of the glasses and slid one over to her. "I owe her a lot and probably would have given up on this whole charade a long time ago, if not for her."

Jackie agreed. She had seen enough of Shelby to get that impression. The woman defined stability and a kick-ass sensibility. "I like her. She's a strong woman."

"Too much at times," he said. "Much like you."

She snorted, nearly spitting ice cream back into the carton. "You comparing me and Shelby? There's a laugh."

"And why not? You are both tenacious and headstrong, independent, a bit self-righteous, and fiercely devoted to those you care about."

Nothing witty came to mind for her to come back with. Her face abruptly felt warmer. "You know, you don't have to be nice to me. You're protecting the agent who thought you were a murderer a couple days ago. I haven't been very nice to you at all."

"I've got nothing against you, Jackie, other than wishing you had decided to stay out of things. Besides, life has been kicking you around enough lately."

God, where's the tequila when you want it? I'm usually drunk off my ass with most guys at this point. Hell, we aren't usually in the kitchen unless it's naked on the floor. "Okay, so now what? I should probably give Gamble a call and see what's up."

"He'll call if anything develops. I think he's afraid of what you'd do to him if he didn't." He laughed softly. "Generally, though, vampires watch TV, read books, or maybe go for swims like everyone else around here."

Jackie had no need to look to know her face had turned a shade redder. *I just got that damn image out of my head, too.* "You always such an ass?"

"Usually," he said, heading toward the kitchen door. "How about some piano? That's always relaxing for me. I'm curious about what drives you to play because I'd not really pictured you as the type."

Jackie hurried after him. "And what sort of woman do you picture playing the piano?"

Nick began ascending the stairs to the loft without turning to speak. "It's not a male-female thing. I just didn't see you as the creative type, that's all."

She couldn't tell if it was a subtle slap or a backhanded compliment. "That sort of stuff doesn't come out as an FBI agent." *Why the hell am I defending myself to him? This is ridiculous. I should just march back to the bedroom and lock the door until morning, or, better yet, get him to drive me back home. I've got no business being with this piano-playing, gourmet-cooking, blood-sucking, heavenly coffee-brewing vampire sheriff.* Jackie stared at her feet, watching them step one after the other up the stairs. *Fuck. You're an idiot, Jackie.*

"I have to agree," Nick said, setting his wine down on a coaster atop the piano. "You're all hard lines and sharp edges on the job. I see a different person now."

Jackie laughed. "Now that I've been clubbed in the head and nearly had my knee torn out?"

He gave her a pained smile. "No, not that. Please. Sit down."

Jackie stared down at the other half of the bench seat, which actually amounted to about a third of the space. She would be right up against him then. The smell of leather would be far stronger. The musk scent of his Mennen Speed Stick would be mere inches away, and those damn eyes would be right there, sneaking sideways glances at her while she played.

"I'd rather just watch you play, if you don't mind."

Nick eyed her for a moment. "You sure you're feeling okay?"

"I said I was fine, damnit, just a little warm, is all."

"All right then, sit. I insist," he said, patting the seat.

She crossed her arms over her chest. "Insist? You really think you're in a position to insist on anything from me, Sheriff?"

Nick rolled his eyes at her. "Christ. Sit down and play the piano with me. It'll relax those frenetic nerves you have going and maybe ease the pain in your heart for just a few minutes."

Fucker. How am I supposed to say no to that? Jackie found herself sitting down before her mind had finished deliberating the subject. "I don't play nearly as good as you do."

"Does it matter?"

"No, I guess not." She stared at the keys, feeling his gaze on her, the closeness of his body. She could not make herself look at those eyes. "What shall we play?"

"You choose," he replied. "I'm not particular, and as long as it's someone known, I'll pick up on it."

"You memorize a lot of songs after a hundred years, I suppose." Jackie laid her hands out over the keys. *Duet. Do I even know one? Will my memory even function to make my fingers play it?* The warm, syrupy feeling had swelled into her head now, leaving an odd, tangy, metallic taste in the back of her mouth. The wine did nothing to get rid of it. It felt like her head floated just above the rest of her body, barely attached. She wanted Nick's cool hands on her face, bringing her mind and body back into one piece.

"You pick," she said, pulling her hands back. "I can't think of anything."

"All right. How about this?"

His fingers moved with deft surety, but with a touch light and soft as a feather. Jackie thought she knew the song, but the notes ringing out of the piano filled her head with color, sound, smells, and the bittersweet taste of tears. Abruptly, the sweet melancholy of the song came to an end.

"Jackie?"

She rubbed her clammy hands on her pants. *Oh, my God, what was that?* "Keep playing. That was so sad and wonderful."

Nick's cool fingertips brushed against Jackie's cheek, and she realized she had begun to cry. Without thinking, Jackie leaned into the touch, and the fingers slid down to cup her chin. He turned her head toward him. "Jackie?"

"What?" *Goddamnit, if you don't kiss me now, I will show you what sharp lines and hard edges are all about.*

"Look at me," he said, voice firm.

Jackie brought her gaze up at last to meet his, locked on like a moth to the flame, charming and deadly both. She could taste his lips against her own, crushing and soft. *I wonder if his tongue is as cool as his hands? Could he make me into his slave if he wanted? Unable to resist his every whim? Fuck, Nick! Kiss me or let go before I do something stupid.*

"Did Shelby do anything to you? Anything to make you feel better?"

She swore she could feel his pulse through the tips of his

fingers, picking up pace against her skin. She nodded. "Said it would have me back on my feet by morning."

He snorted and shook his head. "Probably said you looked good enough to eat as well."

You could eat me right now, Sheriff. Just lay me down on this beautiful, polished piano and eat me right up. Jackie nodded slowly, feeling as if too much movement might indeed make her head float away from her body. "She did." Jackie held up her hands to him, some part of her brain that was normally restrained from active duty brought to the surface on a warm seepage of vampiric goo. "What's the matter, Nick? My blood not good enough for you?"

He leaned back a few inches. "What? That's not even an issue here."

"Shelby wanted it. Why don't you, Nick?"

"She wasn't referring to your blood, Jackie. She had, well, other things in mind."

Jackie wondered if she stood up and sat on the piano keys there before him if he might have a little more compunction to rip her pants off and fuck her brains out. *Just a little. I only need a little. Make me feel so much better.* Some little part of Jackie's mind screamed at her, insisting she get the hell out of there, lock herself in a closet until things settled down, but, apparently, the willpower to use it had gone back down to the kitchen for more ice cream.

"Nick," she said, laying her hand against the rough stubble of his jaw. "I know exactly what she meant, and that's exactly what I want, what I need right now."

He reached up and took her hand off his face. "You're really warm. Shelby did this, damnit. I'm going to kill her."

Jackie guided his hand down to her breast. "She knows what I need, Nick. Is it really that hard? Am I so undesirable?"

"No, it's not that, Jackie. This just isn't the real you here. Shelby did this, filled you with some extra energy to help you heal. It has certain . . . effects." He cleared his throat and removed his hand from her breast.

Jackie stood up and stepped over Nick's legs so that she stood astride him. The keys chimed together in a disharmonious clamor when her butt leaned back into them. "Does it matter?" She laid her hands on his shoulders, squeezing the firm muscle beneath, and found herself strangely and pleasantly oblivious to his fathomless, glowing stare. "I get the impression you don't sleep around much, Nick. When's the last time you had a nice, hard fuck?"

"This isn't the time or place for this discussion, Jackie."

"And you'd prefer to wait until after you're dead?" She leaned forward, fingers digging in until her face was only a few inches from his. It really did look like death back in the depths of those eyes. "I don't want your soul, Mr. Anderson."

Nick stood up, knocking the piano bench over to the floor with a loud clatter against the wooden floor, his hands hooked under Jackie's arms. He pushed her back until she was arched against the front of the piano. "You don't know what you want, Jackie, and I have nothing left to give you."

She sucked in her breath at the quickness with which he had responded, a tingling wash of heat coursing through her at the feeling of being pressed between him and the piano. It was not exactly comfortable, but Jackie didn't notice. He stood over her, staring down at her half-opened mouth, holding her gaze, and Jackie knew his words were only that—just words. *You say it, and you don't want to believe, Nick Anderson. You're just as desperately lonely as I am.* "I know what I want at this very moment. Question is, will you give it to me?"

He leaned farther, pressing his torso against hers. Jackie responded by wrapping her legs around his waist and got rewarded with the feeling of him swelling up against her. Nick's hands gripped the edge of the piano on either side of her, and his mouth hovered perilously and deliciously close to her own. "Jackie . . ."

God! Do you have to be so fucking chivalrous! Just fuck me! Jackie brought her head up and found his mouth. She could feel every little bump and curve of his lips, nibbling them, licking the crease until after a moment he responded, opening to her and letting her tongue swim with his, tasting of wine, sweet and woody. After a few seconds he pulled away, leaving Jackie licking her lips, wanting to taste more.

"Nick, don't stop. Please. I want that mouth all over me."

"No," he said, closing his eyes and pushing back upright. "Damnit, Jackie. I want to, but no, not like this. Not under the influence of the other side."

No, no, no! You bastard. You can't bail now. "I don't care, damnit." She reached for his neck, to pull him back down, but he grabbed her hands in his.

"I do. It'd be like taking advantage of a drunken woman. Come on, a cold shower actually helps the effect go away." He pulled her to her feet and led Jackie to the stairs.

Jackie didn't complain, thinking perhaps she could coax him into the shower with her, but he removed no clothing, only pointing out the bathrobe hanging on the hook behind the door.

"It's Shelby's. She won't mind. Cold water, Jackie. Cold as you can stand it. I'll see you in a few minutes."

Jackie yelled at the first contact, but the pulsing contact from the jets of water did indeed begin to cool her down right away. Gradually, her head floated back to its rightful place on her shoulders, and her will ventured back to take up shop once again. Only then did Jackie feel the mortification of what she had done. What the hell would she say to him now? She had truly wanted him though, sort of. Some part of her had, at least, and Shelby had unleashed it. *How am I going to live this down? Maybe I can just sneak out*

*and walk back to town. I really wanted him. Fuck, what is
my problem? I'm going to have to thank him for saying no.*

It struck Jackie then, beginning to shiver under the cold
spray of the shower, that Nick Anderson was the first guy
that she could remember who had refused to take advantage
of the situation offered to him.

Chapter 43

"Will you give it to me?" The words kept echoing around inside Nick's head. He listened to Jackie finish her shower and then lock herself in the bedroom. Tough not to blame her for that one. Embarrassment was never fun, but he was thankful nonetheless. Nick did not know what he would say to her. Part of him had known what was going on. The symptoms had all been there, but he realized now, after a couple beers and two hours of mindless channel surfing, that he had wanted her. When she had finally irked him enough to push her up against the piano, his body had responded in a way he had not felt in a long time.

He had attempted to call Shelby to give her the piece of mind she deserved for pulling that off on Jackie without mentioning it to him, but she had not answered. It was getting late enough now that it worried him. She should have checked in at least an hour earlier. Gamble had nothing new to pass along. They were all out hunting for Drake. Shelby had been heard from, just not by him. He needed to be out there looking. Somewhere a little girl's life was in grave danger.

Nick wrapped his hand around the beer bottle and felt

the phantom, firm nipple of Jackie's breast pressing through the cotton fabric against his palm. Her skin had been so warm. The desire to knead his fingers into it had been nearly overwhelming. Such a slightly built woman, and she had certainly shown her ability to use it for violence, but her desperate voice had sent his mind in an entirely different direction, wanting to know how that body would work under more desirable circumstances. Nick clicked off the television and headed up to the loft. He needed something to soothe his fraying nerves.

He had made it a whole thirty seconds into a Beethoven piano concerto when the phone rang. His heart skipped a beat when he saw it was coming from the hospital. "Hello?"

Cynthia's voice, groggy and hoarse, whispered in his ear. "Nick?"

"Cyn?" Relief washed through him. "How you doing? It's late, girl. You could have waited until morning."

"Just woke up. I think they pumped a pharmacy into my veins."

"Yeah, you weren't too aware when I saw you earlier."

"Worst migraine of all time," she said and laughed softly. "I thought my head was going to explode."

"Stayed too long on the other side, didn't you? What were you doing poking around in Deadworld, Cyn? This is not a safe time to be doing that." He knew he sounded like a dad scolding a daughter for staying out too late with undesirable friends, but in a way it was how he felt. Losing Cynthia would have been like losing another daughter.

"I know, but I wanted to tell you I found them, Nick. At least, I think so. It's so hard to tell because I can't really see over there. I just hear things."

"I know that, but found who?"

"Some of Drake's victims," she said. "They're trapped, I think."

Nick paused, trying to collect himself. *"Some" means more than one, perhaps many.* "Trapped how? I don't understand."

"Sec," she said, and Nick heard a soda can popping open and a mumbled conversation with a hospital staff person. "I don't either. I think they were inside some . . . place. This big old brute of a guy named Jeffrey was guarding it and took offense at my nosing around.

"Jeffrey?"

"I don't know. The guy was not the brightest. Kept referring to himself in third person. 'Jeffrey not let anyone in. Jeffrey gonna smash your face.' That sort of thing. I tried talking to him, but it was like talking to a brick."

The name rang a bell for Nick. Jeffrey was someone from Drake's past. He had run into Jeffrey back in '32, but the dimwitted thug had been alive then. "Anything else before I come over and smack you for not staying away like I asked you?"

"Promise?"

"Promise to smack you?" *Question is, will I give it to you.* "No. Not funny."

Cynthia sighed. "Fine. Can't give a hospitalized girl a break, can you?"

"Cyn . . . sorry. It's been a very long, frustrating day."

"I'm sorry, too, Nick. Anyway, I got around this nitwit and found a bunch of spirits, those I'd normally think of as lost souls, the ones waiting for something to happen here before they move on, and Drake was with them."

"What?" *Drake has access to his victims after he has already killed them? Dear God.*

"Yeah. At least, I am almost positive that's who it was. English accent, charming voice, and very powerful. I knew the second I heard him I was in trouble so I began pulling out as fast as I could. Reggie showed up though and ran interference long enough for me to get back, but I guess that Jeffrey guy was able to follow me through."

They could all be there, tormented by Drake all this time, waiting for me to arrive and save the day. Nick's hand clenched tightly around the phone. "He can walk among both worlds. Christ."

"Nick . . ." Her voice faded for a moment, and Nick thought she might have fallen asleep, but there was a cough as she cleared her throat before continuing. "If you need any . . . um . . . you know, blood to do this, I—"

"No!" He winced at the tone of his voice. "Sorry, Cyn. I didn't mean to yell. I won't take your blood, no matter what the reason, but thank you."

"Okay. Just thought I'd offer. You know, just in case. Nobody should be allowed to walk among the dead, Nick. It's not right."

"I know. I hope I can stop him."

"Is everything all right back at my house? That idiot was throwing shit all over the place."

Nick swallowed hard. "There was a fire, Cyn. I think it gutted your living room. A lot of smoke damage, I think, but the outside looked pretty intact."

Her voice quavered, on the brink of tears. "Did it look fixable?"

"I think so. It's covered regardless, so don't worry about that now. You can stay out at the ranch until it gets situated if you need to."

Her voice cracked. Nick could tell she was crying now. That was far easier said when it wasn't your house that had burned. "Thanks, Nick. I can probably stay out at Mom's. I'll ask her tomorrow. I'm going to go cry for a while now. You going to be okay over there?"

"For now." *Other than the horny, mortified woman in my spare room.* I'll try to call in the morning and see how you're doing. If we get a break at all, I'll come by and see you."

"Okay." Cyn sniffed and clicked off.

For a moment, he thought the evening could not end on a lower note, but then a short, sharp scream came from down the hall.

Chapter 44

Pale and fanged, black cape swirling about his shoulders like a mist of raven's feathers, Nick had begun to eat at Jackie. Beginning with her toes, he had taken them delicately into his mouth, breaking off each one like a little piece of hard candy. Then, with snakelike effectiveness, he gulped down each leg just short of the point where she really wanted those fangs to bite.

"Eat me, Nick. Oh, yes, eat me." She repeated the absurd refrain over and over while he meticulously devoured her, until on the brink of that sweet bite, he stopped and turned to look over his shoulder. Jackie felt a wave of bone-piercing cold wash through her, and Nick's smiling face froze and shattered into a million tiny pieces.

"Jackie."

Laurel stood at the foot of the bed, her eyes ablaze with an icy fire. Jackie screamed, trying to scramble away, but, of course, her legs were gone, and she could go nowhere. She glared down at the legless bare body and shook her head.

"Jackie."

"I'm sorry," Jackie said, wiping at the tears streaming

down her face. "I couldn't help it. I'm sorry. Please, Laur, forgive me."

"Jackie!"

She awoke finally, sitting bolt upright in the bed, the frightened scream dying as quickly as it had come out. The bedside lamp was still on. She had fallen asleep, lying there contemplating the inevitable conversation she would have to have with Nick. At the foot of the bed, shifting in and out of existence, was the gauzy shape of Laurel's ghost.

Jackie clutched the blanket up to her chest and swallowed the tight ball of fear back down. Her voice, despite the effort, was barely audible. "Laur."

Laurel smiled. Then her brow furrowed in concentration, and her image nearly faded out before growing brighter again. Her voice sounded like it came from the other end of a long corridor, hollow and distant. "Hi, hon. No time . . . talk."

They both turned as the bedroom door swung open. Nick poked his head in, and his eyes grew wide in surprise. "Well, hello, Ms. Carpenter."

"Shut up," Jackie said in a harsh whisper.

Nick stepped in and said nothing. Laurel turned so she could see both of them. "Drake . . . North Shore," she said, bring her hands up to her temples. "Sorry . . . hard. Shelby on the way. Go."

"On the way?" Nick reached into his pocket for his cell, and it began to ring before he pulled it out. "Shel? What the hell . . . Yeah, she's here now. Okay, I'm heading up now. I'll call in a few."

Jackie stared in silence at Laurel. Her brain had shut off. No words came to mind. She tried to blink away the tears filling up her eyes. Laurel did not seem the raging spirit some part of her mind had envisioned when Shelby had told her she would show up again. It was just her. Laurel.

Jackie's friend. And working the case while she slept it away in some stranger's bed.

Laurel turned back to her as Nick pocketed the phone. She smiled. "Go . . . talk later." She stepped forward into the bed, reaching out to Jackie, and then faded out completely.

Jackie reached up to grab her hand and found nothing but an icy-cold breath of air in her grasp. She wiped at the tear that had spilled down her cheek. "Shit."

"I know you'll shoot me if I leave you here, so let's go." Nick stood at the door, standing aside as though waiting for her to go ahead.

She took a deep breath, letting it out in a rush, and swung her legs out of bed. "Give me a sec to throw clothes on."

He nodded. "I'll have the car out front."

A minute later, Jackie stepped out into the cool, misty night air and found herself staring at the open door of a dark purple Porsche 911. The vampire cowboy drove a purple Porsche. She walked over to the driveway and got in, the leather bucket seat snuggling up behind her. "You drive a purple Porsche?"

"It was my wife's favorite color," he said.

"Why don't you drive this thing all the time?"

He shrugged. "Don't generally need to."

"So when do you generally need it?"

Nick backed out onto the road and gave her what she thought might actually be a sly look. "When I want to go really fast. Buckle up, Agent Rutledge."

She just managed to get the strap across her body when her head was forced back into the seat, and the Porsche launched down the road toward North Shore.

Chapter 45

Jackie stared straight ahead in silence while Nick had them weaving in and out of late-night freeway traffic doing about ninety. Gamble had everyone heading up into North Shore, but she knew it would be Shelby and Nick who found Drake. They just needed to be ready to pounce when they did.

Worse, though, was Nick's silence. It made her unable to focus. What was he thinking about earlier? *No big deal? Who the hell is this slut?* Why had Shelby not mentioned the side effects of whatever she had done? Unless of course she wanted the result. Presumptuous bitch.

He downshifted onto an off ramp, slowing enough at a stoplight to make sure no traffic was coming, and turned the corner doing fifty. "About earlier," he said.

Great. Here we go. "Do we have to talk about it now?" *Or ever?*

"No, but I just wanted to say you shouldn't worry yourself over it. It was Shelby's doing."

She looked over at Nick, his features calm, mood unruffled, weaving them through traffic like it was a Sunday drive in the country. Was he truly so unflappable? He had responded to her, hadn't he? Sure, he had stopped, but there had been some response. Or was it that he didn't want to be bothered with the possibilities of what had happened? He was going to let her cop out for him.

"You don't want to talk about it either, do you?"

The phone rang, and Nick slowed to answer. "Anything? What? Already?" The car picked up speed. "Where? Wellington. Got it. We're five minutes away."

"What's going on?" Jackie grabbed the door handle to keep herself from slamming into Nick as he slid around a corner.

"Drake's got her already," Nick replied, mouth set in a grim line.

"What!" Jackie dug up her phone. "Where? I'll call it in."

"One-ninety-first and Wellington, heading south on Wellington. Black Cadillac Escalade."

Jackie called up Gamble, who relayed the information out to everyone on patrol. "Maybe Laurel has him acting sooner than he wanted."

"Maybe, but I doubt it," Nick said. "He's had this planned for a long time, and we aren't really off his timetable. We just may have lucked out. Laurel might have seen what he was doing from the other side. I don't know. And no," he added, "I don't really want to talk about what happened earlier."

An unmarked car with a red flashing light on top went flying through an intersection, and Nick just missed clipping the rear bumper. Two lights farther down, he pulled a hard left, sliding onto the shoulder of the road. The Porsche fishtailed a bit getting back in line on the road.

Jackie glared at him. "Not going to help much if we're dead before we can catch Drake." After Nick failed to say anything, she added, "Don't want to talk about it for my sake or because the whack job of a federal agent turned you on?"

He did look at her this time, and Jackie gave him an innocent, wide-eyed stare. "You aren't a whack job, Jackie."

At the next intersection, a black SUV went sailing through, easily doing ninety to one hundred miles per hour. Right behind was a now very recognizable BMW motorcycle with a black-clad figure hunched low over its handlebars.

"There they are!" She was going to point but found herself slammed up against Nick when he turned across into oncoming traffic, sliding into the opposite shoulder. For a moment, Jackie figured Nick was going to lose it. They slid a good fifty feet sideways, churning up grass and gravel, before he got it back in line with the road, cutting across the opposing lanes again to join the chase. They were two blocks behind already. "God, somebody is going to get killed at this speed."

"I imagine that's his plan," Nick said. "He'd lose us easily enough if he wanted to."

"Can you give us a little fucking credit, please? We aren't amateurs around here, you know."

Nick gave her a sidelong look. "No, but you aren't pros at chasing vampires either."

"Look out!" She cringed as three cars piled into each other at the intersection Drake and Shelby had just passed through.

Nick geared down and turned down the street right before the accident. It was a residential street, and even at the late hour, Jackie could just see someone crossing a street while the Porsche came barreling through at eighty.

"Where're you going?" she wondered as they cut out to a main street, now six blocks off of where they had been.

"Hitting the freeway on-ramp over here."

"You think he's getting on the freeway?"

"He was running out of road going the way he was, and the on-ramp there was six blocks away. I just hope I picked the right direction."

"Hope? You better know what you're doing, Nick."

"Instinct," he said. "He's been messing with me long enough that I have a general sense of what he likes to do."

"And you think he's going to head toward downtown instead of away?"

He nodded, pulling them onto the on-ramp, building up speed. As they climbed up to the level of the freeway, the black Escalade went by, followed once again by Shelby. Nick was up to speed with them in a couple seconds, and just like that, they were right back on Drake.

Jackie shook her head. "Okay, that was good."

Nick gave a little half shrug. "The kiss was better."

Huh? It took a second to register what he had said, and then she felt heat rising to her cheeks. For the moment at least, Nick had gotten the last word in.

Chapter 46

"Why would he be going downtown?" Jackie asked while she braced her feet against the floorboard and clung to the door handle to keep from flipping across into Nick's lap. They were losing ground again on Shelby and Drake, who continued to pull corners at speeds defying physical laws. There had been four wrecks thus far, and more to come if the bastard was going to drive like that through the heart of Chicago's downtown. Traffic there never really died down.

"No idea. We never detected him over here, but that doesn't mean he doesn't have some other place arranged to keep the girl."

"We've got him tracked on air and ground now. He won't be pulling a vanishing act this time," Jackie said, but she didn't sound sure even to herself. "Someone is going to get killed with this kind of chase. You should call off Shelby. Maybe that will slow him down."

"She won't listen to me. You want to tell her?" A bus slammed its brakes as the Escalade and BMW turned a corner in front of it. Sparks went up from the motorcycle as some part of it scraped the asphalt. The bus continued its skid, and Nick was forced to swerve around behind it.

"Goddamnit," he said, barely muttering the words. He turned a one-eighty, facing the Porsche the other way, and sent it over the corner sidewalk, behind the light posts and in front of the doorway to a corner office building.

"Fuck! You're going to kill someone!" Jackie yelled at him.

He slammed on the breaks a moment later, the car coming to a halt halfway down the block. "Don't worry about my driving. I won't hit anyone."

Jackie noticed a second later why Nick had come to a stop. "Where did they go?"

She had no time to consider the options, however. The screeching sound of tires to their left answered the question. An alleyway in the middle of the block disappeared into blackness. The Porsche backed up to where they could see down the narrow street, and Jackie saw—just as Nick did—the looming specter of red eyes rushing at them from the darkness. He threw the car into reverse, gunning the engine, but the reaction came a split second too late as the Escalade bounced across the street and clipped the front of the Porsche, spinning it back around in the opposite direction. Nick swore under his breath and continued to back up, this time toward the escaping taillights of the SUV as it gunned off down the street once again.

When he spun the car back around, Jackie watched the Escalade turn the next corner without the pursuing motorcycle. On top, clinging to the luggage rack of the Escalade, was Shelby's black, leather-clad form.

"Jesus. She's on the fucking roof." Jackie dialed up Gamble, but aerial recon had apparently already informed him. "I'm going to arrest her after this is done. She's a damn civilian. She can't do this shit."

"If anyone has a chance to break up his plan right now, it's her," Nick said and gunned the Porsche back down the street after them.

The Escalade, two blocks ahead, turned short of the next intersection and disappeared from view. Nick slowed as he approached, and Jackie noticed that the last half of the block was comprised of a large multistoried parking structure. Above, a helicopter flew low overhead, and down at the intersection, four federal cars skidded to a halt to block passage.

Jackie keyed in to Gamble again. "Hostage team on standby?"

"They're coming in," he replied. "Fifteen minutes probably."

"Shit, Gamble. That better be enough."

"Let's keep him busy then."

Jackie hung up. "Could this be some kind of trap?"

"If you want out, say so right now," Nick said quickly. "I'm going up there."

"Go," she replied before thinking about it. The three seconds of conversation could have just blown their chance.

The Porsche wheeled into the garage even as she said it, heading in and up the spiral ramp. Above, Jackie heard the sound of squealing tires. The Escalade was still going up. She clutched the door handle while Nick had the Porsche skidding its way up the levels. She wanted to get her gun out, but she was afraid to reach for it and lose her grip. After eight dizzying circles, Nick launched out onto the upper deck and brought the car to a sliding stop.

Halfway across the upper lot, the Escalade stood for a moment in the pale light of an overhead lamp. She noticed the back window had been knocked out. Where was Shelby? An instant later, two flashes went off inside the Escalade in quick succession. Jackie's heart jumped a beat before she opened the door. Nick opened the glove box and pulled out a gun very similar to her own. He stepped out, crouching behind the protection of the front of the car.

Jackie climbed over the driver seat and got out next to Nick, just in time to hear the tires screeching once again.

"Damnit!"

"Tires," Nick said, taking aim with his pistol braced across the top of the hood. "Shoot for the tires."

"There's a little girl in there, you idiot." She kicked at Nick, whose first shot went firing harmlessly off into the night sky. "What are . . . ?" Her voice trailed off when she realized why Nick was shooting.

The Escalade did not turn around. It didn't turn at all. It just kept going, accelerating until it hit the concrete barrier another fifty yards away at the far end of the lot. It had to be going forty by then, maybe more, but that small detail was lost on Jackie as she watched the concrete wall explode outward in a shower of rock and rebar.

For a moment, it hung there, suspended on the edge of nothing, and Jackie began to run, not truly believing what she was seeing. Then the SUV tipped forward, its back end swinging up toward the sky, and it dropped toward the street below.

Chapter 47

Nick let his head slump forward until his forehead rested on the warm hood of his car. The air shook a moment later with the thunderous boom of the Escalade exploding in the street below. He let out a long, slow sigh. "Shit."

Drake and Shelby were gone. He could no longer feel their presence in this world. Drake no doubt had popped back over to the other side before impact. Shelby and the girl, on the other hand . . . Why? Why kill the little girl? It made no sense. He would have wanted to drain her, show Nick the body, and drag him through the end like a long, torturous fingernail pull. Had they really ruined whatever plans Drake had? The whole chase seemed too contrived, too over the top. It had to be a show. So what had happened?

Nick looked up and watched Jackie finish her walk to the edge of the parking platform. She thrust her hands into her pockets, looking down. She looked back toward him for a moment and then back toward the street. *Don't worry, Jackie. That should be the last bit of death bloodying these old hands.*

The sound of squealing tires came up behind, and Nick stood up, putting his gun into his pocket. One of the cars stopped beside him while the other cruised on toward

Jackie. Nick didn't bother to look at who stepped out of the car, but he recognized the voice.

"Hey," Gamble said. "Nick?"

"What?" His voice came out low and harsh. He was not in the mood to discuss anything. "Need a statement or something?"

"No. Just making sure everything was okay up here."

Nick turned and glared down at Gamble, who shrunk back away from his car window. "Peachy. Unless you need me to make one, think I'm going to go home."

"I'll call you if we need you to come in," Gamble said. "Jackie all right?"

"She'll be okay. Don't be surprised if Drake's body isn't down there."

"What?"

"He'll have vanished like before. I'm almost positive."

"So he's still out there somewhere?"

Nick shrugged. "Somewhere." He opened the door to his car and sat down in the seat. The air had become particularly heavy. "I'll be at home. You have my number."

"Um, okay," Gamble said, unsure. "I'll let you know what's going on later."

Nick started up the Porsche and eased it down the exit ramp. He felt a desperate urge to get away. He needed to break something, destroy it into a million little pieces. Then again, did it really matter? Another day or two, and he was going to be dead anyway.

A final glance into the rearview mirror showed the two fed cars on either side of Jackie, who stood with her small fists balled up on her hips watching his car vanish down the exit-ramp tunnel.

Chapter 48

She watched the red taillights of Nick's Porsche vanish into the exit tunnel. "Where the hell is he going?"

"Didn't want to stay," Gamble said. "He sounded a little bit pissed, and to be honest, I really don't want to fuck with that guy. We can call him later for a statement."

Jackie glared at Gamble. "Fucking wimp. His best friend is buried down there in that pile of metal, and he's just going to leave."

Gamble shrugged. "I wouldn't blame him, Jack. Who wants a last memory like that?"

"You know what? Be on my side for a change here." Gamble was right, but still. It was wrong to leave. How could Nick just leave?

"Okay. So go over there later and kick his ass. Get a statement for me while you're at it. It'll save me some time."

Jackie walked around to the passenger side of his car. "I like you better when you aren't an asshole."

Gamble chuckled. "Nice to have you back, Jack."

On the way down he informed her about Nick's claim that Drake would not be there. She started to refute until she remembered that he had done it once already. He could cross over at will, according to Nick. The notion of leaving occurred to her then. She was tired, frayed, but the thought of going home to her apartment didn't sound appealing. In the back of her mind, the thought of Cornelius Drake popping into her bedroom unannounced had her just a little nervous.

Fire crews were already arriving on the scene by the time they drove back down and parked again. The stench of burning fuel and rubber assailed her the moment she stepped out of the car. The Escalade had landed mostly on its back and slightly to the driver's side. There would be no chance of surviving the crash, much less the fire. While the last of the flames were being doused by the streams of water, Belgerman arrived, sleepy-eyed and looking none too pleased with the turn of events.

He gave her a curious glance upon walking up. "You look halfway human again."

Vampire voodoo, baby. "I got some sleep," she said.

He reached up to move the hair off the lump on her head, and Jackie stepped back. "You need more. You got, what, six or seven hours maybe?"

"Enough for now, John. I want to see if Drake's in there."

Belgerman turned and looked at the wreckage. "You don't think he is?"

"Nick said he won't be."

"Ah." Belgerman nodded. "Like before then. This could pose a serious problem."

"Yes, sir," Jackie said, not trying hard to hide the sarcasm. "It does."

It took another twenty minutes for the flames to end, and by that time, Jackie was in the mood for a couple shots. The more she lingered on it, the more she got pissed at Nick. One did not walk away from a scene until the situation was under control, and watching three people tumble off the top of a parking structure and burst into flames at the bottom didn't fall into that category. Then again, Nick Anderson was not part of the investigation. He was a civilian, helping them find a killer. He could come and go as he pleased. Then why was she feeling like he had just left her behind? The notion merely added more fuel to her frustrations.

There were television crews at either end of the scene now, and the entire block was lit up with blinking, swirling lights. Jackie realized her headache was starting to come back, and the lights were not helping one bit. Gamble walked over to the fire chief and got the okay to inspect the wreckage. He stood up from the crushed driver's-side window before Jackie could even make it over.

"Son of a bitch," he said in disbelief.

"No Drake?" Jackie said and stooped down next to him to look for herself.

"No nothing," Gamble said. "They're all fucking gone. What the hell?"

Jackie peered into the melted, dripping cabin, still steaming from the heat. The bodies should have been burned to a crisp, not even recognizable, but the telltale smell of burned flesh was noticeably missing.

"And Mr. Anderson just left the scene?" Belgerman squatted down beside Jackie to verify for himself the impossible. "That's curious."

"I think you should go have a little chat with your vampire and see if he can clue us in," Gamble said.

"He's not my goddamn vampire," Jackie said far more adamantly than she intended.

Belgerman laid a hand on her shoulder. "Jack, go talk to him. Gamble, you go with her just in case, and call it in if anything even slightly suspicious seems to be going on."

"This entire mess is suspicious," Gamble complained but followed Jackie as she stomped off toward his car. "I'm driving!" he called after her.

Chapter 49

It was as good a day to die as any. After so many false starts, Nick had come to realize that it could be any day, and every day was available to him. All he had to do was let go, and the door would open, pulling him through. It had been so tempting, and Nick realized now that even if he had taken the low road and done just that, Cornelius likely awaited him on the other side, too. Alive or dead, he would face the man, and, given the option, he had at least a remote chance of success if he was alive.

After parking the Porsche, he walked directly up to the loft, opening the door to his room of memories. Nick walked slow and purposeful toward the back, stopping every so often to pick up something, one of Agatha's dolls, or a coin from Joshua's collection. He brought up their images, getting dusty and faded with age, recalling the times long past, far simpler times, when the world was a vast, wide-open place, and justice came in the form of a badge and a pair of six-shooters.

Nick picked up the box of matches next to an antique brass candleholder on the small, quilt-covered table and lit a candle for Gwen, staring for a long moment at his painting of her until he could hear her dying voice fresh in his mind once again. He then picked up the painting and moved it away from the wall, revealing a polished, wooden trunk behind it set against the wall. He did the combination on the lock and opened the chest to reveal that which he had stored away for this particular time.

From inside the chest, Nick pulled out the beaten and dusty leather overcoat he would wear riding the range on those cool, fall Wyoming days when the wind would be sharp enough to sting your face. Beside that lay his hat, and Nick had the absurd notion that it would be too small now, shrunken with age, but it fit snug to his scalp, and he took a moment to roll the brim between his fingers, setting its angles and curves to just the proper position. Beneath those lay the oak case carrying his old six-shooters, and Nick laid it down gently on the table beside the candle, breaking the wax seal with his pocketknife and smiling when he saw them, the cherry handles still gleaming with polish, and the metal still shiny with oil from the last time he had removed them to ensure they were still in working order.

He grabbed the leather belt from the bottom of the chest and strapped the guns on, feeling for a brief second like the man he was of old. At least if Drake showed up now, Nick could go down like he had once already, six-shooters blazing in an abysmal, stormy downpour of water and blood. At least this time there was nothing else left for Drake to take.

"Just me this time, you miserable old bastard," Nick said and walked out of the room.

After making a pot of coffee, Nick took his mug out onto the deck and sat in his chair, polishing the old guns and sipping the hot brew until it was gone. He was covered in a fine mist by then, the night skies growing more saturated by the hour. It would be a nice, solid rain before long, he figured.

Nick's thoughts turned to Shelby. In the end, she had done what he could not, and it still was not enough. If both of them had, would the results have been any different? Would that have been something Drake would have not guessed? Did he plan his actions around Nick's rigid, moral code?

"Pigheaded, obstinate, stupid fucking code, more like," he said, repeating Shelby's words. The woman had never been afraid to express her feelings toward him about anything. For him, against him, or just in plain disagreement, she had always been straightforward and honest. That directness had been one of the main reasons he had fallen in love with the woman. It still amazed Nick that she stuck around, and now she had died because of him. Twice.

Jackie was like her in a lot of ways. Straightforward, a no-bullshit kind of woman. Not the stunning beauty Shelby was, and in fact, nearly the opposite, having a definite tomboyish quality to her. But it was that attractive, rumpled, stumbling-around-in-your-flannels-with-a-mug-of-coffee look that hit a soft spot for him. Shelby had known better than he, but it was too late for that. It was better to get rid of those thoughts before he became even more morose than he was already.

Nick picked up one of his pistols from his lap and aimed it at a distant fence post, imagining it could be Drake's head, standing there with that thin, bloodless grin. His shot caught the corner of the post, and Nick grumbled to himself. How had he gotten so rusty?

He took aim again, this time with more focus, and caught it square, blasting off the top two inches of the post in a shower of splintery debris. He smiled. It felt good to hold his guns again, and, better still, the crack of gunfire took his mind off things better left unthought of. Lifting up the other gun, Nick took aim and fired again at the next post.

Chapter 50

They parked on the side of the road short of Nick's driveway. Jackie would have said an hour ago that her suspicions about Nick Anderson and Shelby Fontaine were long gone, but now, after the vanishing act, she had a whole new set of questions. Could this Drake guy have literally made them all vanish? She did not want to entertain what that might mean. Maybe he had vanished, and Shelby had followed him. Was it an ability all vampires had? Jackie needed some answers.

She stepped out of the car to the sound of a gunshot. Jackie ducked behind the open door, and Gamble came out to do the same, his gun drawn.

"You see where?" he whispered.

"No."

Three seconds later there was another shot fired. No flash of muzzle fire in the dark. No sound of ricocheting bullets. They were both still standing.

"Around back?"

Jackie nodded. "Sounds like. You go around to the far corner. Wait for my signal."

He nodded and went off at a slow jog, half crouched along the edge of the road and then across Nick's drive. Another shot had Gamble dropping to a knee, pointing his gun toward the house, but there was still no indication of attack. Jackie quietly closed the car door and moved along the thick row of rhododendrons and oaks lining the property. A walk up to the garage window indicated Nick was likely home. The dinged-up Porsche was parked inside. Another shot made her jump, and she moved quickly to the back corner of the house.

A dark figure, overcoat flapping in the night breeze, cowboy hat pulled low over his eyes, stood on Nick's deck. He had two guns in his hands, two huge fricking guns, and Jackie watched him raise up one and squeeze off a shot into the yard. In the dim light provided from the inside lights, another fence post blew its top. It took Jackie a moment to register the image she was seeing.

"Nick?" she called out. "Mind putting down the guns?"

He turned, the pistols hanging loose at his side. "Agent Rutledge," he said. "They send you for the statement, or just back to get your things?"

Why did he sound just a little off to her? Jackie didn't like the feeling she was getting from him. "Both. Can you put the damn pistols away, please?"

He hesitated for a moment, but she could see Gamble creeping up silently from behind. "Agent Gamble, any louder, and you might as well announce you're sneaking up on me."

Gamble stopped at the edge of the deck. "Christ. You hear better than a fucking dog."

Jackie watched Nick pull back the edges of his coat and slide the pistols into holsters at each hip. It was then in the light that she caught the glint of a shining star pinned to his shirt. Sheriff. *He's wearing his goddamn sheriff outfit. What the hell?* "What are you doing, Nick?"

"A little target practice," he said with half a smile. There was no amusement in the rest of his face.

"And the sheriff costume? What's going on?"

Nick turned and made for the back door, moving with slow and purposeful steps. "Nostalgia, Ms. Rutledge. Nothing more." He slid the glass door open and walked inside, leaving it open behind him.

Gamble waved a hand in Nick's direction, a questioning look on his face, and Jackie frowned at Nick's retreating figure. He was going into the kitchen now, slow, with shoulders drooping. It began to dawn on Jackie then what she was seeing. *Nostalgia, my ass. I can't even fucking believe it.* Anger knotted up her gut. "Go ahead and wait in the car, Gamble. I want a few private words with Mr. Anderson."

"What?" Gamble rolled his eyes. "You're going to kick the vampire's ass, and I have to go wait in the car?"

She cocked her head, narrowing her gaze. "I'm going to kick your ass if you don't shut up."

He shook his head and began to walk off the deck.

"Leave your com open just in case though."

"Yeah, don't worry," he said. "It is."

Jackie found Nick pouring a cup of coffee at the kitchen counter. He looked completely out of place in the kitchen's modern decor, and surprisingly appealing in the leather duster and cowboy hat.

"So what's the real deal here, Nick? What's going on?" She wanted to come right out with it, but it would be better to hear it out of his own mouth.

He poured a second cup and pushed it across the counter toward her, but Jackie left it untouched. "Just what I said. Nostalgia."

She bit her lip to keep the epithets at bay. "You dress up in your cowboy outfit and blast away your fence posts when feeling nostalgic?"

"Among other things," he said simply and sipped at his coffee. "One hundred eighty years provides a number of things to be nostalgic about.

He would not say it. Jackie realized he wouldn't. "You're so full of shit."

"Pardon?"

She walked up to him, stabbing a finger at his chest, anger roiling up into her throat, full of rage now, not only at him, but herself as well. "You're giving up. You're waiting for Drake to come take you away."

"He won't be taking me anywhere."

"Oh, really?" She stepped back, arms crossed over her chest. "And you have a plan now?" She waited for a whole second before continuing. "I didn't think so. You just plan on going down with guns blazing away at something you can't kill." The look on his face was all the agreement she needed. "Coward. A hundred forty years of chasing this fucker, and you're going to lame out in the end."

"Coward?" Nick's eyes narrowed imperceptibly at her, a dim glint beneath the low brim of his hat. "I'm not real sure you're in a position to be making any claims regarding cowardice, Ms. Rutledge."

Jackie's mouth dropped open for a moment. "Are you calling me a coward, too, cowboy?"

"Not about this," he said, voice low. "But you've got something you're afraid to face, and it sure makes you hate men."

"That's absurd," she said, suddenly finding herself on the defensive. The rage began to melt away into blubbering self-doubt. "I don't hate men at all."

"Don't trust them then? Afraid of them?"

"Look, Nick, I didn't come here to argue our personal faults."

He stepped across the floor toward her, and Jackie found herself eye to eye with the sheriff's badge. It did indeed look like the genuine article.

He arched an eyebrow, pulling Jackie's glare up to his

glowing eyes. "Well, you sure started out that way, and now you're chickening out."

Jackie reached up to slap him, and Nick caught her wrist in his hand. "I'm not a coward, Jackie. I'm tired. I've come to the end, and I've failed. It's disappointing that I let down those I promised to get justice for. If you have a problem with the fact I choose to go out the same way I came into this nightmare, then so be it, but do not call me a coward."

"Then let's get him," she said defiantly, wishing he would let go and stop looking down at her. His eyes had gone from a glint to a soft glow. "I can't let him get away with killing you, or anyone else, so quit trying to get everyone out of the way who wants to help. That's just stupid pigheadedness."

"And why do you care so much, Jackie? Tell me that." He still held her wrist, as though keeping her in his grip might force her to answer. "People like you don't do this because they want to. It's because they need to."

"People like me?" She yanked her hand away from him, and he let her go. "What the fuck is that supposed to mean? I catch guys who are the lowest of the low, the sickest, most twisted minds around who deserve to be taken out or put away. I like justice just as much as you do, Sheriff."

Nick looked at her for a long moment and then nodded once, stepping around the counter to sit himself down on a bar stool. "Noble of you." He smiled, but it was wistful and sympathetic.

Jackie hated that smile.

"So who was the guy who got away?"

"What?" She knew what he was asking, but it shocked her that he would ask.

"Who ruined your life that drives you to such extremes and keeps you from ever being happy?" He tipped his hat up, a curious brow cocked over one eye. "Who's your Drake, Jackie?"

For a moment, all she could do was stare at him in silence. Indecision froze her. How had the conversation turned to this? It was the last thing she needed to be doing. She had little doubt, however, that Nick thought Shelby and the girl were dead. There was no reason to stay any longer.

Yet Jackie made no move to go. She sucked in a deep breath, holding it, looking at Nick. *This is dumb. Stupid, dumb, idiotic conversation, and I should get my ass back to the car.* "My stepfather."

Nick watched her in silence, making no move to agree or respond.

"He was a cop, and he abused my mother until she killed herself."

Still, Nick sat in silence, waiting and wondering.

"He told me I would end up just like her."

Nick sat up straight again, reached over, and handed Jackie her coffee. "Ah, well, I am sorry you had to endure someone like that, and that your mother came to such a sad end, but you won't."

She frowned at his presumptuousness. "Are you a psychoanalyst as well?"

"No," he said with a slow shake of his head. "I've been around a while though, and I know you had your moment there a couple days ago, and you survived. You won't let yourself get to that point again, because it's a scary place to be, and you want to get your life back."

Jackie sipped her coffee to hide the disbelief. The damn bastard was far more perceptive than he looked. Who knew men could pay that close attention? "And what about you, Nick?" She waved her hand at his outfit. "What do you want?"

He gave her a wistful smile, his eyes crinkling at the edges. "I want justice. I want to move on from all this, for it to be done." He set his mug down on the counter and stood up. "What I want at the moment is the answer to a question that's been plaguing me for the past few hours."

He stepped up in front of her, and Jackie gulped down her mouthful of coffee. *A few hours ago? What happened a few . . . Oh, damn. He can't be serious.* She looked up at him, the bemused smile still turning up the corner on one side of his mouth, and felt his hand remove the coffee cup from her own. *Oh, my God! He is!* "What . . . um, what question is that?"

Nick inched closer to her, and Jackie inched back until she found the wall behind her. "I'm curious," he said, holding her gaze while one hand reached up and tucked an errant wisp of hair behind her ear. "How much was Shelby, and how much was really you?"

Where are a dozen shots of tequila when you need them? He stood toe to toe with her now, looming above in the cowboy hat and the thick leather duster, two pistols the size of her arm at his hips. The brush of his fingertips along her scalp, trailing down behind her ear, sent a wave of prickly goose bumps down her spine. *I can duck out of this, I still can, damnit! God, this is stupid. What the fuck are we doing?* The thoughts tumbled through Jackie's brain in a befuddled mess. She could not remember the last time she had been sober for this kind of thing.

"Mostly her," she finally whispered, trying to lick a hint of moisture back to her lips.

His hand cupped the back of her head, the fingers laced into the short waves of hair, and Jackie held her breath for a brief moment, terrified of the awareness of thoughts and emotions that alcohol had always drowned in its lovely, numbing sea.

She had been prepared for fierce, hard desperation, or a warm snake of a tongue dancing down her throat. Jackie didn't expect the first soft brush of lips, barely a kiss at all, a hesitant introduction of his lips to hers. She opened her eyes after a moment to find his face inches away, looking at her with eyes that saw far more of her than she deemed reasonable.

"You're trembling," he said. The other hand reached up and cupped her cheek, and Jackie found herself in a very defenseless position. "In a good or bad way?"

Some small part of Jackie's brain was screaming, "Groin him and run!" But in another, the strong, vibrant voice of Laurel came to her, and Jackie remembered the offhand promise she had made. "Good, I think."

She closed her eyes, and this time, perhaps for the first time, Jackie let herself be held by those hands, giving in to it instead of bracing herself against it. The lips were still soft, but there was no hesitation as he kissed her this time, and Jackie could feel the hunger. His teeth gave a gentle tug on her lower lip, and that slight relenting of her mouth to his broke down whatever will remained to resist, and Jackie brought her arms up around Nick's neck and invited his tongue into her mouth for a fervent, burning waltz.

After a few seconds or an hour, Nick pulled away from the embrace. "I believe you answered my question, Agent Rutledge." He had a pleased smile on his face, but the eyes stared with far more than amusement and didn't look to be entirely focused on her eyes.

That was completely unfair. Jackie leaned against the wall and slowly let out her breath. This was not what she was here for. Not at all. She could not decide if she was terrified or just wanted to strip him down to the gun belt and play "ride 'em, cowboy." The fact she even considered the notion was scary enough. And exciting.

"Good. Glad to help. Now answer my question, because it's why I came over here."

He picked up his coffee cup and took another swallow. "Hmmm?"

"Why would there be no bodies in that SUV?"

Nick nearly choked on his coffee. "What?"

His reaction looked real enough. "Drake's Escalade. It burned to a crisp, but when we looked inside, it was empty. So I know how Drake got out, but what about Shelby and the little girl?"

Nick sat back down on the bar stool. "Damn. He must have dropped the girl off somehow and took Shelby with him, unless she figured out how to do it herself. Or maybe she crossed over with the girl?"

"The alley!" Jackie remembered now. "He pulled into an alley for, like, five seconds and then nearly ran us over coming out."

"Maybe," Nick said. The phone rang, and he pulled his cell phone out of the duster's pocket. He frowned at the caller ID before opening up the phone. "Hello?"

Jackie could hear a man's voice on the other line. It sounded vaguely English.

Nick's eyes narrowed. His mouth drew into a thin crease. "Hello, Cornelius."

Chapter 51

"Nicholas! My old friend. You gave it a good go of things that time. I must say I was actually impressed with your efforts." He chuckled softly into Nick's ear, and Nick found himself clenching his teeth so hard his jaw had begun to hurt.

Jackie's eyes were wide in surprise. She mouthed the words "Keep him on the phone" to him. Nick nodded. He knew they had bugged his phone, and he had let it remain on just this off-chance occurrence.

"Sometimes we just get lucky," he replied. "Where's she at, Drake? You can dispense with the niceties."

"Would you be referring to Ms. Fontaine or little Agatha?"

Nick closed his eyes for a moment and took a deep breath. Every time around, he had needed to put up with the reminders, and Drake had made sure to provide them, occasionally in far more detail than necessary. "Let's stick with the girl for now."

"Of course, of course. Far more noble to try to save the child. I could always count on you to be an honorable man, Nicholas. That is what has made this so entertaining, you know. And in the end, that is what the game comes down to, is it not? Where does honor stand in relation to vengeance, my good sheriff?"

Wordy fucking bastard. "The honorable thing is justice, and in your case, Drake, that goes beyond the hangman's noose. So would you care to tell me where she is so we can have this little showdown you've been dreaming of for a hundred years? Or are you going to pop back through the doorway again?"

Drake laughed, high-pitched, and sounding very nonsinister for a five-hundred-year-old vampire. "Caught you off guard with that one, didn't I? I wish I could have seen the look on your faces. Priceless, to be sure."

"I don't really have expectations about you anymore, Cornelius. This scheme is tiring and stale, and I'm ready for its conclusion. I am curious though. How much blood does it take to cross over?"

"You will have to learn that trick on your own, and I believe you have grown far too moral to pursue that course of action."

"Keeps me human at least," Nick said, not trying to hide the menace in his voice.

Drake laughed. "Now, now, Sheriff. Taking the high ground again? I knew it would be your undoing, but as I said at the first, I shall say at the last. If you wish to win this game, dear boy, you shall have to be that which you are not. Nonetheless, you've had a sporting chance, and one cannot say I did not give you the opportunities, Nicholas."

"You always were the thoughtful one," Nick replied.

"I dare say we would have gotten along splendidly under other circumstances, but we got off on a bit of the wrong foot back then."

"That would be stating it mildly, yes. Anyway, about this sporting chance. What have you got in mind this time?"

Drake huffed, sounding offended. "I've already given it to you. You haven't proven very adept at finding me, which

I shall admit is rather difficult these days, but I had the good graces to call and chat so your fine lass there could trace the call. Really, Nicholas. I'm not stupid, and neither are you, so please do not insult me. We are nearly done, and then perhaps you can have a few words with Gwendolyn before I drain your souls completely away."

Nick gripped his phone so hard his hand began to tremble. "You aren't invincible, Drake, so get over yourself. I know you can die, and you shall."

There was a brief pause, and then Drake's voice returned, sounding muted and distant. "Ask the sister, dear girl. I'm busy with a call just now." He was back a moment later. "Oh, someday, when I've tired of everything, perhaps. But not from you, Nicholas. You haven't got what it takes. So come alone, unless of course you wish for this to all end badly. I have followed the rules, and I expect you to do the same. Not my fault you lost your taste for blood, now, is it?" He chuckled, and Nick barely restrained himself from smashing the phone down on the counter. "Well, that should be enough time, don't you think, Ms. Rutledge? Tsk-tsk if you dropped the ball on this one. See you soon, Nicholas. I am looking forward to it."

The phone went dead, and Nick clapped it shut, shoving it back into his pocket. "Oh, I'm sure you are, you little prick."

Jackie was already on her own phone, having listened to most of the conversation by leaning up next to Nick's ear. He could still smell the clean scent of her hair.

"Did they get it?" Her mouth scrunched up in disgust at the reply. "Almost? Fuck! What do you mean almost? Where?" She shook her head. "Fine, whatever. Just keep everyone out of the area until we track down his location. I'll contact you then." She slammed the phone down on the counter. "God, I work with idiots, I swear."

"It's okay. It'll be enough. What area?"

"Wicker Park," she said. "That going to be good enough?"

"It will be. Drake leaves nothing to chance. He figured you might not narrow his location down exactly, so he gave us a clue."

"He did?"

Her forehead wrinkled up between her eyebrows, a cute trait Nick had failed to notice before. There was more and more about this woman he found appealing. Kissing her may have been a mistake, he realized. He had wanted to know, though, figuring it might be the only chance he would ever get to see, and he had been right: It had not been mostly Shelby.

"Did you hear when Drake moved away from the phone? It was hard to make out."

Jackie nodded. "I couldn't make out what he said."

"He said 'ask the sister.'"

"A church?" She looked stunned. "The fucker has been hiding out in a church?" She picked her phone back up to dial downtown.

"Jackie, keep them away. Seriously," Nick said, laying a hand on her arm. "They get close, and the girl is dead. There is no sneaking up here."

She nodded. "I know. Gamble! I need church addresses in that area you gave, and keep everyone out. If anyone is in the area, get them out now. I'll let you know more when we get over there. Call me with addresses when you get them." She shoved the phone into her pocket. "Ready to go, Nick?"

"Yeah." He found himself smirking at her again. This woman, whom he sensed being on the verge of quaking in her boots, didn't think twice about jumping into the jaws of death. He wanted to kiss her again for luck.

"What? What's with the look?"

"Nothing important. Let's go get this done."

Chapter 52

They were in her Durango, and Jackie could not get comfortable riding shotgun in her own car. On a casual drive, perhaps, but they were heading toward a confrontation with something more and less than human, and not being behind the wheel tugged on the strings of control. The closer they got, the more nervous she became, which was very unlike her. When did she ever get nervous chasing down the bad guys? She never even thought about it, but now it began weighing on her with each passing second. This was no ordinary bad guy. The guy could take them out quicker than she could down three shots.

"Why a church?" she wondered. "Crosses and holy water are yet another myth, I take it?"

"And we like garlic, too. Go figure," Nick said with a smile.

"Smart-ass."

He shrugged, whipped around a pair of cars using the emergency lane, and clocked her Durango up to a hundred on an open stretch of freeway. A light rain was falling, and Jackie swore they were going to hydroplane at any moment. "That goes without saying, I suppose."

Gamble called back a moment later and began to run

through a list of possible churches in the area. On the fourth one, Nick stopped her.

"That one. That's it," he said. "Has to be."

"I'll call you back when we verify," she said to Gamble and clicked off. "You sure?"

"That was the name of his church back in 1934. He was a minister back then, too. Easy access to victims."

"God, that's sick."

He shrugged. "Practical if you are looking for easy prey."

Prey. One little word, and Jackie was reminded that Nick was not quite what he appeared, a dying man in need of blood to stay alive. "Did you ever get used to . . ."

"No, Jackie. I hate it. It's a very difficult thing to live with," he said plainly.

"Shelby says . . . said it's very addictive."

"It is, but for all the power it gives, it makes you weak."

"Ah. I think I see." Jackie had not really thought of it like that. Of course, when did she ever think about such things? But Nick was right. You had to take the life from people in order to get the strength, and no matter how you sliced that pie, it was bad. "Can we kill him?"

"Sure," Nick said, nodding once. "Drake's powerful, but not invincible. He can bleed like everyone else, but the power can heal with amazing speed, as Shelby showed you."

Jackie could not argue with that, but she was not sure she would do it again knowing how it affected a person.

"If you see him, you don't think or ask questions. You just shoot. Got it?"

Jackie snorted. "That's about as ass-backward an order as you can give, Sheriff, but I got no problem with that, unless he's holding that little girl."

"Fair enough, but shoot him a lot. There is no such thing as overkill with this guy. A nice shot to the temple will likely just have him spitting the bullet back at you."

"Christ, Nick. Seriously?"

"I'm not joking. With real blood, the control over the body is phenomenal. If we get him, you empty that gun of yours into him, and you shoot for damage, not to kill. Blow his goddamn head apart if you can, take a leg off. Concentrate your shots and put the biggest fucking hole in him you can. Feel free to take out any and all anger."

They were cruising by downtown, the first vestiges of light encroaching on the charcoal sky. The skyline was an eerie sight, a dark and ragged maw of teeth filled with leery, weeping eyes. Soulless concrete, glass, and steel. Some found it full of life, exciting, vigorous, a life unto itself, but Jackie could never quite get that feeling from the city. *Why do I even live here?* At the moment, it felt filled with an inexplicable taint. Death, it seemed, was everywhere, and they were now going after its master.

"Jackie? You okay?"

"I just have a bad feeling about this, is all."

"I'd be worried if you weren't scared," he replied.

"Did I say I was scared?"

"You didn't have to," Nick said. "I could see it in the way you were looking out the window just then."

"Well, pay more attention to the road then, damnit." He was exasperating. It was almost like having . . . Laurel in the car. "Sorry. You're right. I'm a bit worried about this, and I'm still not used to doing anything without Laur around. It's just . . . strange."

"I know. Nothing will be the same around here without Shelby either. She kept me on my toes. I will truly miss her."

"Let's deal with Drake first. This is dragging me down."

"Agreed. Sorry."

The Durango smoked its tires suddenly as Nick took them through a red light and pulled a hard right against the oncoming traffic. The sound of crunching metal and exploding glass could be heard behind them, but Jackie was too busy bracing herself in the seat. "What the hell?"

Nick wove in and out of the early morning traffic, thankfully light. Doing eighty in a thirty-five could get you in trouble. His hands were clenched on the steering wheel as he focused on the road ahead, mouth set in a grim and furious line. "He's feeding."

"On the little girl? Now?" Jackie had the image of a young girl with strawberry-blond hair zip-tied to a stainless-steel table under the intensity of a fluorescent light, a bright tube of red flowing out of her arm, an innocent life draining away into another. "Shit, Nick. Drive faster."

The First Hope Church of Christ had lights on when they pulled into the parking lot. The clock on the Durango read 5:47 AM. Nick had a sinking feeling that the "sister" mentioned in the earlier phone call might likely be inside. A sign hanging over the main double doors read FIRST HOPE DAY CARE. A SAFE AND LOVING ENVIRONMENT FOR YOUR CHILD. SIGN UP NOW! Around the corner of the parking lot loomed a dark, converted Victorian home. The placard hanging between two posts in the small yard had the words TANENBAUM'S FUNERAL HOME in elegant, gold script.

The sense of Drake permeated the air so heavily Nick could not decide where exactly it was coming from.

"Should we really be parking right out front?" Jackie said, leaning forward and staring out the front window at the church and then over at the funeral home.

The edge of fear in her voice had faded. It was resolute, determined now in spite of the fear he knew lay beneath. It was a good sign. He could count on her. "Doesn't matter. He knows we're here."

"That's a relief."

"Where would you go if you wanted to drain a body of blood?" he asked her, getting out of the Durango and walking toward the funeral home.

Jackie caught up to him a moment later, Glock held firmly in one hand. "Funeral home would be my bet, too. Maybe we should split—"

"No," he said, insistent. "We stay together, or you stay in the car. No choice this time, Jackie.

"What, you going to cuff me to the steering wheel?"

"If that's what it takes. You can't face this guy alone, Jackie. No."

She was passed arguing the point. "Okay, we stay together. You better be right."

Nick hoped so as well. He drew a six-shooter from its holster and held it loosely but ready at his side as they approached the house. The inside was black as pitch and was beginning to feel about as thick with the sense of the dead. He could sense ghosts in the area. It had to be the place. "I really wish you would stay back at the car," he told her.

"There's a girl dying in there, Nick. Let's go." At the foot of the front steps she paused. "Maybe we should go around back?"

Nick shook his head. He knew they were running dangerously low on time. They could only be so careful now if the girl was going to be saved. "Last chance, Jackie. Please go back and wait."

She jabbed a finger at his ribs. "Do you want to get this guy or not?" Jackie reached for the handle and jiggled the door. "Shit, locked."

The door was a framed stained-glass window depicting some religious symbolism Nick paid little attention to as he flicked the barrel of his revolver through, sending shards of glass tumbling inward to the floor. He reached in and opened the door. "No, it's not."

Jackie leaned up against the door frame, gun held up between both hands, ready to go in. Nick swung the door in and stepped inside, scanning the entry along the barrel of his gun. Jackie turned and bolted over to the archway leading into the living room on the right side of the house. Once inside, it was not as dark as it had appeared. The growing light outside provided enough to see inside, and the front of the home was empty. She peered in and then stepped into the former living room, which now appeared to be an elegant seating room filled with Victorian furnishings. Stairs in front of them went up to the second floor, while the doorway to the left opened into what looked to be the front office. Above, a delicate chandelier of gold and glass hung high up over their heads.

The smell was unsettlingly sterile.

Jackie motioned at him and pointed up the stairs and then toward the floor. Where would they have the embalming equipment? Basement was the logical choice. Nick pointed at the floor, and Jackie nodded agreement, walking across the entry toward him. From above, Nick heard a soft creak and groan, as though perhaps someone were walking directly overhead. The sound was followed by the short, sharp sound of a fizzle.

Short-circuited wiring. Nick leaped forward, shoving Jackie back toward the sitting room, and the chandelier crashed to the center of the floor, showering Nick in tiny shards of glass.

"Son of a bitch!" Jackie muttered, climbing back to her feet.

"All right?" Nick kicked off the mangled light and stood up, shaking the glass off his coat.

She nodded. "Yeah, thanks. I—"

"Oh, good show. The sheriff saves the poor damsel in distress." Drake's voice was hollow, echoing from out of the ventilation ducts.

Nick glanced around and caught the faint, wispy glow of a ghost drifting back through the wall in the rear of the sitting room. "The show is just starting, Drake!" Nick shouted into the room. "I won't miss this time."

"Well, he's in here at least," Jackie said, sounding a bit more like her usual pissed-off self.

"Waiting and ready," Nick added. So far, so bad, Nick figured. Cornelius had it all choreographed, and it was up to Nick to figure out a way to alter the game plan in their favor, but so far, nothing brilliant was coming to mind. He pointed toward the office, and Jackie nodded. They approached, guns out and ready.

The room was empty of the living or dead, with a doorway leading down a short hallway toward the back of the house. Likely the former kitchen, and that meant the entry to the basement.

Nick shouldered up to Jackie to whisper in her ear. "If he's feeding when we find the girl, I'll try to grab her. You put as many holes in Drake as you can, and whatever you do, do not look him in the eye. There should be a back door here close by. We'll get out that way if we can." Jackie nodded once and kept her gaze focused on the hall.

The hall had a small bathroom on one side and an oversize closet that was floor-to-ceiling coffin samples, dozens of doll-sized miniatures to pretend your loved ones were getting buried in. Past that was the kitchen, beyond which a door in the back led to what was likely the former mud room. A door led out, and another led down. Next to the door, a small electric lift sat waiting where the dumb-waiter likely was.

Drake's hollow, distant voice came drifting up through the vents once again. "Dear boy, you are dallying. This cute little thing is getting droopy-eyed. I would think for your last effort you would be giving it that one hundred and ten percent. Agatha deserved no less. I would have done the same for my boy, were he alive today, but, alas, he is not."

Nick reached over and grabbed the mudroom door's handle. "Be wary. We're walking into a trap." She nodded, and Nick opened the door. At that moment, the ringing thrum of Deadworld began to abate. "Damnit. He's stopped feeding."

The heavy, metal basement door was unlocked, and Nick shoved it open and leaped down to the landing. Jackie tried to run after.

Summoning up the bit of extra strength he could, Nick braced himself for the landing so he would keep from slamming into the opposite wall. He had both guns out pointing out across the basement floor when his feet touched down.

A single fluorescent light burned in the middle of the room, an all-too-familiar setup. Its blue-white glare cast a ghostly cone of light down on the cadaver's table, upon which the Agatha lookalike lay. She was still clad in Winnie the Pooh pajamas, and her listless arm hung over the side of the table, fresh blood dripping from the small puncture in her arm.

Of Drake, there was no immediate sign. Guns held out before him, Nick leaped the last six stairs to the floor. Behind him, Jackie stopped on the landing, crouched down on the balls of her feet, Glock scanning across the room.

"Cover me," he said and ran over to the little girl. *Be alive! Please, just be alive!* Nick picked up the dangling arm, his fingers clamped across her wrist, and he found a faint pulse. "She's alive!"

"Where the hell is he?" Jackie said in a hushed voice.

Nick dug in his pocket for his pocketknife. The girl's other wrist and ankles were bound with the familiar zip-ties. "I don't . . ." He stopped after taking a single step. Above them, at the top of the stairs, the basement door slammed shut. It was followed by the loud and unmistakable sound of a dead bolt being slid into place. And then the light went out. "Shit."

Jackie squeezed off two quick shots. "Fuck! Nick, it's a solid steel door. What the hell?"

"Call Gamble now, Jackie." The trap had been sprung. The question was just how tightly were they being held?

"Gamble? Get them here. Now. Fire, ambulance, everyone. We're locked in the basement of Tanenbaum's Funeral Home."

In the pitch blackness, Nick fumbled around for the girl's hands and feet, hoping he did not cut her skin getting her free.

"Nick? You smell something?"

He did the moment she said it. Smoke. "Yeah. Something's burning."

The dim light of her cell phone came back on. "Gamble! Tell them the building is likely on fire, so the sooner the better. No. The power is out down here, I have no fucking idea how we're getting out. Yes, I tried! It's a metal fucking door. Just get them over here!"

"Keep the cell on, Jackie. We can use the light to see with."

She began to walk toward him, but a thunderous boom shook the house, knocking her down the last three steps to the floor.

Floating through the foul air, Drake's voice quietly taunted. "Speed, dear boy. Once again, you have gone for the rescue over the kill. I'd hoped just this once you would give in on that choice, but it seems you will be stubborn to the end. I am still the gentleman, however, and have given you one last chance. Figure it out, and perhaps we shall dance again. You are too predictable, my friend. Good-bye. I shall see you on the other side."

Drake's laughter faded into the smoky darkness.

"There has to be another door out of here," Jackie said.

There should be, and odds were it was securely sealed like the other one. "There should be windows though," Nick answered. "Painted over, maybe. If they're big enough we might be able to push the girl through."

"Okay," she said, moving over to a wall and stumbling over something metal on the floor. "Ow! Goddamnit." Her voice had a tinge of panic to it, and Nick could hardly blame her for that one. Trapped in a burning building was not high on his choices of ways to go.

Smoke was beginning to thicken in the air. Another boom, and there came the sound of something crashing on the floor above. The second-floor ceiling perhaps? If they had looked upstairs first, they might have found whatever materials Drake had situated to take the house down.

Carrying the girl in one arm, Nick felt his way along the back wall, lined with stainless-steel counters and cupboards. There had been a full-sized door for something over on this end of the room.

"Hey, I found a window!" Jackie called out. "And it's maybe six inches wide. We'll never get her through this, Nick."

"Okay," he said, finally finding the door that had been to the left of the stairs and across the room from the foot of the cadaver table. "Office or storage room here. Maybe an extinguisher inside." Not that it would do them a lot of good in the end. It might buy them a minute or two. Holding the girl, Nick kicked the door in and was greeted by a shimmering wall of heat and bright flame. He turned his back to the fire to protect the girl. "Christ. The ceiling is down in here."

That meant the first floor was already engulfed in flames—likely began the moment they came downstairs. They needed that basement door opened. It was only a six-foot span across to the back door through the mudroom. Even with the house on fire, they could make that leap without dying. Probably. Jackie had the same thought.

"Gamble! We need that basement door unlocked, or you're going to have a very crispy agent down here." She coughed several times against the thickening smoke. "Yeah,

I realize the place looks like an inferno, but we're dead if it doesn't get open. Got it?"

To emphasize her point, another explosion shook the house, and this time part of the ceiling did collapse, bringing down a pile of flaming furniture from the sitting room. It narrowly missed Jackie, and she jumped back, a short scream escaping her lips. "Oh, my God. Nick! Any brilliant ideas?"

The fire lit up the room, allowing them to see at least, and Nick saw one last door past the office. It was large and metallic, with a handle much like one might find on an upright freezer. "Come on. In here," he said, pointing at the cadaver fridge. "It might buy us some time."

"That's crazy. We'll cook in there."

"The floor is going to fall on us out here, Jackie. Move it."

Nick ran over to the door and pulled the handle open. Even with the power off, the room inside was still cool relative to the rest of the basement. Once inside, Jackie was hesitant to shut the door all the way.

"Jackie. It's forty degrees in here. Close the door."

"But . . . Nick, it'll be a goddamn oven."

"It will be, but it gives us the most time."

"Shit." She pulled the latch shut, and they were closed inside. "Let's hope they put out the fire before it can cook us."

Nick gently laid the girl down on the floor, squatting beside her. He took off his hat and set it down over the wide, staring, and empty eyes. "Yeah, let's hope."

"Oh, no. Damnit, no!"

He could see that courage and determination, the desire to rescue the girl, which had been driving Jackie past the fear of everything else, slowly evaporate from her gaze. Nick rubbed a hand over his scalp. "I wish you'd have stayed outside, Jackie."

She did not respond. Jackie was staring over the top of

his head at the back of the freezer. Nick turned and realized the open-mouthed silence had nothing to do with the death of the girl. Oozing her way through the small ventilation grate in back of the ceiling was the faded, distorted form of Laurel.

Chapter 53

Oh, my God. Why is she here? We're about to fucking die, that's why. Laurel's ghostly image barely made itself present, a poorly lit hologram of her friend. She bent down immediately and passed her hand through the body of the young girl, a frown stretching the dark lines of her mouth. When she spoke, her voice sounded like it came from the end of a long tunnel.

"Nick," she said, her words spaced out with apparent effort, "you must come. We need you."

He stood up, hands thrust into his pockets. "We're trapped here, Laurel."

"Nick. You know how."

"No!" he answered abruptly. In the dead silence of the freezer, it made Jackie's stomach jump.

"Laur, can you help us?" She had no idea what a ghost could do for them, but maybe she knew something they did not. "Nick? What's going on?"

Laurel's foggy image faded to almost nothing for a moment but then sprang back with brief, brilliant intensity. "You must!" Her finger jabbed out at Nick, and she watched him take a hesitant step backward.

She could not see his face, but a second later, his shoulders visibly sagged. "I can't do that, Ms. Carpenter. There must be another way."

Her head shook. "No time. I'll help, but hurry."

Jackie tapped Nick on the shoulder, and he whirled around on her, startled. For the first time, she saw something she didn't think possible in those depthless eyes. He looked afraid, which was the last thing Jackie needed to reassure her fraying nerves.

"Care to explain what the hell you're talking about?"

Nick dropped back to his knees, reaching out to lift the hat and brush a strand of hair off the little girl's face. "Blood. It's all about blood."

Something stung Jackie's eye, and she reached up to realize it was sweat. Looking behind her on the wall by the door, the thermostat already read seventy-eight degrees. "Blood. What's blood got do with our current situation?"

Nick stood up, moving with the effort of an old man. His face had gone into that unreadable zone again, except perhaps a droop in his eyes. Sadness? Haunted? Regardless, not a look Jackie was going for, under the circumstances.

"Laurel wants me to take us over."

"Over where? Outside?"

"No, Jackie. Over to the other side. Deadworld."

Jackie glanced over at Laurel. Was she out of her mind? The look she gave Jackie brought a lump to her throat.

"Please, hon. Be brave. It's your only chance."

"Don't we sort of have to be . . . dead for that?"

"No," Nick said. "Drake has been doing it, so presumably I can do it as well."

"I'm no vampire though," Jackie replied. Her mind was still trying to wrap around the notion of going to the "other" side. What did that mean exactly? It was an apples-and-oranges arrangement. Then again, Laurel's ghost was standing here in front of her. The dead could walk among the living.

He gave her a reluctant shrug. "Technically, that shouldn't matter."

Jackie grunted. "Technically. You aren't sounding too sure of yourself, Sheriff, but it's now . . . ninety-four degrees in here. We need to try something, so I vote yes for hanging out with Laurel for a while."

"Jackie, I can't do it without blood."

"Okay. Well . . ." The obvious now smacked Jackie square in the gut. He needed *her* blood. "You need some of my blood."

"I might need a lot of your blood, and even then I have no guarantees anything will work."

"But Laur thinks it will. She said she will help."

Laurel nodded behind Nick. "Yes. It can work. It's the only way."

She took a deep breath. Laur would never steer her wrong about anything. "If she says go for it, then go for it, Nick. We have to try. And I'll have you shoot me before I roast to death in here."

"Jackie," Nick said, stepping up close to her. He reached up, taking her face in his hands. Compared to the air in the sealed room, they were wonderfully cool. "Look me in the eye and tell me you're okay with this. I have to drink your blood, and it may kill you."

"I'm good," she answered back, trying desperately to actually sound that way. "Are you?"

He licked his lips, prepared to say something, but then Jackie felt herself pulled up to her toes, and Nick's mouth crushed down against hers. No soft hesitation this time. No pleasant little meeting of the mouths. It was just some heady mix of desperation, need, fear, and desire. After a few seconds he pulled back, but his hands still held her. He smiled. "Better now, thanks. Look at me, Jackie. If you look close enough you might actually see the door to the other side."

She stared hard into his eyes, wondering. "Really? You can see that?"

"If you know how to look, but I want you to know this won't hurt much at all, just a bit of weakness, maybe a little light-headedness, and then, hopefully, we'll be good, and Laurel will help me through this."

Jackie nodded. "Okay. Sounds good." The wide doe eyes said different.

"Now, keep your eye on Laurel. Not much else here to look at, and it might soothe your fear a bit."

Jackie's voice sounded dreamy, almost far away. "I'm not afraid though."

Laurel smiled at her. "It won't take long, hon. You'll hardly even realize."

"What happens then?"

"This is kind of a plan-as-you-go scenario. Let's just get you out of here first."

There was a dull pain in the crook of her right arm, and then pressure—soft, warm pressure. Out of the corner of her eye, Jackie could see Nick's head against her elbow. She knew it was happening now, but it all felt so far away. "He did that vampire thing on me again, didn't he?"

Laurel nodded. "Better that way, sweetie. Just keep watching me, talking to me, and then we'll go when Nick is ready."

"I like him, you know."

"Yeah, I can see that."

"And I miss you horribly."

"I know. I miss you, too."

"And I still love you, Laur. Really, but just . . . well, not like you wanted me to. I'm sorry."

"Hush. You can't be sorry about that."

Tears spilled down Jackie's cheeks, feeling distant and far, like she was watching someone else cry. A part of her knew it was Nick's doing, hypnotizing her, and, sadly, she had trusted him without hesitation. How embarrassing was that? They were tears of remorse, regret, and terror. Whatever might happen next, at the moment she was dying, her blood draining into Nick's suckling mouth.

"God, I'm scared, Laur. I don't want to die. Fuck, this really sucks." Laurel's image swam in her view, two, then three of her dancing across the back of the freezer. Her elbow began to ache, and she could feel the blood in her body ebbing toward Nick's drinking mouth, drawn like a pool of liquid iron to a magnet. "Nick! Please make this work. Please, please, please don't let me die like this."

"It's okay, baby," Laurel's voice cooed in her ear. "Hang in there a little longer. We're almost ready."

"Laur? I can't see you!"

"Shhhh. All done, sweetie. Rest now. I'll see you on the other side."

Jackie sank to her knees, head lolling over against Nick's shoulder, a chaotic jumble of thoughts pouring through her head, as they are wont to do when death encroaches. Most were full of anger and regret, but not of dying. Her life had not been what she wanted, consumed with pursuing demons she could not catch, filled with a need for revenge over losing something she had never really had. Ironic that Laurel had been there all those years, ready to give it, and Jackie had been oblivious, and even if she had leaned in that direction, the fear of herself would have kept her silent. Who would love her if they were really let in?

Goddamnit. I want another shot. God, Goddess, or whoever the fuck you are. If you give a shit about my sorry ass, please get me back alive. I can do better, I swear. I . . . I . . . Wow, Nick really smells good.

A warm blanket of darkness swaddled her in the blessed relief of nothingness.

Chapter 54

Nick blinked away the tears. He had managed to stay focused on his own feelings until Jackie's panicky fear peaked. Why did something so despicable have to feel so damn good? He was sucking the life from this woman, and all he could think about was how sweet she tasted. His cock was so hard it hurt, but he had kept those images mostly stuffed into the background. He had wallowed in that kind of thing before, but at least whatever shreds of willpower he had could keep those thoughts at bay. Finally, Jackie's pleas faded into unconsciousness, and she slumped forward. Nick eased her to the floor, his mouth still buried against her arm.

Laurel pushed and nudged at him, her cold, ethereal hands caressing his hair, rubbing at his temples. "Goddess be damned, Nick. Quit resisting so hard. Let me in."

"Hmmm?" It was all he could manage to say in response without lifting his mouth free from Jackie. It was difficult to hear her over the growing howl of the wind coming from the other side. The sound existed only in his head, but it was real nonetheless, a bitter, icy chill that came along with the incredible surge of power that filled his body.

"Relax, you stupid cowboy. Focus on the good things.

Shelby told me how real blood makes you feel, so let go of the guilt for two seconds so I can get in."

Get in. Why does she need to do that? And how the hell can anyone relax while drinking blood from anyone? Focus on the good things. I'm not a savage. I'm not a loathsome animal. Focus on good things. The sweet taste of Jackie's skin. How wonderful it would be to be inside her, kissing the crook of her elbow instead of sucking upon it.

"There," her voice said from within his head now. "Was that so hard? Okay, get us through, Nick. We need to hurry. I'm going to amplify your power to open the door. Nick? Stop drinking! She's going into shock."

He pulled his mouth away, clamping his hand over the open knife wound. Sweat was dripping down his face from the heat inside the freezer. "Is it going to be enough?"

"Let's find out," she said. "And hurry. This is very difficult for me, too."

Nick picked up Jackie, holding her tightly against him, and let the natural order of things follow, the order he had interrupted so many years ago in order to get his revenge. Now, ironically enough, he was letting it all go. The door yawned open, wider and wider, the breath of the dead blowing him through, but Jackie was not coming, not just yet, as she had not reached that brink, and Nick could feel her body slowly slipping from his grip.

"Laurel. Now would be a good time to kick it up a notch." Nick dug his fingers into Jackie, clenching as hard as he could. She was not ready yet, and he didn't have the force to get her through.

"Imagine a safe place, Nick. A safe place to take Jackie."

His home was the only place he would take her. It was the only place he felt might be remotely defensible against Drake. "I can't hold her much longer here, Ms. Carpenter." Despite the strength of his grip, Jackie was slowly beginning to pull away. Even as close as she was to death. That little bit of life was enough to offset the pull of the dead.

Then Laurel's whispering voice grew inside his head, slowly overtaking the howl of Deadworld. She was chanting, and Nick could not make out the words, or they were in a language he didn't understand, but just like she had claimed, the door stretched itself, becoming more elastic, the louder her voice became.

Home. Take us home.

They broke free of that boundary, falling into the black void between the world of the living and that of the dead, a cold so intense Nick felt sure his bones would splinter apart into a million icy shards.

Take us home. Make her safe, please, God, if you exist and are there at all, get her through this. I beg of you.

The blackness began to fade into gray, a substanceless fog that gave Nick no sense of location. The howling wind of the doorway had faded, and it was now eerily quiet. There was the faintest whispering in the background. "Laurel?"

"Shhhh," came the reply still echoing around inside his head. "Home. Keeping thinking of home. Almost there."

Nick did his best to keep the images of his house fresh, the piano loft where he spent so many hours of his recent life, and where Jackie had felt compelled to kiss him. He desperately wanted a chance to do that again. "Trying."

"Shhhh. No talking. They'll hear you."

She went back to her quiet chanting, and Nick wondered what she was talking about, but the whispers grew louder then, becoming nearly discernible voices. They were angry voices and many, but the words were jumbled, except for one, which he could make out because it was louder than all the rest. "Vampire."

Laurel's voice took on a fearful edge, the chanting becoming more frantic, and Nick took the cue and zeroed in on his house, the living room sofa, a fire, Jackie there, alive and healthy, sipping on a cup of the nuclear coffee he had made. Safe, comfortable, and home.

Something pushed at Nick's back, and for a split second he panicked, thinking perhaps that crowd of voices was upon them, but then it took on more substance and feel, pressing against his back and legs, and Jackie's body took on more weight against him as the gray fog dissipated into a serene background wash of color over everything. He was sitting on the sofa in his living room before his stone fireplace. It was a washed-out version of it, but his house nonetheless.

Resting against his chest, Jackie's pale, bluish lips appeared to be kissing his shirt. Nick shifted and turned, easing her cold body down on the cushions, and pressed a pair of fingers against the soft flesh of her throat. For a moment, panic fluttered through his stomach, but then he felt her pulse, weak but still there. They had made it for now, but how long did Jackie really have?

Chapter 55

Cold. Aching, biting cold. Did the dead feel cold? Jackie's eyes blinked open, seeing little but foggy white nothingness, and groaned at the icy grip of the giant hand that clamped down on her body when she attempted to move.

"Hey, hon." Laurel's face immediately moved into view. "How do you feel?"

Laurel looked solid enough to touch. Jackie smiled, which even made her mouth hurt. "It's fucking cold. My entire body hurts."

She leaned down and kissed Jackie's cheek, her lips the barest whisper against her skin. "I figured. I wasn't quite sure if you'd make it or what would happen once you got here."

Here. The other side. So Nick had managed to bring them across. "Am I dead?"

Laurel shook her head. "No, not yet, but I don't think you can stay here long. The living aren't supposed to be here."

"How long?"

It was Nick's voice, and Jackie realized he was sitting behind Laurel on a couch. Things looked oddly familiar. Jackie turned and noticed the massive slate fireplace of Nick's living room. "This looks like Nick's place."

"A few hours maybe?" Laurel said with a shrug. "And, yes, hon. It's Nick's. We needed a safe place to come to."

Jackie reached out tentatively and tried to touch Laurel's arm but was disappointed to see her fingers pass right through, disappearing for a moment before reappearing on the other side. How creepy was that? She shivered. "Heat doesn't work around here, I take it?"

"We'll get you back as soon as we can," Nick said.

Jackie stared at him for a moment, those depthless eyes surprisingly readable in the ghostly gray gloom. Laughter almost bubbled out of her mouth. "You don't have a fucking clue, do you?"

He stared at her in silence and then finally offered up a grim smile. "No. This is all new to me. I'm hoping Laurel knows what she's doing."

"I'll get us to Drake," she replied, "but after that, it's up to you."

"We need to figure out how to get Jackie back first."

Laurel's answer was simple. "You have to take her back."

"What?" He didn't bother hiding the chagrin in his voice. "I don't have the power to do that now. It took most of what I had to get us here."

Laurel reached down and brushed a wisp of hair from Jackie's face. "I know. You'll have to get it back from Drake."

Nick slumped back on the couch. "Ah. And I thought it would be something difficult."

Jackie struggled to sit up. Every movement felt sluggish, as if she were moving through water. "I wanted to kill him anyway."

"I don't even know if he can be killed here," Nick said. "The rules I knew don't seem to apply anymore."

"It's not his blood you want, Nick. You want his power. He takes it from the spirits here, draining their souls away to give him strength to pass back and forth."

"Okay, and if it's not through blood, just how do I do that?"

Laurel looked at a loss. "I don't know, but we'll figure it out."

Jackie shivered again. The cold was seeping deeper into her bones by the minute. If this kept up, she would hardly be able to move, let alone function in this place of the dead. "So, where's he at?"

"At the moment, I'm not sure," Laurel said. "But he keeps everyone locked away inside the Hancock building."

Nick snorted. "Seriously? I hadn't thought him so corporate."

"That's almost thirty miles from here," Jackie lamented. "I can't walk that far unless there's a ghost version of that Porsche sitting in the garage."

"No cars." Laurel stood up, backing around the coffee table that sat in the middle of the *U* shape of the sofas. She looked at both of them. "I just will myself to where I want to go. It's very easy here. Crossing over, not so much. I'm hoping it's an effect of this place and doesn't require actually being dead to work."

Jackie clutched her arms tightly across her chest in an effort to ease the chill. Teleport? Her life force was crystallizing inside her body, thin shards of death forming in an unbreakable lattice. She could barely move, much less *will* herself somewhere. "I don't know how to do that kind of shit, Laur."

Nick leaned forward, hands resting on his knees. The aggravating, indifferent look he usually presented had disappeared. He looked . . . worried? Scared? God help them if he had lost his nerve now. "Maybe you should stay here while we get Drake. It'll be safer for you here."

I'm not dying alone in this place. Jackie shook her head. "Screw that. If I'm going to be dead in a couple hours, I don't really want to do that alone."

"Then try to see if you can do it," Laurel said. "If not, we'll have to carry you there."

Jackie forced herself to sit up straight. "I don't want to hurt our chances of getting him."

"It's fine, hon. Just try something simple like moving over to the couch next to Nick. Picture yourself seated next to him, focus your thoughts on wanting to sit next to him, and visualize everything you can about it."

Nick leaned back, one arm laid out across the back cushion. Jackie eyed the spot on the couch next to him, and the probable warmth that might be obtained snuggled into the crook of his body. *Okay, not so hard to think about.* Jackie closed her eyes and wished for that simple, comforting embrace. It might not help, but at least it would feel good, and far better than his mouth licking and sucking at the hole in her arm. It would be nice to die without that lingering image and sensation squirming in her gut.

"Jackie, relax." Laurel's voice was a soothing whisper of wind in her ear. "Quit squinting. It's a mental thing, not physical."

Jackie took a deep breath, the tightening muscles in her chest failing to provide much air, and let it out in a rush. "Relaxing. Sitting next to Nick. Warm body. Warm, fucking body."

Jackie felt a nudge, a soft push from behind, as if the whole couch were tipping her toward Nick, and then his firm, depressingly cool arm came around her. Jackie put her hands out against him to push away, but the strength appeared to have dissipated from her body. He held her tightly, the big hand planted firmly on her hip, pulling her close.

"Holy shit," she said in a rush. "I did it."

Laurel clapped. "Awesome, hon."

"Did you help her, Laurel?"

"Shut up, you dumb cowboy." She huffed at him. "I gave

her a little nudge, but that was it. You did it mostly on your own, babe."

"Great," Jackie said but felt no elation at the feat. Her body hurt too much to feel good about anything. "Now what? I'm still about as useful as a wet noodle."

"I'm going to go check out the Hancock building and see where we need to go," Laurel replied. "We need a safe place to arrive."

Nick shifted against Jackie but kept his arm snugly against her body. "And what if they're waiting? Maybe we should just all go now."

Laurel shook her head. "No. I can handle getting away from Drake's goons. He's not back yet, but he might be soon, so we need to hurry."

"You sure?" Nick sounded skeptical. Given what she had witnessed from Drake, Jackie felt the same way.

"Nick, you are as different here as you are in the living world. Trust me, if Drake was back, I'd know." Laurel straightened up and closed her eyes. "See you soon. Be ready."

Without a chance to even wish her luck, Laurel vanished from sight. A shiver rippled through Jackie's body again, clenching her body into an even harder knot. "Shit."

"She'll be back," Nick said. "She knows what she's doing."

"Any clue what you're going to do when you get there?"

He was silent for a moment. "No."

"You don't give a dying girl much confidence."

"We'll get you back home, Jackie."

Yeah, right. She did not voice the opinion, and let herself sag against Nick's chest, feeling a swell of tears push up behind her eyes. "This isn't how I want to go."

"You aren't going to die in this place," he said, his arm pulling her more snugly against him.

Tears welled up, and Jackie tried to blink them away. Somehow even blinking was painful. "You don't know that.

I can tell I'm dying here, Nick. Don't placate me, you'll piss me off."

"All right," he said, a mixture of sympathy and annoyance in his voice. "You're dying, and I am truly sorry for that. This mess is mine, and I tried to keep you out of it, but that didn't happen. I don't know how the hell we're getting out of here, but I'm going to do my damnedest to get you back and patched up."

Jackie started to laugh and then groaned at the pain it induced. "Better, and don't blame yourself. You warned me, but that didn't really matter, now, did it?"

"No, I suppose not. You're too pigheaded to do what's best for you."

"Fuck you. Am not."

He chuckled. "It's okay. It's one of your more endearing qualities."

"You're an obstinate prick, too, you know."

The sarcasm in his voice vanished. "See, perfect match. No wonder I like you."

"I find that hard to believe."

"You don't like yourself much, do you, Agent Rutledge?"

"Are we having a counseling session now? Because I'm not in the mood."

"No, but you sell yourself short. There's a lot about you to like, regardless of what's happened to you. You think Laurel would love you otherwise?"

"Laurel was . . . is my friend. You're supposed to love them despite their faults."

"Exactly."

"And your point is?"

"You're a good person. You're smart, attractive, and stand up for what you feel is right. You also are stubborn enough to chase down injustice, no matter the cost." He paused, and it was quiet enough that Jackie could hear him swallow. He continued, much quieter. "All the women I've loved have been like that."

"Thanks, I think." *Did he just say he loves me? That can't be right.* "I'll admit, you're not like any guy I've ever met before." She wished the comfort of leaning into his body would provide more relief. She liked the feeling, but her body refused to relax. If anything, her shivering just kept getting worse.

"I'll take that as a compliment."

Jackie put her arm around Nick's waist, hugging herself to him. "It is. God, why can't you vampires be warmer? This sucks so bad."

His arm shifted behind her back, and Jackie felt herself roll over in his lap until she looked up into his face. "Look at me, Jackie." He tapped a finger next to those radiant blue eyes. "Let me try to ease that pain a bit."

"You going to hypnotize it away, Sheriff?"

He shrugged. "I can try. It hurts to see you like this. I want to try."

Jackie's eyes watered up again, and a tear trickled down her temple. "You stop this shivering, and I'll kiss you right now."

"Deal," he said and brought his lean, strong hands down to cup her face. "Just keep looking up here, Jackie. Think calm, warm thoughts. Wrap yourself up in a blanket by the fire. Bask in the afternoon sun. Trust me. My warmth is yours."

His face inched down toward hers as he spoke, and Jackie tried to think warm thoughts. A fire would have been a wonderful thing about now, if it would indeed have made a difference. She continued to look into the bottomless depths of those eyes, sensing that they were beginning to glow brighter the longer and deeper she stared. His hands did indeed feel slightly warmer—not much, but any warmth in this place was a blessing.

"I think it's working," she said, her voice a whisper from somewhere far away.

"Good," Nick replied, his mouth an inch above hers. "I was looking forward to that kiss."

Smart-ass. The thought dwindled away beneath the warm caress of his mouth. It was not a kiss full of lust, but the soft, lingering brush of affection and care that did more to warm her then anything sexual. Jackie could hear his voice in her head, a quiet, repetitive chant to relax, breathe, and feel the warmth of his skin against her own.

The shivering began to subside. Her muscles unclenched to some degree, at least so that her body no longer screamed in pain with every movement. Sadly, and all too soon, the contact with his mouth ended.

Nick's face still hovered above hers, the eyes glowing with luminous blue light. "Better?"

Jackie nodded. "I feel drunk."

"I know. Can't do much about that. Think you can move okay now?"

"Yeah, but I don't want to. It feels good to lay here like this."

Nick smiled down at her. "Wish you could, but we need to move."

"Why?"

Laurel's voice startled her. "Drake's still on the other side, but he's got his goons out in force. He must know something went awry with his plans. I can't find a safe spot for us outside."

Nick eased Jackie up into a sitting position next to him. "Meaning what? Inside?"

"Yes. We need to get by the front doors."

"I have no idea what the inside of the Hancock building looks like, Laurel."

She nodded. "I know, but you know what someone in there looks like."

"Does it work like that? You can travel to a person as well as a place?"

"You can go where your mind wills, Nick. Different rules. Can you remember what your wife looked like?"

Jackie felt him stiffen against her, his voice a whisper. "What?"

"Your wife. Gwendolyn, I think? Can you still envision her strongly?"

Jackie looked over at Nick, who stared in silence at Laurel, his mouth a thin, pale line. She recalled the room up behind his office, filled with all the memorabilia from his old life and family, obsessive in its detail. Then there was the painting. Oh, yeah, he could envision her strongly. Question was, did he want to go there?

Jackie touched his arm. "Nick? You okay?"

He turned toward her in slow-motion, eyes glassy and distant. One shoulder offered a barely discernible shrug. "Yeah. Just not what I was expecting. I haven't seen her in . . . a long time." He turned back to Laurel. "You sure she's there?"

"You think Drake would let them go before you got here? Isn't the point here to make you suffer as much as possible?"

Nick's back stiffened. "You make a good point, Ms. Carpenter. Thank you."

Laurel smiled. "Get cold feet at the last moment, Sheriff, and I'll kick your ass."

Nick's mouth puckered in consternation. "Not sure she's going to want to see me."

"Nonsense," she replied. "She loved you, didn't she?"

"Yeah, I suppose she did."

Jackie recalled what Nick had said about the events of his wife's death. Would *she* ever get over something like that? Much like him, she would blame herself, no doubt about that. But Gwendolyn had wanted him to do it. The children, on the other hand . . . Jackie laid her hand on Nick's thigh. "She'll be glad to see you, Nick. They all will."

He stared at her for a moment, the eyes locking on to hers and holding her perfectly still. There was a brief look of anger there, a "don't be a presumptuous bitch" gaze that melted away as quickly as it had come. "Unlikely, but thanks."

"She won't blame you," Jackie said. It was not a certainty, but she felt reasonably sure that this Gwendolyn would know exactly how Nick would be feeling and act accordingly. "I wouldn't."

He said nothing, but his mouth relaxed, one corner flickering with a smile, and he turned back to Laurel. "All right, I'll try to take us to her and see what happens."

"Great," Laurel said, walking over to the couch. "Nick, hold on to Jackie and focus. I'll help give you the strength to get us there."

Nick stood up and offered Jackie his hand. "You ready to do this?"

"Could I ever be?" She reached up and let Nick pull her up to her feet. Her body swam in syrup, sluggish but, thankfully, not shaking any longer.

"He'll get us there, hon," Laurel said. "Just concentrate on Gwendolyn."

Nick's hand squeezed Jackie's. "I'll get us there. Trust me."

The surety of his words brought little comfort. They were walking into a death trap with no plan for getting out. Then again, she was dying. A few hours, and the life in her would freeze into a solid block. There was nothing in this wretched place to make sticking around worthwhile. Worse, she could die and find herself in the same place.

"Okay. I guess." She put her arms around Nick's waist and held him tight. His body had the same musty, dry smell as the air around them. Laurel's cold presence closed in behind.

"Let's go, Nick," Laurel said, her voice in Jackie's ear.

A voice, lost somewhere in the haze that filled her brain, was screaming to her to wait, that she was not ready at all, but Jackie knew they had little choice or time.

Nick's arms pressed against her, one at the small of her back, the other cupping her head against his chest. "Relax, Jackie. Let's get this prick."

Jackie closed her eyes and imagined the Hancock building in her mind, an iconic symbol in the Chicago skyline, sleek, black, and—in this shrouded ghost land—full of death. After a little extra help from Laurel, they were off.

Chapter 56

The trip to the Hancock building likely took seconds to complete, but it was more than enough time for a thousand panicked thoughts to bounce at random off each other inside Nick's head. The worst being the dreaded notion that his family would be far from pleased to see him again, ghosts full of rage and hate for abandoning them in this place and failing to save them back when he had a legitimate chance to. A part of him was convinced they would attempt to kill him for what he had done and since become. What was there to understand? He had let them down in the worst way imaginable and been unable to bring them the justice and peace they deserved. If they wanted him dead, Nick was ready to accept that fate.

Except there was the dying woman in his arms. What would they say when he left to try to save her? Because if there proved to be a chance to do it, as Laurel stated, he would leave them again to save her. Jackie was still alive, and his family was not. After all these years, would they understand? A part of him was ready to just say, "Screw it," and spend what remained of his time in the arms of his family. It had a certain appeal. He was tired of all this and ready for it to end, but the sheriff inside would not and could not stop. It would be selfish of him to relinquish the badge at the very end, not to mention cowardly. Yes, as much as it would break his heart, Nick knew that no matter what awaited him in the Hancock building, he would leave them all to save the one among them who still lived. There would be no living with himself to do otherwise. He only hoped his family would understand.

All the fears were moot, however, if Drake killed him before he had a chance to do anything. Failing again before all of those who had come before would be the last and worst slap in the face.

Nick could feel them before they arrived, a swarming mass of spiritual energy, some of which had a pang of familiarity. There were dozens of them, but none so significant or intense as the one he zeroed in on, which Laurel pushed them toward, and that Nick found himself standing before in a dissipating swirl of bone-cold mist. His throat constricted, and for a moment he might as well have been dead, given the frozen state of his heart.

Gwendolyn stood before him, straightening her gray, homespun dress about her legs. She stared directly at Nick as he tried to orient himself. There was no sign of the former mutilation Drake had inflicted upon her. She looked much the same as the day she had gone, only pale and ashen. A smile turned up the corners of her bluish lips, not even the vaguest sign of animosity in the lines of her face.

"Hello, my love." Her hands reached out for his, full of acceptance and forgiveness. "We've been expecting you."

Shouts of "Sheriff!" and "It's Mr. Anderson!" echoed through the cavernous room, with a few assorted variations of his name used at different times over the decades. The crowd shifted and drifted toward him, apparently eager to catch sight of the man who had brought them all to an early grave. A nervous twinge gripped Nick's gut, but he refused to move. If his fate was to die at the hands of those he had failed, so be it. He deserved no less.

"Nick, it's all right," Gwen's voice said, so painfully sweet in his ears. "We're all glad you are here."

"And about fucking time, too," an all-too-familiar voice chided. Shelby stepped out from the crowd behind Gwen and moved up beside her. She didn't look much better off than Jackie. Her arms were crossed tightly over her chest, the usual brilliant red of her mouth washed out to the color of old, dried blood. "I wasn't sure you'd make it."

He gulped, trying to get the vaguest hint of moisture back in his mouth. She honestly and truly stood right there before him. His Gwen, with none of the rage and anger he had feared for all these years. Shelby's presence barely registered. The rest were little more than a gray wash of fog. Gwen's hand reached out and touched his, cold fingers grasping his own. The lack of warmth mattered little. The touch jolted Nick's heart back into action, and he blinked away the tears.

"Gwen." His voice cracked. It was all he could manage to say. He pulled her into an embrace, burying his face in her hair. For the few seconds it lasted, she didn't feel at all cold and lifeless but warm and comforting, smelling of fresh baked bread and a smoky fire, the scents that always greeted him upon his return home each evening. Her arms wrapped around him, and Nick felt the same measure of desperation and relief in her touch. "God, how I've missed you," he whispered.

Her voice was hushed against his shoulder. "Too much, love, too much."

Nick pulled back to look Gwen in the eye. She was serious. "Why would you say that?"

The faintest smile touched her lips. "Shelby told me about your room over the garage."

He turned his gaze to Shelby, who only stared back with

her usual unflappable stare and an arched brow, daring him to say something. What was there to say? "I couldn't forget," he said. "I couldn't afford to have the memory of you fade, not while Drake was still alive."

Gwen nodded and kissed Nick's cheek. "I know. Let's hope we can bring this to an end now. I'm ready to move on from this place. I'm also curious why you've brought a living soul here. She can't stay, Nick. She'll die."

"I know. Drake left us no choice. We were dead on the other side."

"I thought as much. So is this the detective Shelby told me about?"

"Jackie," Jackie interjected, voice quivering with the chatter of teeth. "Agent Jackie Rutledge."

Gwen turned and gave her a nod of acknowledgment. "I'd say welcome, Ms. Rutledge, but this is no place to welcome anyone."

She gave Gwen a little wave, and Nick grimaced at the visible shaking of her arm. "You should sit down, Jackie, conserve your strength."

"I'm . . . fine, thanks."

Gwen stepped over to her, her hand brushing through the edge of Jackie's arm. "Dear, you better sit before you fall over. Now is not the time to be stubborn. Save it for Nick. He likes that."

Jackie collapsed, cross-legged on the floor, the fight to argue obviously gone. "He should love me, then."

Gwen's mouth quirked at the corner, her glance flickering over to Nick, who could not hold her gaze and looked away. Having the three women he had had any kind of involvement with over the past century and a half gathered around him at the same time was just a little bit disconcerting. Gwen stood up from Jackie and faced him, her look bemused.

"That's the least of your worries right now, Sheriff."

Nick swallowed hard. "No, Gwen, it's not that, really. I will always—"

"Nicholas," she said, placing her hands upon his shoulders. "Don't." She brought a finger up to his lips to emphasize the point. "I know, but you will promise something right now before Cornelius makes his way back and this all comes to some kind of end."

He nodded once. "You know I'd promise you anything."

Gwen smiled. "When . . . when you get back, you will move on, and place me in that part of your mind filled only with good memories."

"But you're—"

"Shut up," she said. "You will put me there and get me out of that place of guilt and obsession you have been wallowing in for all these years."

"Gwen, that's not how . . ." Nick stopped, cut off by her look and the grim knowledge that she was right. Was it even possible to not live in that place anymore? Could there be anything after this? A normal life was such a far and distant memory that Nick could not be sure he would even know how to live one. His gaze fell to Jackie, shivering on the floor, huddled around herself as tightly as she could manage.

Gwen shook him gently. "Promise me, damn you, so I can finally move on."

The words were a slap to the head. The notion she had wanted to and could not move on because of him had never occurred to Nick. Was everyone here waiting as well? "All right, I promise."

She kissed him. "Good, thank you."

The rest of the crowd was gathering in close now, looking as though their long-lost brother had finally returned home. It hit him then, what Gwen had said, and who he now realized were missing. "The children? Are they here?"

"No," she replied, her features turning at once from stern

to sad. "They moved on a long time ago, Nicholas. I couldn't let them stay here, not with Drake. I helped them let go."

Tears welled up in his eyes, realizing that, ghosts or not, he had truly wanted to see them again. "That's good. They don't belong in this place. Nobody does." There were murmurs of assent among the crowd, and Nick finally turned and looked at them all, acknowledging them for the first time. Most he recognized, and there was not an angry face among them. They were glad the sheriff was back in town, such that it was.

"What's the plan, Sheriff?" someone asked.

"How do we get him?"

Yes, exactly. How did they get Drake? What possible tools did Nick have at his disposal here, other than a couple guns? They needed something positive, but as he stared out over the sea of hopeful, eager faces, hoping that something brilliant would spring to mind, that something would be different this time, Nick realized he had nothing. He had nothing to give them.

"Folks," he began, but faltered. The usual sheriff's bravado, the confidence he had so long ago to bring the bad guys to justice, had been beaten out of him by the continual years of failure.

"Nick." Gwen's cold hand touched his arm. "I have a notion about what might—"

"Ah, Nicholas!" Drake's voice boomed like hollow thunder through the room.

Nick had felt him the moment he entered, a cold wash of stinking dread invading all his senses. He was there, standing in a doorway on the far side of the large room, the blood-red tie shining like a beacon against his black pinstripe suit. The crowd of ghosts instinctively parted, leaving an open path between them.

"Finally, you surprise me. Good show, I say. I am pleased."

Nothing in Drake's voice sounded pleased, and Nick did the only thing he could think to do. Pushing the flaps of his coat aside, Sheriff Nicholas Anderson drew his old six-shooters and prepared for the end.

Chapter 57

Jackie did what any self-respecting agent would do when confronted by the man who had killed her partner and friend. She emptied her Glock into the man's body, though her aim was not nearly so lethal, given her trembling hands.

"Die, you son of a bitch," she said through gritted teeth, pulling the trigger for several rounds even after the clip had emptied.

Drake had begun to walk forward but stopped, flinching for just a moment at the initial shots. He stood there, a faint smile on his withered face, as if the bullets were little more than annoying mosquitoes. Small, pasty white smears appeared where the bullets hit him, one on his stomach, a pair in the chest, another in the throat, and finally beneath the cheekbone. When she had finished, he glanced at Jackie, a "what do you know about that?" look on his face, and then adjusted the suit on his thin frame and continued stepping forward.

"Fuck," she muttered and let the now useless weapon clatter to the floor beside her.

"It would seem, my dear agent, that real bullets have little effect in the world of the dead, but the thought is appreciated just the same."

Above her, Nick did nothing but stand at the ready, the handheld cannons aimed in Drake's direction. To Jackie, it appeared comically out of place. If bullets could do nothing, what the hell was Nick going to do to him? She watched the ghostly crowd cower back from Drake's presence as though he had some dead-repelling force field around him. Their fear was palpable. A few more steps, and Drake stopped, still a good twenty meters away.

At Nick's side, Gwen spoke quietly. "Nicholas, listen to me."

Behind Jackie, Shelby spoke to Nick with grim determination. "I'll handle the goons, babe. Focus on him."

Drake, meanwhile, casually scanned the crowd, his hand tracing a slow arc from left to right. The act had the crowd of ghosts shrinking back in terror. When his arm stopped and the fingers curled up into a "come here" motion, he smiled and said, "Miranda Davenport, it is time to move on. Come, child. Come."

The young, faded form of a woman stepped from the crowd and walked toward Drake as though his order could not be denied. There appeared to be no hesitation in her steps. Why, Jackie wondered, would anyone willingly approach that thing? Perhaps it was some kind of hypnosis. Perhaps he had control over all of them in some way in this place. If so, they all were more than screwed.

Miranda Davenport did not stop when she got close to Drake but instead walked right up to his outstretched hand. Her back was to Jackie, but her distance indicated Drake's hand had pushed directly into her body. The pale, faded form shuddered, and Miranda's head arched back, her mouth open to scream, but no sound issued forth. Her body kept bending, folding awkwardly back, quaking against Drake's stiffened arm. For a moment, Jackie swore he was pulling the dress from her body, but as the woman's body stretched and contorted, she realized with horror that the

woman's body was being drawn directly into Drake's outstretched hand. The body lost shape, folding down until it
appeared her back had snapped in two, and then shrank and
evaporated until finally she was gone, drawn up into
Drake's body like the result of some soul-sucking vacuum
cleaner.

Jackie looked over at Laurel, who still crouched beside
her. "Jesus, Laur. What the fuck was that?"

She shook her head. "I think he just consumed her soul."

Drake shrugged his shoulders and gave his neck a soft,
twisting pop, the smile on his face a bloodless, sinister line.
"You see, Nicholas? Even in death, my victims feed me. I
have more power than your morally rigid soul could possibly fathom." He began to walk forward again with slow, de-
liberate steps. "I knew from the beginning your righteous
constraint would keep you from ever doing what needed to
be done. You've never had a chance, dear boy. Smart blokes
know you only play games you are guaranteed of winning."

"This game isn't over yet, Cornelius," Nick grated, but
Jackie could sense the lack of confidence in his voice. Who
would blame him after seeing that?

Gwen's hands clasped around Nick's then, finally drawing his attention away from Drake. "My love, we can help.
We're ready to move on from this. You just have to be willing to let us go."

He turned, the twisted sneer on his face melting away
when he looked down at Gwen. "What are you talking about?"

Drake laughed. "Are you so dense as all that, Nicholas?
They accepted their fate long ago, unlike you, who has
proven stubborn to a fault." He gave a mirthless chuckle,
stretching out his arms to encompass the crowd. "In the
end, my friend, you cannot accept what you are, and the fact
that you are here, still living, makes it so much the sweeter.
Now then, Ralph Morris, come to me and accept your fate."

The man stepped from the crowd, approaching Drake

with no resistance. Jackie turned her gaze away. Watching the process had slimy worms of dread crawling around in her gut. She would kill herself before going out like that. But, then, did it matter one way or the other? Being slowly consumed by the chill of death could not be much worse. The ache was getting excruciating, thin shards of ice being driven into the marrow of her bones. She would be lucky if she could get to her feet now.

"Laur, if this doesn't go well, take me back. I don't want to die here like this."

"If it comes to that," she whispered, "but we aren't done here yet."

"He's going to suck us up one by one until Nick is the only one left."

"It's Nick's move right now, just hold on a bit longer, hon."

Above Jackie, Gwen's voice was quietly insistent. "Nicholas, let me go. Don't let him take me like that."

"I won't let him, not again."

"No, love. Now." She reached up and touched Nick's face. "Let me go, and I can help you. We all can."

It took Jackie a moment to realize what she meant. Nick's expression confirmed her suspicion. Gwen wanted him to suck them up just like Drake was doing, and the shock on Nick's face said it all.

His voice was barely audible. "No! Gwen, there must be another way."

Drake called upon another ghost to feed his twisted soul.

"Nicholas, you're our only hope of leaving on our own terms. Don't let me die at his hand a second time."

Nick's face went slack. The dread in his stare was painful to watch, and Jackie knew what he must be thinking. *How can I destroy my wife again to stop this killer?* Drake's chuckle froze the air in her lungs.

"Just cannot stand to step into those shoes, can you, Nicholas? Cannot dare to be like your old friend Cornelius."

Gwen took Nick's face in her ashen hands. "You could never be like him, love. It's one of the reasons I love you so much, but this is the right thing to do, and the time is now."

"Touching, Gwendolyn," Drake said. "Just the right amount of sentimentality to end our little affair, but I believe it is time. Come. Come to me."

He motioned with his hand toward Gwen, and to Jackie's surprise, she stepped away from Nick, her hands still held to cup his face. Nick's jaw went slack, his eyes wide with terror. It was not a look Jackie would have ever expected to see on his face. Three steps toward Drake, and Nick holstered a gun and reached out to his dead wife.

"Gwen."

She paused, looking back over her shoulder at him. "Sheriff." Her tone had an imploring quality to it, but Jackie saw something else in her look, one of stern reminder that Nick was indeed the sheriff and still possessing those qualities that had made him so.

Nick closed his eyes, and Jackie watched a tear squeeze out beneath one lid. He mouthed "I love you" and then opened his eyes again. "Come back, Gwen. Be with me, now and forever."

She smiled and turned fully back around. Jackie looked over at Drake and saw him take a stumbling step forward in surprise. "Gwendolyn! To me. Now."

Gwen hesitated for a moment, a painful wince on her face, and then continued toward Nick. She reached for his hand, but instead of the welcoming grasp and twine of fingers, her fingers stretched out toward his, becoming long tendrils of gray smoke that crept up her arm, until her shoulder and head began to distort like warm putty being pulled down into a funnel. Seconds later, her feet left the floor, following the rest of her rushing wisp of a body, and disappeared into Nick's trembling hand.

"No!" Drake lunged forward, his usual dead-calm

countenance momentarily transformed by wide-eyed shock. The look vanished a second later, and Jackie could see that the man genuinely looked pissed. Nick had ruined the game plan.

Jackie thought to smile at the small victory, pleased that Nick had overcome the weight of his burdened soul and done what needed to be done. However, stretching her facial muscles felt like thorny, cold nettles rolling beneath her skin. Her chest was so frosted with death it was beginning to constrict on itself. Breathing, she suddenly realized, was becoming difficult.

"Laur," she said, her tongue feeling thick in her mouth. "I think I'm in trouble here."

Laurel had begun to stand with Drake's abrupt approach but then squatted back down. The look on her face confirmed Jackie's repetitive thought. *I'm dying.* "You need to hold on a bit longer."

Jackie huddled her knees up against her chest. "I'm trying."

"Boys, gather up the rest of them. I'll handle the sheriff." Drake waved his hands at the group of ghosts that huddled toward them, surrounding Nick.

Shouts from the group began to go up. "Take me next, Sheriff!"

Nick still had a look of shock on his face. He stared at his hand, flexing the fingers, and Jackie wondered if he could continue taking the souls. Her question was answered a moment later when an elderly woman stepped before him, inches from his extended arm, grim determination etched into her lined face.

"Kill him," she said.

A moment of silence descended on the room, a collectively held breath, waiting to see if Nick's self-loathing would win out in the end over the desire for justice. The creased line of the old woman's mouth turned up at the corner, and Nick reached out to touch her. A second later, she was gone.

Before the last traces of her vanished up Nick's arm, Drake let out an angry roar and charged. Nick drew his six-shooter with the other hand and got off three rounds before Drake crashed into him and sent them flying backward across the room.

Chaos erupted all around Jackie.

Laurel took Jackie's face in her hands. "Listen to me. When the time comes, you'll have to let me take you back. You'll have to let me in there, understand?" Jackie was not sure that she did, but nodded anyway. "Shel, get her out of the way." Laurel leaped to her feet and, without looking back, ran toward one of Drake's goons.

"C'mon, Jack," Shelby said, grunting as she hooked her hands under Jackie's arms and began to pull her back toward the outer wall of windows opposite the main door, which opened into the center of the building. "Fuck, girl. We need to get you out of here."

Jackie tried to help, but her muscles were so clenched with shivering cold that movement was impossible. It took all her effort just to force her chest to expand and let air into her lungs. Just when they needed her the most, she was failing like she had twenty years before when she sat, huddled and shivering, behind her bedroom door, listening to her mother's pleas for help. Unlike then, having the courage to act would do little good. There was just too little life left in her.

Nick flew back across the room, slamming into the thick glass wall of windows so hard a spiderweb of cracks flared out around him. Jackie could feel the vibration clear through Shelby's body. He dropped to one knee, managing still to keep one hand outstretched for the ghosts of his past to continue their relentless surge into his body.

"Too little, too late, my friend," Drake barked as he

marched toward Nick's prone body. "You do not even know what to do with the power you have at your disposal." He paused long enough to draw in another victim, but Nick was taking them in as fast as they could reach him.

To their left, Laurel rode around on the back of one of Drake's brutes, hands clawing at his face. He spun in circles, hands pummeling backward in a vain attempt to knock her off. The other one stopped his attack on the crowd pushing toward Nick to help out. If anything, it was biding Nick a few extra seconds of time.

Jackie could only watch in mute, gasping silence, unable to do anything except force her lungs to keep breathing.

Another thud vibrated her body when Drake slammed Nick up against a cement support column along the wall. He had Nick by the lapels of his duster, pushing him up off the floor. Nick's hands were clamped around Drake's wrists, pulling at them to break the hold. For a moment, at least, they were locked together in an equal struggle.

"Boys!" Drake glanced over at the ongoing fight between the goons and Laurel. "You bloody fools."

Nick let go abruptly, hands flashing out to box Drake's ears. The move got him back to the floor but did nothing to break the hold. A smirk twitched at the corner of Drake's mouth—appreciated, perhaps, of Nick's effort—but an instant later his head snapped forward, butting into Nick's nose with a crunching pop of bone and gristle. Blood erupted from the broken nose, draining over Nick's face, leaving him sagging against the glass wall.

Still, the ghosts came, a great wall of writhing gray appendages. Jackie could not even discern solid bodies anymore. Her vision had begun to blur.

"Come to me, Laurel. Your time is now."

Her name brought Jackie's vision back into focus. Drake's hand beckoned toward her best friend, whose love for her had been beyond what she had ever felt deserving of. Like the flick of a light switch, Laurel's attack on the bodyguard ceased, and she dropped back to the floor. She did not look at Drake, her face contorted with the effort to resist his will. Her gaze was directed squarely at Jackie.

"Jackie . . ."

No! Jackie struggled to sit up, putting her hands on the floor to push herself up, but there was nothing. She could no longer feel anything, as if her arms had vanished from the elbow down. She could not let Drake take Laurel a second time. She could not fail again.

Let me in, hon, before it's too late.

Laurel walked across the room now, approaching Drake in slow, resisting steps. Jackie began to cry. She could not even yell for her to stop. Be stronger, damnit!

Trust me! Just let go. Let it all go.

What had she said? *You'll have to let me in there.*

"Laurel Carpenter! You will come to me now." Drake's voice was more insistent than it had been previously. One hand pressed tightly up against Nick's chest while the other beckoned.

Laurel's face contorted, lips creased into a razor-thin line, but she continued the inexorable march toward Drake's outstretched hand.

Jackie glanced over at Nick, who struggled to shake the cobwebs out of his head. The ghosts had paused, apparently too afraid to approach the now-angered Cornelius Drake.

Shelby's voice was an urgent hiss in her ear. She could barely feel the fingers digging into her shoulders as Shelby pushed her forward to get up. "Fucking Drake. I've got to help her."

The pressure on her released, and Jackie slumped over to the floor. This was it. She was going to die alone on the stone-cold floor in this wretched world of the dead, no peace, and no comforting hand holding hers as she faded away into darkness. This was not how it was supposed to be, not at all.

Laur, I love you. Just take me out of this place.

The blessed relief of her friend's touch welcomed her into the end.

Chapter 58

Laurel vanished. One moment she was there, struggling against Drake's coercive pull, and the next she was gone.

"What?" Drake appeared to be as perplexed as Nick was angry.

The distraction was all the time Nick needed, however, as the crushing weight of Drake's powerful hand eased from his chest. Pulling together the raw, spiritual energy that had been surging into his body, Nick was able to bring his left arm across his body with hammerlike force to Drake's elbow. The reprieve allowed much needed oxygen back into his lungs.

If Drake had not taken Laurel, where in hell had she gone to? She was their way back. If she was gone, they were as good as dead, and all this was moot.

Out of the corner of his eye, Nick saw Shelby come barreling at Drake. She must have realized as well the seriousness of Laurel's disappearance. Behind her, Jackie lay prone on the floor, curled up in the fetal position, unmoving. It occurred to him then that Shelby was not hell-bent for Drake because of Laurel, but because Jackie had finally died. The one truly living being in this cold and barren Deadworld, and he had let her slip away, unable to overcome the fear of what he was. Too little too late.

Drake turned back; the hand once outstretched to get Laurel balled into a fist to smash Nick in the face. The half second Nick spent staring at Jackie's unmoving body would have been enough for it to land, but Shelby took Drake out at the knee, buckling him to the floor.

The ghosts, ready for the opportunity, rushed in upon Nick, flowing up his arm in a mad rush of energy. It was almost enough to fry his synapses. The kinds of things possible with such power were limitless, far more than he had imagined back in the days of drinking real blood. The prospect was terrifying. Shrouding it all in a smoldering, dark haze was the image of Jackie's dead body. Such power meant nothing now. He had wanted only to save her, get her back to the world of the living where she might be saved. She deserved no less. It was his fault for letting her get dragged into this mess. He should have forced her out, broken the law, tied her up, or taken whatever means necessary to ensure her safety. He should have done a lot of things that had been necessary. Now, however, only one necessity remained.

Nick leaped on top of Drake, funneling the raw energy into his clenched fists, burying them again and again into the pale, haughty face. The rage and frustration of the decades suffered at the man's relentless vengeance poured out of him, finding release but little solace or satisfaction in the rupturing of skin and cracking of bone his fists inflicted.

After the seventh or eighth punch, Drake's broken mouth twisted into a smile. "You can't kill me here, Nicholas. Your friends are dead or dying. Good show, though. I did not believe you had it in you."

Nick clamped his hands around Drake's head, thumbs digging into those soulless gray eyes. "You'll die, you fucking bastard, even if I have to twist your withered head right off your body." He began to bear down, pushing against the force of Drake's will that worked to pry his fingers free. "Even if I burn myself away, you're going to burn up with me."

Drake's hands locked onto Nick's wrists, squeezing down against the bones, and Nick could feel the pressure building, beginning to grind bone and ligament together.

Behind him, Shelby's voice was strained. "Goddamnit, Nick. Hurry up."

She was clamped around Drake's legs, but her strength had waned with the time among the dead. Her help would not last much longer. Nick pushed back with everything he had, hoping to crush Drake's skull. His thumbs ground down, fluid beginning to seep out.

A lightning jolt of pain flew up his arm along with the sound of cracking bone. Cornelius had begun to break his left wrist. The smile on Drake's face remained unflinching even as blood begin to drip from his sockets. Doubt crept into Nick's mind. Perhaps the vampire could not be killed in this place. A few more seconds, and it would not matter. His wrist was going to give out, and his viselike grip around Drake's skull would fail.

Then something was on his back. For an instant Nick thought it one of the goons come over to try to pry him off, but the voice in his ear could not have been any sweeter, any more of a relief to his guilt-ridden conscience.

"Take us out, Nick. Now!"

Jackie. But the words were Laurel's. Somehow Laurel was in control. Her voice whispered through all the rampant energy supercharging his body, urgent and insistent. "Cynthia," she said. "Hospital." Jackie's arms wrapped around his neck, and Nick understood where they needed to go.

Open the door and push them all through. Nick let her in, using her guidance to open the doorway back to the world of the living. The change of focus diverted his energy away from Drake's crushing grip, and Nick felt his wrist give way, grinding to pieces beneath his skin.

For the first time, Drake's victorious smile faltered. Going back through did not appear to be on his list of options. He tried to throw them off, push them aside before that door could be opened.

Pushing three people from one world to the other had been rough, but now there were five, one of whom was doing his best not to go through. They had to overcome not only the tension of the doorway itself being pushed open beyond its rightful bounds, but Drake's panicked efforts to pull it closed. For the first time in 180 years, Nick realized he had more strength than his nemesis. The unharnessed energy, with which he had been unsure how to focus before, exposed itself with its true power. The power did not give him the ability to wreak havoc upon another, but the power to manipulate that fabric of time, space, and spirit between the living and the dead.

The door yawned opened beneath them, and Nick rolled over into it, his good hand hooked into the bones of Drake's face. Jackie's body clung to his back, and Shelby wrapped herself about his legs as the pull of the other side stretched him. The pathway was hardly big enough to let them through, but the tug of life grabbed a hold of the part of him that still lived, conforming his body to it, bending and twisting bones and stretching him to the point of breaking as they were drawn through.

Laurel's voice yelled in his head, full of a panicked urgency. *Push, Nick! You've got to push us through.*

I'm trying. The door was meant for one, not five.

She's almost dead. Get us through. Now, damn you.

Like he did this every day, just dragging people around between the lands of the living and the dead. It didn't help that one of them had a very strong desire not to go through.

Push as he might, however, the doorway was not big enough. All the focus in the world could not direct enough energy to widen the opening. They were not going to make it.

You're trying too hard, Nick. Let us go.

The voice was not Laurel's this time. It might have been Gwen's, or some conglomeration of all the spirits that swam through his veins. Laurel had spoken of it before when they had traveled through. But to just let it go now, when using spirits' energy was all that was giving them the chance to get out, made Nick hesitate. Everything had been put into his hands. Jackie was on the verge of death, and vindication for all that had happened, all that he had done, surged within him. He was finally able to do something to right these wrongs, and he had to just let it all go? If this was wrong, there would be no strength left to do anything, and they would all be dead.

The time to ponder was gone. Fate, he supposed, would have to decide. He could only hope the dead were right. Nick relinquished control, effectively letting go of his grip on the door. For a moment, they were all pulled back, swayed toward Deadworld by Drake's force of will.

The dead within Nick dispersed from his body in a blinding flash of white light, pulling at every cell from the inside out. It was the intense, painful relief of pulling a knife from a wound, at once agonizing and then a flood of relief.

Awareness of his body and everyone around him began to dissipate. Fog and darkness seeped into his pores, filling every opening, saturating him down to the marrow with a cold that felt like it must have come from the dead void of space itself. Nick wanted to scream, tried to, but he could not tell if he actually did. Was this it? Had death finally come to embrace him, mocking him in the end with this final failure? The moment lasted a second or eternity. There was no point of reference. He could only hope and pray.

Nick fell through, tumbling into the nothingness between the worlds, the desperate grips of those around him clinging for dear life. At the last, he focused his awareness on the one good hand he had left. If there was any justice left in the world, its grip would not fail.

Chapter 59

Bright light. Bright fucking light. *Shit, I died.* The grogginess of sleep distorted Jackie's perception for a moment as consciousness finally took a hold of her body. The sticky crust around her eyes gave way at last, however, and she blinked at the streaming rays of sunshine coming in through a hospital window. A chrome pipe rose above her next to the bed, dangling a clear bag of fluid. Okay, it sure as hell was not heaven.

Looking down at the sterile baby-blue blanket covering her body, Jackie noticed a sleeping figure in a green overstuffed chair. Nick's head leaned back against the top, lolling to one side, snoring softly. A glance to the other side of the room revealed that she was in a single room. What the hell had happened? Did it matter? She was actually warm. How long had he been sitting there?

"Nick . . ." Her voice cracked, mouth dry and parched as bone.

His head snapped up, wide awake in an instant. His eyes were puffy and dark. A single Band-Aid bridged the gap between them. "Jackie! You're awake."

"Yeah," she said. God, it hurt to talk. "Water?"

He leaped to his feet. "No problem. Be right back."

Nick bolted out the door, which Jackie found amusing until she heard him shout, "Nurse! She's awake. She's goddamned awake."

Before she had time to really ponder the ramifications of his excitement over her just waking up, a pair of nurses and a doctor came hustling into the room. The next two hours went downhill from there. God, she hated the fucking hospital. At least they had brought water. By then, half the crew from headquarters had come by to see her, hardly able to move as she was and with tubes running into her arm. A parade of doctors and nurses had stormed in and out, poking and prodding, and the whole time, Nick had sat there in his chair, elbows on his knees and chin resting on his hands, watching her intently. Occasionally, a bemused smirk would cross his face when she would finally get frustrated at the hospital staff and tell them to leave her the fuck alone. The sun no longer beamed through the window when quiet made its blessed descent on the room.

"Thanks for the water, Nick," she said, trying in vain to find a comfortable position in which to lie. She settled on her right side, the left arm laying down her side. The pink, welted line of the wound at her elbow smiled back at her, remarkably healed.

She should have died, they said, flatlined for three minutes before being brought back. Nobody had provided any worthwhile information, least of all Nick, who had remained more or less silent the entire time other than greeting those who came to visit. Belgerman had said nothing, other than stating that he was thankful she was alive and would be fired if he saw her in the office within a month. "Don't come back until you are ready," he had said. Ready. Was one ever ready to go back to work after something like this? She just wanted some answers.

"Sorry," Nick replied. "I was just . . . very pleased to see you awake again."

"Has it really been five days?"

He nodded. "Seven, counting our time on the other side."

"But . . . how?"

"I don't know." Nick gave her a nonchalant little shrug. "Time doesn't work the same over there, I guess."

Yeah, whatever. Nothing would be the same after that place. "Drake's dead though, right? I mean, really and truly dead?"

"Yes. When we came back, he was so full of holes even his power couldn't save him." Nick absently flexed his right hand. "Don't worry, we made sure."

Jackie thought better of getting any clarification on that one. "Good. That fucker needed to die."

Nick smiled. "Yes, he did indeed."

"I guess I owe you one now."

"No. No, Jackie you don't. I'm just glad we got you back. It was more Laurel than me anyway."

Laur. Jackie had hardly thought about her since waking up. Fresh tears stung her eyes. More than anything, she wished her friend was with her now. "I'm going to miss her."

Nick got to his feet and picked up the tissue box sitting on the side table next to the chair. He set it down on the serving table next to her bed. "I don't think she's gone, not yet anyway."

Jackie pulled out a tissue and wiped at the tears running down onto the pillow. "You know what I mean."

"I do," he agreed. "And I'm truly sorry."

Jackie knew he did not speak of her death. She wadded up the tissue and threw it at him. "You couldn't have stopped us, Nick. You really think you could have done anything to keep us away?"

He walked back over and sat down, sagging back in the chair. "No, probably not."

"No probably about it, Sheriff. Not everything in this world is your fault."

"Okay, okay. Relax, please. You're right, just a bad habit."

"Not bad," she said, letting her head fall back into the pillow. The small effort had sapped what strength she had regained. "Just wrong." They were silent for several seconds. She didn't want to argue with him. He had saved her life, after all, and here he was, just sitting in her hospital room, and had been for, what? Hours? Days?

"Have you been sitting here the whole time, just watching me?"

"Off and on," he said. "I felt it was important that someone was here when you came around."

"It could have been weeks, for all you knew."

He smiled that oddly reassuring, law-enforcement smile that said he knew better. "No. I knew it would be soon."

"What, you can see into my head or something? One of your little vampire tricks?"

"Something like that."

"I'll bet all the girls love that."

Nick sighed. "It's not something I generally do with anyone."

"Because you're too good for that, I suppose?" The look he gave her made Jackie flinch. "Sorry. I'm tired and bitchy."

"There has to be a connection of some kind for it to work."

"Connection? Can you ever directly answer anything I ask you, Nick?"

He chuckled. "Fine. There has to be an emotional bond, some trust, for it to work."

"So we have a bond then?"

"Apparently, we do." He got up and picked up the water

pitcher from her bedside table. "Get some rest, Jackie. You need it. You'll be out of here by tomorrow afternoon."

"Know that for a fact, do you?" A bond. What did one make of a bond to an 180-year-old vampire sheriff?

"You'll be out of here the second you're able, and not a second later." He grinned and set the water pitcher back down. "Back in a minute."

Jackie watched his solid, bruised figure leave. Damnit, there was a bond. She closed her eyes, pushing his image out of her mind. What the hell was she going to do about this? With everything? Her job was fucked. Her best friend was dead. She had almost died. Where did you go from there? The question faded into the oblivion of sleep before Nick returned.

The following afternoon, she was more than ready to leave. If one more person marveled at her recovery, she was going to deck them. Shelby, at least, had come along, exhibiting her usual charm. Then the doctors fell all over themselves to get things signed off. When they finally cleared Jackie, she sent Nick off to bring the car around front.

"He really likes you, you know," Shelby said after the hospital-room door closed behind him. "You couldn't have paid me to sleep in that fucking chair for five days. No offense."

Jackie stopped packing her overnight bag that someone had brought in with a change of clothes. "He was here the whole time?"

"Yep. Our sheriff is about as loyal a dog as they come. I had to make him go home and take a shower after the first two." She laughed at Jackie. "Don't look so surprised. You guys have been through a lot."

She tried to imagine sitting there in that green hotel-lobby chair for five straight days. *Would I have been that dedicated?* For Laurel. She would have done it for Laurel because Jackie had loved her more than anyone. God. Not even possible that was why Nick had done it for her. It was just the circumstances.

"He just wanted to make sure someone was around when I woke up, someone who knew what happened."

Shelby patted her arm. "Guess that's why he never asked me to take the chair for a while."

Jackie pulled a Northwestern sweatshirt over her head and zipped the bag. "Can we not discuss this right now?"

"Sure thing, hon. Just saying is all, and I know Nick. There's something there."

Jackie shouldered the bag. "Can we go?"

They stopped at the gift shop on the way out, and Shelby bought a bouquet of flowers. Jackie thought for a moment she might be giving them to her, but Shelby said nothing, just smiling with those perfect, brilliantly red lips. Nick waited with the car doors open when they stepped out of the hospital side entrance.

"Get in," he said, pulling the bag from Jackie's shoulder. "We move fast, they won't even notice we've left."

Jackie looked around but saw nobody out of the ordinary. "They who?"

"There's more than a few folks around interested in how you vanished from the basement of a burning funeral home and reappeared two days later," Shelby replied. "You can go around front and conduct an interview or ten if you want."

Jackie quickly ducked into the backseat of the car and hunkered down. What a nightmare that would be. She had not even considered that possibility. "Let's go."

They wound through the city's streets, still wet from an early morning rain. It was cool and breezy, a typical early fall day in Chicago. Nothing, however, felt typical anymore. Jackie had seen things no living person had any business seeing. She was getting a ride home from a couple vampires, one of whom she could not decide what to think of. The man, a good-looking one at that, had saved her life. By itself, that had some potential right there. A couple weeks ago, it would have made for a rollicking, drunken night of sex, and then it would have been back to work the next day, out of sight and out of mind. But now?

Life had shifted in a very peculiar direction, and Jackie could not decide what to make of it. Begrudgingly, she had to admit there was something there with Nick, and it could easily be chalked up to the intensity of circumstance, but there was something more. Yet was it really there, or just because she wanted it to be there, needed it to be there? She could not go back to her old life and ways. That Jackie no longer existed, the one who had bled out into the mouth of the man sitting in the front seat. What was left? Did it matter?

Jackie stared at the bouquet in the seat next to her, bright and summery in color, an overabundance of daisies packed into its tightly wound band.

"What are the flowers for?"

Shelby looked back with a sympathetic smile. "Laurel."

Before she could wonder why, Nick turned his car into the driveway of the Montrose Cemetery. She stared out the window, row after row of marble stones filing past. They made their way to the back of the property, where it butted up against the edge of the LaBagh Woods. In a few more weeks it would be a beautiful setting with the trees changing into their fall dress. When Nick stopped the car, Jackie could plainly see their destination a few meters off into the manicured lawn, where a mound of flowers still adorned a fresh grave.

For a long minute, Jackie could only stare out the window at it. The finality of everything, of what had happened to them, the unheeded warning to leave all this alone, grew out of the ground before her in an absurdly mocking pile of cheerful color. She began to cry.

"Go," Shelby said.

Nobody had mentioned the funeral or that she had missed it. The tears would not stop. While she still had any nerve left to get out of the car, Jackie picked up the bouquet from the seat and stepped out. The air had become oddly still and silent. At the foot of the grave, Jackie stopped, holding the flowers limply in one hand. Such a trifling thing to bring them here, a wholly inadequate gesture to someone who had been so much more than just her friend. She wiped at the tears with the back of her other hand, throat too constricted to force out any words. Not that any words could convey her feelings at that moment.

"They're pretty," Laurel said. "Daisies are my favorite flower."

Jackie knelt down and set them at the edge of the others, managing at last to force out a single, choked word. "Hi."

"It was a lovely funeral," Laurel said. "Pernetti even cried like a baby."

Jackie's clipped laugh came out more as a sob. "Sorry I missed it."

"It's okay," Laurel said. "Better this way anyway."

Probably so. They might have carted her off if she had begun to have a conversation with the dead. "I'm so lost now, Laur. It's like I'm treading water out in the middle of the ocean. I don't know where to go from here."

"I know. I wish I had an answer for you, but I don't."

"You always had the answers."

Laurel gave her a sad, sympathetic smile. "Even if I had them, I can't give them anymore, hon. You have to find your own way, leave all that old stuff behind, and start fresh. You've got a second chance at life now. Don't be afraid."

Afraid. None of the old terrors compared to this. "Do I

deserve another chance?" She had not thought to ask the question, but it came out before she realized.

"Don't," Laurel snapped back, pointing an accusatory finger. "I wouldn't be here if you didn't, so stop. You deserve it as much as anyone I've ever known. I wouldn't have loved you if you didn't deserve the best life has to give."

Jackie sniffled and wiped the tears away again. "Okay, fine. I deserve it. So what happens now?"

"I don't know. How about you go home and have a bath? Give Bickers some love. He misses you."

"God, I totally forgot about him. He's probably peed in every corner of my apartment."

Laurel laughed. "He's fine. You'll be fine. Do something that will make you happy."

Happiness was the furthest thing from Jackie's mind at that moment. "I don't see that happening any time soon."

"There's a little bit of it waiting right back there in the car."

"What? Nick? I . . . I don't really know what to think of that man."

"Then don't. Just do. He's looking for the same things you are."

"And what is that?"

"Hon, quit being dense, and quit being afraid of liking him. You'd be good for each other."

It struck Jackie then that Nick was the first guy Laurel had ever said that about. "He freaks me out. He's so fucking intense, and there's that whole . . . blood thing."

"And your point is?"

What was her point? She had none. The thought of something real with someone freaked her out more than anything else. "Fine, I'll think about it."

"No. Didn't I say to stop thinking about it?"

"All right! Christ. Casper, you aren't."

Laurel grinned. "Feeling better though, aren't you?"

The morose black veil that had been covering Jackie had lifted, though it still hovered at the fringes, ready to fall. "I suppose. Thanks, Laur. I just wish you were still here. I still feel so . . ." She shrugged. *Guilty* did not even come close.

"If I forgive you every day, will that help?"

Jackie snorted. "Yeah, it would."

"Okay, then. I forgive you. It wasn't your fault, and you weren't to blame, and I still love you."

Tears welled up again. "Better. I love you, too."

"Now go. Cemeteries depress you. I'll see you again soon."

Laurel faded into the ground, but Jackie stood there a while longer staring down at the grave. Her friend's body was buried down there, but she was not truly gone. How could you really say good-bye? It wasn't right. Still, the pain of Laurel's missing presence was there, and Jackie knew it would be for a long time to come. It just had to be dealt with. She had to move on.

Back in the car, Jackie closed the door. "You can take me home now."

"You okay?" Shelby reached her hand over the back of the seat, an open offer of comfort there for the taking, if Jackie wanted it.

Jackie smiled at her, grateful for the gesture, took her hand, and squeezed briefly before letting go. "Thanks. Yeah, I think I'm good for now."

Shelby nodded and turned back around. "Good. Let's get out of here."

Jackie stared out the window, watching the mound of flowers until they had faded from view. *Move on. Don't think about it, just do.* "Nick?"

He looked at her in the rearview mirror. "Yeah?"

"What're you doing Saturday night?"

"Huh?"

"Saturday. Are you available on Saturday night?"

"Available? What do you mean?"

Shelby's fist flashed across the seat and struck him on the shoulder.

"Ow! What the hell?"

"I swear you're an idiot sometimes," Shelby scolded. "Just say yes, for fuck's sake."

They stopped at an intersection, and he turned to look back at Jackie, those faintly glowing eyes studying her with disarming intensity. She managed to hold his gaze, forcing herself not to look away. He turned back and set the car in motion once again.

"How's seven o'clock?"

"Seven's fine." She took a deep breath and let it out to calm the butterflies. It was a step forward, and that was the only direction she could look now.

Jackie Rutledge has come to realize how
thin a line separates the living and the dead,
and her view of the world will never be the same again.
Follow her further adventures in the next book
of the DEADWORLD series,
a Kensington paperback on sale October 2011.

Turn the page for a special preview!

Prologue

Detective Thomas Morgan threw the empty pill bottle out of his cruiser into the manicured hedge dividing a pair of Sterling Heights, half-a-million-dollar homes. The bitter pill in his mouth was beginning to dissolve, so he reached and grabbed the cold remnants of his McDonald's coffee and washed it down.

Had to be the last one for a while, if not for good. Beverly had been getting suspicious of late. Money was funneling in and out of the bank account too rapidly and gradually working its way toward zero. And, let's face it, the shit was too good to be taking indefinitely. Morgan had seen it more times than he cared to remember. He was turning into an addict, or maybe he already was, if truth be told. Perhaps it was pilfering from his daughter's college fund that had finally clued him in. Oxycontin was not more important than his daughter's future. Tom felt disgusted with himself. Desperation was ugly and weak. He was turning into what he dreaded most: a bad cop.

Morgan turned the corner into a swirling mass of crime-scene color. Four cop cars blocked off the street leading to a two-story, tudor-style house that looked like every sixth or seventh house in the upscale neighborhood. Small groups of residents clumped together on the sidewalk and across the street, wrapped up in robes, blankets, or jackets, morbid curiosity getting the better of the cool and damp October morning. Everyone, it seemed, loved a good murder.

And, apparently, this one was very good, in the way people judged horror movies based on how disturbing the death scenes were. Morgan pulled up behind the roadblock and got out of his car. On the opposite side, he spotted Frank Wysocki's vehicle. Tom frowned. Sock would be less than pleased that Tom had not been immediately available to pick him up. When Tom found him sitting on the front porch, hands hanging loosely over his knees and looking pale as milk, Morgan figured this murder was not just very good, it was Oscar caliber.

"Sock, man. You lose your lunch?"

"Where the fuck you been, Tom? Don't stick me with this shit." He wiped the back of his hand across his mouth and then through his receding, graying hair. "Your jalapeno-eating, hairy black ass can take the upstairs. I'll take the nice and cheery guy with his brains blown across the wall."

Tom moved quickly to get out of Sock's sight. "Hey, no problem. Sorry for the delay. I was away from the phone for a few." He gave Sock a pat on the shoulder and walked up the front step. Worse than a brain mural? Morgan did not like the sound of that, because it usually meant children were involved.

"You're always away from the fucking phone," Sock said, but Tom was already through the front door and chose to ignore him.

He pulled a pair of neoprene gloves from his coat pocket and considered stepping back out for a mask, but that would mean raising Sock's ire once again, and so Tom decided to let it slide. It was just a bit of the old blood and death. Just breathe through the mouth and tune the emotions out. It took practice to get good at that, but was essential for homicide.

Morgan upgraded his assessment when he reached the end of the foyer, which opened into a living room to the right. There was a lot of blood, and one could only call it a living room in the loosest of terms. A Hispanic male slumped over on a leather sofa in sweats and a U of C T-shirt. He was in decent shape, until someone had put a slug in his head and redecorated the wall with bits of his brain matter. The smell of it was thick and pungent in the air, so the guy had been dead a few hours at least. As for the rest of the living room, every last piece of furniture and decoration had been smashed to pieces, demonstrating a level of violence far in excess of that needed to ransack the place.

Initial impression: crime of passion. Someone had been very upset about something or someone. The rest was up to Sock for now. Morgan continued walking toward the staircase and had to stop to get out of the way of a young beat cop hustling to get to the front lawn before he puked. *Welcome to homicide, kid. Sometimes it ain't cool or fun.* Needless to say, it put Morgan on edge. Even strong stomachs had their limits. He kept his breath coming through his mouth only and climbed the stairs two at a time.

The temperature dropped a good ten degrees by the time he reached the landing. No draft blew through the house, however. If some dumbshit had opened a window to air out a crime scene before the evidence guys had done their job, he was going to give someone a reason to be sick.

Disbelieving voices, low and muttering, came from the room at the end of the hall that doubled back from the top of the stairs. Tom walked by a workout room with weights and a treadmill and then a spare bedroom. Items were knocked over and broken, more like an afterthought than an actual effort to destroy.

And still the temperature turned colder. Morgan thrust his hands into the pockets of his leather coat and forced his breath to slow and get shallower. The stench had taken on a different tone. Someone had spilled their guts onto the floor. He had seen it before with knife and bullet wounds. Gut deaths were some nasty shit.

Morgan paused when he reached the door. Goose bumps ran down his spine. He closed his eyes and tried to will away the nervous knot in his stomach. This had happened a couple other times in the past, on the verge of stepping into a crime scene he would never truly walk away from. Some crimes had a way of burning themselves indelibly upon your soul, and no effort could scour it clean. They changed you, and you had to hope you were strong enough not to let it take you down a dark path that might end your life or at least your career as a cop.

This was going to be one of those crimes.

Two officers had handkerchiefs over their mouths. They were staring across the room, which Morgan found obscured by a corner of wall marking the entry into the room. He cleared his throat, and both of them jumped, wide-eyed, glazed with fear and then relief.

"The fucking cavalry has arrived!" one of them said, raising his fists into the air. "This is brutal shit, man. It's all yours, detective—"

Morgan stuck his arm across the entry, blocking his escape. "I'll need one of you to stay," he replied. "Draw straws or something." He took a step around the corner and stopped dead. "Jesus motherfucking Christ!"

"Brutal, man, I warned you," the first said. The other just nodded, refusing to pull the cloth from his mouth.

Morgan waved at the second guy. "Go. Brutal boy can stay."

"Aw, shit, detective. Come on."

He narrowed his gaze at the cop, mouth drawing into a thin line. Morgan did "angry face" very well. "You're staying. Greenie over there can go puke now. Go!" The other hurried out, and Morgan slowly turned back around to face the bed on the opposite wall. "What a goddamned mess."

"I told you, detective," came the muffled reply. "Brutal. Sick fuck."

Morgan swallowed down the bile in his throat. He had abruptly forgotten to watch his breathing and sucked in a lungful of the putrid air. The woman on the bed had been gutted and had the same dark hole in her forehead as the dead man downstairs. Dark splotches of blood and matter coated the headboard and wall behind her. The rest of her was just a grizzly mound of red straight out of a horror movie. From the neck down, Morgan hardly recognized the rest as having been human. Whoever had attacked her had not just cut her open, they had actively yanked her insides out.

"You touched anything over there, officer?"

"No, sir," he said. "I'm not getting close to that. Blood on the floor around the bed, too. Maybe not just hers."

Morgan nodded and stepped toward the end of the bed. The woman lay slumped against the headboard, pillows pushed to the side. Her legs were pushed apart at an uncomfortable-looking angle, with her hands clenched in her lap. Likely, she was alive when her gut had been split open. So much for anger. They had a genuine psychopath on their hands. Still, Morgan eyed the mass of organs and entrails spilled out on the bed. They did not look quite right, far more mass than should have been coming out of the human body. Given the blackening, pulpy mass in the chest cavity, the lungs and heart were still tucked up inside. So why did this look all wrong?

Careful of the blood spatter on the floor, Morgan stepped around the corner of the bed and moved in for a closer look, holding his breath as he did.

"You see something, detective?"

Morgan waved him off, leaning over the body. He started to reach down, to pull some of the gore aside, but froze, inches away. Something tiny and far too recognizable lay buried with the bloody remains. He stood up, staring at it in disbelief. "Ah, fuck me, man."

"What is it?"

It couldn't be. Sweet Lord above, let it not be. Morgan leaned back over, his hand trembling. He slipped his gloved hand beneath what might have been kidney and lifted, exposing a miniature arm and hand with its tiny fingers to go along with the face he could not believe he was seeing. Morgan's heart thumped like a mad drummer in his chest.

LEAVE MY BABY ALONE! The voice burst inside his head, a screaming, rage-filled bomb.

Morgan stumbled back, clutching at his head. "God . . . damn . . ."

"Sir? What the hell?" The officer rushed over to Morgan, gripping an arm to steady him.

Tom gasped, sucking in the foul air, sure that any moment he would be spewing his coffee all over the floor. "Pregnant," he said, shrugging off the hand and making for the door. "She was pregnant!"

"Ah, shit," the officer said with quiet shock.

Morgan stumbled down the hall, grasping at the rail to keep his balance. He had to get out.

He killed my baby! He killed him. He must die. Must die! Help me kill him. You must!

Morgan tripped and fell going down the stairs, clutched at the handrail and kept himself from somersaulting down to the bottom, but only managed to delay the fall. He did a tumbling, rolling slide over the last dozen stairs before thudding onto the hardwood floor of the foyer. Someone had torn the babe right out of her womb, massacred her flesh and left the infant to rot away in the wake of blood. The voice was right. Someone would have to die for this.

YES. You will help me. He must die.

Morgan struggled back to his hands and knees. "Get out of my head."

No. You will help me. My baby needs justice.

What was this shit? The Oxycontin was fucking with him, causing hallucinations. That had to be it.

Let me in, Detective Thomas Morgan. You will help me get justice.

"Tom, you okay?" Sock was kneeling beside him. "What the hell is going on?"

Sock's voice sounded hollow, distant. Tom's muscles were weak and trembling. "Sock? She was . . . The vic . . ." Morgan sagged sideways into Sock, who grabbed a hold to keep him upright.

"I know, man. Sucks to be us, huh?"

Sock's voice faded into the distance, coming down a long tunnel. "Sock . . ." *Sweet Jesus, help me.*

You are too weak, Thomas Morgan. I will gut them and splatter their fucking brains all over their walls. My baby boy will have justice!

"What is it, Tom? You need me to get someone in here?"

Morgan sat up and stretched his neck from side to side. He pushed away from Sock and slowly staggered back to his feet. "No. I don't need anyone. I'm good. I'm going to kill them, every last one of them."

"That's the spirit," Sock said, slapping him on the back.

"Yes," Morgan said and grinned. "It is."

Chapter 1

Jackie woke from her recurring dream of the past two weeks where she had been chasing down Laurel through the shrouded, gray streets of Chicago's Deadworld. Laurel continually stayed ahead of her, slipping into the swirling fog, only to reappear moments later. *Sorry.* A simple yet significant word. If Laurel would only stop so Jackie could say it, but she led her on a never-ending game of cat and mouse, taunting and teasing, until the end, when waking finally peeled back the layers of tequila-induced sleep, and Laurel would stop in those crystallized final moments of dreams, when everything was painfully real.

"I don't love you anymore!" The damning statement came with such force it physically knocked Jackie backward. No matter what she did, she could not get the apology out of her mouth before the depressing light of day intruded and sent the dream scattering away, back into the recesses of her mind.

Jackie lurched up from the couch to the buzz of her doorbell, driving tiny little spikes into her throbbing skull. Bickerstaff blinked at her from atop one of the couch cushions.

"Shit. Go away!"

The cat leaped off and jumped for a safer perch atop the piano, hidden among the empty tequila and wine bottles, half-empty glasses, and open Chinese-food containers.

"Not you, dummy." The buzzer rang again, followed moments later by her ringing phone. Jackie put her hands to her ears. "Oh, my God."

She swung her feet off the couch and pushed herself up. Her head weighed fifty pounds. The motion knocked over the carton of fried rice in her lap, sending the remains spilling across the floor.

"Damnit!" Jackie brushed rice off the couch. She needed at least one clean spot in her apartment. The answering machine finally picked up.

"Jackie? You awake? I'm downstairs. I know you're home."

The voice brought Jackie to her feet, feeling like a wobbling, overstuffed bobblehead. It was Belgerman.

"Oh. Oh, fuck." Jackie turned, looking quickly around her apartment to see if she might be able to sweep the collected crap of two weeks' worth of slumming and depression out of sight from John. There was shit everywhere. And she realized the litter box was officially too full. He could not come in. Could. Not. Likely, he'd just fire her on the spot.

Jackie made her way through the clothes on the floor, spilled mail off her entry table, and hit the intercom button for the downstairs entry. "S–sir?" She was forced to clear her throat to get the word out. "What are you doing here?"

"I stopped by on my way in to give you a file you might want to look at before you come back."

"A file? For what?"

"Your new partner," he said. "Figured you might like to get a head start on him so you can be a bit more up to speed when you come back."

Jackie let her head sag against the wall. New partner.

Holy hell. The thought had been completely gone from her mind. "Let me get something on, and I'll come down and get it."

"Just buzz me up, Jack. I'll hand it to you."

And see my place? I don't think so. "That's okay, sir. Just give me one sec."

"Jack! For Christ's sake. We could have been done already. Buzz me up."

Jackie jumped at the startlingly loud volume of his voice and hit the button without even thinking. "Shit." She was standing there in a knee-length T-shirt that stated ALL GOOD THINGS COME IN SMALL PACKAGES. Jackie opened the hall closet and pulled out an overcoat—a button-down, belt-at-the-waist, traditional khaki-colored raincoat that had been a gift from Laurel on Jackie's first day on the job. She couldn't even remember the last time she'd worn it. She yanked it off the hanger and barely got it wrapped around her as Belgerman walked up to the door. She stepped halfway out and held the door closed against her foot. A couple inches of space did not afford much of a view, or so she hoped.

"Looks like I woke you up, Rutledge." He smirked at her appearance. "If I didn't know better, I'd say you were rather happy to see me."

It took Jackie a moment, looking down at herself, to realize what he was getting at. It looked as though she might be naked beneath the overcoat. She could feel her cheeks begin to flush. "You did, sir, but that's okay. I should probably be getting up now anyway."

He glanced at the door. "Hiding someone in there, are you?"

"What? Oh. God, no. I was just sleeping, sir. I'm not much of a morning person. Sorry."

He laughed kindly. "Don't be. I was just giving you shit.

You going to keep me standing out here in the hall like your local Jehovah's Witness?"

Jackie glanced back into her dumping ground of an apartment. It was not the home of a well-adjusted agent. It was an embarrassment. "The place is kind of trashed. I haven't really done any cleaning since I've been off. If it's all the same, sir, I'd rather you didn't see it this way."

Belgerman looked over her head through the crack in the door. "I've never pictured you as the neat and tidy sort, Jackie. And you're talking to a guy who lived on his own until he was thirty-two. I've seen and lived in my share of trash heaps, so quit worrying."

She winced, keeping a firm grip on the door handle. "I know, but, uh . . . it's bad."

John rolled his eyes. "How many times have I been out here, Jackie?"

"You've never been here, sir."

"Exactly," he said. "I don't care if you've been punching holes in the walls. I know how hard this is. I've been there. I lost a partner to some gunrunners about fifteen years ago. One of the shittiest times of my life. I think I can see past the mess. Honestly, I'm curious. I'm not your father."

Jackie looked up into his very fatherly eyes. He'd always had some of that feel about him. She had more respect and admiration for his work than anyone. And somewhere, buried in the vaults of her mind, a twelve-year-old girl desperately wished she could have had a father just like him. Her shoulders slumped, and Jackie let go of the door.

"Don't say I didn't warn you," she said and stepped back in to give him access. She wanted to run and hide, shut herself away in her room and make him put the file down and leave. After closing the door, she found him standing at the threshold of the living room.

"So this is the infamous piano," he said.

Jackie leaned against the wall behind him, arms crossed

over her chest. *Please, please, please don't ask me to play.* "Yeah, that's it. Doubles as a bar."

There were three empty tequila bottles sitting on top, a half-empty bottle of red wine, half a dozen Chinese-food cartons, and a mostly eaten package of Oreos. None of this would have been so bad if it weren't for the pair of flies eagerly buzzing around the treasure trove. If he didn't go in any farther, he would miss the kitchen, where every last dish and cup sat unwashed in the sink and overflowing onto the counter.

"You have a cat?" Belgerman turned to face her at last. His face was slack, noncommittal.

Jackie looked around but didn't see Bickerstaff. This only meant one thing. He had smelled the cat—or, rather, the cat box. Another one of those things she had been meaning to get to, but it had never made it on the to-do list above drinking or channel surfing. He had to be thinking she was completely disgusting.

"Bickerstaff," she said. "Big, fat tabby."

He smiled. "That's not a name you came up with, is it?"

"He was a gift from Laur."

John nodded. "I figured. Been a rough couple weeks."

It was a statement of fact. He knew. What could she say? "It has. I'm . . . spinning my wheels here, sir. I, um . . . I don't know how not to work."

"You've never taken more than two days' vacation in eight years, Jackie."

"Really?" That fact had never occurred to her. Vacations were not something she had needed or wanted.

"It's good to take time away from the bureau on occasion. Helps maintain perspective," he said. "But losing your partner and friend is not the way to do it."

Where was he going with this? "No. Guess I'm living proof of that."

"It will get easier, Jackie. Not in a few days or even months, but it'll happen."

Months. She could not handle months of this. "How did you deal with it, sir? When you lost your partner, I mean?"

He chuckled. "I worked. A lot."

Jackie nodded and said nothing. Work would be good. Work would get her out of this depression pit and give her something worth doing. More importantly, work would occupy her brain enough to keep every damn thing from reminding her that Laurel was dead and no longer a part of her everyday life. And where the hell was she anyway? Two weeks and not a peep. She thought she had felt her presence several times, but no appearances. Even a "Hello, how are you?" would have been nice.

"I also spent time away from my house," he added. "Movies, golf, a Cubs game, anything that would provide a distraction. You sit around drinking all day, it just festers and gets worse."

She winced. It certainly did not look like things were getting better. "It um . . . looks worse than it is, sir. I haven't been downing gallons of booze a day. I've just been a slob."

"Not here to judge, Jackie. We all have our ways of dealing with pain. I don't want to see you making things worse though. If it's too much of a struggle—"

"No!" Her voice was too loud, desperate. "I mean, I'm getting there. I'll get out more, do . . . something. You're right. Distractions would be good."

John nodded, his eyes sweeping around the room again. "You want to start coming in again, Jackie? Office stuff, mind you, no investigating until your thirty days are up, but if you want to be in the office around the guys and distract yourself with some paperwork, I think that would be doable."

"Seriously?" She wanted to hug him. "That would be

great. I need to get out of here, and there's plenty for me to do that doesn't involve chasing bad guys."

"Would give you a chance to get used to your new partner also, before you're back out in the field."

"Yeah. That would be a good idea," she said. New partner. The two words sounded completely alien. "So who is it? Anyone I know?"

Belgerman handed her the file. "His name is Ryan Mc-Manus, out of the San Francisco office. Mostly gang-enforcement stuff, but wants to do homicides. Steady, levelheaded guy. I think he'll suit you."

Jackie stared at the name printed on the folder tab. It should have said *Laurel Carpenter*. "Can I come in tomorrow then?"

"This decision isn't entirely mine, Jackie. You need to get Tillie's agreement as well."

Aunt Matilda, the office shrink—the wise old lady who had the uncanny knack for knowing exactly what you didn't want to talk about, and to whom Jackie owed visits. Tillie had extorted future visits from her after Laurel had died in order for Jackie to stay on the case. Nobody in the world terrified her more.

"Great. So much for that idea." Jackie made no effort to hide her annoyance.

John laughed. "I think she'll be amenable to you coming back, as long as she knows you won't be out in the field. She's dealt with partner loss before. She knows how hard it is, Jackie. Besides, aren't you seeing her today anyway?"

"Shit!" She had completely forgotten. "What time is it?"

Belgerman looked at his watch. "Nine forty."

"Fuck! Fifty minutes." Jackie hurried toward her bedroom. "You could have said something sooner! I look like shit."

"You look fine," he said. "You want a ride in?"

"No, I'm good. I'm going to shower right quick. I'll see you there, sir."

He chuckled. "I'll see myself out then. Just remember to remain calm, Jackie. Tillie only needs to see you're not losing it."

"Okay, thanks." *So, lie through my teeth,* Jackie thought. For two weeks that was all she had been doing. But this was a chance to get out of the hellhole of her apartment. She needed to work, needed the routine of her life to return, because outside of work, she had nothing—she was nothing. She only had to convince the omniscient, brain-scanning Dr. Erikson this wasn't the case.